PRAISE FOR THE
GRISHAVERSE

'A master of fantasy'
THE HUFFINGTON POST

'The best magic universe since Harry Potter'
BUSTLE

'This is what fantasy is for'
THE NEW YORK TIMES BOOK REVIEW

'[A] world that feels real enough to have its own passport stamp'
NPR

'The darker it gets for the good guys, the better'
ENTERTAINMENT WEEKLY

'Sultry, sweeping and picturesque . . . Impossible to put down'
USA TODAY

'There's a level of emotional and historical sophistication
within Bardugo's original epic fantasy that sets it apart'
VANITY FAIR

'Bardugo crafts a first-rate adventure, a poignant romance,
and an intriguing mystery!'
RICK RIORDAN, BESTSELLING AUTHOR
OF THE PERCY JACKSON SERIES

KING
OF
SCARS

Also by Leigh Bardugo

The Shadow and Bone Trilogy

Shadow and Bone

Siege and Storm

Ruin and Rising

The Six of Crows Duology

Six of Crows

Crooked Kingdom

The Language of Thorns

Also available

Six of Crows Collector's Edition

KING

OF
SCARS

LEIGH BARDUGO

Orion

ORION CHILDREN'S BOOKS

First published in Great Britain in 2019 by Hodder and Stoughton

1 3 5 7 9 10 8 6 4 2

Text © Leigh Bardugo 2019
Jacket art © Leigh Bardugo 2019

Book design by Ellen Duda
Map art by Sveta Dorosheva

The moral rights of the author have been asserted.

A CIP catalogue record for this book is available from the British Library.

HB ISBN 978 1 5101 0445 7
TPB ISBN 978 1 5101 0566 9

Printed and bound in Great Britain by Clays Ltd, Elcograf S.p.A.

The paper and board used in this book are from
well-managed forests and other responsible sources.

MIX
Paper from
responsible sources
FSC
www.fsc.org   FSC® C104740

Orion Children's Books
An imprint of Hachette Children's Group
Part of Hodder and Stoughton
Carmelite House
50 Victoria Embankment
London EC4Y 0DZ

An Hachette UK Company
www.hachettechildrens.co.uk

At the foot of the Petrazoi lies a small swamp that smells potently of feet and rancid cooking oil.
It is known as the Armpit and its fumes cause dizzy spells, vomiting, and fervent prayers to Sankt
Bozkho the Minty. Forced to camp there overnight and desperate for relief, an army regiment
begged a passing witch for help. A generous sort, she cut off their noses and replaced them
with crow beaks and they were grateful for it. Steal this book and you will stink worse than
this swamp—and no passing witch will help you.

For Morgan Fahey—
wartime general
peacetime consigliere
dearest friend
(mostly) benevolent queen

THE GRISHA

SOLDIERS OF THE SECOND ARMY
MASTERS OF THE SMALL SCIENCE

CORPORALKI
(THE ORDER OF THE LIVING AND THE DEAD)
Heartrenders
Healers

ETHEREALKI
(THE ORDER OF SUMMONERS)
Squallers
Inferni
Tidemakers

MATERIALKI
(THE ORDER OF FABRIKATORS)
Durasts
Alkemi

THE
WANDERING
ISLE

THE BONE ROAD

JELKA

VILKI

NOVYI
ZEM

WEDDLE

Reb
Harbor

Eames
Harbor

SHRIFTPORT

EAMES
CHIN

COFTON

SOUTHERN
COLONIES

The
True Sea

KETTERDAM

BELENDT

KERCH

KING

OF
SCARS

THE
DROWNING
MAN

1

DIMA

DIMA HEARD THE BARN DOORS slam before any-
one else did. Inside the little farmhouse, the kitchen bubbled like a
pot on the stove, its windows shut tight against the storm, the air in
the room warm and moist. The walls rattled with the rowdy din of
Dima's brothers talking over one another, as his mother hummed and
thumped her foot to a song Dima didn't know. She held the torn
sleeve of one of his father's shirts taut in her lap, her needle pecking
at the fabric in the uneven rhythm of an eager sparrow, a skein of
wool thread trailing between her fingers like a choice worm.

Dima was the youngest of six boys, the baby who had arrived late
to his mother, long after the doctor who came through their village
every summer had told her there would be no more children. *An unexpected blessing*, Mama liked to say, holding Dima close and fussing over

him when the others had gone off to their chores. *An unwanted mouth to feed*, his older brother Pyotr would sneer.

Because Dima was so small, he was often left out of his brothers' jokes, forgotten in the noisy arguments of the household, and that was why, on that autumn night, standing by the basin, soaping the last of the pots that his brothers had made sure to leave for him, only he heard the damning *thunk* of the barn doors. Dima set to scrubbing harder, determined to finish his work and get to bed before anyone could think to send him out into the dark. He could hear their dog, Molniya, whining on the kitchen stoop, begging for scraps and a warm place to sleep as the wind rose on an angry howl.

Branches lashed the windows. Mama lifted her head, the grim furrows around her mouth deepening. She scowled as if she could send the wind to bed without supper. "Winter comes early and stays too long."

"Hmm," said Papa, "like your mother." Mama gave him a kick with her boot.

She'd left a little glass of kvas behind the stove that night, a gift for the household ghosts who watched over the farm and who slept behind the old iron stove to keep warm. Or so Mama said. Papa only rolled his eyes and complained it was a waste of good kvas.

Dima knew that when everyone had gone to bed, Pyotr would slurp it down and eat the slice of honey cake Mama left wrapped in cloth. "Great-grandma's ghost will haunt you," Dima sometimes warned. But Pyotr would just wipe his sleeve across his chin and say, "There is no ghost, you little idiot. Baba Galina was lunch for the cemetery worms, and the same thing will happen to you if you don't keep your mouth shut."

Now Pyotr leaned down and gave Dima a hard jab. Dima often wondered if Pyotr did special exercises to make his elbows more pointy. "Do you hear that?" his brother asked.

"There's nothing to hear," said Dima as his heart sank. The barn door . . .

"Something is out there, riding the storm."

So his brother was just trying to scare him. "Don't be stupid," Dima said, but he was relieved.

"Listen," said Pyotr, and as the wind shook the roof of the house and the fire sputtered in the grate, Dima thought he heard something more than the storm—a high, distant cry, like the yowl of a hungry animal or the wailing of a child. "When the wind blows through the graveyard, it wakes the spirits of all the babies who died before they could be given their Saints' names. *Malenchki.* They go looking for souls to steal so they can barter their way into heaven." Pyotr leaned down and poked his finger into Dima's shoulder. "They always take the youngest."

Dima was eight now, old enough to know better, but still his eyes strayed to the dark windows, out to the moonlit yard, where the trees bowed and shook in the wind. He flinched. He could have sworn—just for a moment, he could have sworn he saw a shadow streak across the yard, the dark blot of something much larger than a bird.

Pyotr laughed and splashed him with soapy water. "I swear you get more witless with every passing day. Who would want your little nothing of a soul?"

Pyotr is only angry because, before you, he was the baby, Mama always told Dima. *You must try to be kind to your brother even when he is older but not wiser.* Dima tried. He truly did. But sometimes he just wanted to knock Pyotr on his bottom and see how *he* liked feeling small.

The wind dropped, and in the sudden gust of silence, there was no disguising the sharp slam that echoed across the yard.

"Who left the barn doors open?" Papa asked.

"It was Dima's job to see to the stalls tonight," Pyotr said virtuously, and his brothers, gathered around the table, clucked like flustered hens.

"I closed it," protested Dima. "I set the bar fast!"

Papa leaned back in his chair. "Then do I imagine that sound?"

"He probably thinks a ghost did it," said Pyotr.

Mama looked up from her mending. "Dima, you must go close and bar the doors."

"I will do it," said Pyotr with a resigned sigh. "We all know Dima is afraid of the dark."

But Dima sensed this was a test. Papa would expect him to take responsibility. "I am not afraid," he said. "Of course I will go close the doors."

Dima ignored Pyotr's smug look; he wiped his hands and put on his coat and hat. Mama handed him a tin lantern. "Hurry now," she said, pushing up his collar to keep his neck warm. "Scurry back and I'll tuck you in and tell you a story."

"A new one?"

"Yes, and a good one, about the mermaids of the north."

"Does it have magic in it?"

"Plenty. Go on, now."

Dima cast his eyes once to the icon of Sankt Feliks on the wall by the door, candlelight flickering over his sorrowful face, his gaze full of sympathy as if he knew just how cold it was outside. Feliks had been impaled on a spit of apple boughs and cooked alive just hours after he'd performed the miracle of the orchards. He hadn't screamed or cried, only suggested that the villagers turn him so the flames could reach his other side. Feliks wouldn't be afraid of a storm.

As soon as Dima opened the kitchen door, the wind tried to snatch it from his grip. He slammed it behind him and heard the latch turn from the other side. He knew it was temporary, a necessity, but it still felt like he was being punished. He looked back at the glowing windows as he forced his feet down the steps to the dry scrabble of the yard, and had the awful thought that as soon as he'd left the warmth of the kitchen his family had forgotten him, that if he never returned, no one would cry out or raise the alarm. The wind would wipe Dima from their memory.

He considered the long moonlit stretch he would have to traverse past the chicken coops and the goose shed to the barn, where they sheltered their old horse, Gerasim, and their cow, Mathilde.

"Faced with steel saw blades," he whispered, brushing his hand over the new plow as he passed, as if it were a lucky talisman. He wasn't sure why the blades were better, but when the plow had arrived, those were the words his father had proudly repeated to their neighbors, and Dima liked the strong sound of them. There had been long arguments at the kitchen table about the plow, along with all the king's agricultural reforms and what trouble or hope they might bring.

"We're on our way to another civil war," Mama had grumbled. "The king is too rash."

But Papa was pleased. "How can you worry with your belly full and the roof patched with fresh tar? This was the first year we were able to harvest enough of our crops to sell at market instead of just keeping ourselves fed."

"Because the king cut Duke Radimov's tithe to a scrap of what it was!" Mama exclaimed.

"And we should be sorry?"

"We will be when the duke and his noble friends murder the king in his bed."

"King Nikolai is a war hero!" said Papa, waving his hand through the air as if trouble could be banished like pipe smoke. "There will be no coup without the army to back it."

They talked in circles, debating the same things night after night. Dima didn't understand much of it, only that he was to keep the young king in his prayers.

The geese honked and rustled in their shed, riled by the weather or Dima's nervous footsteps as he passed. Ahead, he saw the big wooden barn doors swaying open and shut as if the building were sighing, as if the doorway were a mouth that might suck him in with a single breath. He liked the barn in the daytime, when sunlight fell through the slats of the roof and everything was hay smells, Gerasim's snorting, Mathilde's disapproving moo. But at night, the barn became a hollow shell, waiting for some terrible creature to fill it—some cunning thing that might let the doors blow open to lure a foolish boy outside. Because Dima *knew* he had closed those doors. He felt certain of it, and he could not help but think of Pyotr's *malenchki*, little ghosts hunting for a soul to steal.

Stop it, Dima scolded himself. *Pyotr unbarred the doors himself just so you would have to go out in the cold or shame yourself by refusing.* But Dima had shown his brothers and his father he could be brave, and that thought warmed him even as he yanked his collar up around his ears and shivered at the bite of the wind. Only then did he realize he couldn't hear Molniya barking anymore. She hadn't been by the door, trying to nose her way into the kitchen, when Dima ventured outside.

"Molniya?" he said, and the wind seized his voice, casting it away. "Molniya!" he called—but only a bit louder. In case something other than his dog was out there listening.

Step by step he crossed the yard, the shadows from the trees leaping and shuddering over the ground. Beyond the woods he could see the wide ribbon of the road. It led all the way to the town, all the way to the churchyard. Dima did not let his eyes follow it. It was too easy to imagine some shambling body dressed in ragged clothes traveling that road, trailing clods of cemetery earth behind it.

He heard a soft whine from somewhere in the trees. Dima shrieked. Yellow eyes stared back at him from the dark. The glow from his lantern fell on black paws, ruffled fur, bared teeth.

"Molniya!" he said on a relieved sigh. He was grateful for the loud moan of the storm. The thought of his brothers hearing his high, shameful yelp and running outside just to find their poor dog cowering in the brush was too horrible to contemplate. "Come here, girl," he coaxed. Molniya had pressed her belly to the ground, her ears flat against her head. She did not move.

Dima looked back at the barn. The plank that should have lain across the doors and kept them in place lay smashed to bits in the brush. From somewhere inside, he heard a soft, wet snuffling. Had a wounded animal found its way into the barn? Or a wolf?

The golden light of the farmhouse windows seemed impossibly far away. Maybe he should go back and get help. Surely he couldn't be expected to face a wolf by himself. But what if there was nothing inside? Or some harmless cat that Molniya had gotten a piece of? Then all his brothers would laugh, not just Pyotr.

Dima shuffled forward, keeping his lantern far out in front of him. He waited for the storm to quiet and grabbed the heavy door by its edge so it would not strike him as he entered.

The barn was dark, barely touched by slats of moonlight. Dima edged a little deeper into the blackness. He thought of Sankt Feliks' gentle eyes, the thorny apple bough piercing his heart. Then, as if the storm had just been catching its breath, the wind leapt. The doors behind Dima slammed shut, and the weak light of his lantern sputtered to nothing.

Outside, he could hear the storm raging, but the barn was quiet. The animals had gone silent as if waiting, and he could smell their sour fear over the sweetness of the hay—and something else. Dima knew that smell from when they slaughtered the geese for the holiday table: the hot copper tang of blood.

Go back, he told himself.

In the darkness, something moved. Dima caught a glint of moonlight, the shine of what might have been eyes. And then it was as if a piece of shadow broke away and came sliding across the barn.

Dima took a step backward, clutching the useless lantern to his chest. The shadow wore the shredded remains of what might have once been fine clothes, and for a brief, hopeful moment, Dima thought a traveler had stumbled into the barn to sleep out the storm. But it did not move like a man. It was too graceful, too silent, its body unwinding in a low crouch. Dima whimpered as the shadow prowled closer. Its eyes were mirror black, and dark veins spread from its clawed fingertips as if its hands had been dipped in ink. The tendrils of shadow tracing its skin seemed to pulse.

Run, Dima told himself. *Scream.* He thought of the way the geese came to Pyotr so trustingly, how they made no sound of protest in the scant seconds before his brother broke their necks. *Stupid*, Dima had thought at the time, but now he understood.

The thing rose from its haunches, a black silhouette, and two vast wings unfurled from its back, their edges curling like smoke.

"Papa!" Dima tried to cry, but the word came out as little more than a puff of breath.

The thing paused as if the word was somehow familiar. It listened, head cocked to the side, and Dima took another step backward, then another.

The monster's eyes snapped to Dima, and the creature was suddenly bare inches away, looming over him. With the gray moonlight falling over its body, Dima could see that the dark stains around its mouth and on its chest were blood.

The creature leaned forward, inhaling deeply. Up close it had the features of a young man—until its lips parted, the corners of its mouth pulling back to reveal long black fangs.

It was smiling. The monster was smiling—because it knew it would soon be well fed. Dima felt something warm slide down his leg and realized he had wet himself.

The monster lunged.

The doors behind Dima blew open, the storm demanding entry. A loud *crack* sounded as the gust knocked the creature from its clawed feet and hurled its winged body against the far wall. The wooden beams splintered with the force, and the thing slumped to the floor in a heap.

A figure strode into the barn in a drab gray coat, a strange wind lifting her long black hair. The moon caught her features, and Dima cried harder, because she was too beautiful to be any ordinary person, and that meant she must be a Saint. He had died, and she had come to escort him to the bright lands.

But she did not stoop to take him in her arms or speak soft prayers or words of comfort. Instead she approached the monster, hands held out before her. She was a warrior Saint, then, like Sankt Juris, like Sankta Alina of the Fold.

"Be careful," Dima managed to whisper, afraid she would be harmed. "It has . . . such teeth."

But his Saint was unafraid. She nudged the monster with the toe of her boot and rolled it onto its side. The creature snarled as it came awake, and Dima clutched his lantern tighter as if it might become a shield.

In a few swift movements, the Saint had secured the creature's clawed hands in heavy shackles. She yanked hard on the chain, forcing the monster to its feet. It snapped its teeth at her, but she did not scream or cringe. She swatted the creature on its nose as if it were a misbehaving pet.

The thing hissed, pulling futilely on its restraints. Its wings swept once, twice, trying to lift her off her feet, but she gripped the chain in her fist and thrust her other hand forward. Another gust of wind struck the monster, slamming it into the barn wall. It hit the ground, fell to its knees, stumbled back up, weaving and unsteady in a way that made it seem curiously human, like Papa when he had been out late at the tavern. The Saint tugged on the chain. She murmured something, and the creature hissed again as the wind eddied around them.

Not a Saint, Dima realized. *Grisha.* A soldier of the Second Army. A Squaller who could control wind.

She took the shawl from her shoulders and tossed it over the creature's head and shoulders, leading her captured prey past Dima, the monster still struggling and snapping.

She tossed Dima a silver coin. "For the damage," she said, her eyes bright as jewels in the moonlight. "You saw nothing tonight, understood? Hold your tongue or next time I won't keep him on his leash."

Dima nodded, feeling fresh tears spill down his cheeks. The Grisha raised a brow. He'd never seen a face like hers, more lovely than any painted icon, blue eyes like the deepest waters of the river. She tossed him another coin, and he just managed to snatch it from the air.

"That one's for you. Don't share it with your brothers."

Dima watched as she sailed through the barn doors. He forced his feet to move. He wanted to return to the house, find his mother, and bury himself in her skirts, but he was desperate for one last look at the Grisha and her monster. He trailed after them as silently as he could. In the shadows of the moonlit road, a large coach waited, its driver cloaked in black. A coachman jumped down and seized the chain, helping to drag the creature inside.

Dima knew he must be dreaming, despite the cool weight of sil-ver in his palm, because the coachman did not look at the monster and say *Go on, you beast!* or *You'll never trouble these people again!* as a hero would in a story.

Instead, in the deep shadows cast by the swaying pines, Dima thought he heard the coachman say, "Watch your head, Your Highness."

2

ZOYA

THE STINK OF BLOOD HUNG heavy in the coach.
Zoya pressed her sleeve to her nose to ward off the smell, but the
musty odor of dirty wool wasn't much improvement.

Vile. It was bad enough that she had to go tearing off across the
Ravkan countryside in the dead of night in a borrowed, badly sprung
coach, but that she had to do so in a garment like this? Unacceptable.
She stripped the coat from her body. The stench still clung to the silk
of her embroidered blue *kefta* beneath, but she felt a bit more like
herself now.

They were ten miles outside Ivets, nearly one hundred miles from
the safety of the capital, racing along the narrow roads that would
lead them back to the estate of their host for the trade summit, Duke
Radimov. Zoya wasn't much for praying, so she could only hope no
one had seen Nikolai escape his chambers and take to the skies. If

they'd been back home, back in Os Alta, this never would have happened. She'd thought they'd taken enough precautions. She couldn't have been more wrong.

The horse's hooves thundered, the wheels of the coach clattering and jouncing, as beside her the king of Ravka gnashed his needle-sharp teeth and pulled at his chains.

Zoya kept her distance. She'd seen what one of Nikolai's bites could do when he was in this state, and she had no interest in losing a limb or worse. Part of her had wanted to ask Tolya or Tamar, the brother and sister who served as the king's personal guards, to ride inside the carriage with her until Nikolai resumed his human form. Their father had been a Shu mercenary who had trained them to fight, their mother a Grisha from whom they'd both inherited Heartrender gifts. The presence of either twin would have been welcome. But her pride prevented it, and she also knew what it would cost the king. One witness to his misery was bad enough.

Outside, the wind howled. It was less the baying of a beast than the high, wild laugh of an old friend, driving them on. The wind did what she willed it, had since she was a child. Yet on nights like these, she couldn't help but feel that it was not her servant but her ally: a storm that rose to mask a creature's snarls, to hide the sounds of a fight in a rickety barn, to whip up trouble in streets and village taverns. This was the western wind, Adezku the mischief-maker, a worthy companion. Even if that farm boy told everyone in Ivets what he'd seen, the townspeople would chalk it up to Adezku, the rascal wind that drove women into their neighbors' beds and made mad thoughts skitter in men's heads like whorls of dead leaves.

A mile later, the snarls in the coach had quieted. The clanking of the chains dwindled as the creature seemed to sink farther and farther into the shadows of the seat. At last, a voice, hoarse and beleaguered, said, "I don't suppose you brought me a fresh shirt?"

Zoya took the pack from the coach floor and pulled out a clean white shirt and fur-lined coat, both finely made but thoroughly rumpled—appropriate attire for a royal who had spent the night carousing.

Without a word, Nikolai held up his shackled wrists. The talons had retracted, but his hands were still scarred with the faint black lines he had borne since the end of the civil war three years ago. The king often wore gloves to hide them, and Zoya thought that was a mistake. The scars were a reminder of the torture he had endured at the hands of the Darkling—and the price he had paid alongside his country. Of course, that was only part of the story, but it was the part the Ravkan people were best equipped to handle.

Zoya unlocked the chains with the heavy key she wore around her neck. She hoped it was her imagination, but the scars on Nikolai's hands seemed darker lately, as if determined not to fade.

Once his hands were free, the king peeled the ruined shirt from his body. He used the linen and water from the flask she handed him to wash the blood from his chest and mouth, then splashed more over his hands and ran them through his hair. The water trickled down his neck and shoulders. He was shaking badly, but he looked like Nikolai again—hazel eyes clear, the damp gold of his hair pushed back from his forehead.

"Where did you find me this time?" he asked, keeping most of the tremor from his voice.

Zoya wrinkled her nose at the memory. "A goose farm."

"I hope it was one of the more fashionable goose farms." He fumbled with the buttons of his clean shirt, fingers still shaking. "Do we know what I killed?"

Or who? The question hung unspoken in the air.

Zoya batted Nikolai's quaking hands away from his buttons and took up the work herself. Through the thin cotton, she could feel the chill the night had left on his skin.

"What an excellent valet you make," he murmured. But she knew he hated submitting to these small attentions, hated that he was weak enough to require them.

Sympathy would only make it worse, so she kept her voice brusque. "I presume you killed a great deal of geese. Possibly a shaggy pony." But had that been all? Zoya had no way of knowing what the monster might have gotten into before they'd found him. "You remember nothing?"

"Only flashes."

They would just have to wait for any reports of deaths or mutilations.

The trouble had begun six months earlier, when Nikolai had woken in a field nearly thirty miles from Os Alta, bloodied and covered in bruises, with no memory of how he'd gotten out of the palace or what he'd done in the night. *I seem to have taken up sleepwalking*, he'd declared to Zoya and the rest of the Grisha Triumvirate when he'd sauntered in late to their morning meeting, a long scratch down his cheek.

They'd been concerned but baffled. Tolya and Tamar were hardly the type to just let Nikolai slip by. *How did you get past them?* Zoya had asked as Genya tailored away the scratch and David carried on about somnambulism. But if Nikolai had been troubled, he hadn't shown it. *I excel at most things*, he'd said. *Why not unlikely escapes too?* He'd had new locks placed on his bedroom doors and insisted they move on to the business of the day and the odd report of an earthquake in Ryevost that had released thousands of silver hummingbirds from a crack in the earth.

A little over a month later, Tolya had been reading in a chair

outside the king's bedchamber when he'd heard the sound of breaking glass and burst through the door to see Nikolai leap from the window ledge, his back split by wings of curling shadow. Tolya had woken
Zoya and they'd tracked the king to the roof of a granary fifteen miles
away.

After that, they had started chaining the king to his bed—an
effective solution, workable only because Nikolai's servants were not
permitted inside his palace bedchamber. The king was a war hero,
after all, and known to suffer nightmares. Zoya had locked him in
every night since and released him every morning, and they'd kept
Nikolai's secret safe. Only Tolya, Tamar, and the Triumvirate knew
the truth. If anyone discovered the king of Ravka spent his nights
trussed up in chains, he'd be a perfect target for assassination or
coup, not to mention a laughingstock.

That was what made travel so dangerous. But Nikolai couldn't
stay sequestered behind the walls of Os Alta forever.

"A king cannot remain locked up in his own castle," he'd declared
when he'd decided to resume travel away from the palace. "One risks
looking less like a monarch and more like a hostage."

"You have emissaries to manage these matters of state," Zoya had
argued, "ambassadors, underlings."

"The public may forget how handsome I am."

"I doubt it. Your face is on the money."

Nikolai had refused to relent, and Zoya could admit he wasn't
entirely wrong. His father had made the mistake of letting others
conduct the business of ruling, and it had cost him. There was a balance to be struck, she supposed, between caution and daring, tiresome as compromise tended to be. Life just ran more smoothly when
she got her way.

Because Nikolai and Zoya couldn't very well travel with a trunk
full of chains for inquisitive servants to discover, whenever they were

away from the safety of the palace, they relied on a powerful sedative to keep Nikolai tucked into bed and the monster at bay.

"Genya will have to mix my tonic stronger," he said now, shrugging into his coat.

"Or you could stay in the capital and cease taking these foolish risks."

So far the monster had been content with attacks on livestock, his casualties limited to gutted sheep and drained cattle. But they both knew it was only a question of time. Whatever the Darkling's power had left seething within Nikolai hungered for more than animal flesh.

"The last incident was barely a week ago." He scrubbed a hand over his face. "I thought I had more time."

"It's getting worse."

"I like to keep you on your toes, Nazyalensky. Constant anxiety does wonders for the complexion."

"I'll send you a thank-you card."

"Make sure of it. You're positively glowing."

He's faring worse than he's letting on, thought Zoya. Nikolai was always freer with compliments when he was fatigued. It was true, she did look splendid, even after a harrowing night, but Zoya knew the king couldn't care less about her appearance.

They heard a sharp whistle from outside as the carriage slowed.

"We're approaching the bridge," Zoya said.

The trade summit in Ivets had been essential to their negotiations with the nations of Kerch and Novyi Zem, but the business of tariffs and taxes had also provided cover for their true mission: a visit to the site of Ravka's latest supposed miracle.

A week ago, the villagers of Ivets had set out behind Duke Radimov's ribbon-festooned cart to celebrate the Festival of Sankt Grigori, banging drums and playing little harps meant to mimic the instrument Grigori had fashioned to soothe the beasts of the forest before his martyrdom. But when they'd reached the Obol, the wooden bridge that spanned the river gorge had given way. Before the duke and his vassals could plummet to the raging whitewater below, another bridge had sprung up beneath them, seeming to bloom from the very walls of the chasm and the jagged rocks of the canyon floor. Or so the reports had claimed. Zoya had put little stock in the tales, chalked them up to exaggeration, maybe even mass delusion—until she'd seen the bridge for herself.

She peered out the coach window as they rounded the bend in the road and the bridge came into view, its tall, slender pillars and long girders gleaming white in the moonlight. Though she'd seen it before and walked its length with the king, the sight was still astonishing. From a distance, it looked like something wrought in alabaster. It was only when one drew closer that it became clear the bridge was not stone at all.

Nikolai shook his head. "As a man who regularly turns into a monster, I realize I shouldn't be making judgments about stability, but are we sure it's safe?"

"Not at all," admitted Zoya, trying to ignore the knot in her stomach. When she'd crossed over it with the twins earlier that night, she'd been too focused on finding Nikolai to worry about the bridge holding up. "But it's the only way across the gorge."

"Perhaps I should have brushed up on my prayers."

The sound of the wheels changed as the coach rolled onto the bridge, from the rumble of the road to a steady *thump, thump, thump*. The bridge that had so miraculously sprung up from nothing was not stone or brick or wooden beam. Its white girders and transoms were bone and tendon, its abutments and piers bound together with ropy bundles of gristle. *Thump, thump, thump*. They were traveling over a spine.

"I don't care for that sound," said Zoya.

"Agreed. A miracle should sound more dignified. Some chimes, perhaps, or a choir of heavenly voices."

"Don't call it that," snapped Zoya.

"A choir?"

"A miracle." Zoya had whispered enough futile prayers in her childhood to know the Saints never answered. The bridge had to be Grisha craft, and there was a rational explanation for its appearance, one she intended to find.

"What would you call a bridge made of bones appearing just in time to save an entire town from death?" asked Nikolai.

"It wasn't an entire town."

"Half a town," he amended.

"An unexpected occurrence."

"The people might feel that description falls short of this marvel."

And it was a marvel—at once elegant and grotesque, a mass of crossing beams and soaring arches. Since it had appeared, pilgrims had camped at either end of it, holding vigil day and night. They did not raise their heads as the coach rolled by.

"What would you call the earthquake in Ryevost?" Nikolai continued. "Or the statue of Sankta Anastasia weeping tears of blood outside Tsemna?"

"Trouble," Zoya said.

"You still think it's the work of Grisha using *parem*?"

"How else could someone create such a bridge or an earthquake on demand?"

Jurda parem. Zoya wished she'd never heard the words. The drug was the product of experimentation in a Shu lab. It could take a Grisha's power and transform it into something wholly new and wholly dangerous, but the price for that brief bit of glory was addiction and eventually death. It might make it possible for a rogue

21

Fabrikator to shake the earth or for a Corporalnik to make a bridge out of a body. But to what end? Could the Shu be using Grisha slaves to destabilize Ravka? Could the Apparat, the supposed spiritual counselor to the crown, be involved? Thus far, he had only declared that he was praying over the incidents and planned to stage a pilgrimage to the sites. Zoya had never trusted the priest, and she had no doubt that if he could find a way to stage a miracle, he could also find a way to use the spectacle to his own advantage.

But the real question, the question that had brought them to Ivets, was whether these strange happenings around Ravka were tied to the dark power that sheltered inside Nikolai. The occurrences had begun right around the same time as Nikolai's night spells. It might be a coincidence, but they had come to Ivets in the hope of finding some clue, some connection that would help them rid Nikolai of the monster's will.

They reached the other side of the bridge, and the reassuringly ordinary rumble of the dirt road filled the coach once more. It was as if a spell had lifted.

"We'll have to leave Duke Radimov's today," said Nikolai. "And hope no one saw me flapping around the grounds."

Zoya wanted to agree, but since they'd made the journey . . . "I can double your dose of Genya's tonic. There's another day left in negotiations."

"Let Ulyashin handle them. I want to get back to the capital. We have samples from the bridge for David. He may be able to learn something we can use to deal with my . . ."

"Affliction?"

"Uninvited guest."

Zoya rolled her eyes. He spoke as if he were being plagued by a bilious aunt. But there was an important reason for them to stay in Ivets. She had been wary of the trip, skeptical of the bridge, fearful of

22

the risks, but she'd also known the trade summit presented them with a good opportunity—a certain Hiram Schenck and his two marriageable daughters.

She tapped her fingers against the velvet seat, uncertain of how to proceed. She'd hoped to orchestrate a meeting between Nikolai and the Schenck girls without him realizing that she was meddling. The king did not like to be led, and when he sensed he was being pushed, he could be just as stubborn as . . . well, as Zoya herself.

"Speak, Nazyalensky. When you purse your lips like that, you look like you've made love to a lemon."

"Lucky lemon," Zoya said with a sniff. She smoothed the fabric of her *kefta* over her lap. "Hiram Schenck's family accompanied him to Ivets."

"And?"

"He has two daughters."

Nikolai laughed. "Is that why you agreed to this trip? So that you could indulge in your matchmaking?"

"I agreed because someone has to make sure you don't eat anyone when your *uninvited guest* gets peckish in the middle of the night. And I am not some interfering mama who wants to see her darling son wed. I am trying to protect your throne. Hiram Schenck is a senior member of the Merchant Council. He could all but guarantee leniency on Ravka's loans from Kerch, to say nothing of the massive fortune one of his pretty daughters will inherit."

"How pretty?"

"Who cares?"

"Not me, certainly. But two years working with you has worn away my pride. I want to make sure I won't spend my life watching other men ogle my wife."

"If they do, you can have them beheaded."

"The men or my wife?" said Nikolai.

"Both. Just make sure to get her dowry first."

"Ruthless."

"Practical. If we stayed another night——"

"Zoya, I can't very well court a bride if there's a chance I may turn her into dinner."

"You're a king. You don't have to court anyone. That's what the throne and the jewels and the title are for, and once you're married, your queen will become your ally."

"Or she may run screaming from our wedding bower and tell her father I began by nibbling on her earlobe and then tried to consume her actual ear. She could start a war."

"But she won't, Nikolai. Because by the time you two have said your vows, you'll have charmed her into loving you, and then you'll be her problem to take care of."

"Even *my* charm has its limits, Zoya."

If so, she had yet to encounter them. Zoya cast the king a disbelieving glance. "A handsome monster husband who put a crown on her head? It's a perfect fairy tale to sell to some starry-eyed girl. She can lock you in at night and kiss you sweetly in the morning, and Ravka will be secure."

"Why do you never kiss me sweetly in the morning, Zoya?"

"I do nothing sweetly, Your Highness." She shook out her cuffs. "Why do you hesitate? Until you marry, until you have an heir, Ravka will remain vulnerable."

Nikolai's glib demeanor vanished. "I cannot take a wife while I am in this state. I cannot forge a marriage founded on lies."

"Aren't most?"

"Ever the romantic."

"Ever *practical*."

"Kerch bridal prospects aside, we need to escape before Schenck can question me more closely about the *izmars'ya*."

Zoya cursed. "So the twins were right—there was a leak at our old research facility." The *izmars'ya* were ships that traveled beneath the surface of the water. They would be vital to Ravka's survival as the Fjerdan navy grew, especially if Nikolai could arm them as he had planned.

"It seems so. But the Kerch don't know how far along we are, at least not yet."

Those words did little to cheer Zoya. The Kerch already had enough leverage against Ravka. Schenck wouldn't have raised the topic of the *izmars'ya* with the king lightly. What did he intend to do with this new intelligence?

Another sharp whistle sounded from outside the carriage, two quick notes—Tolya's signal that they were approaching the gatehouse.

Zoya knew there would be some confusion among the guards. No one had seen the coach ride out, and it bore no royal seal. Tolya and Tamar had kept it at the ready well outside the duke's estate just in case Nikolai slipped his leash. She'd gone to find them as soon as she realized he was missing.

They'd gotten lucky tonight. They'd found the king before he'd strayed too far. When Nikolai flew, Zoya could sense him riding the winds and use the disruption in their pattern to track his movements. But if she hadn't gotten to that farm when she had, what might have happened? Would Nikolai have killed that boy? The thing inside him was not just a hungry animal but something far worse, and she knew with absolute surety that it longed for human prey.

"We cannot go on this way, Nikolai." Eventually they would be found out. Eventually these evening hunts and sleepless nights would get the best of them. "We must all do what is required."

Nikolai sighed and opened his arms to her as the coach rattled to a stop. "Then come here, Zoya, and kiss me sweetly as a new bride would."

So much for propriety. Thanks to Zoya's late-night visits to make sure the king was safely restrained in his chambers, the gossip was already thick that their relationship was more than political. Kings took mistresses, and worse things had been rumored about leaders before. Zoya just hoped the Schenck girls were the open-minded sort. The king's reputation could withstand a bit of scandal; it would not survive the truth.

Zoya took a second flask from the pack and dabbed whiskey at her pulse points like perfume before handing it to Nikolai, who took a long swig, then splashed the rest liberally over his coat. Zoya ruffled her hair, let her *kefta* slip from one shoulder, and eased into the king's arms. The charade was necessary, and it was an easy role to play, sometimes too easy.

He buried his face in her hair, inhaling deeply. "How is it I smell like goose shit and cheap whiskey and you smell like you just ran through a meadow of wildflowers?"

"Ruthlessness."

He breathed in again. "What *is* that scent? It reminds me of something, but I can't place what."

"The last child you tried to eat?"

"That must be it."

The door to the coach flew open.

"Your Highness, we hadn't realized you'd gone out tonight."

Zoya couldn't see the guard's face, but she could hear the suspicion in his voice.

"Your king is not in the habit of asking for anything, least of all permission," said Nikolai, his voice lazy but with the disdainful edge of a monarch who knew nothing but easy gratification.

"Of course, of course," said the guard. "We had only your safety in mind, my king."

Zoya doubted it. Western Ravka had bridled under the new taxes and laws that had come with unification. These guards might wear the double eagle, but their loyalty belonged to the duke who ran this estate and who had thrown up opposition to Nikolai's rule at every turn. No doubt their master would be thrilled to uncover the king's secrets.

Zoya summoned her most plaintive tone and said, "Why aren't we moving?"

She sensed the shift in their interest.

"A good night, then?" said the guard, and she could almost see him peering into the coach to get a better look.

Zoya tossed her long black hair and said with the sleepy, tousled sound of a woman well tumbled, "A very good night."

"She only play with royals?" said the guard. "She looks like fun."

Zoya felt Nikolai tense. She was both touched and annoyed that he thought she cared what some buffoon believed, but there was no need to play at chivalry tonight.

She cast the guard a long look and said, "You have no idea." He chortled and waved them through.

As the coach rolled on, Zoya felt the faint tremor of Nikolai's transformation still echoing through him and her own exhaustion creeping over her. It would be too easy to let her eyes close, to rest her head against his chest and give in to the illusion of comfort. But the price for such indulgence would be too high. "Eventually the monster will be found out," she said. "We've had no luck in finding a cure or even a hint of one. Marry. Forge an alliance. Make an heir. Secure the throne and Ravka's future."

"I will," he said wearily. "I'll do all of it. But not tonight. Tonight let's pretend we're an old married couple."

If any other man had said such a thing, she would have punched him in the jaw. Or possibly taken him to bed for a few hours. "And what does that entail?"

"We'll tell each other lies as married couples do. It will be a good game. Go on, wife. Tell me I'm a handsome fellow who will never age and who will die with all of his own teeth in his head. Make me believe it."

"I will not."

"I understand. You've never had a talent for deception."

Zoya knew he was goading her, but her pride pricked anyway. "How can you be so sure? Perhaps the list of my talents is so long you just haven't gotten to the end."

"Go on, then, Nazyalensky."

"Dearest husband," she said, making her voice honey sweet, "did you know the women of my family can see the future in the stars?"

He huffed a laugh. "I did not."

"Oh yes. And I've seen your fate in the constellations. You will grow old, fat, and happy, father many badly behaved children, and future generations will tell your story in legend and song."

"Very convincing," Nikolai said. "You're good at this game." A long silence followed, filled with nothing but the rattling of the coach wheels. "Now tell me I'll find a way out of this. Tell me it will be all right."

His tone was merry, teasing, but Zoya knew him too well. "It will be all right," she said with all the conviction she could muster. "We'll solve this problem as we've solved all the others before." She tilted her head up to look at him. His eyes were closed; a worried crease marred his brow. "Do you believe me?"

"Yes."

She pushed away from him and straightened her clothes. False-hoods were inevitable, maybe even necessary between a husband and wife. A general and her king could ill afford them.

"See?" she said. "You're good at this game too."

3

NINA

NINA CLUTCHED HER KNIFE and tried to ignore the carnage that surrounded her. She looked down at her victim, another body splayed out helpless before her.

"Sorry, friend," she murmured in Fjerdan. She drove her blade into the fish's belly, yanked up toward its head, seized the wet pink mess of its innards, and tossed them onto the filthy slats where they would be hosed away. The cleaned carcass went into a barrel to her left, to be cleared by one of the runners and taken off for packaging. Or processing. Or pickling. Nina had no idea what actually happened to the fish, and she didn't much care. After two weeks working at a cannery overlooking the Elling harbor, she didn't intend to eat anything with scales or fins ever again.

Imagine yourself in a warm bath with a dish full of toffees. Maybe she'd just fill the bathtub with toffee and be really decadent about the endeavor. It could become quite the rage. Toffee baths and waffle scrubs.

Nina gave her head a shake. This place was slowly driving her mad. Her hands were perpetually pruned, the skin nicked by tiny cuts from her clumsy way with the filleting knife; the smell of fish never left her hair; and her back ached from being on her feet in front of the cannery from dawn until dusk, rain or shine, protected from the elements by nothing but a corrugated tin awning. But there weren't many jobs for unmarried women in Fjerda, so Nina—under the name Mila Jandersdat—had gladly taken the position. The work was grueling but made it easy for their local contact to get her messages, and her vantage point among the fish barrels gave her a perfect view of the guards patrolling the harbor.

There were plenty of them today, roaming the docks in their blue uniforms. *Kalfisk*, the locals called them—squid—because they had their tentacles in everything. Elling sat where the Stelge River met the Isenvee, and it was one of the few harbors along Fjerda's rocky northwest coast with easy access to the sea for large vessels. The port was known for two things: smuggling and fish. Coalfish, monkfish, haddock; salmon and sturgeon from the river cities to the east; tilefish and silver-sided king mackerel from the deep waters offshore.

Nina worked beside two women—a Hedjut widow named Annabelle, and Marta, a spinster from Djerholm who was as narrow as a gap in the floorboards and constantly shook her head as if everything displeased her. Their chatter helped to keep Nina distracted and was a welcome source of gossip and legitimate information, though it could be hard to tell the difference between the two.

"They say Captain Birgir has a new mistress," Annabelle would begin.

Marta would purse her lips. "With the bribes he takes he can certainly afford to keep her."

"They're increasing patrols since those stowaways were caught."

Marta would cluck her tongue. "Means more jobs but probably more trouble."

"More men in from Gäfvalle today. River's gone sour up by the old fort."

Marta's head would twitch back and forth like a happy dog's tail. "A sign of Djel's disfavor. Someone should send a priest to say prayers."

Gäfvalle. One of the river cities. Nina had never been there, had never even heard of it until she'd arrived with Adrik and Leoni two months ago on orders from King Nikolai, but its name always left her uneasy, the sound of it accompanied by a kind of sighing inside her, as if the town's name was less a word than the start of an incantation.

Now Marta knocked the base of her knife against the wooden surface of her worktable. "Foreman coming."

Hilbrand, the stern-faced foreman, was moving through the rows of stalls, calling out to runners to remove the buckets of fish.

"Your pace is off again," he barked at Nina. "It's as if you've never gutted fish before."

Imagine that. "I'm sorry, sir," she said. "I'll do better."

He cut his hand through the air. "Too slow. The shipment we've been waiting for has arrived. We'll move you to the packing room floor."

"Yes, sir," Nina said glumly. She dropped her shoulders and hung her head when what she really wanted to do was break into song. The pay for packing jobs was considerably lower, so she had to make a good show of her defeat, but she'd understood Hilbrand's real message: The last of the Grisha fugitives they'd been waiting for had made it to the Elling safe house at last. Now it was up to Nina, Adrik, and Leoni to get the seven newcomers aboard the *Verstoten.*

She followed close behind Hilbrand as he led her back toward the cannery.

"You'll have to move quickly," he said without looking at her. "There's talk of a surprise inspection tonight."

"All right." An obstacle, but nothing they couldn't handle.

"There's more," he said. "Birgir is on duty."

Of course he is. No doubt the surprise inspection was Captain Birgir's idea. Of all the *kalfisk*, he was the most corrupt but also the sharpest and most observant. If you wanted a legal shipment to get through the harbor without being trapped forever in customs—or if you wanted an illegal bit of cargo to avoid notice—then a bribe for Birgir was the cost.

A man without honor, said Matthias' voice in her head. *He should be ashamed.*

Nina snorted. *If men were ashamed when they should be, they'd have no time for anything else.*

"Is something amusing?" Hilbrand asked.

"Just fighting a cold," she lied. But even Hilbrand's gruff manner put a pang in her heart. He was broad-shouldered and humorless and reminded her painfully of Matthias.

He's nothing like me. What a bigot you are, Nina Zenik. Not all Fjerdans look alike.

"You know what Birgir did to those stowaways," Hilbrand said. "I don't have to tell you to be careful."

"No, you don't," Nina said more sharply than she meant to. She was good at her job, and she knew exactly what was at stake. Her first morning at the docks, she'd seen Birgir and one of his favorite thugs, Casper, drag a mother and daughter off a whaler bound for Novyi Zem and beat them bloody. The captain had hung heavy chains around their necks weighted with signs that read *drüsje*— witch. Then he'd doused them in a slurry of waste and fish guts from the canneries and bound them outside the harbor station in the blazing sun. As his men looked on, laughing, the stink and the promise of

32

food drew the gulls. Nina had spent her shift watching the woman trying to shield her daughter's body with her own, and listening to the prisoners cry out in agony as the gulls pecked and clawed at their bodies. Her mind had spun a thousand fantasies of murdering Birgir's harbor guards where they stood, of whisking the mother and daughter to safety. She could steal a boat. She could force a ship's captain to take them far away. She could do *something*.

But she'd remembered too clearly Zoya's warning to King Nikolai about Nina's suitability for a deep-cover mission: "She doesn't have a subtle bone in her body. Asking Nina not to draw attention is like asking water not to run downhill."

The king had taken a chance on Nina, and she would not squander the opportunity. She would not jeopardize the mission. She would not compromise her cover and put Adrik and Leoni at risk. At least not in broad daylight. As soon as the sun had set, she'd slipped back to the harbor to free the prisoners. They were gone. But to where? And to suffer what horrors? She no longer believed that the worst terror awaiting Grisha at the hands of Fjerdan soldiers was death. Jarl Brum and his witchhunters had taught her too well.

As Nina followed Hilbrand into the cannery, the grind of machinery rattled her skull, the stink of salt cod overwhelming her. She wouldn't be sorry to leave Elling for a while. The hold of the *Verstoten* was full of Grisha that her team—or Adrik's team, really—had helped rescue and bring to Elling. Since the end of the civil war, King Nikolai had diverted funds and resources to support an underground network of informants that had existed for years in Fjerda with the goal of helping Grisha living in secret to escape the country. They called themselves Hringsa, the tree of life, after the great ash sacred to Djel. Nina knew Adrik had already received new intelligence from the group, and once the *Verstoten* was safely on its way to Ravka, Nina and the others would be free to head inland to locate more Grisha.

Hilbrand led her to his office, shut the door behind them, then ran his fingers along the far wall. A click sounded and a second, hidden door opened onto the Fiskstrahd, the bustling street where fishmongers did their business and where a girl on her own might avoid the notice of the harbor police by simply disappearing into the crowd.

"Thank you," Nina said. "We'll be sending more your way soon."

"Wait." Hilbrand snagged her arm before she could slip into the sunshine. He hesitated, then blurted out, "Are you really her? The girl who bested Jarl Brum and left him bleeding on a Djerholm dock?"

Nina yanked her arm from his grip. She'd done what she had to do to free her friends and keep the secret of *jurda parem* out of Fjerdan hands. But it was the drug that had made victory possible, and it had exacted an awful price, changing the course of Nina's life and the very nature of her Grisha power.

If we'd never gone to the Ice Court, would Matthias still be alive? Would my heart still be whole? Pointless questions. There was no answer that would bring him back.

Nina fixed Hilbrand with the withering glare she'd learned from Zoya Nazyalensky herself. "I'm Mila Jandersdat. A young widow taking odd jobs to make ends meet and hoping to secure work as a translator. What kind of fool would pick a fight with Commander Jarl Brum?" Hilbrand opened his mouth, but Nina continued, "And what kind of podge would risk compromising an agent's cover when so many lives are on the line?"

Nina turned her back on him and waded into the human tide. *Dangerous.* A man who lived his life in deep cover shouldn't be so careless. But Nina knew that loneliness could make you foolish, hungry to speak something other than lies. Hilbrand had lost his wife to Brum's men, the ruthless *drüskelle* trained to hunt and kill Grisha. Since then, he'd become one of King Nikolai's most trusted operatives in Fjerda. Nina didn't doubt his loyalty, and his own safety relied on his discretion.

It took Nina less than ten minutes to reach the address Hilbrand had given her, another cannery identical to the buildings bracketing it—except for the mural on its western side. At first glance, it looked like a pleasant scene set at the mouth of the Stelge: a group of fishermen casting their nets into the sea as happy villagers looked on beneath a setting sun. But if you knew what to look for, you might notice the white-haired girl in the crowd, her profile framed by the sun as if by a halo. Sankta Alina. The Sun Summoner. A sign that this warehouse was a place of refuge.

The Saints had never been popular among the people of the north—until Alina Starkov had destroyed the Fold. Then altars to her had begun to spring up in countries far outside Ravka. Fjerdan authorities had done their best to quash the cult of the Sun Saint, labeling it a religion of foreign influence, but still, little pockets of the faithful had bloomed, gardens tended in secret. The stories of the Saints, their miracles and martyrdoms, had become a code for those sympathetic to Grisha. A rose for Sankta Lizabeta. A sun for Sankta Alina. A knight skewering a dragon on his lance might be Dagr the Bold from some children's tale—or it might be Sankt Juris, who had slain a great beast and been consumed by its flames. Even the tattoos that ran over Hilbrand's forearms were more than they seemed—a tangle of antlers, often worn by northern hunters, but arranged in circular bands to symbolize the powerful amplifier Sankta Alina had once worn.

Nina knocked on the cannery's side door, and a moment later it swung open. Adrik ushered her inside, his glum face pale beneath his freckles. His features were pleasant enough, but he maintained a relentlessly defeated demeanor that gave him the look of a melting candle. Instantly, Nina's eyes began to water.

"I know," said Adrik dismally. "Elling. If the cold doesn't kill you, the smell will."

"No fish smells like that. My eyes are burning."

"It's lye. Vats of it. Apparently they preserve fish in it as some kind of local delicacy."

She could almost hear Matthias' indignant protest: *It's delicious. We serve it on toast.* Saints, she missed him. The ache of his absence felt like a hook lodged inside her heart. The hurt was always there, but in moments like these, it was as if someone had seized hold of the line and pulled.

Nina took a deep breath. Matthias would want her to focus on the mission. "They're here?"

"They are. But there's a problem."

She'd thought Adrik seemed more morose than usual. And that was saying something.

Nina saw Leoni first, bent over a makeshift crate desk beside a row of vats, a lantern near her elbow, her ordinarily cheerful face set in hard lines of determination. The twists of her hair were knotted in the Zemeni style, and her dark brown skin was sheened with sweat. On the floor next to her, she'd cracked open her kit—pots of ink and powdered pigments, rolls of paper and parchment. But that made no sense. The emigration documents should have been long since finished.

Understanding came as Nina's eyes adjusted and she saw the figures huddled in the shadows—a bearded man in a muskrat-colored coat and a far older man with a thick thatch of white hair. Two little boys peeked out from behind them, eyes wide and frightened. Four fugitives. There should have been seven.

Leoni glanced up at Nina, then at the fugitive Grisha, offering them a warm smile. "She's a friend. Don't worry."

They didn't look reassured.

"Jormanen end denam danne näskelle," Nina said, the traditional Fjerdan greeting to travelers. *Be welcome and wait out the storm.* It wasn't totally appropriate to their situation, but it was the best she could offer. The men seemed to relax at the words, though the children still looked terrified.

"Grannem end kerjenning grante jut onter kelholm," the older man said in traditional reply. *I thank you and bring only gratitude to your home.* Nina hoped that wasn't true. Ravka didn't need gratitude; it needed more Grisha. It needed soldiers. She could only imagine what Zoya would make of these recruits.

"Where are the other three?" Nina asked Adrik.

"They didn't meet their handler."

"Captured?"

"Probably."

"Maybe they had a change of heart," said Leoni, opening a bottle of something blue. She could always be counted on to find a positive outcome, no matter how unlikely. "It isn't easy to leave all you love behind."

"It is when all you love smells of fish and despair," Adrik grumbled.

"The emigration papers?" Nina asked Leoni as gently as she could.

"I'm doing my best," Leoni replied. "You said women don't travel alone, so I wrote up the indentures as families, and now we're short two wives and a daughter."

Not good at all. Especially with *kalfisk* crawling all over the docks. But Leoni was one of the most talented Fabrikators Nina had met.

In recent years, the Fjerdan government had begun to watch their borders more closely and prohibit travel for their citizens. The authorities were on the lookout for Grisha attempting to escape, but they also wanted to slow the tide of people traveling across the True Sea to Novyi Zem seeking better jobs and warmer weather, people willing to brave a new world to live free of the threat of war. Many Ravkans had done the same.

Fjerda's officials especially didn't like to let able-bodied men and prospective soldiers emigrate and had made the necessary papers almost impossible to fake. That was why Leoni was here. She was no ordinary forger but a Fabrikator who could match inks and paper at a molecular level.

Nina pulled a clean handkerchief from her pocket and dabbed Leoni's brow. "You can manage this."

She shook her head. "I need more time."

"We don't have it." Nina wished she didn't have to say so.

"We might," Leoni said hopefully. She had spent most of her life in Novyi Zem before traveling to Ravka to train, and like many Fabrikators, she had never seen combat. Fabrikators hadn't even been taught to fight until Alina Starkov had led the Second Army. "We can send word to the *Verstoten*, ask them to wait until—"

"It's no good," Nina said. "That ship has to be out of port by sunset. Captain Birgir is planning one of his surprise raids tonight."

Leoni let out a long breath, then bobbed her chin at the man in the muskrat-colored coat. "Nina, we'll have to pass you off as his wife."

It wasn't ideal. Nina had been working at the harbor for weeks now, and there was a chance she'd be recognized. But it was a risk worth taking. "What's your name?" she asked the man.

"Enok."

"Those are your sons?"

He nodded. "And this is my father."

"You're all Grisha?"

"Just me and my boys."

"Well, lucky you, Enok. You're about to acquire me as a wife. I enjoy long naps and short engagements, and I prefer the left side of the bed."

Enok blinked and his father looked positively scandalized. Genya had tailored Nina to look as Fjerdan as possible, but the demure ways of northern women were far more exhausting to master.

Nina tried not to pace as Leoni worked and Adrik spoke quietly to the fugitives. What had happened to the other three Grisha? Nina picked up the discarded emigration documents, priceless sets of papers that would never be used. Two women and a girl of sixteen missing. Had they decided a life in hiding was better than an uncertain future in a foreign land? Or had they been taken prisoner? Were they somewhere out there, scared and alone? Nina frowned at the papers. "Were these women really from Kejerut?"

Leoni nodded. "It seemed simpler to keep the town the same."

Enok's father made a sign of warding in the air. It was an old gesture, meant to wash away evil thoughts with the strength of Djel's waters. "Girls go missing from Kejerut."

Nina shivered as that strange sighing filled her head again. Kejerut was only a few miles from Gäfvalle. But it all might mean nothing.

She rubbed her arms, trying to dispel the sudden cold that settled into her. She wished Hilbrand hadn't mentioned Jarl Brum. Despite all she'd been through, it was a name that still had power over her. Nina had defeated him and his men. Her friends had blown Brum's secret laboratory to bits and stolen his most valuable hostage. He should have been disgraced. It should have meant an end to his command of the *druskelle* and his brutal experiments with *jurda parem* and Grisha prisoners. And yet somehow, Brum had survived and continued to thrive in the highest ranks of the Fjerdan military. *I should have killed him when I had the chance.*

You showed mercy, Nina. Never regret that.

But mercy was a luxury Matthias could afford. He was dead, after all.

It seems rude to mention that, my love.

What do you expect from a Ravkan? Besides, Brum and I aren't done.

Is that why you're here?

I'm here to bury you, Matthias, she thought, and the voice in her head went silent, as it always did when she let herself remember what she'd lost.

Nina tried to shake the thought of Matthias' body, preserved by Fabrikator craft, bound up in ropes and tarp like ballast, hidden beneath blankets and crates on the sledge that waited back at their boardinghouse. She'd sworn she would take him home, that she would bury his body in the land he loved so that he could find his way to his god. And for nearly two months they had traveled with that body, dragged that grim burden from town to town. She'd had countless opportunities to lay him to rest and say her goodbyes. So why hadn't she taken them? Nina knew Leoni and Adrik didn't want to raise the issue with her, but they couldn't be thrilled to be members of a months-long funeral procession.

It has to be the right place, my love. You'll know it when you see it.

But would she? Or would she just keep marching, unable to let him go?

Somewhere in the distance, a bell rang, signaling the end of the workday.

"We're out of time," said Adrik.

Leoni didn't protest, just stretched and said, "Come dry the ink."

Adrik waved his hand, directing a warm gust of Squaller air over the documents. "It's nice to be useful."

"I'm sure you'll come in very handy when we need to fly kites."

They exchanged a smile, and Nina felt a stab of irritation, then wanted to kick herself for being so unfair. Just because she was miserable didn't mean everyone else should be.

But as they all set out toward the docks with the fugitives in tow, Adrik began giving them instructions, and Nina felt her temper spike again. Though he was her commanding officer, she'd lost the habit of taking orders during her time in Ketterdam.

Leoni and Adrik led the way to the *Verstoten*. They were conspicuous but in a way that fit with the tumult of the harbor—a Zemeni woman and her husband, a merchant couple with business on the docks. Nina slipped her arm through Enok's and hung back slightly with her new family, keeping a careful distance.

She rolled her shoulders, trying to focus, but that only served to sharpen the edge of her tension. Her body felt wrong. Back in Os Alta, Genya Safin had tailored her to the very brink of what her skills would allow. Nina's new hair was slick, straight, and nearly ice white; her eyes were narrower, the green of her irises changed to the pale blue of a northern glacier. Her cheekbones were higher, her brows lower, her mouth broader.

"I look uncooked," she'd complained when she'd seen the milky depth of her new pallor.

Genya had been unmoved. "You look Fjerdan."

Nina's thighs were still solid, her waist still thick, but Genya had pushed back Nina's ears, flattened her breasts, and even changed the set of her shoulders. The process had been painful at times as the bone was altered, but Nina didn't care. She didn't want to be the girl she'd been, the girl Matthias had loved. If Genya could make her someone new on the outside, maybe Nina's heart would oblige and beat with a new rhythm too. Of course, it hadn't worked. The Fjerdans saw Mila Jandersdat, but she was still Nina Zenik, legendary Grisha and unrepentant killer. She was still the girl who craved waffles and who cried herself to sleep at night when she reached for Matthias and found no one there.

Enok's arm tensed beneath her fingers, and she saw that two members of the harbor police were waiting at the gangway that led onto the *Verstoten*.

"It's going to be fine," murmured Nina. "We'll see you all the way onto the ship."

"And then what?" Enok asked, voice trembling.

"Once we're out of the bay, I'll take a rowboat back to shore with the others. You and your family will travel on to Ravka, where you'll be free to live without fear."

"Will they take my boys? Will they take them away to that special school?"

"Only if that's what you wish," said Nina. "We're not monsters. Not any more than you are. Now hush."

But part of her wanted to turn around and stride right back to the safe house when she saw that one of the guards was Birgir's champion thug, Casper. She tucked her face into her coat collar.

"Zemeni?" Casper asked, glancing at Leoni. She nodded in reply.

Casper gestured to Adrik's missing arm. "How'd you lose it?"

"Farming accident," Adrik replied in Fjerdan. He didn't know much of the language, but he could speak bits and pieces without a Ravkan accent, and this particular lie was one he'd told many times. Nearly everyone they met asked about his arm as soon as they saw the pinned sleeve. He'd had to leave the mechanical arm David Kostyk had fashioned for him back in the capital because it was too recognizable as Grisha handiwork.

The guards asked them the usual series of questions—How long had they been in the country? Where had they visited during their stay? Did they have knowledge of foreign agents working inside Fjerda's borders?—then waved them through with little ceremony.

Now it was Enok's turn. She gave his arm a squeeze and he stepped forward. Nina could see the sweat beading at his temple, feel the slight tremor in his hands. If she could have snatched the papers away and given them to the guards herself, she would have. But Fjerdan wives always deferred to their husbands.

"The Grahn family." Casper peered at the papers for an uncomfortably long time. "Indentures? Where will you be working?"

"A *jurda* farm near Cofton," said Enok.

"Hard work. Too hard for the old father there."

"He'll be in the main house with the boys," said Enok. "He's gifted with a needle and thread, and the boys can be runners until they're old enough for the fields."

Nina was impressed by how easily Enok lied, but if he'd spent his life hiding as a Grisha, he must have had plenty of practice.

"Indentures are difficult to come by," mused Casper.

"My uncle secured them for us."

"And why is a life breaking your back in Novyi Zem so preferable to one spent doing honest work in Fjerda?"

"I'd live and die on the ice if I had my way," said Enok with such fervor Nina knew he was speaking the truth. "But jobs are scarce and my son's lungs don't like the cold."

"Hard times all around." The guard turned to Nina. "And what will you do in Cofton?"

"Sew if I'm able, work the fields if need be." She dipped her head. She could be subtle, damn it. No matter what Zoya thought. "As my husband wishes."

Casper continued to look at the papers, waiting, and Nina nudged Enok with her elbow. Looking as if he might be sick all over the docks, Enok reached into his pocket and drew out a packet stuffed with Fjerdan currency.

He handed it to Casper, who lifted a brow. Then the guard's face broke into a satisfied smile. Nina remembered him watching the gulls tear at the Grisha chained in the sun, their beaks bloodied with bits of skin and hair.

Casper waved them through. "May Djel watch over you."

But they hadn't set foot on the gangway when Nina heard a voice say, "Just a moment."

Birgir. Couldn't they catch a bit of luck? The sun hadn't even set. They should have had more time. Enok's father hesitated on the gangway next to Leoni, and Adrik gave Nina the barest shake of his head. The message was clear: *Don't start trouble.* Nina thought of the other Grisha fugitives packed into the hold of the ship and held her tongue.

Birgir stood between Casper and the other guard. He was short for a Fjerdan, his shoulders sloped like a bull's, and his uniform fit so impeccably that Nina suspected it had been professionally tailored.

She kept behind Enok and whispered to the boys, "Go to your grandfather." But they didn't move.

"It was a hard day's travel for all of us," Enok said to Birgir amiably. "The boys are eager to get settled."

"I'll see your papers first."

"We just showed them to your man."

"Casper's eyes aren't nearly as good as mine."

"But the money—" protested Enok.

"What money was that?"

Casper and the other guard shrugged. "I don't know about any money."

Reluctantly, Enok handed over the papers.

"Perhaps," said his father, "we could reach a new arrangement?"

"Stay where you are," ordered Birgir.

"But our ship is about to depart," Nina tried from behind Enok's shoulder.

Birgir glanced at the *Verstoten*, at the boys tugging restlessly on their father's hands. "They're going to be a handful cooped up for a sea journey." Then he looked back at Enok and Nina. "Funny the way they cling to their father and not their mother."

"They're scared," said Nina. "You're frightening them."

Birgir's cold eyes traveled over Adrik and Leoni. He smacked the indenture papers against his gloved palm. "That ship isn't going anywhere. Not until we've seen every inch of it." He gestured to Casper. "There's something off here. Signal the others."

Casper reached for his whistle, but before he could draw breath to blow, Nina's arm shot out. Two slender bone shards flew from the sheaths sewn into the forearms of her coat—everything she wore was laced with them. The darts lodged in Casper's windpipe, and a sharp wheeze squeaked from his mouth. Nina twisted her fingers and the bone shards rotated. The guard dropped to the dock, clawing at his neck.

"Casper!" Birgir and the other guard drew their guns.

Nina shoved Enok and the children behind her. "Get them on the boat," she growled. *Don't start trouble.* She hadn't, but she intended to finish it.

"I know you," Birgir said, training his gun on her, his eyes hard and bright as river stones.

"That's a bold statement."

"You work at the salmon cannery. One of the barrel girls. I knew there was something wrong about you."

Nina couldn't help but smile. "Plenty of things."

"Mila," Adrik said warningly, using her cover name. As if it mattered now. The time for bribes and negotiations was over. She liked these moments best. When the secrets fell away.

Nina flicked her fingers. The bone shards dislodged from Casper's windpipe and slid back into the hidden sheaths on her arm. He flopped on the dock, his lips wet with blood, his eyes rolling back in his head as he struggled for breath.

"*Drüsje*," Birgir hissed. *Witch.*

"I don't like that word," Nina said, advancing. "Call me Grisha. Call me zowa. Call me death, if you like."

Birgir laughed. "Two guns are pointed at you. You think you can kill us both before one of us gets a shot off?"

"But you're already dying, Captain," she crooned gently. The bone armor the Fabrikators had made for her in Os Alta was a comfort and had proven useful more times than she could count. But sometimes she could feel death already waiting in her targets, like now, in this man who stood before her, his chin jutting forward, the brass buttons on his fine uniform gleaming. He was younger than she'd realized, his golden stubble patchy in places, as if he couldn't quite grow a beard. Should she be sorry for him? She was not.

Nina. Matthias' voice, chiding, disappointed. Perhaps she was doomed to stand on docks and murder Fjerdans. There were worse fates.

"You know it, don't you?" she went on. "Somewhere inside. Your body knows." She drew closer. "That cough you can't shake. The pain you told yourself was a bruised rib. The way food has lost its savor." In the day's fading light she saw fear come into Birgir's face, a shadow falling. It fed her, and that strange sighing inside her grew louder, a whispering chorus that rose, as if in encouragement, even as Matthias' voice receded.

"You work in a harbor," she continued. "You know how easy it is for rats to get into the walls, to eat a place up from the inside." Birgir's pistol hand dipped slightly. He was watching her now, closely—not with his sharp policeman's eyes but with the gaze of a man who didn't want to listen, but who had to, who must know the end to the story. "The enemy is already inside you, the bad cells eating the others slowly, right there in your lungs. Unusual in a man so young. You're dying, Captain Birgir," she said softly, almost kindly. "I'm just going to help you along."

The captain seemed to wake from a trance. He raised his pistol, but he was too slow. Nina's power already had hold of that sick cluster of cells within him, and death unfurled, a terrible multiplication. He might have lived another year, maybe two, but now the cells became a black tide, destroying everything in their path. Captain Birgir released a low moan and toppled. Before the remaining guard could react, Nina flicked her fingers and drove a shard of bone through his heart.

The docks were curiously still. She could hear the waves lapping against the *Verstoten*'s hull, the high calls of seabirds. Inside her the whispering chorus leapt, the sound almost joyful.

Then one of Enok's boys began to cry.

For a moment, Nina had stood alone with death on the docks, two weary travelers, longtime companions. But now she saw the way the others were watching her—the Grisha fugitives, Adrik and Leoni, even the ship's captain and his crew leaning over the railing of the ship. Maybe she should have cared; maybe some part of her did. Nina's power was frightening, a corruption of the Heartrender power she had been born with, twisted by *parem*. And still it had become dear to her. Matthias had accepted the dark thing in her and encouraged her to do the same—but what Nina felt was not acceptance. It was love.

Adrik sighed. "I'm not going to miss this town." He called up to the ship's crew. "Stop staring and help us get the bodies on board. We'll dispose of them when we reach open water."

Some men deserve your mercy, Nina.

Of course, Matthias. Nina watched Enok and his father lift Birgir's body. *I'll let you know when I meet one of them.*

Adrik held his tongue until they were in the little rowboat headed back to shore. They would make land in one of the coves north of Elling and hike back to their lodgings to collect their things.

"There's going to be trouble when those men are discovered missing," he said.

Nina felt like a child being scolded, and she didn't appreciate it. "Good thing we'll be long gone."

"We won't be able to operate out of this port anymore," added Leoni. "They're going to tighten security."

"Don't take his side."

"I'm not taking sides," said Leoni. "I'm just making an observation."

"Did you want to give up the whole ship? Did you want to give up the Grisha in the hold?"

Adrik adjusted the rudder. "Nina, I'm not angry at you. I'm trying to figure out what we do next."

She leaned into her oars. "You're a little angry with me."

"No one's angry," said Leoni, matching Nina's pace. "We freed a ship full of Grisha from that horrible place. And it's not like Birgir and his *kalfisk* goons didn't have plenty of enemies on the docks. They could have run into trouble with anyone during their *surprise inspection*. I call this a victory."

"Of course you do," said Adrik. "If you can find a way to put a sunny spin on something, you will."

It was true. Leoni was like cheer in a bottle—and not even months in Fjerda had dimmed her shine.

"Are you actually *humming*?" Adrik had once asked incredulously when they'd been forced to spend an hour digging their sledge out of the mud. "How can you be so relentlessly optimistic? It isn't healthy."

Leoni had stopped humming to give the question her full consideration as she tried to coax their horse to pull. "I suppose it's because I almost died as a child. When the gods give you another look at the world, best enjoy it."

Adrik had barely raised a brow. "I've been shot, stabbed, bayoneted, and had my arm torn off by a shadow demon. It's done nothing for my disposition."

It was true. If Leoni was sunshine walking, Adrik was a doleful storm cloud too put-upon to actually rain.

Now he cast his eyes at the spangle of stars above them as he steered the rowboat toward shore. "The *Verstoten* will have to be repainted, given new documentation and a new history. We'll have to shift our operations to another port. Maybe Hjar."

Nina gripped her oars. King Nikolai had sent the *Verstoten* to dock and trade in Elling for the better part of a year before Adrik's team had begun their mission. It was a familiar vessel that had drawn scarce attention. A perfect cover. *Had* she acted too hastily? Captain Birgir had been a greedy man, not a righteous one. Maybe she'd wanted to see him dead a little too much. But she'd been like this since Matthias died—fine one moment, then ready to snarl and snap like a wild thing.

No, like a wounded animal. And like a wounded animal, for a time, she had gone to ground. She'd spent months at the Little Palace, rekindling old friendships, eating familiar food, sitting by the fire in the Hall of the Golden Dome, trying to remember who she'd been before Matthias, before a glowering Fjerdan had disrupted her life with his unexpected honor, before she'd known that a witchhunter might shed his hate and fear and become the boy she loved. Before he'd been taken from her. But if there was a way back to the girl she had been, she hadn't found it. And now she was here, in Matthias' country, in this cold, hostile place.

"We'll go south," Leoni was saying. "It's only going to get colder. We can work our way back here in a few months, when good old Captain Birgir has been forgotten."

It was a reasonable plan, but the whispering chorus in Nina's head rose, and she found herself saying, "We should go to Kejerut, to Gäfvalle. The fugitives who didn't make it to the safe house didn't just change their minds."

"You know they were most likely captured," said Adrik.

Tell them the truth, my love.

"Yes, I do," said Nina. "But you heard what that old man said. Girls go missing from Kejerut."

Tell them you hear the dead calling.

You don't know that, Matthias.

It was one thing to hear her dead lover's voice, quite another to claim she could sense . . . what exactly? She didn't know. But she didn't think the whispering in her head was just imagination. Something was pulling her east to the river cities.

"There's another thing," said Nina. "The women I worked with claimed the river up near Gäfvalle had gone sour, that the town was cursed."

Now she had Adrik's attention. What had she once said to Jesper back in Ketterdam? *Do you know the best way to find Grisha who don't want to be found? Look for miracles and listen to bedtime stories.* Tales of witches and wondrous happenings, warnings about cursed places— they were signposts to things that ordinary people didn't understand. Sometimes there was little more to it than local lore. But sometimes there were Grisha hiding in these places, disguising their powers, living in fear. Grisha they could help.

Tell them the truth, Nina.

Nina rubbed her arms. *You're like a dog with a bone, Matthias.*

50

A wolf. Did I ever tell you about the way Trassel would destroy my boots if I didn't tie them up in a branch out of his reach?

He had. Matthias had told her all kinds of stories to keep her distracted when she'd been recovering from the influence of *parem*. He'd kept her alive. Why hadn't she been able to do the same for him?

"Curses, spoiled rivers," continued Nina. "If it's nothing, we head south and I'll buy you both a good dinner."

"In Fjerda?" said Adrik. "I won't hold you to it."

"But if I'm right . . ."

"Fine," Adrik said. "I'll send word to Ravka that we need to establish a new port, and we'll head to Gäfvalle."

The whispers quieted to a gentle murmur.

"Nina . . ." Leoni hesitated. "There's open land out there. Beautiful country. You could find a place for him."

Nina looked out at the dark water, at the lights glittering on shore. *Find a place for him.* As if Matthias were an old armoire or a plant that needed just the right amount of sun. *His place is with me.* But that wasn't true anymore. Matthias was gone. His body was all that remained, and without Leoni's careful maintenance, it would have long ago given way to rot. Nina felt the press of tears in the back of her throat. She would *not* cry. They'd been in Fjerda two months. They'd helped nearly forty Grisha escape Fjerdan rule. They'd traversed hundreds of miles of barren field and snowy plain. There had been plenty of places to lay Matthias to rest. Now it had to be done. It would be done. And one of her promises to him would be fulfilled.

"I'll see to it," she said.

"One more thing," said Adrik, and she could hear the command in his voice, so different from his usual dismal tone. "Our job is to find recruits and refugees. Whatever we discover in Gäfvalle, we are not there to start a war. We gather intelligence, open communication, provide a path to escape for those who want it, and that's all."

"That's the plan," said Nina. She touched her fingers to the spikes of bone in her gloves.

But plans could change.

NIKOLAI

DESPITE ZOYA'S PROTESTS, Nikolai had refused to remain in Ivets. The beginnings of a plan had formed in his mind, and he didn't want to waste another day languishing at a trade summit. He wasn't interested in Hiram Schenck or his marriageable daughters, and the next time Nikolai conversed with a member of the Kerch Merchant Council, it would be on his own terms.

To that end, though he had plenty of business awaiting him in the capital, his first stop had to be at Count Kirigin's. He needed to collect a bit of information along with his most valued Fabrikator—and, as a rule, if one had the opportunity to visit a pleasure palace, one should. Especially if said pleasure palace served as cover for a secret laboratory.

The elder Count Kirigin was a West Ravkan merchant who had made vast sums of money trading arms and intelligence—and anything else that wasn't nailed down—to Ravka's enemies. But his son had served with Nikolai in Halmhend, and in exchange for getting to keep his considerable fortune as well as avoiding the disgrace of being stripped of his title and seeing his father thrown in jail forever for treason, the younger Kirigin had pledged both money and fealty to the crown. A more than reasonable bargain.

Nikolai's demands had been unorthodox: Kirigin was already a bit of a rake. Now he was to live decadently, spend wildly, and maintain a reputation as a notorious libertine and social climber. The young count had taken to the role with zeal, staging elaborate parties renowned for their debauchery and doing his best to buy his way into the homes of Ravkan nobles who possessed more illustrious titles and older if less plentiful fortunes. He dressed absurdly, drank excessively, and dithered about with such stupid good cheer that his name had become synonymous with both wealth and buffoonery: *Oh, the Gritzkis' son is a terror and unlikely to make much of himself, but at least he's not a Kirigin.*

This was why, when Kirigin bought a vast swath of land just east of Os Alta, no one blinked. *Of course Kirigin wants to be close to the capital,* they whispered in sitting rooms and salons. *Trying to curry favor with the king and the old families, no doubt. But what man of sense and breeding would ever let his daughter near that upstart?* And when Kirigin commissioned some Zemeni mastermind to design a pleasure compound for him like none ever seen on Ravkan soil—complete with earthworks that required the hiring of thousands of men to dig a valley where there had been none before, a wine cellar said to stretch for a mile underground, and a vast lake that required Grisha Tidemakers to fill it and took days to cross by boat? Well, no one batted an eye. They shook their heads when Kirigin took up hot-air ballooning and laughed behind their hands when the meadows where he launched excursions were so frequently plagued by fog. *Wasteful, grotesque, obscene*, they chorused. And all hoped for invitations to one of Kirigin's spectacular fetes.

Kirigin dubbed his magnificent compound Lazlayon, the Gilded Hollow—though it was so often cloaked in mists and damp that it was usually referred to as the Gilded Bog—and the parties he threw there were indeed legendary. But they were also part of a grand lie, a lie essential to Ravka's future.

As it turned out, Kirigin's wine cellar ran for five miles, not one, and it was not a wine cellar at all but an underground bunker devoted to weapons development. The lake was used for prototypes of undersea craft and Nikolai's new naval warfare ventures. The dense fog that shrouded the valley was frequently helped along by Grisha Squallers to provide cover from prying eyes and Fjerdan air surveillance. The ballooning meadow was in fact an airfield; the elaborate gardens hid two long, straight runways for testing experimental aircraft; and the frequent fireworks Kirigin staged disguised the sound of rifle fire and shelling.

There was, of course, no mysterious Zemeni architect. Nikolai had designed the Gilded Bog himself—though young Count Kirigin's fortune had paid for its construction. The king visited occasionally as a party guest, to ride or hunt or drink Kirigin's excellent wines. But more often, he arrived in secret through one of his own private entrances and went immediately to see to the progress of his latest endeavor.

Nikolai always felt a sense of excitement as he entered the Gilded Bog. The palace at Os Alta was full of ghosts. His father's crimes. His mother's failings. The memory of his brother's body bleeding on the floor as the Darkling's shadow soldiers smashed through the windows of the Eagle's Nest. But Lazlayon was Nikolai's creation. Here, for a short time, the demon that ruled his nights and troubled his dreams retreated, held at bay by logic, the hope of progress, and the happy pastime of building giant things meant to explode. But the Gilded Bog was not only a playground for his inventions—it was also where the strengths of the First and Second Armies, of traditional weaponry and Grisha power, would be forged into something new.

Hopefully, thought Nikolai as he and Tolya reached the front steps of the main house. *Or it's where I'll spend the last of Ravka's war chest and have nothing to show for it but a pile of rusty propellers and a chilly lake that makes for mediocre sailing.*

Ravka was many things to him: a grand lady who required constant courting, a stubborn child unwilling to stand on its own, and most often, a drowning man—the more Nikolai struggled to save it, the harder it fought. But with the help of the scientists and soldiers at the Gilded Bog, he might just drag his country to shore yet.

"Your Highness!" Kirigin said as he swept down the stairs to greet Nikolai. His orange hair had been arranged in a sleek coiffure, and he was turned out in a violet coat and gold brocade wholly inappropriate to the hour. Beside Tolya dressed in stolid olive drab and mounted on his towering stock horse, Kirigin looked like an actor in the wrong play. "How can I be expected to prepare the best entertainments when you give me no notice of your arrival?"

"Ah, Kirigin," said Nikolai, ignoring the formality of the count's bow to embrace him and slap him on the back. "I know you like to improvise."

"A visit to the wine cellar is the perfect place to start. Do come inside."

"Tolya and I would prefer to have a ride around your grounds. Will you be stocking game for the season?"

"Of course, Your Highness. We must have sport to keep us warm this winter, and if not, the three hundred bottles of Kerch brandy I've laid my hands on should do the trick."

For Saints' sake. Nikolai sometimes worried that Kirigin had taken to his role as a reprobate with a little too much enthusiasm. "Just don't get the entirety of my cabinet soused," he said. "I need a few coherent ministers on hand."

"Of course, of course," said Kirigin, peering down the drive, the hope clear on his face. *Poor fool.*

"Zoya has gone directly to the capital."

Kirigin cleared his throat. "It's of no matter to me. I just wondered if I should have that cordial she likes waiting. Is Commander Nazyalensky well?"

"Pretty as a picture and brimming with spite."

"She is lovely, isn't she?" said Kirigin dreamily. "I'll leave you to it, then. And if you would . . . send her my regards?"

"All Saints," rumbled Tolya. "She'd have you for breakfast."

The count grinned. "Might not be such a bad way to go, eh?"

"Kirigin, old friend," said Nikolai, "you're a good fellow. Why not find yourself a nice girl who likes hunting and can feel warmly toward a wastrel?"

Kirigin shuffled his feet like a schoolboy. "I just can't help but feel that Commander Nazyalensky's icy demeanor masks a tender spirit."

Tolya snorted. "She'll pulp your heart and drink it."

Kirigin looked aghast, but Nikolai suspected Tolya was right. He'd come to recognize the bizarre phenomenon of Zoya's beauty, the way men loved to create stories around it. They said she was cruel because she'd been harmed in the past. They claimed she was cold because she just hadn't met the right fellow to warm her. Anything to soften her edges and sweeten her disposition—and what was the fun in that? Zoya's company was like strong drink. Bracing— and best to abstain if you couldn't handle the kick.

Nikolai hoisted himself back into the saddle. "Commander

Nazyalensky's icy exterior masks an even icier interior, but I will most certainly let her know you wish her health."

He nudged his horse into a trot and Tolya followed suit. They made their way along the white gravel path that ran parallel to the eastern side of the main house. Through the windows, Nikolai heard music from the parlors and gaming rooms. He glimpsed bodies swathed in silk and jewels and saw a man wearing nothing but an admiral's hat and beating a large pot with a spoon as he ran down the hall.

Tolya's scowl was deep enough to sow seeds in. "The crown shouldn't be associated with such displays."

"Perhaps not," conceded Nikolai. "But the Ravkan people like their leaders with just a touch of the unseemly about them. They don't trust a man of too much virtue."

Tolya narrowed his golden eyes. "And you really trust a man of so little?"

"I know you don't approve. But Kirigin has played the part I've asked him to. He may not be the brightest fellow, but he's loyal."

"He can't possibly think Zoya would spare him her time."

"Let us pray she never does. Poor Kirigin would be better off trying to waltz with a bear."

Even so, Nikolai thought neither Zoya nor Tolya gave the young count enough credit. Kirigin's affability and lack of ambition hid a good heart. He was an honorable man with romantic ideas of duty to his country and profound shame over the way his father had conducted himself—something with which Nikolai could sympathize. Nikolai was acutely aware of his own father's reputation. It was one of the many reasons he kept his public visits to Lazlayon to a minimum. From the moment he'd contemplated taking the throne, Nikolai had known he would have to be a better man than his father and a better king than his brother could have ever hoped to be. Vasily had been killed by the Darkling, and Nikolai had done his best to grieve for him, but the truth was that his brother's untimely death had proved quite timely indeed.

Nikolai was pleased to see two groundskeepers emerge from the hedges as soon as he and Tolya left the gravel path. Kirigin's entire staff, from scullery maid to groom to head housekeeper, was made up of the king's spies.

"Any falcons in the skies?" Nikolai called, using the code that would allow them to pass without triggering security protocols.

"No, but we hear there are foxes in the woods," one of the men replied, and they returned to their work.

The codes changed each week and were just one of the ways they kept the real business of the Gilded Bog secure.

The southern shore of the lake was heavy with unnatural mist, and only when he and Tolya had passed through the haze did they see the docks bustling with both Grisha and First Army engineers. The waters were arrayed with the latest prototypes of Nikolai's hydrofoil fleet. The real fleet would be constructed at a hidden base on Ravka's coast—small gunners and huge transportation ships that could carry everything from troops to aircraft. Assuming Nikolai could some-how find the money to finance the project. Not even Kirigin was rich enough to modernize an entire navy.

Nikolai would have liked to stay and watch the tests, but he had other priorities today. He and Tolya tethered their horses by one of the moss-covered grottoes and entered the caves. The air should have been moist, but the grotto was not a real one, and the humidity in the labs and the passageways inside was strictly regulated by Squallers. Nikolai found the appropriate notch in the stone by a cluster of fake salt lilies and punched his thumb into the divot. The stone shifted, revealing a brass chamber. He pulled a lever, the door clanked shut, and he and Tolya were descending, down, down, six stories into the earth to Kirigin's infamous "wine cellar." It could be reached from hidden elevators located throughout the property.

"I hate this part," muttered Tolya. "Feels like being buried."

Nikolai knew Tolya had almost been killed in a cave-in during his time with the Sun Summoner. "You should wait above. Watch them test the new engines. I could use a report on their success."

He tightened the knot that restrained his long black hair, and folded his huge tattooed arms. "Tamar says fears are like weeds. They grow wild if left unattended."

Well and good for Tamar—Tolya's twin was essentially fearless. "So forcing yourself underground is a bit of light gardening?"

Tolya gritted his teeth. "If I don't face it, I'll never get over it."

Nikolai chose to hold his tongue. If the sweat on Tolya's massive brow and his clenched jaw were any indication, these excursions beneath the earth were doing him no good at all. But the war had left all of them with wounds, and Tolya had the right to tend to his as he saw fit. Nikolai flexed his fingers in his gloves and thought of the black scars staining his fingers. *Would I have the courage to look the monster in the eye?* He truly didn't know.

When the doors to the elevator opened, they exited to another brass chamber, their passage blocked by a thick steel door. Nikolai set to opening the Schuyler combination locks he'd learned about from a certain master thief in Ketterdam. A moment later, the door swung open and he was home.

The laboratories were separated into four main divisions, though all of them worked together as needed: artillery and body armor, naval warfare, aerial warfare, and the labs devoted to trying to develop both an antidote to *jurda parem* and a strain of the drug that might allow Grisha to heighten their powers without making them addicts. His first stop was always the labs. He spoke briefly to his

Alkemi to confirm what he'd suspected regarding the antidote based on their last report, and collected a tiny vial of the stuff to share with the Triumvirate. Nikolai wanted something concrete to dangle before his advisers, given what he intended to propose.

It took them a little longer to find David Kostyk, since the Fabrikator worked in every division of the laboratory. But eventually they discovered him hunched over a set of blueprints by the vast tanks where the latest prototypes of their new submersibles were being built in miniature. The sleeves of his purple Fabrikator's *kefta* were threadbare, and his poorly cut brown hair gave him the appearance of a shaggy dog deep in thought.

Through the glass, Nikolai saw the most recent version of his *izmars'ya*, his underwater fleet. On land, they looked clumsy: wide, flat, and ungainly, like someone had taken a quality piece of metal and pounded it into a winged pancake. But beneath the surface, they became something elegant, sinuous predators that glided through the depths, their movements guided by Tidemakers, their crews provided with breathable air through a combination of Squaller power and a filter that had taken Nikolai and David the better part of a year to perfect. The real challenge would be arming the fleet. Only then would his ships become a true school of sharks. After that? It wouldn't matter how many warships Ravka's enemies built. The *izmars'ya* would be able to move through the world's oceans unseen and attack without ever surfacing. They would change the face of naval warfare.

David looked up from where he was consulting with Nadia Zhabin over the pendulum-and-valve system they were developing for missile targeting. "They're testing the surface engines today," he said.

"And good morning to you, David."

"Is it morning?"

"The sunrise was my first indication," said Nikolai. "How do the new missiles look?"

"We're still trying to get them to maintain course," said Nadia, her pale, pointed features tinged blue from the light reflecting off the tank. She was a Squaller who had fought beside the Sun Summoner with her younger brother, Adrik, but she'd shown her true potential in weapons design. She'd been integral in the development of the *izmars'ya.* "I think we're close."

Though the inventor in Nikolai thrilled at the news, his enthusiasm was tempered by the conversation he'd had with Hiram Schenck back in Ivets. He could practically feel the Kerch breathing down his neck, and it wasn't a sensation he relished.

Nikolai had two rules for his Nolniki—the scientists and soldiers who labored at the Gilded Bog, his Zeroes who were neither First nor Second Army but both. Above all else, be thieves. Take the work of their enemies and turn it against them. It didn't matter if Ravka got to the technology first as long as they found ways to make it better. The Fjerdans had developed an engine to drive wagons and armored tank battalions, so the Ravkans had made it powerful enough to move massive ships. The Fjerdans had built steel aircraft that didn't require Squaller skill to pilot, so Ravka's Fabrikators stole the design and constructed sleeker flyers in safer, lighter aluminum. The second rule? Be fast. Fjerda had made huge leaps in military technology over the last year—how he did not yet know—and Ravka had to find a way to keep pace.

Nikolai tapped the blueprints on the table. "If the fuel tests for the surface engines go well, how long until the *izmars'ya* are operational?"

"A matter of weeks," said Nadia.

"Excellent."

"But we can't put anything into production without more steel."

"And you'll have it," Nikolai promised. He could only hope he was telling the truth.

"Thank you, Your Highness," Nadia said with a smile and a bow.

Somehow she still had faith in her king, but Nikolai wasn't sure if he found her ready confidence reassuring or worrisome. He had always found a way to keep the rusty, ramshackle machine that was Ravka grinding along—by finding that extra bit of money when they needed it most, making the right alliance at the right time, cobbling together some invention that would make their meager standing army a match for the vast forces commanded by the enemies at their borders. For Nikolai, a problem had always presented an opportunity no different than the one offered by a Fjerdan engine. You stripped it down to its parts, figured out what drove it, then used those pieces to build something that worked for you instead of against you.

The demon disagreed. The demon wasn't interested in problem-solving or statecraft or the future. It was nothing but hunger, the need of the moment, what could be killed and consumed.

I'll find a way. All his life, Nikolai had believed that. His will had been enough to shape not only his fate but his own identity. He had chosen what he wanted people to see—the obedient son, the feckless rogue, the able soldier, the confident politician. The monster threatened all of that. And they were no closer to finding a way to drive the thing out than they had been six months ago. What was there to do but keep moving? Lesser animals whined and struggled when they'd been caught in a snare. The fox found a way out.

"David, did you sleep here last night?" Nikolai asked.

The Fabrikator frowned. "I don't think so."

"He spent the night here," Nadia clarified. "He didn't actually sleep."

"Did *you*?" asked Nikolai.

"I . . . dozed for a bit," Nadia replied evasively.

"I'm taking you home to Tamar."

"But I need her for the fuel tests," David objected.

"And I'm taking *you* home to Genya," added Nikolai.

"But—"

"Don't argue, David. Makes me want to blow something up to assert my authority. I need the Triumvirate together. And I'm going to need you and Nadia to start work on a new prototype of the *izmars'ya*."

Nadia brushed her blond hair from her eyes. "I can start now, Your Highness."

"Don't go running off to display your excessive competence just yet. I want you to make sure this particular prototype doesn't work."

David began rolling up his blueprints, carefully arranging his pens and instruments. "I don't like it when he doesn't make sense."

Nadia raised her brows. "I assume Your Highness has a reason?"

I always do. He would drag the drowning man to shore kicking and screaming if he had to—no matter what the demon demanded.

"I'm going to stage a little play," said Nikolai, already imagining a moonlit lake and all the glorious chaos he intended to incite there. "That means I need the right props."

5
NINA

GÄFVALLE.

The closer they drew to the town, the harder it was to ignore the rustling whispers in her head. Sometimes Nina could swear she heard voices, the dim shapes of words just beyond understanding. Other times the sound dwindled to the rush of wind through reeds.

Tell them, my love.

But what was there to tell? The sound might be nothing. It might be an auditory hallucination, some remnant of her bout with *parem*.

Or it might be the dead, drawing her on.

The town itself was located in the shadow of a low mountain range, beneath the hulking shape of what had once been a fort and then a munitions factory lodged into the cliffside high above it. It didn't take long to realize that the old factory had been recommissioned for something new—the traffic of wagons and men traveling in and out of the facility made that clear—but for what?

There were no proper inns, only a public house with two guest rooms that were already occupied. The owner told them that the convent up the hill sometimes boarded lodgers.

"Ladies at the convent there take in washing for the soldiers," he said. "They don't mind having a few extra hands around for chores."

"Must be busy these days with the old factory running," said Nina in Fjerdan. "Good for business."

The owner shook his head. "Soldiers came in about a year ago. Didn't hire any locals, poured their filth into the river."

"You don't know that," said a heavyset woman shelling peas at the bar. "The river was full of runoff from the mines before the soldiers started up the smokestacks again." She cut a long glance at Nina and the others. "Don't pay to speak trouble to strangers."

They took the hint and headed out to the main street. It was a surprisingly pretty town, the buildings small and snug, their roofs peaked, their doors brightly painted in yellow, pink, and blue.

Leoni gazed up the mountain to where the old factory loomed, its big square buildings pocked with dark windows. "They could just be manufacturing rifles or ammunition."

Adrik's expression was bleaker than usual. "Or some of those new armored tanks they're so fond of."

"If that's the case, we'll have some intelligence to pass along to the capital," Nina said. She hoped that wouldn't be all.

Nina was surprised to glimpse signs of the Saints here, in places she knew were not dedicated to the Hringsa network. She had seen them on the road too—altars bearing the symbol of Sankta Alina instead of Djel's sacred ash tree, an icon of Sankt Demyan of the Rime perched in a shop window, two thorny boughs crossed above a door to signify the blessing of Sankt Feliks. There had been talk of miracles and strange happenings throughout Ravka, and it seemed new fervor for the Saints had taken hold in Fjerda as well. It was risky to be so public about heresy with soldiers close by, but perhaps these were small acts of rebellion for the townspeople who resented the military men standing watch up at the factory.

The convent was located on the northern outskirts of town, almost directly down the slope from the factory. It was a round slab of milk-white stone with a turreted roof that made the building look like a tower in search of a castle. The large chapel it abutted was constructed of sturdy, rough-hewn logs and fronted by an entrance of ash branches woven into complicated knots.

They left their sledge in the stables and rang the bell at the convent's side door. A young woman in the embroidered pale blue pinafore of a novitiate answered, and a moment later they were meeting the Wellmother. The older woman wore dark blue wool and had a round, apple-cheeked face, her skin deeply lined, as if it had been pleated into neat, pallid folds instead of wrinkled by age.

Nina made the introductions, explaining that she was serving as a translator for a merchant couple selling their wares, and asked if they might stay somewhere on the property while exploring the area.

"Do they have any Fjerdan at all?"

"*Bine*," said Adrik. *Some.*

"*De forenen*," added Leoni with a smile. *We're learning.*

"And where is your husband?" the Wellmother asked Nina.

"Gone to the waters," Nina said, dropping her eyes to the silver ring on her hand. "May Djel watch over him."

"Not a soldier, then?"

"A fisherman."

"Ah. Well," she said, as if dissatisfied with such a bloodless death. "I can give you and the Zemeni woman rooms on the bottom floor near the kitchens. But her husband will have to stay in the stables. I doubt he'd be much harm to the girls," she said with a glance at the pinned sleeve of Adrik's coat, "but even so."

It was the kind of thoughtless comment people often made around Adrik, but all he did was smile pleasantly and offer up payment for the week with his remaining hand.

The Wellmother instructed them on the routine of the convent as she led them through the dining hall and then down to the stable. "The doors are locked at ten bells every night and are not reopened until the morning. We ask that you keep to reading or silent meditation at that time so as not to disturb the girls at their studies."

"Are they all novitiates?" Nina asked.

"Some will become Springmaidens. Others are here to be educated until they return to their families or husbands. What are you transporting under there anyway?" the Wellmother asked, lifting the corner of the tarp attached to the sledge.

Nina's instinct was to slap the woman's hand away. Instead, she stepped forward eagerly and reached for the ties securing the tarp. "This couple has invented a new form of rifle loader."

Right on cue, Leoni drew a colorful pamphlet from her coat. "They're affordably priced, and we're projecting big sales in the new year," she said. "We're looking for a few small investors. If you'd like a demonstration—"

"No, indeed," the Wellmother said quickly. "I'm sure they're most impressive, but I'm afraid the convent's finances are simply too tight for, uh . . . speculative ventures."

It never failed.

"We serve our meals at six bells following morning prayers—which you are of course encouraged to join—and in the evening again at six bells. Bread and salt are available in the kitchens. Water is rationed."

"Rationed?" asked Nina.

"Yes, we draw from the well at Felsted, and that requires quite a journey."

"Isn't Gjela closer?"

The Wellmother's plump lips pursed. "There are many ways in which we show service to Djel. The trip provides good opportunity for quiet contemplation."

River's gone sour up by the old fort. So the Wellmother didn't want her charges drinking from this tributary of the river, but she also wasn't willing to discuss it. It was possible the Springmaidens were just laundering soldiers' uniforms, but it was also likely they knew what was happening at the factory.

As soon as the Wellmother had gone, Adrik said, "Let's walk."

Nina checked the lashings of the tarp and they headed up the side of the mountain, setting a leisurely pace and making a show of chattering loudly in Zemeni. They paralleled the road that led to the factory, but they took time to point out birds and stop at vistas overlooking the valley. Three tourists out for a walk and nothing more.

"Will you be all right in the stables?" Leoni asked as they made their way through a grove of pines.

"I'll manage," said Adrik. "A one-armed lecher can still prey upon the horses. The Wellmother never thought of that."

Leoni laughed and said, "It's the wolves who go unseen that eat the most sheep." Adrik snorted but he looked almost pleased.

Behind them, Nina rolled her eyes. If she was going to be forced to continue a mission with two people starting this dance of cautious compliments and sudden blushes, it might well kill her. It was one thing to find happiness and lose it, quite another to have someone else's happiness thrust at you like an unwanted second slice of cake. Then again, she'd never refused a second slice of cake. *This will be good for me*, she told herself. *Like green vegetables and lessons in arithmetic. And I'll probably enjoy it just as much.*

Eventually they picked their way to a gap in the trees that over-looked the entrance to the factory. At the sight of it, the rustling of voices rose in her mind, louder than the wind shaking the pines. Two soldiers were posted at the huge double doors, and there were more stationed along the parapets.

"It was a fort before it was a factory," Nina said, pointing to what looked like old niches carved into the stone walls. A large reservoir sat behind the main building, and she wondered if the water was used for cooling whatever machinery was operating inside.

"It's a good strategic vantage, I suppose," said Adrik in his dreary voice. "High ground. A safe place to shelter in an attack or when the river spills its banks."

The might of Djel, thought Nina. *The Wellspring, the wrath of the river.*

Two smokestacks belched gray-blue smoke into the late-afternoon sky as they watched a covered wagon roll up to the gate. It was impos-sible to tell what passed between the guards and the driver.

"What do you think is in that wagon?" asked Adrik.

"Could be anything," said Leoni. "Ore from the mines. Fish. Bushels of *jurda*."

Nina ran her hands over her arms and glanced at the smokestacks. "Not *jurda*. I would smell it." Small doses of ordinary *jurda* had helped her to survive her ordeal with *parem* but had left her with an acute sensitivity to it. "What do you think?" she asked Adrik. "Do we stay?"

"I think I want a look inside that fort, but I'll settle for knowing what the hell they leaked into the water."

"It could be from the mines," said Leoni.

"If it were the mines, the fishermen would have rioted to have them shut down. Fear is keeping the townspeople quiet."

"Let's draw samples of the water," Leoni said. "If I can isolate the pollutants, we might be able to figure out what they're doing inside the fort."

"You're equipped for that?" Adrik said.

"Not exactly. I came prepared to forge documents, not test for poisons. But I could probably rig something up."

"If I told you we needed magical dust to make me vomit peppermints, you'd probably say you could *rig something up*."

"Probably," Leoni replied with a grin. "I'd just have to try."

Adrik shook his head in disbelief. "I'm getting tired even contemplating it."

"I'll need time," said Leoni, and Nina saw a troubled shadow pass over her face. "Poisons are tricky work."

"We can't stay here too long without drawing suspicion," said Adrik. "There's not enough trade passing through to justify it. And I don't want us snowbound if a bad storm hits."

"I know," Nina said. She had pushed them to come here, and she hoped they had more to find than a recommissioned munitions factory. "Give it a week."

A silence followed, and Nina sensed the shared concern that passed between Leoni and Adrik.

Leoni touched Nina's hand gently. "Nina . . ." she began, and Nina knew what she was going to say.

The whispering rose in her head again, but Nina ignored it. Instead, she looked out at the valley, at the dense forest, the gleaming tributary slicing through the trees like a glittering chain in a jewel box, the tidy little town bisected by the road. It did not feel like enemy territory here. It felt like a quiet place where people came to build their homes and try to make a life for themselves, where the business of soldiers and wars was nothing but an intrusion.

In another life, she and Matthias might have made their home in a place like this. They would have argued about how close they should live to a city. Nina would have longed for people and excitement; Matthias would have grumbled for quiet. They would have found a way to compromise. They would have argued and kissed to make up. But where would they have ever felt safe together? In Fjerda? In Ravka? Was there anyplace they would have truly been free and happy? Another life, another world.

It's time, Nina. Return me to my god.

Nina drew in a long breath and said, "I'll need two days to take him where the water is clean."

Saying the words was like feeling her heart split, the heavy swing of the axe, the blade sinking past bark to the soft white wood.

"You shouldn't go alone," said Adrik without enthusiasm. He sounded like he was contemplating putting on a sodden pair of socks.

"I can go by my—"

A noise sounded from somewhere below. They stilled, bodies tense, waiting. Silence, and then a shout.

"The meadow," whispered Nina.

Adrik started down the hill and signaled for them to follow, his glum demeanor vanishing in an instant as the hardened fighter emerged. They kept to the shadows, moving with care, creeping closer.

"Soldiers," hissed Leoni, peering through the branches.

A group of young men in gray Fjerdan uniforms were gathered around the stream, shouting at one another. Two were on horseback; the others had dismounted and were trying to calm a horse that had somehow gotten spooked and thrown its rider. Nina could see the soldier's boot had caught in the stirrup and he was being dragged through the stream as the horse cantered back and forth in the shallows, barely missing the soldier's head with its hooves. All it would take was a single heavy strike and the boy's skull would be crushed.

"We should help them," said Leoni.

"We should get back to the safety of the town," said Adrik. "They'll manage."

"And that's one less Fjerdan soldier to plague us," Nina said beneath her breath.

Nina.

Adrik and Leoni stared at her. Adrik looked like a mourner in search of a wake, and even Leoni's usual sunshine was clouded with worry.

She didn't approve. Adrik didn't approve. Hell, in her heart, Nina didn't approve either.

But since Matthias had left her—been *taken* from her—Nina had lost the part of her that cared. What was the point of it all? You saved one life only to see another taken. The good perished. And the bad? Nina looked at the young Fjerdans in their uniforms, killers in the making. What right did they have to survive when her Matthias, her beautiful barbarian, was gone?

Nina.

She wished she could clap her hands over her ears and tell him to leave her alone. But that was the last thing she wanted.

Must you insist I stay human? she complained silently.

I know how strong you are, Nina. My death will not be the thing that defeats you.

"What are we even supposed to do?" Nina said aloud.

"I know my way around horses," Leoni offered.

Adrik rolled his eyes. "Here we go."

"It will ingratiate us with the locals," insisted Leoni, already pushing through the trees. "We could use some soldier friends."

"Soldier friends?" Nina asked incredulously.

"Come on," said Adrik. "If we leave Leoni to her own devices, she may invite them to a slumber party."

"*Gedrenen*," yelled one of the soldiers as they entered the clearing. *Strangers.* He sounded like a child.

"Can we be of help?" Nina called in Fjerdan.

73

"No!" he cried from the riverbank. "Stay back!"

That was when Nina realized they weren't men at all—they were young women dressed as Fjerdan soldiers.

Nina held up her hands to try to make peace. "Let us help your comrade. My Zemeni friend knows horses." She really hoped that was the case and not just Leoni's optimistic take on *I once pet a pony.*

Leoni walked to the edge of the stream, making a low nickering sound and murmuring in Zemeni. She moved slowly left, then right, arms spread wide.

"I need rope," she said quietly, without looking away from the horse.

One of the riders came forward. She had to be six feet tall and was all wiry muscle. Her skin had the warm, tawny brown cast that usually indicated Hedjut ancestry this far north, and a few wisps of russet hair were visible beneath her army-issue cap. Now that they were closer Nina could see their uniforms were all too big, ill fitting. *Stolen.*

The tall girl's chin jutted forward. She was around Nina's age, and whatever fear she had at being discovered, she was hiding it well. She tossed the rope to Nina, who passed it to Leoni, keeping her distance. What were these girls doing? Women didn't serve in the Fjerdan military. They didn't ride often, and when they did, they certainly didn't ride astride. They didn't even wear trousers, just heavy skirts intended to preserve their modesty.

The girl caught in the stirrups moaned, struggling to right herself in the shallows. She had straw-yellow hair that had come loose around her shoulders, and she was bleeding badly from a cut on her forehead. But she was alive and her skull was still in one piece—for the moment.

Leoni kept her eyes fastened on the horse as she twisted the rope into a lasso. She swung it in gentle, lazy loops, her voice continuing that low, soothing murmur as they all stood watching. Then, without breaking her rhythm, she tossed the lasso in a gentle arc. It landed perfectly over the horse's head, and the beast reared with a high whinny. Leoni moved left and right again, turning the rope, leaning back, using her strength but not fighting. At last the horse settled.

The tall girl who had given Nina the rope stepped forward, but Leoni gave a quick shake of her head.

"Let her be," Nina said quietly. A flush spread over the girl's sharp jaw.

Leoni approached the horse slowly and rested her hand on its neck, stroking its mane down to the withers. "Something scare you?" she said in Zemeni, cautiously making her way around the horse's flank. She bent to the stirrup but gestured to the girl lying glazed-eyed in the water to stay still. She didn't want to risk the horse shying again. Nina hoped the girl was conscious enough to understand. "Nothing to worry about," murmured Leoni.

She released the girl's boot from the stirrup, then quickly tugged on the rope and led the horse away.

For a long moment the fallen girl lay in the water. Then she released a sob and pushed herself up. Her companions ran to her, pulling her from the stream.

Leoni brought the horse to where Nina was standing with the tall girl. "Any idea what spooked him?" she asked in Zemeni.

Nina translated, but the tall girl didn't respond, she just narrowed her coppery eyes. "What are you doing out here?"

"Other than saving your friend's life?" Nina replied mildly.

"I hardly think she would have died."

"No? Just bled until she passed out from her concussion or until that horse trampled her into a coma?"

"We had it under control," she insisted. Then she glanced up at the trees. "You came from the northern woods. There's nothing up there."

"So we soon learned. We're new to these parts. Is exploring considered a crime in Gäfvalle?"

"There's a vantage of the factory up that way."

"Ah!" said Nina, and turned to Adrik and Leoni. "The building we saw was some kind of factory." Best to keep to their ruse in case any of these women spoke a little Zemeni. She turned back to the tall one. "We thought it looked a bit like a fort. What is it they make there?" she asked innocently.

"It isn't my business and I doubt it's yours. You're staying at the convent?"

Just how much *did* this girl know, and why was she so hostile? Maybe she was a soldier's sister, raised to be suspicious. Nina's hands twitched, and she felt the bone shards shift. She didn't want to hurt this girl, but she would if she had to. The last thing they needed was someone running home to talk about the strangers in the woods who had been spying on the factory. Then the tall girl clenched her fists and said, "I . . . Will you not tell the Wellmother you saw us here?"

Suddenly, the girl's defensiveness made more sense. The stolen uniforms. The excursion into the woods in the middle of the day. She had been trying to go on the attack, but she was legitimately frightened of being discovered.

"You're novitiates?" Nina asked.

"We're all being educated at the convent. Some will marry. Some will become Springmaidens and give their lives to Djel." She didn't sound like either prospect excited her.

Nina adopted a more serious mien and realized it was Matthias' manner she was mimicking. "Riding astride, wearing trousers, cavorting in the woods with no chaperone . . . It would be irresponsible for us not to say something to the Wellmother, especially given the generosity of our hosts."

The tall girl turned ashen, and Nina felt a stab of guilt. If she really was close to Nina's age, she was too old to be a novitiate. All of them were. Were these the outsiders, then? The girls who hadn't been chosen for brides? What happened to Fjerdan women who didn't find a place as wives or mothers? Ravka was broken in many ways, but at least there Nina had been allowed to train as a soldier, to become what she was meant to be.

Free to fight and die alongside your men?

Yes, Matthias. Free.

What would he have made of these girls in their stolen clothes?

"Where did you get those uniforms?" Nina asked.

"The laundry. The soldiers send their clothes to the convent for cleaning."

"Then you're a thief too," said Nina. She might feel for these girls, but she wasn't about to break cover for them.

"We were only borrowing them! It was a lark. We won't do it again."

Nina doubted that. This wasn't the first or the last time these girls would "borrow" uniforms or horses. From a distance, they could maintain the ruse that they were soldiers out to train and roam the countryside with a freedom they would never otherwise enjoy. But at what risk? Nina couldn't imagine the punishment if they were discovered.

"What say you, Adrik?" Nina asked, deferring to the man in the party as a proper Fjerdan girl would—even if he was a foreigner.

Adrik cast a judgmental eye over the novitiates, pretending to consider. "Very well. Let us not speak of this day."

Nina nodded to the tall girl, whose shoulders sagged in relief.

The others looked relieved too as they pulled their injured friend onto a saddle.

"Get her home and healed," Nina said with the prim superiority of a student who would never, ever break the rules. "You should say thanks tonight in your prayers to Djel that he would tolerate such recklessness in his servants."

The tall girl bowed. *"Djel jerendem."* She mounted her horse.

"And we had better not see you out here again!" said Adrik in clumsy Fjerdan.

"No, sir. Of course not," said the girl, but as she turned, Nina glimpsed the defiant spark in her copper eyes. The others might be cowed, but not this girl. She had a different kind of heart. She would ride. She would hunt. She would fight when she could. And that was how she would stay alive.

When the novitiates had gone from the clearing, Nina said, "They're not going to talk."

"No," said Adrik. "They were clearly terrified that we'd be the ones to speak to the Wellmother. Let's fill our canteens. We can take the samples back to the stables."

But Nina wasn't quite ready to leave the mountain. The whispering had started again, and she wasn't going to ignore it this time. "I want to take another look at the factory."

"Why?"

How to answer that? "I . . . I just think there might be more to see." The chorus inside her sighed.

Adrik looked skeptical. "Go, but be careful. And do *not* engage on your own, understood?" Nina nodded, but apparently Adrik saw something he didn't like in her expression. "Nina, do not engage. If you're caught, it will put all of our operations here in Fjerda at risk. That is an order, not a request."

"Yes, sir," Nina said, and she managed it without a hint of the frustration she felt. Obedience had never been one of her strong points, and she'd been making her own decisions for far too long. But she wanted to be a soldier for Ravka, and that meant learning to do what she was told all over again.

Trassel didn't like following my orders. I bribed him with bits of steak.

Really, Matthias? Should I just try biting Adrik the next time he annoys me? I am not a wolf. I am a gently bred lady . . . though steak does sound good.

"Leoni and I will take samples here and at the tributary closer to town," Adrik said, and Nina was glad he couldn't read her mind. "Be back before dark."

Nina headed into the trees, taking her time cutting back to the factory on the off chance she was observed. She didn't follow the road this time. Instead she listened to the whispers, and she didn't think she was imagining their excitement as she scaled the mountain, letting them guide her farther east. Their anticipation drove her tired legs onward, the rustle growing louder, the sound of a crowd chattering its excitement before the start of a play. Or perhaps an execution.

It was almost sunset when she finally saw the fort come back into view. *Why does adventure always involve so much hiking?* she wondered. She'd somehow tracked behind the building so that she was on the far side of it, closest to the eastern wing. At this angle she could see there was a dirt road that led to another gate, two bored-looking guards bracketing it. This part of the factory seemed to have fallen into disrepair. Some of the windows were broken, and she saw no signs of occupation.

She also had a better view of the reservoir, its retaining wall carved into the shape of a giant ash tree, its branches and roots radiating in thick, twisting bulges of hewn stone. No doubt it had been blessed when the dam had been built. Wherever water was used or contained, the Fjerdans said prayers, at mills and in harbors, in the great northern mines where holy words were carved into the ice every season. A round sluice gate sat at the base of the dam, and Nina could see refuse in the mud that surrounded it. Soiling Djel's waters was considered a crime punishable by death in Fjerda. Perhaps these soldiers weren't particularly religious.

There was nothing to see here, but the whispering in Nina's head had risen to a clamor, and now she could hear that the voices were not excited—they were anguished.

Nina reached out with her power, the thing that *parem* had created within her. She felt the flow of the invisible river that no man could contain. It was death, a cold and inevitable tide, and when she focused, she could sense where it rushed and where it eddied. She let her mind dive into that cold, seeking those voices.

Where are you? she asked the darkness. *Who are you?*

She gasped as the current seized her, as if to drag her along, to pull her into the deep. The wailing inside her rose like a terrible flood. Death wanted to claim her. She could feel it. And did some part of her want to let it have its way?

Nina, come back.

The water did not feel cold anymore.

It felt kind. Like a welcome.

Nina. Do not give in to the tide.

Nina's eyes flashed open. The world of the living enveloped her again—birdsong, the wet scent of the soil beneath her boots, the sound of small creatures moving through the brush.

She looked at the hulking shape of the factory and felt a deep chill sink into her bones. The voices had receded, but she could still hear them crying. She knew who they were. Women and girls in the hundreds. All of them dead.

Here, on this mountaintop, Nina was surrounded by graves.

6
NIKOLAI

NIKOLAI AND TOLYA BROUGHT David and Nadia back to the capital by way of the underground tunnel that stretched from the Gilded Bog all the way to the grounds of the Grand Palace— fifteen miles of travel far beneath the surface of the earth. Poor Tolya muttered to himself the entire way. In verse.

Nikolai would have liked to spare Tolya and his own ears the trauma of the journey, but his head of security had insisted he was fine. Besides, Nikolai had received word that the crowd of pilgrims camped outside the city walls had grown in recent days and that some were demanding an audience with the king. All he needed was for an overzealous zealot to hurl himself beneath the hooves of one of the royal riders. Nikolai didn't intend to make any martyrs today.

They emerged behind a noisy manmade waterfall not far from the royal stables, the path to it monitored by two of Nikolai's most trusted palace guards. In their white-and-gold uniforms, dark hair parted neatly on the side, both of their faces cast in the solemn disinterest of soldiers at attention, the guards might have been brothers, but they couldn't have been less alike in disposition. Trukhin was always laughing and full of bravado; Isaak was so shy he often struggled to make eye contact.

The guards registered no surprise as Nikolai's party appeared from between the hedges.

"Trukhin," Nikolai said. "What excitement did I miss on my travels?"

Trukhin's stern expression gave way instantly to an easy smile. "Welcome back, Your Highness. Not much to report here, though an Inferni did set fire to the woods behind the lake."

Sounds like Kuwei. Nikolai admired the Shu boy's gift for mayhem. Especially because the young Inferni was Zoya's problem to manage. "That doesn't sound too bad."

Trukhin's grin turned rueful. "I believe the minister of defense was caught in the blaze. But he suffered no injuries."

"As long as no one set fire to the minister of finance. *Cav anenye?*" Nikolai asked Isaak in Zemeni. He had discovered the guard's gift for languages during his service at Halmhend and encouraged Isaak to foster those talents.

Isaak bowed slightly. "Your accent is coming along nicely, Your Majesty."

"Don't coddle me, Isaak."

The guard cleared his throat. "Well, the Zemeni word for *day* is *can*, not *cav*. Unless you meant to ask how my donkey is going."

"I wish your donkey well, but you should always feel free to correct me when I make mistakes."

"Yes, Your Highness," Isaak said uncomfortably.

"Don't worry," said Nikolai as they turned their backs on the gardens and headed toward the Grand Palace. "It doesn't happen often."

Easy words. Old words. Harder to prove true with every passing day.

Through the trees, Nikolai glimpsed the gilded terraces of the Grand Palace, stacked like the frosted layers of the world's most expensive tea cake. His ancestors had enjoyed an excess of everything—except good taste. But he would not be stopping there just yet. He veered left toward the Little Palace instead, passing through the woods and emerging to the sight of its golden domes, the gleaming blue lake with a tiny island at its center visible just beyond.

Nikolai had spent plenty of time here, and yet there was something about this place—the soaring towers, the ancient wooden walls inlaid with mother-of-pearl and carved with every manner of flower and beast. He always felt he was traveling into foreign territory, leaving the new world behind for someplace where dark bargains might be struck. He should probably stop reading novels.

Grisha were everywhere in their brightly colored *kefta*—uniforms Tolya and Tamar had resolutely refused to wear, opting for the olive drab of First Army soldiers instead. The twins kept their arms bare, their deep bronze skin tattooed with the markings of the Sun Saint.

Zoya and Genya were already waiting in the war room.

"You're late," said Zoya.

"I'm the king," said Nikolai. "That means you're early."

For most state matters, the Grisha Triumvirate attended Nikolai at the Grand Palace, in the same room where he met with his ministers and governors. But when they needed to talk—really talk without fear of being overheard—they came here, to the chambers the Darkling had built. He was a man who had excelled at keeping secrets;

the war room had no windows and only a single entrance that couldn't be accessed without breaching the Little Palace itself. The walls were lined with maps of Ravka made in the old style. They would have enchanted Nikolai as a child—had he ever been allowed anywhere near the place.

"We're in trouble," Nikolai said without preamble, and settled himself in a chair at the head of the table with a cup of tea perched on his knee.

"Saying we're in trouble is like saying Tolya is hungry," replied Zoya, ignoring Tolya's scowl and pouring herself tea from the samovar. "Am I supposed to be surprised?"

She had dressed in the blue wool *kefta* that most Etherealki wore in cold weather, silver embroidery at its cuffs and hem, gray fox fur at its collar. She showed little sign of fatigue despite the days and nights of travel that had brought them back to Os Alta. Zoya was always a general, and her impeccable appearance was part of her armor. Nikolai glanced at his perfectly shined boots. It was a trait he respected.

"But this is particularly delicious trouble," he said.

"Oh no," groaned Genya. "When you talk that way, things are always about to go horribly wrong." Her *kefta* was Corporalki red, only a shade darker than her hair, its cuffs embroidered in dark blue—a combination worn only by Genya and her regiment of Tailors. But the cuffs and hem of Genya's *kefta* were also detailed with golden thread to match the sun emblazoned over her eyepatch in remembrance of Alina Starkov. Nikolai had added the sun in ascendance to his own Lantsov heraldry, a gesture he could admit had been driven by the need to court public opinion as much as by personal sentiment. Still, it sometimes felt like Alina was trailing them from room to room, her presence as tangible as the heat of a summer sun, though the girl was long gone.

Nikolai tapped his spoon against his cup. "David and Nadia are close to perfecting the weapons system on the *izmars'ya*."

David didn't bother to look up from the reading he'd brought with him—a treatise on osmotic filters that Nikolai had found most helpful. "You're right, Genya. This must be very serious trouble."

Genya cocked her head to the side. "Why do you say that?"

"He's starting with the good news."

Nikolai and Zoya exchanged a glance, and Zoya said, "Hiram Schenck approached the king at the trade summit in Ivets. The Kerch Merchant Council knows about our underwater fleet."

Tamar pushed back her chair in frustration. "Damn it. I knew we had a leak at the old facility. We should have moved to Lazlayon sooner."

"They were going to find out eventually," said Tolya.

David mumbled, "There are peaceable applications for the submersibles. Research, exploration."

He'd never liked to think of himself as a maker of weapons. But they couldn't afford to be so naive.

Tamar leaned against the wall and propped up her heel. "Let's not pretend we don't know what the Kerch intend to use our sharks for."

Hiram Schenck and the merchants of the Kerch Council claimed they wanted the *izmars'ya* as a defensive measure against their Shu neighbors and the possibility of Fjerdan blockades. But Nikolai knew better. They all did. The Kerch already had a target in mind: Zemeni ships.

The Zemeni had been building up their navy and establishing their own trade routes. They no longer needed Kerch ports or Kerch vessels, and for the first time, the mighty Kerch, who had ruled the seas and the world's trade undisputed for so long, had competition to worry about. Not only that, but the Zemeni had advantages the

Kerch couldn't match—extensive farmland, timber, and mines of their own. If Nikolai was honest, he was jealous of the way the young country had thrived. This was what a nation could do without enemies at their borders, unburdened by the constant threat of war.

But if the Kerch Merchant Council obtained the plans to Ravka's fleet of sharks, there would be no quarter for Zemeni ships. They could be attacked anywhere, and the Kerch would regain their monopoly of the seas—a monopoly that had made them one of the wealthiest and most powerful nations in the world, despite their tiny size.

"The Zemeni have been strong allies," said Tolya. "They've lent us aid, stood with us when no one else would."

Tamar folded her arms. "But they can't forgive our loans. The Kerch control Ravka's debt. They could cripple us with the stroke of a pen."

Nikolai contemplated the map before him. Shu Han to the south. Fjerda to the north. Ravka caught between them. If Ravka couldn't maintain its borders, his nation would become little more than a battleground between two great powers—and Nikolai had promised his people peace, a chance to rebuild. Both the Fjerdans and the Shu possessed vast standing armies, while the Ravkan army was depleted from years of waging war on two fronts. When Nikolai had taken command of Ravka's forces after the civil war, he had known they could not match their enemies' numbers. Ravka could only survive by using innovation to stay one step ahead. His country did not want to be at war again. *He* did not want to be at war again. But to build flyers, ships, or weapons in any quantity that would matter, they needed money and access to resources that only Kerch loans could provide. The decision seemed simple—except no decision was ever simple, even if one was willing to put thoughts of honor and allies aside.

"You're both right," Nikolai said. "We need the Zemeni and we need the Kerch. But we can't choose two partners in this dance."

"All right," said Zoya. "Who do we want to go home with when the music stops?"

Tamar tapped her heel against the wall. "It has to be the Kerch."

"Let's not make any rash decisions," said Nikolai. "Pick the wrong partner and we could be in for a disappointing night."

He removed a vial of cloudy green liquid from his pocket and set it on the table.

Zoya drew in a sharp breath and Genya leaned forward.

"Is that what I think it is?" asked Zoya.

Nikolai nodded. "Because of the information we gleaned from Kuwei Yul-Bo, our Alkemi are close to perfecting an antidote to *parem*."

Genya pressed her hands together. There were tears in her single amber eye. "Then—"

Nikolai hated to quell her hope, but they all needed to understand the reality of the situation. "Unfortunately, the formula for the antidote requires huge amounts of *jurda* stalks. Ten times the number of plants it would take to create an ounce of *jurda parem*."

Zoya picked up the vial, turned it over in her hands. "*Jurda* only grows in Novyi Zem. No other climate will sustain it."

"We need an antidote," said Tamar. "All of our intelligence points to the Shu and the Fjerdans being closer to developing a usable strain of *parem*."

"More Grisha enslaved," said Zoya. "More Grisha used as weapons against Ravka. More Grisha dead." She set the vial back on the table. "If we give the Kerch the plans to the *izmars'ya*, we'll lose Novyi Zem as an ally and our chance to protect our Grisha—maybe the world's Grisha—from *parem*." With a tap of her finger, she set the vial spinning in a slow circle. "If we say no to the Kerch, then we won't have the money to adequately arm and equip the First Army. Either way we lose."

Genya turned to Nikolai. "You'll make a diplomatic trip, then. Visit the Kerch, visit the Zemeni. Do that thing you do where you use too many words to say something simple and confuse the issue."

"I'd like nothing better than another opportunity to talk," said Nikolai. "But I'm afraid I have more bad news."

Genya slumped in her chair. "There's more?"

"This is Ravka," said Zoya. "There's always more."

Nikolai had known this moment was coming, and yet he still wished he could make some kind of excuse and bring the meeting to a halt. *So sorry, friends. I'm needed in the greenhouses on a matter of national security. No one else can prune the peonies.* Though everyone here knew what had been happening to him, it still felt like a dirty secret. He did not want to let the demon into the room. But this had to be said.

"While Zoya and I were away, the monster took hold of me again. I broke free at the duke's estate and made a delightful sojourn to a local goose farm."

"But the sleeping tonic—" Genya began.

"The monster is getting stronger." There, now. He'd said it. Not a bit of waver to his voice, not even the barest note of worry, though he wanted to choke on the words.

Genya shuddered. Better than anyone, she understood the darkness living inside Nikolai. It was tied to the *nichevo'ya*, to the very monsters that had terrorized her. The Darkling had set his shadow soldiers upon her when she betrayed him. She had lost an eye to his creatures, and their bites had left her body covered in scars that could not be tailored away. Nikolai still marveled at the particular cruelty of it. The Darkling had known that Genya valued beauty as her shield, so he had taken it from her. He had known that Nikolai relied on his mind, his talent for thinking his way out of any situation, so he'd let the demon steal Nikolai's ability to speak and think rationally. The Darkling could have killed either of them, but he had wanted to punish them instead. He might have been an ancient power, but he certainly had a petty streak.

"David," Genya said, her skin pale beneath her scars. "Is that possible? Could it be getting stronger?"

David brushed his shaggy brown hair back from his eyes. "It shouldn't be," he said. "Not after it was dormant for so long. But the power that created the presence inside the king wasn't ordinary Grisha power. It was *merzost*."

"Abomination," murmured Tolya.

"Are we calling it a presence now?" asked Nikolai. "I preferred 'monster.' Or 'demon.' Even 'fiend' has a nice ring." *The monster is me and I am the monster.* And if Nikolai didn't laugh at it, he was fairly sure he'd go mad.

"We can name it Maribel if it suits you," Zoya said, pushing away her empty cup. "It doesn't matter what we call it, only what it can do."

"It matters if we're misunderstanding its nature," said David. "You've read Grisha theory, Morozova's journals. Grisha power cannot create life or animate matter, only manipulate it. Every time those limits are breached, there are repercussions."

"The Shadow Fold," said Nikolai. The swath of darkness crawling with monsters had split Ravka in two, until Alina Starkov had destroyed it during the civil war. But the wound remained—a wasteland of dead sand where nothing green took hold, as if the Darkling's power had leached the very life from the land. *Merzost* had created the Fold, the creatures inside it, as well as the Darkling's shadow soldiers—and it was the same power that the Darkling had used to infect Nikolai.

David shrugged. "That power is unpredictable."

"We don't know what may happen next," said Nikolai. "Usually a thrilling proposition, less so when a demon may take over my consciousness and try to rule Ravka by gnawing on my subjects." How did the words come so easily—even as he contemplated losing his mind and his will? Because they always had. And he needed them. He needed to build a wall of words and wit and reason to keep the beast at bay, to remember who he was.

To rid himself of the monster, Nikolai had allowed himself to be subjected to extreme heat and cold. He had brought in bewildered Sun Summoners to use their power on him with no discernible result except the sensation that he was being gently roasted from the inside. His agents had scoured libraries the world over and retrieved the journals of the legendary Fabrikator Ilya Morozova after months of excavation in the rubble of the Spinning Wheel—all with nothing to show for it but frustration. That frustration had led him to Ivets, to the bone bridge, in some futile attempt to draw a connection between the darkness within him and the strange happenings around Ravka. Maybe he'd been hoping the Saints would present him with a miracle. But thus far, divine intervention had been in short supply.

"So you see the problem," he said now. "I cannot travel without risking exposure, but I cannot stay in hiding at the capital without drawing suspicion and risking Ravka's future with the Zemeni and the Kerch. Did I not promise particularly delicious trouble?"

"I'm sorry," said Genya. "Exactly what is delicious about this?"

"The way we're going to get out of it." Nikolai slouched back in his chair and stretched his legs, crossing them at the ankle. "We're going to throw a party."

"I see," said Zoya. "How drunk am I expected to get before this all starts looking better?"

"I fear there isn't enough wine in all of Kirigin's cellars," conceded Nikolai. "And I regret to say we'll need to be sober for this. The Kerch, the Zemeni, the Fjerdans, and the Shu—we're going to bring them all here. We're going to stage a little performance so that they know Ravka and its king are in perfect health."

"Is that all?" said Zoya. "Will you be taking up juggling as well?"

"Don't be ridiculous," Nikolai replied. "I already know how to juggle. Literally and figuratively. We'll renew our alliance with the Zemeni—"

"But the Kerch—" Genya began.

"And we'll give the Kerch a secret look at our prototype of the *izmars'ya*."

"We will?" asked David.

"It will be an utter catastrophe, of course. Perhaps a nice explosion, some flying metal. Maybe we can pretend to drown a few sailors. Whatever will convince the Kerch our sharks aren't seaworthy and buy us the most time." Nikolai could almost feel the demon recede, feel its claws retract, driven back by the prospect of a course of action. "We're going to get all of those diplomats and merchants and politicians under our roof. We get everyone talking, and then we listen. Zoya, we'll need your Squallers to create an acoustic map so we have ears everywhere."

"I don't like that," said Tolya.

"I knew you wouldn't," said Nikolai.

"It isn't ethical to spy on one's own guests."

"And that is why your sister is the head of my intelligence network. Kings need spies, and spies can't afford to fiddle about with ethics. Do you have a problem with overseeing an eavesdropping campaign, Tamar?"

"Not in the least."

"There you have it."

Tamar considered. "I like the idea of tackling them all at once, but what possible reason could we have for bringing our enemies and allies beneath this roof that won't draw even more suspicion?"

"We could celebrate your Saint's day," said Genya enthusiastically. "Sledding, bonfires—"

"No," said Nikolai. "I don't want to wait for the Feast of Sankt Nikolai." He certainly couldn't count on the demon to delay. "The party will take place six weeks from now. We'll call it . . . the Festival of Autumn Nonsense or something like that. Celebrate the equinox, gifts of the harvest, very symbolic."

"*Six weeks?*" exclaimed Genya. "We can't possibly organize an event of that size in such a short time. The security concerns alone—"

Nikolai winked at her. "If I had anyone but Genya Safin in charge, I might be worried."

Zoya rolled her eyes. "She doesn't need your flattery. She already thinks enough of herself."

"Let him go on," said Genya. "David never gives me pretty compliments."

"Don't I?" asked David. He patted his pocket absently. "I have the list of your good qualities you gave me somewhere."

"You see what I endure."

"I need to keep Genya happy," said Nikolai, "or she may turn on me."

"*I* may turn on you," said Zoya.

"Oh, that's unavoidable. But you're immune to compliments."

Zoya lifted a shoulder. "Then I suggest gifts of jewels and cash." She rose, and he could see her mind at work, the general contemplating her attack. She paced slowly before the map, the Fold appearing and disappearing behind her. "If we're going to bring these powers here, we need to have a better reason than a festival of gourds and wheat sheaves."

"Zoya," Nikolai warned. He knew exactly what she was thinking.

"This is the perfect opportunity for you to find a bride."

"Absolutely not."

But Zoya had the smug look of a woman who had won an argument before it had begun. "As you said, you can no longer travel, so it's essential that prospective brides come to you."

He shook his head. "I cannot take a bride. The risks are too great."

"That's exactly why you must," said Zoya. "We can bring these powers together. I even believe you have the charm and guile to out-maneuver our enemies. But how much time can you buy us? Six months? A year? Then what, Your Highness?"

"It *is* an ideal reason to bring them all here," said Genya.

Nikolai grimaced. "I *knew* you would turn on me. I just didn't think it would be so soon."

"Nikolai," Zoya said quietly, "you said the monster is getting stronger. If that's true, this may be your best chance."

Your only *chance.* The words hung unsaid.

Ravka needed a queen. Nikolai needed an heir.

And yet every part of him rebelled at the thought of marriage. He did not have time to properly court someone with so much work to be done. He did not want to wed someone he barely knew. He did not dare reveal his secrets to a stranger. The danger to the woman he chose would be too great. All good reasons. All convincing excuses. But the monster had set the clock ticking.

Nikolai looked around the room. These people knew him as no one else did. They trusted him. But the demon lurking inside him might change all that. What if it grew stronger and continued to erode his control, to eat at the will that had guided him for so long? *Abomination.* He remembered the way Genya had shuddered. What if *he* was the drowning man and it was Ravka he would drag down with him?

Nikolai drew in a long breath. Why put off the inevitable? Surely there was something to be said for the firing squad instead of slow torture. "We'll need to come up with a list of candidates," he said.

Zoya grinned. "Done." She really was ready to be rid of him.

"You're going to manage this like a military campaign, aren't you?"

"It *is* a military campaign."

"My ministers and ambassadors will have their suggestions too."

"We'll invite them all," said Genya, drawing pen and ink toward her, unable to disguise her excitement. "We can house everyone at the palace. Just think of all the dinners and teas and dancing."

"Just think of all the dinners and teas and dancing," said David glumly.

Genya set her pen aside and seized his hands. "I promise to let you hide in your workshop. Just give me five events and one banquet."

"Three events and one banquet."

"Four."

"Very well."

"You're a dreadful negotiator," said Nikolai. "She would have settled for two."

David frowned. "Is that true?"

"Absolutely not," said Genya. "And do shut up, Your Highness."

"We'll need to run additional checks on all palace security," Nikolai said to Tolya. "Anticipate that every servant, every guard, every lady-in-waiting will be a potential spy or assassin."

"Speaking of which," said Tamar. "Dunyasha Lazareva is dead."

The Lantsov pretender. "Who got her?"

"Not one of ours. All I know is they found her splattered on the cobblestones outside the Church of Barter after the auction."

Troubling. Had she been in Ketterdam to hunt him? She wasn't the only pretender to the Lantsov throne. Every few months it seemed a new person cropped up to declare that they were a lost Lantsov heir, someone who insisted they'd escaped the Darkling's slaughter of the royal family, or who claimed to be a by-blow of Nikolai's father—which, given the old king's behavior, was entirely plausible. Of course, Nikolai might very well have less right to the Ravkan throne than half of them. He was the greatest pretender of them all.

"There will be another," said Zoya. "Someone else to claim the Lantsov name. All the more reason to produce an heir and secure the throne."

"I said I would choose a bride, and I will," Nikolai said, trying not to sound quite as petulant as he felt. "I'll even get down on one knee and recite some love poetry if you like."

"I could make some selections," offered Tolya, looking genuinely happy for the first time since they'd gone underground at the Gilded Bog.

"An excellent idea. Keep it short and make sure it rhymes."

Nikolai looked again at the old map of Ravka—violent, hopeless, unappeasable in its constant need. Ravka was his first love, an infatuation that had begun in his lonely boyhood and that had only deepened with age. Whatever it demanded, he knew he would give. He'd been reckless with this country he claimed to love, and he could no longer let his fear dictate Ravka's future.

"Send the invitations," he said. "Let the great royal romance begin."

The rest of the day was spent in meetings with ministers, making plans for roads and aqueducts they could not afford, writing letters to the Kerch to request extensions on their loans, and finishing correspondence with everyone from the ruling Marchal of the Wandering Isle to the admirals in his navy requesting funds for repairs to the existing Ravkan fleet. All of it required concentration, finesse, and infinite patience—and all of it was less onerous than the work of finding a queen. But eventually evening came and Nikolai was forced to face Zoya and her army of prospective brides.

Nikolai and his general worked alone in his sitting room, a fire crackling in the tiled grate. The chamber still bore his father's stamp—the double eagle wrought in gold, the heavy carpets, the curtains so laden with brocade they looked as if they could be melted down and pressed into coins.

Zoya's list went on and on, girl after girl, a march of willing maidens.

"The brides are meant to be cover for our meetings with the Kerch and the Zemeni," he said. "Perhaps we could make this an opening gambit, less an engagement than a prelude to an engagement."

Zoya straightened the papers before her. "Two birds with one stone, Your Highness. It's a matter of efficiency. And expectation. You need a bride, and right now, you're still a worthy prospect."

"Right now?"

"You're still young. You have all of your teeth. And Ravka's military hasn't yet been trounced into the ground. Your hesitation is distinctly unkingly. It isn't like you."

It wasn't. He excelled at decisions. He enjoyed them. It was like clearing the deadfall from a forest so that you could see an open path. But when he thought of choosing a wife, the branches crowded in on him and he found himself glad to be left alone in the dark. Perhaps not alone, precisely. He very much enjoyed the quiet of this room, the warmth of the fire, and the steel-spined harpy seated across from him.

Zoya snapped the paper she was holding to get his attention. "Princess Ehri Kir-Taban."

"Second in line for the Shu throne, yes?"

"Yes, and one of our most ideal prospects. She's young, amiable, and wildly popular among her own people. Very gifted on the *khatuur*."

"Twelve strings or eighteen?"

"Why does it matter?"

"It's important to have standards, Nazyalensky. Are you so sure the Shu will send her?"

"The invitation will be to the royal family. But given the way the people adore Princess Ehri, I suspect her older sister wouldn't be sorry to see her out of the country. If they send one of the younger sisters . . ." She shrugged. "We'll know they aren't serious about an alliance. But a Shu bride would free us from the need for Kerch gold."

"And how long do you suppose Ravka would remain independent after such a marriage? The Shu wouldn't need to invade. We'd be hand-lettering an invitation."

"There is no perfect choice," said Zoya.

"Who's next?"

She sighed and handed him another dossier. "Elke Marie Smit."

Nikolai glanced down at the file. "She's barely sixteen!"

"She's from one of the most powerful families in Kerch. Besides, Alina was only a few years older when you threw away the Lantsov emerald on her."

"And so was I at the time." Thinking of Alina always smarted. He knew he'd been a fool to propose to her. But at the time he'd been more in need of a friend than a political ally. Or at least it had felt that way.

Zoya leaned back and cast him a long look. "Don't tell me you're still mourning the loss of our little Sun Saint?"

Of course he was. He'd liked Alina, maybe he'd even started to love her. And maybe some arrogant part of him had simply expected her to say yes. He was a king, after all, and a passable dancer. But she'd known the Darkling better than anyone. Maybe she'd sensed what was festering inside him. Years had passed, and yet her rejection still stung.

"Never had a gift for pining," Nikolai said. "Though I do like to show off my profile by staring mournfully out of windows."

"Elke Marie Smit's parents will still marry her off, probably to some merchant. I'm sure she'd be better pleased with a king."

"No. Next?"

"Natasha Beritrova," said Zoya.

"The Baroness Beritrova?"

Zoya looked studiously at the paper. "That's the one."

"She's *fifty*."

"She's a very well-off widow with lands near Caryeva that could prove essential in any southern campaign."

"No, Zoya."

Zoya rolled her eyes but picked up another paper. "Linnea Opjer."

"No."

"Oh, for all the Saints and their suffering, Nikolai. Now you're just being difficult. She's twenty-three and, by all accounts, beautiful, even-tempered, has a talent for mathematics—"

Nikolai flicked a piece of lint from his cuff. "I'd expect nothing less of my half sister."

Zoya stilled. She glowed like a painted icon in her *kefta*, the firelight clinging to her like a halo. He swore no woman had ever looked better in blue. "So it's true, then?"

"As true as any story," Nikolai said. The rumors of his bastardy had circulated since well before his birth, and he'd done his best to make peace with them. But he'd only ever spoken the truth of his parentage to one person—Alina Starkov. Why was he telling Zoya now? When he'd told Alina, she'd reassured him, said he would still make a great king. Zoya would offer no such kindness. But still he unlocked the top of his desk and removed the miniature his mother had passed along to him. She'd given it to him before she'd been forced into exile, when she'd told him who his father really was—a Fjerdan shipping magnate who had once served as emissary to the Grand Palace.

"Saints," Zoya said as she stared down at the portrait. "The likeness—"

"Striking, I know." Only the eyes were different—tiny daubs of blue instead of hazel—and the beard, of course. But looking at the miniature was like gazing into the future, at a Nikolai grown a bit older, a bit graver, with lines at the corners of his eyes.

Zoya hurled it into the fire.

"Zoya!" Nikolai shouted, lunging toward the grate.

"What kind of fool are you?" she spat.

He reached his hand out, but the flames were too high, and he recoiled, his rage igniting at the sight of the tiny canvas melting in its frame.

He whirled on her. "You forget yourself."

"That portrait was as good as a loaded gun pointed at your heart." She jabbed her finger into his chest. "Ravka's heart. And you would risk it all for what? Stupid sentiment?"

He seized her hand before she could jab him again. "I am not one of your boys to be trifled with and lectured to. I am your king."

Zoya's blue eyes flashed. Her chin lifted as if to say, *What is a mortal king to a queen who can summon storms?* "You are my king. And I wish you to *remain* my king. Even if you're too daft to protect your claim to the throne."

Maybe so, but he didn't want to hear it. "You had no right."

"I am sworn to protect you. To protect this realm. I had every right." She yanked her hand from his. "What if Magnus Opjer came to this palace? Or was invited to some banquet with you in Kerch? All it would take is a single glance for people to know—"

"They already know," Nikolai said, feeling suddenly weary. "Or they've guessed. There have been whispers since before I was born."

"We should consider eliminating him."

He clenched his fists. "Zoya, you will do no such thing. I forbid it. And if I find you've acted without my consent, you will lose your rank and can spend the rest of your days teaching Grisha children how to make cloud animals."

For a moment, it looked like she might lift her hands and raise a storm to blow the whole palace down. But then she bobbed a perfect curtsy that still somehow conveyed her contempt. "Of course, *moi tsar.*"

"Are you really so ruthless, Zoya? He is an innocent man. His only crime was loving my mother."

"No, his crime was bedding your mother."

Nikolai shook his head. Leave it to Zoya to cut right to the truth. Of course, he had no way of knowing if there had ever been love between his mother and his true father, but he hoped there had been something more than lust and regret.

He plucked his wineglass from his abandoned dinner tray and drank it to the dregs. "One day you will overstep and I will not be so forgiving."

"On that day you may clap me in irons and throw me in your dungeons." She crossed the room, took the glass from his hands, and set it on the table. "But tonight it is you who wears chains."

Her voice was almost kind.

Nikolai released a sigh. "After the business of this evening, it will be a relief."

He unlocked his bedchamber. Servants were allowed access to clean only under Tolya and Tamar's supervision and only once a week. He had no personal valet and attended to his own bath.

Though it had become his nightly prison, the room itself was a sanctuary, maybe the only place in the palace that truly felt like it belonged to him. The walls were painted the deep blue of the sea, and the map above the mantel had been taken from the cabin he'd once occupied as Sturmhond, when he'd disguised himself as a privateer and sailed the world's oceans aboard the *Volkvolny*. A long glass stood propped on a tripod by the bank of windows. He couldn't see much through it—the stars, the houses of the upper town—but even having it there gave him some sense of peace, as if he might one day put his eye to it and see the heaving shoulders of a great gray sea.

"Salt water in the veins," one of his crewmen had told him. "We go mad if we're too long onshore." Nikolai would not go mad, at least not from being landlocked. He had been born to be a king, even if his blood told a different story, and he would see his country to victory again. But first he had to make it through the night.

He sat down at the edge of the bed, removed his boots, and clamped the iron fetters around each of his ankles, then lay back. Zoya waited and he was grateful for it. It was a small thing to be the one to chain himself, but it allowed him to keep control for a short time longer. Only when Nikolai had fastened the fetter to his left wrist did she approach.

"Ready?"

He nodded. In these moments, her ruthlessness made it all a bit more bearable. Zoya would never indulge him, never shame him with pity.

She tugged on the special lock that David had rigged. With a sudden clanking whir, three chains shot across his body at the knees, midriff, and shoulders. He was strong when the beast came upon him, and they could take no chances. He knew this, should be used to the experience of restraint, and still all he wanted was to struggle.

Instead, he kept his easy demeanor and offered up his right wrist to Zoya. "And what are your plans for the evening, darling jailer? Headed to a secret rendezvous?"

Zoya blew out a disgruntled breath as she bent to fasten the last fetter and check the security of the locks. "As if I have the time."

"I know you go somewhere late at night, Zoya," he prodded. He was curious but also eager for distraction. "You've been seen on the grounds, though no one seems to know where you go."

"I go a lot of places, Your Highness. And if you keep prying into my personal life, I'll have some suggestions as to where *you* can go."

"Why keep your dalliance a secret? Is he an embarrassment?" Nikolai flexed his fingers, trying to even his breathing. Zoya turned her head and the lamplight caught the crescent of her cheekbone, gilding the dark waves of her hair. He'd never quite managed to make himself immune to her beauty, and he was glad his arms were chained to the bed or he might have been tempted to reach for her.

"Keep still," she snapped. "You're worse than a child given too many cakes."

Bless her poison tongue. "You could stay, Zoya. Entertain me with lively tales of your childhood. I find your spite very soothing."

"Why don't I ask Tolya to soothe you by reciting some poetry?"

"There it is. So sharp, so acerbic. Better than any lullaby." As the last lock clicked home, her sleeve slid back, revealing the silver cuff that circled her wrist, pieces of bone or what might have been teeth fused with the metal. He had never seen her without it and wasn't even sure if it could be removed. He knew a bit about amplifiers. He had even helped Alina secure the scales of the sea whip, the second of Morozova's legendary amplifiers. But he could admit there was a whole universe he didn't know. "Tell me something, Nazyalensky. David said transgressing the boundaries of Grisha power has repercussions. But doesn't an amplifier do just that? Is *parem* any different?"

Zoya brushed her fingers over the metal, her face thoughtful. "I'm not sure *parem* is so different from *merzost*. Like *merzost*, the drug requires a terrible sacrifice for the power it grants—a Grisha's will. Even her life. But amplifiers are something else. They're rare creatures, tied to the making at the heart of the world, the source of all creation. When an amplifier gives up its life, that is the sacrifice the universe requires. The bond is forever forged with the Grisha who deals the killing blow. It's a terrible thing, but beautiful as well. *Merzost* is—"

"Abomination. I know. It's a good thing I have such a fondness for myself."

"All Grisha feel the pull toward *merzost*, the hunger to see just what we might do if we had no limits."

"Even you?"

A small smile touched Zoya's lips. "Especially me. Power is protection." Before Nikolai could ask what she meant, she added, "But the price for that particular kind of power is too high. When the Darkling tried to create his own amplifiers, the result was the Fold." She held up her arm, the cuff glinting in the lamplight. "This is enough for me."

"The shark teeth worn by the twins," mused Nikolai. "Genya's kestrel bones. I've heard the stories behind all of them. But you've never told me the tale of the amplifier you wear."

Zoya raised a brow. In the space of a breath, the contemplative girl was gone and the distant general had returned. "Steel is earned, Your Highness. So are stories." She rose. "And I believe you're stalling."

"You've found me out." He was sorry to see her leave, whatever guise she wore. "Good night, Commander."

"Good night, King Wretch."

He would not beg Zoya to stay. It was not in his nature to plead with anyone, and that was not the pact they shared. They did not look to each other for comfort. They kept each other marching. They kept each other strong. So he would not find another excuse to get her talking again. He would not tell her he was afraid to be left alone with the thing he might become, and he would not ask her to leave the lamp burning, a child's bit of magic to ward off the dark.

But he was relieved when she did it anyway.

7
ZOYA

ZOYA ROSE WHEN THE SKY WAS STILL DARK.
She would see to the morning's business before she made the walk to
the Grand Palace to unlock Nikolai. A week had passed since they'd
arrived back at the capital, and to her relief, the king's monster had
made no more appearances.

Tamar and Nadia were already waiting in the common room outside her chambers, seated at the round table that had once belonged
to the Darkling's personal guard. Nadia was still in her blue dressing
gown, but Tamar was in uniform, arms bare, axes glinting at her
hips.

"Reports of two more *khergud* attacks," said Tamar, holding up a
sheaf of papers covered in tight scrawl.

"I need tea," said Zoya. How could the world be falling apart
before sunrise? It wasn't civilized. She poured herself a glass from the

samovar and took the documents from Tamar's hand. There were more spread across the table. "Where did they strike this time?"

"Three Grisha taken from Sikursk and eight more south of Caryeva."

Zoya sat down hard. "So many?" The Shu had used their stores of *jurda parem* to develop a new kind of warrior: soldiers tailored by Grisha Fabrikators, honed to greater strength, given wings, weighted fists, unbreakable bones, and heightened senses. They called them *khergud*.

"Tell her the rest," said Nadia.

Zoya's gaze locked on Tamar. "There's more?"

"This *is* Ravka," said Tamar. "The Grisha near Sikursk were traveling undercover. Either the Shu knew about the mission—"

"Or Nina was correct and these new soldiers really can somehow sniff out Grisha," finished Nadia.

"Nina warned us," said Tamar.

"She did, didn't she?" said Zoya bitterly. "How fortunate, then, that our good king sent our chief source of information on these Shu soldiers thousands of miles away."

"It was time," said Tamar. "Nina was lost in her grief. It will do her good to be of use."

"What a consolation that will be when she's captured and executed," Zoya retorted. She pinched the bridge of her nose. "The Shu are testing us, pushing farther into our territory. We have to push back."

"With what?" Nadia asked. "A stern warning?"

"It would be one thing if we could target them at home," said Tamar. "But my sources have had no luck discovering the locations where they're creating and training the *khergud* soldiers."

Zoya's stomach knotted when she thought of those bases, of the Grisha "volunteers" the Shu had addicted to *parem* to create these monstrosities. She reached for another file. "Are these the dissections?" Tamar nodded. The bodies of two *khergud* soldiers had been retrieved from Ketterdam and brought back to the Little Palace for study. Tolya had objected, claiming it was wrong to "desecrate" a fallen soldier's body. But Zoya had no patience for fine feeling when their people were being stolen from within their very borders.

"This metal," Zoya said, pointing to the notes David had made in the margin of one of the detailed anatomical sketches created by the Corporalki. "The one they're using to plate the bones. It's not just Grisha steel."

"It's an alloy," said Nadia. "They're combining Grisha steel with ruthenium. It's less malleable but more durable."

"I've never heard of it before."

"It's extremely rare. There are only a few known deposits around the world."

Tamar leaned forward. "But the Shu are getting it from somewhere."

Zoya tapped her finger to the file. "Find the source. Track the shipments. That's how we'll figure out where the *khergud* are being made."

Tamar ran her thumbs over her axes. "When we do, I'm leading the attack."

Zoya nodded. "I'll be right beside you."

Nadia grinned. "And I'll be watching your back."

Zoya hoped it would be soon. She was itching for a fight. She glanced at the clock on the mantel. It was time to wake the king.

A cold mist had crept over the grounds in the night, covering the trees and stone paths in a veil of cloud. She passed through the woods, beneath a canopy of twisting branches. They would bloom white, then pink, then red as blood when spring came, but for now they were only gray wood and thorns. She emerged to the manicured hedges and sprawling lawns that surrounded the Grand Palace, lanterns casting light over the still-dark grounds in muzzy halos. The palace looked like a bride before her wedding, its white stone terraces and golden statues cloaked in mist. It should have been peaceful, this soft gray hour before dawn. But all she could think of was the *khergud*, the Zemeni, the Fjerdans, the Kerch.

Each day she worked with new recruits at the Little Palace and managed the affairs of the Second Army. It had grown under her command, slowly recovering from the wounds the Darkling had dealt them—wounds that had almost been death blows. *How could he do it?* She still wondered. The Darkling had built up the strength of the Second Army over generations, adding to its numbers, improving its training, solidifying his own influence. He had cultivated the talents of young Grisha, helped them to develop their skill. He had raised them like children. And when his children had misbehaved? When his coup attempt had failed and some of the Grisha had dared to stand with Alina Starkov against him? He'd murdered them. Without hesitation or remorse. Zoya had watched them fall. She'd almost been among them.

Almost, she reminded herself as she climbed the palace steps. *But I survived to lead the army he built and nearly destroyed.* Zoya had vowed to make the Second Army a power to be reckoned with again. She'd gone deeper within the borders of Fjerda and the Shu Han, pierced the shores of the Wandering Isle and the frontiers of Novyi Zem in search of Grisha who might wish to learn to fight and who might give their allegiance to Ravka. She was determined to capitalize on that growth, to assemble a force greater than what even the Darkling had raised. But that wouldn't be enough. She intended to find a way to protect Grisha throughout the world so no one would ever have to live in fear or hide their gifts again—a governing body with representatives from every nation to hold their countries accountable, a guarantee of rights and of punishment for anyone who tried to imprison or harm her kind. For that dream to be anything more than a pleasant fantasy, Ravka would have to be strong—and so would its king.

As Zoya strode through the Grand Palace halls to Nikolai's chambers, she cast a look at two servants lingering outside his door that sent them shrinking up against the wall like frightened anemones.

She knew the way they sighed over their poor king. *He's never been the same since the war*, they whispered, swooning and dabbing their eyes whenever he was near. She couldn't blame them. Nikolai was rich, handsome, and beset by a tragic past. Perfect daydream fodder. But with her luck the king would ignore the suitable prospective brides she'd found, fall for a common housemaid, and insist on marrying for love. It was just the kind of contrary, romantic nonsense he was prone to.

She greeted Tolya, rang for a breakfast tray, then entered the king's bedroom and threw open the curtains. The morning light had turned pale and rosy.

Nikolai cast her a baleful glare from his place among the pillows. "You're late."

"And you're chained to a bed. Perhaps not the best time to be critical."

"It's too early in the morning to threaten a king," he said grumpily.

She sank down beside him and began the work of unshackling him. "I'm at my most murderous on an empty stomach."

Zoya was grateful for the chatter. It was meaningless, but it filled the silence of the room. They'd slipped back into an easy routine after the near disaster in Ivets, but she could never quite accustom herself to this intimacy—the dawn quiet, the rumpled sheets, the tousled hair that made Nikolai look less a king than a boy in need of kissing.

Entertain me with lively tales of your childhood, he'd said to her. Zoya doubted the king would be amused by her stories. *Should I tell you about the old man my mother wanted to marry me off to when I was nine years old? Should I tell you what happened on my wedding day? What they tried to do to me? The damage I left in my wake?*

Zoya finished the business of freeing him from his bonds, taking care to touch his sleep-warmed skin as little as possible, then left the king to wash and dress.

A moment later a knock sounded on the sitting room door and a servant entered with hot tea and a tray of covered dishes. Zoya didn't miss the furtive glance in her direction as he scurried away. Perhaps she should simply give in to the rumor that she was Nikolai's mistress and let people talk. At least then she could skip the predawn trek from the Little Palace and sleep in.

Nikolai sauntered into the sitting room, golden hair combed neatly, boots shined, impeccably attired as always.

"You look well rested," she said sourly.

"I barely slept, and I woke with a crick in my back that feels like Tolya played lawn tennis with my spine. But a king does not hunch, Zoya dear. Are you eating my herring?"

She popped the last bite into her mouth. "No, I have *eaten* your herring. Now——"

Before Zoya could begin to address the business of the day, the door flew open and Tamar entered, followed by her brother, golden eyes glinting, both of them fully armed.

"Tell me," Nikolai said, all hint of his easy manner gone.

"There's trouble with the pilgrims camped outside the city walls. The Apparat doesn't like anything this new cult has to say. He's called the Priestguard to the lower town."

Zoya was on her feet in an instant. The Apparat was meant to serve as spiritual counselor to the king, but he was a traitor and a troublemaker through and through.

Nikolai took a quick swig of his tea and rose. "Are our people in position?"

Tolya nodded. "We have Heartrenders in plain dress interspersed throughout the crowd and snipers in position along the walls and the nearest hillside. There's not much cover, though."

"You knew this would happen?" Zoya asked Nikolai as she followed him and the twins back through the palace corridors.

"I had a feeling."

"And you made no move to stop him?"

"How?" said Nikolai. "By barricading him in the chapel?"

"I've heard worse ideas. He has no standing."

"But he has the means, and he knows I won't challenge him outright with armed troops."

Zoya scowled. "The Priestguard should have been disbanded long ago." They were warrior monks, both scholar and soldier, and there was no question their loyalty lay with the Apparat, not their king.

"Unfortunately, that would have caused riots among the common people, and I'm not keen on riots. Unless they involve dancing, but I believe those are usually referred to as parties. What kind of party is this, Tamar?"

"We've had our people circulating with the pilgrims every day and reporting back. They've been mostly peaceful. But this morning one of their preachers got them riled up, and the Apparat must not have liked what he heard."

The king's soldiers were waiting by the double-eagle fountain with additional horses in tow.

"No uniformed soldiers will move past the lower wall without my say-so," Nikolai commanded. "The Grisha are only there for crowd control unless I give the signal. Keep the snipers in position, but absolutely no one is to act without direct orders from me, understood?"

The king had the right to command his forces as he saw fit, and Zoya trusted the twins to make the best possible use of their Heartrenders to protect the crown, but Zoya's temper still bristled at the fact that they'd been put in this position. Nikolai was too fond of compromise. The Apparat had betrayed everyone who'd ever been foolish enough to trust him. He was a snake, and if she'd had her way, he and his Priestguard lackeys would have been offered two choices after the civil war—execution or exile.

They mounted and were headed through the gates when Nikolai said, "I need you calm, Zoya. The Apparat isn't fond of the Grisha Triumvirate to begin with—"

"I weep."

"And outright hostility from you won't help. I know you don't approve of allowing the priest to remain in the capital."

"Of course you should keep him here. Preferably stuffed above my mantel."

"A stirring conversation piece, no doubt, but we can't afford to make him a martyr. He has too much sway among the people."

Zoya ground her teeth. "He is a liar and a traitor. He was instrumental in deposing your father. He tried to keep Alina and *me* captive beneath the earth. He never lent you support during the war."

"All true. If I ever need to study for a history exam, I know who to come to."

Why wouldn't he listen? "The priest is dangerous, Nikolai."

"He's more dangerous if we can't see what he's doing. His network is far-reaching, and his sway with the people is something I can do nothing to combat directly."

They passed through the gates and on to the streets of the upper

112

town. "We should have held a trial after the war," Zoya said. "Made his crimes known."

"Do you really believe it would have mattered? Even if Alina Starkov herself rose from the Fold ensconced in sunlight to denounce him, the Apparat would still find a way to survive. That's his gift. Now put on your most devout face, Zoya. You make a darling heretic, but I need you looking pious."

Zoya ordered her features into a facsimile of calm, but the prospect of dealing with the Apparat always left her caught between rage and frustration.

Nikolai had rebuilt the royal chapel on the palace grounds after the war and had it consecrated by the Apparat himself—a gesture of reconciliation. It was the site of Nikolai's coronation, where the Lantsov crown had been set upon his head and the moth-eaten but supposedly sacred bearskin of Sankt Grigori had been laid upon his shoulders. The painted triptych panels of the Saints had been pulled from the rubble and refurbished, the gold of their halos burnished brightly—Ilya in Chains, Lizabeta of the Roses. Alina had been added to their number with her white hair and antler collar so that now fourteen Saints watched over the altar, assembled like a serene choir.

Zoya had barely made it through the coronation. She couldn't help but think of the night the old chapel had fallen, when the Darkling had slaughtered most of the Second Army, the very Grisha he had spent his life claiming he would protect. If not for Tolya and Tamar, the war would have ended that night. And Zoya could admit that the Apparat's forces had played their part too, holy warriors known as the Soldat Sol, young men and women dedicated to the worship of the Sun Saint, many of whom had been endowed with her power in the final battle with the Darkling on the Shadow Fold. That little miracle had cemented Alina's legacy—and unfortunately bolstered the power of the Apparat as well. It was hard not to suspect he had something to do with the bone bridge at Ivets and the spate of strange happenings throughout Ravka.

As they passed over the bridge and into the streets of the lower town, Zoya could hear the crowds outside the double walls, but it was only when they'd dismounted and reached the top of the battlements that she got a good look at the people gathered below. She heard her own gasp, felt shock travel through her like a slap. These were not the ordinary pilgrims who journeyed across the country to pay homage to their Saints; they were not the sun cult that had grown up around Alina Starkov and that often came to the palace walls to honor her. These people wore black. The banners they raised were emblazoned with the sun in eclipse—the Darkling's symbol.

They'd come here to praise the man who had torn Zoya's life apart.

A young cleric stood on a rock. He had the long, wild hair of the Priestguard, but he wore black, not brown. He was tall and bony, and she doubted he could be much older than twenty.

"We begin in darkness," he cried to the swaying crowd, "and it is to darkness we return. Where else are the rich man and the poor man made equal? Where else is someone judged for nothing but the purity of his soul?"

"What is this drivel?" Zoya demanded.

Nikolai sighed. "This is the Cult of the Starless Saint."

"They worship—"

"The Darkling."

"And just how many followers do they have?"

"We're not sure," said Tamar. "There have been rumblings of a new cult but nothing like this."

The Apparat had caught sight of the king and was making his way along the battlements. Zoya could see the Priestguard arrayed behind him, wearing robes bearing Alina's golden sun—and armed with repeating rifles.

"Better and better," muttered Zoya.

"Your Majesty." The Apparat bowed deeply. "I am honored you would make time to lend me your support. I so rarely see you in the chapel. I sometimes fear you have forgotten how to pray."

"Not at all," said Nikolai. "Just not much for kneeling. Plays havoc on the joints. You've brought armed men to the city walls."

"And you can see why. You've heard this blasphemy? This vile heresy? They want the church to recognize the Darkling as a Saint!"

"Who is this new cleric to you?" Zoya said, striving to keep her tone even. "Was he a member of the Priestguard?"

"He is the lowest form of traitor."

You would know, she thought grimly. "So that's a yes?"

"He's a monk," confirmed Tamar. "Yuri Vedenen. He left the Priestguard a year ago. My sources don't know why."

"We can discuss the boy's provenance another time," said Nikolai. "If you let the Priestguard loose, you risk causing a bloodbath and making a whole slew of new martyrs, which will only validate their cause."

"You cannot ask me to permit this heresy—"

Nikolai's voice was cold. "I *ask* nothing."

The Apparat's already waxen face paled further. "Forgive me, Your Highness. But you must understand, this is not a matter for kings to decide. It is a battle for Ravka's very soul."

"Tell your men to stand down, priest. I will not have more blood shed in the capital." Nikolai did not wait for the Apparat's reply but descended the battlements. "Open the gates," he commanded. "The king rides out."

"Are you sure this is wise?" murmured Tamar. "I've heard the talk in this camp. These pilgrims aren't fond of you."

"Perhaps they just haven't gotten to know me. Stay close. Tolya, you make sure those Priestguard don't get any ideas. Try to keep them separated from my soldiers. I don't need to cause a riot of my own."

"I'm coming with you," said Zoya.

Nikolai cast her a long look. "I'm all for reckless choices, Zoya, but this is a delicate matter. You will have to bite your tongue."

"Until it bleeds." She wanted a closer look at the people gilding the Darkling's memory. She wanted to remember each of their faces.

The gate rose and a hush descended as the king rode out of the city and into the crowd. The pilgrims might not care for Ravka's young ruler, but there were plenty of people who had come to the capital on other business, to trade or visit the lower town. To them, Nikolai Lantsov was not just a king or a war hero. He was the man who had restored order after the chaos of the civil war, who had granted them years of peace, who had promised them prosperity and worked to see it done. They went to their knees.

Re'b Ravka, they shouted. *Korol Rezni*. Son of Ravka. King of Scars.

Nikolai raised his gloved hand in greeting, his face serene, his bearing erect, sliding from the role of commander to born nobility in the blink of an eye.

Some of the black-clad pilgrims knelt with the rest of the crowd, but a few remained standing, gathered around their bony prophet, who stood defiant upon an outcropping of rock. "Traitor!" he shouted as Nikolai approached. "Pretender! Thief! Murderer!" But his voice trembled.

"I've certainly been busy," said Nikolai. They rode closer, forcing the pilgrims to move aside until the monk stood alone atop the rock to face Nikolai.

Maybe younger than twenty, Zoya thought. The monk's narrow chest rose and fell rapidly. His face was long, his skin pale except for two hectic spots of color on his cheeks that gave him the look of a boy with a fever. His eyes were a melancholy green at odds with the fervor in them.

"What is on his chin?" Zoya whispered to Tamar.

"I believe he's trying to sprout a beard."

She peered at his long face. "He'd have better luck trying to grow a horn in the middle of his forehead."

The monk flapped his black sleeves like a crow about to take flight. "Tell your false priest to do what is right and recognize the Starless One as a Saint."

"I'll consider it," Nikolai said mildly. "But first I must ask that you join me for breakfast."

"I will not be wooed! I will not be bribed!"

"Yes, but will you have tea or coffee?" A titter rose from the crowd, the smallest release of tension.

The boy raised his hands to the skies. "The Age of Saints has come! The signs appear from the permafrost to the Sikurzoi! Do you think I will be swayed by your glib words and friendly demeanor?"

"No," said Nikolai gently, and dismounted. Zoya and Tamar exchanged a glance. If this was all some elaborate setup for an assassination attempt, then the king was playing his part very well. "May I join you?"

The young monk blinked, flustered. "I . . . I suppose?"

Nikolai hoisted himself onto the rock. "I don't expect you to be wooed or bribed or swayed by my admittedly winning demeanor," he said so quietly that only the monk and Zoya and Tamar could hear. "But you may be swayed by the sniper stationed behind that gentle knoll—do you see it? Excellent spot for picnicking—with orders to burst your head like a summer melon if I lift my right hand." Nikolai raised his hand and the boy flinched, but the king merely adjusted the lapel of his coat.

"I would gladly be martyred——"

"You won't be martyred . . . Yuri, is it? You'll be a mistake. That bullet will graze my shoulder and I'll make sure to fall very dramatically to the ground. The shooter will confess to being an assassin who wished to murder the Lantsov king. Maybe he'll even say he was loyal to the cause of the Starless Saint."

"But that . . . that's preposterous," the monk sputtered.

"Is it more preposterous than the king of Ravka putting himself in the path of a sniper's bullet in order to rid the kingdom of an upstart monk? Because that, my friend, is quite a story." Nikolai extended his hand. "Come to breakfast. My cook makes a marvelous pork loin."

"I don't eat meat."

"Of course you don't," Zoya said. "It's animals you object to killing, not people."

"The Darkling——"

"Spare me your sermons," she hissed. "It is only my loyalty to the king that keeps me from pulling the air from your chest and crushing your lungs like hollow gourds."

"I've seen her do it," said Nikolai. "Makes a funny sound."

"Kind of a pop?" said Tamar.

"Wetter," Nikolai said. "More of a squelch."

"I'll go," said the monk. "But if I am not returned to my followers safe and unharmed, there will be blood in the streets. There will——"

"Please let me do it," said Zoya. "No one will miss him."

"Don't be silly," said Nikolai. "I'm sure he has a mother. Right, Yuri? Nice woman. Lives in Valchenko?"

Yuri touched his hand to his chest as if the king had struck him. Apparently Tamar's spies had gathered plenty of intelligence on this boy.

"I know," said Nikolai, patting the monk on the shoulder. "Most disconcerting to realize you're gambling with lives other than your own. Shall we?"

Yuri nodded and Nikolai turned to the crowd.

"We will meet," he declared, voice booming. "We will talk." He shrugged. "Perhaps we will argue. But Ravkans need agree on nothing more than the drinking of tea."

A ripple of laughter passed through the people, still kneeling but grateful now, relieved. Tamar gave the monk her horse and they rode back through the gates.

As soon as they were inside, the Apparat rushed toward them, flanked by Priestguards. "We will take him into custody. I have many a question for this heretic——"

"Yuri Vedenen is my guest," said Nikolai pleasantly.

"I insist that I be present at his interrogation."

"What a peculiar name for breakfast."

"You cannot possibly mean to——"

"Tolya," Nikolai said, "take our guest to the Iris Suite and make sure he is adequately fed and watered. I'll join you shortly." They waited for the monk to be escorted away. It was clear the Apparat was desperate to speak, but before he could open his mouth, Nikolai swung down from his horse. "Priest," he said, and now his voice held the low, angry thrum of a temper barely leashed. "Do not think that because I've let you live this long, I cannot change my mind. Accidents happen. Even to men of faith."

"Forgive me, Your Highness. But . . . a creature like this cannot be trusted."

"Pray go on," said Zoya. "I'd like to see if an excess of irony can actually kill a man."

"Why did the monk abandon the Priestguard?" asked Nikolai.

"I don't know," admitted the Apparat. "He was a scholar, a good one. Better than that. His theories were unorthodox but brilliant. Then a year ago he vanished without explanation. Until he reappeared on our doorstep preaching this absurd gospel."

"Do we know where the cult originated?"

"No," said the Apparat. He sighed. "But I think it was inevitable the people would seek to make the Darkling a Saint."

"Why?" said Zoya. "The common people had no love for him."

"In life, no. In death, a man may become anything at all. He possessed great power and died grandly. Sometimes that is enough."

It shouldn't be. After everything he did.

"Very well," said Nikolai. "We will grant the monk an audience and see what he has to say."

The Apparat's eyes protruded almost comically from his head. "You cannot mean to speak with him, to lend his cause such credibility! It is the height of recklessness!"

Though Zoya might well have agreed with the priest, she still wanted to seize his filthy robes and shake him until he recognized he was talking to his king and not some supplicant. Not that *she* was particularly compliant when it came to Nikolai, but it was the principle of the thing.

Nikolai remained unruffled, his temper forgotten. "Calm yourself, priest. I have no intention of seeing the Darkling called a Saint. But if we can make a friend of this boy, we should, and I intend to get all of the information I can from him in the process."

"My followers will not like it," said the Apparat with false regret. "I, of course, understand the need for diplomacy, but they may fear the spiritual corruption of their king."

"What a tragedy that would be. Perhaps there is a way to appease them and compensate you for this difficult day."

The Apparat bristled. "The Saints have no need of gold."

Nikolai looked scandalized. "Nothing so crass."

"Well," said the Apparat, making a great show of thinking. "Ulyosk and Ryevost are in need of new churches. The people need to know the king shares their faith, and such a gesture will help strengthen their faith in their ruler."

After a long moment, Nikolai bobbed his chin. "You will have your churches."

"They are the Saints' churches, Your Highness."

"Then please inform the Saints."

"Does a king bow so easily to a man with no title?" Zoya asked as they rode away. She had said she would bite her tongue, and she had, but it had left her temper boiling. "You are helping the Apparat build his network of spies. You are making him stronger."

"At some point, you might consider treating me as something other than a fool. Trust me, Zoya. You may come to enjoy it."

"That's what Tamar said about absinthe."

"And?"

"It still tastes like sugar dipped in kerosene."

Zoya cast a glance over her shoulder and saw the priest watching them from the city gates, his eyes as dark as pits. Nikolai might joke all he liked, but every concession they made to the Apparat felt like a misstep. The old king, the Darkling, Alina Starkov—they'd all bargained with the priest, and all of them had paid in blood.

Zoya spent the rest of her day overseeing a new squadron of Squallers and sending orders to the outposts along the southern border. She hoped the Grisha forces there would be able to guard against a possible Shu attack. She dined in the Hall of the Golden Dome beside Genya and David, listening with one ear to Genya's plans for the arrival of their international guests as she thumbed through a summary of David's work with Kuwei Yul-Bo. The young Inferni sat at a table surrounded by other young Grisha. His late father had created *parem*, and Kuwei had done his best to share his knowledge of that work with David and the other Fabrikators attempting to alter the addictive side effects of the drug. But he was less a scientist than a soldier. Though Genya had tailored him slightly, Kuwei's gifts as an Inferni were his greatest disguise; no one in the Shu Han had known of his abilities. He had chosen a new name when he'd come to the Little Palace: Nhaban. It meant "rising phoenix" in Shu. The boy was as pretentious as he was gifted.

After dinner she managed another hour of work before she ventured to the Grand Palace to lock Nikolai in for the night and then allowed herself to retire to her chambers. They had once belonged to the Darkling. Genya and David had refused them when they'd assumed their duties in the Triumvirate, but Zoya had gladly occupied the spacious rooms. She was happy to take anything that had once been his, and she had swung the first hammer when it was time to tear down the old furnishings and remake the space to her liking. A gesture. She wasn't about to let her hands get calloused and had left the real effort to the workmen. It had taken long months and considerable Fabrikator craft to fashion the rooms to her taste, but now the domed ceiling showed a sky thick with cloud, and the walls had been treated to look like a storm-swept sea. Few people noticed the little boat that had been painted into one of the six corners, or the flag it flew with two tiny stars. And no one who did would have known what it meant.

Zoya washed and dressed for bed. There had been a time when she had been able to sleep deeply beneath the domes of the Little Palace, but that was before the Darkling's coup. He had shattered her belief that nothing could touch this place, this home that had once been a haven. Now she slept lightly—and woke instantly at the sound of a knock on her chamber door.

The monk, she thought. *I knew we shouldn't have let him into the palace.*

But as soon as Zoya slid the bolt and opened the door, Tamar said, "Nikolai is out."

"Impossible," Zoya protested, though she was already reaching for her boots.

Tamar's brows rose as Zoya tossed a coat over her nightdress, cobwebs of silver silk that flickered like lightning in a storm cloud when the lamplight struck the sheer fabric just right. "Who did you dress for tonight?" she asked.

"Myself," snapped Zoya. "Do we know where he headed?"

"Tolya saw him fly west toward Balakirev."

"Anyone else?"

"I don't think so. No alarm sounded. But we can't be sure. We're lucky this didn't happen in the summer."

When the sun never properly set and anyone would be able to see a monster in the skies.

"How?" Zoya asked as she nudged a panel in the wall and it slid open to reveal a long flight of stairs. When she'd had her chambers refurbished, she'd had a tunnel dug to connect it to the network of passages beneath Os Alta. "Those chains are reinforced with Grisha steel. If he's gotten stronger—"

"They weren't broken," said Tamar from behind her. "They were unlocked."

Zoya stumbled and nearly toppled down the stairs. *Unlocked?* Then someone knew Nikolai's secret? Had sought to sabotage their work to keep it undiscovered? The implications were overwhelming.

Long moments later they were pushing into the basement of the Convent of Sankta Lizabeta. Tolya waited in the gardens with three horses.

"Tell me," Zoya said as she and Tamar mounted.

"I heard glass breaking," Tolya replied. "When I ran inside, I saw the king take flight from the window casement. No one had come or gone through his door."

Damn it. Then had the monster somehow managed to pick the locks? Zoya kicked her horse into a gallop. She had a thousand questions, but they could worry about how Nikolai had gotten free once they'd retrieved him.

They rode hard over the bridge and through the streets of the lower town. At a signal to the guards, they thundered through the gates and Os Alta's famous double walls. How far had Nikolai gotten? How far would he go? Better that he flew away from the city, away from anywhere heavily populated. Zoya reached for the invisible currents that flowed around them, higher and higher, seeking the disruption on the wind that was Nikolai. It was not only the weight and size of him but the very wrongness of him that brushed against her power. *Merzost.* Abomination. The taint of something monstrous in his blood.

"He's still headed west," she said, feeling his presence bleed across her senses. "He's in Balakirev." A pretty little spot. One of the favored places for Grisha to visit for sleigh rides and festivals in better times.

They slowed their horses as they approached the outskirts of town and the dirt roads gave way to cobblestones. Balakirev slept, its windows dark and houses quiet. Here or there Zoya saw a lantern lit through the glass, a mother tending to a fussy infant, a clerk working late into the predawn hours. She turned her awareness to the skies and gestured the twins forward. Nikolai was moving toward the town center.

The main square was silent, lined by the courthouse, the town hall, the grand offices of the local governor. Stone paths radiated from a large fountain, where Zoya knew the women would come to do their washing. A statue of Sankt Juris stood at its center, his lance piercing the heart of a great dragon as water cascaded from the back

124

of the beast's wings. Zoya had always hated that particular story. The great warrior Juris seemed like a big bully.

"The roof," she whispered, pointing to the town hall. "I'll watch the perimeter."

Tamar and Tolya slipped silently from their horses, shackles in hand, and disappeared into the building. If Nikolai took flight, she could try to bring him down or at least track him. But dawn was coming on. They had to move quickly.

She waited in the shadows, eyes trained on the spires of the town hall. The night felt too still. Zoya had the uncomfortable sense that she was being watched, but the shops and buildings surrounding the square showed no signs of life. High above, the roofline of the town hall seemed to shift. A shadow broke from the roof, wings spread against the moonlit sky. Zoya lifted her hands and prepared to bring Nikolai down, but he circled once, then settled on the towering spike of the church's bell tower.

"Damn it."

Tolya and Tamar would be racing up the stairs of the town hall only to find their quarry escaped. If Zoya attempted the church stairs, Nikolai could well make another leap and be long gone before she reached the top. The sky was already turning gray, and if he broke for open countryside they might never catch him. There was no time to hesitate.

She eyed the open notches in the stonework of the bell tower. Even with her amplifier, she'd never managed the control necessary for flight. Only Grisha flush with the effects of *jurda parem* could accomplish that feat.

"This is going to hurt," she muttered, and spun her hands in tight circles, summoning the current, then arced her arms. The gust hit her from behind, lofting her upward. It took all her will to resist the urge to pinwheel her arms and let the wind take her higher. She thrust her hand forward and the gust threw her toward the gap in the stone—too hard, too fast. There was no time to adjust her aim.

Zoya covered her head and face, then grunted as her shoulder cracked against the edge of a column. She tumbled to the floor of the bell tower in a graceless heap and rolled to her back, trying to get her bearings.

There, high above, perched in the eaves, she caught the glint of the monster's eyes in the dark. She could just make out his shape. His chest was bare, his torn trousers slung low on his hips. His taloned feet curved over the beams of the bell tower.

A low growl reached her, seemed to reverberate through the floorboards. Something was different tonight. *He* was different.

Oh Saints, she realized. *He's hungry.*

In the past Zoya had been slower to find Nikolai, locating him after he had hunted and fed. *He's never killed a human before*, she reminded herself. Then amended, *That we know of.* But she felt, in her bones, that tonight she was the prey.

Like hell.

She pushed to her feet and hissed in a breath at the throb in her shoulder. She'd dislocated it, maybe broken the bone. Pain rolled through her in a wave that set her stomach churning. Her right arm was useless. She'd have only her left arm to summon with, but if Adrik could do it, so could she.

"Nikolai," she said sternly.

The growl stopped, then picked up again, lower and louder than before. A tendril of fear uncurled in her belly. Was this what it was to be a small creature pinned helpless in the wood?

"*Nikolai*," she snapped, not letting her terror enter her voice. She thought it might be a very bad thing if he knew she was afraid. "Get down here."

The growl rippled and huffed. Almost like a laugh.

Before she could make sense of that, he launched himself at her.

Zoya threw up her hand and a blast of wind pummeled the creature, but her attempt had only half the strength of her usual summoning. It drove him backward and he struck the wall, but with little force.

She saw the monster register her injury, her weakness. It drew in a long breath, muscles tensing. How many nights had she kept it from its fun? How long had it been waiting for a chance to hurt her? She needed help.

"Tolya!" she shouted. "Tamar!" But could they even hear her at such distance? Zoya eyed the bell.

The monster lunged. She dove right and screamed as her injured shoulder hit the slats, but threw her other arm up with all the force she could muster, begging the storm to answer. Wind seized the bell and sent its massive metal shell swinging. The clapper struck, a rever-berant clang that shuddered through her skull and made the monster snarl. The bell struck a second time, far more weakly, before it slowed its arc.

Zoya was sweating now, the pain turning her vision black at the edges. She dragged herself toward the wall.

Nikolai—the monster—was prowling toward her in a low crouch, its clawed feet silent over the slats of the floor, the movement eerily inhuman. It was Nikolai and yet it was not Nikolai. The elegant lines of its face were the same, but its eyes were black as ink. The shadows of its wings seemed to pulse and seethe.

"Nikolai," she said again. "I'm going to be furious if you try to eat me. And you know what I'm like when I'm mad."

Its lips drew back in a smile—there was no other word for it—revealing needle-sharp fangs that gleamed like shards of obsidian.

Whatever was stalking her was not her king.

"Captain," she tried. "Sturmhond." Nothing. It stalked closer.

"Sobachka," she said. *Puppy*, the nickname he'd had as a child, one she'd never used with him before. "Stop this."

From somewhere far below she heard a door slam. Tolya? Tamar? It didn't matter. They weren't going to make it in time. Zoya could summon lightning, but without both arms to control the current, she knew she would kill him.

She raised her arm again. The gust drove the creature back, but its claws gripped the wooden floor and it plowed forward, wings pinned tight to its body, dark gaze focused on her.

It batted her good arm aside, hard enough that she thought it might have broken that bone too. The wind fell away and the monster's wings flared wide.

It opened its mouth—and spoke.

"Zoya."

She flinched. The monster did not speak. It could not. But it wasn't even the shock of speech coming from the creature's lips that so frightened her. That was not Nikolai's voice; it was soft, cool as glass, familiar.

No. It couldn't be. Fear was clouding her mind.

The creature's lips parted. Its teeth gleamed. It seized her hair and yanked her head back as she struggled. It was going to tear her throat out. Its lips brushed the skin of her neck.

A thousand thoughts crowded into her mind. She should have brought a weapon. She shouldn't have relied on her power. She shouldn't have believed she wasn't afraid to die. She shouldn't have believed that Nikolai would not harm her.

The door to the bell tower slammed open and Tamar was there, Tolya behind her. Tamar's axes flew. One lodged in the creature's shoulder, the other in the meat of one of its wings. The thing turned on them, snarling, and Tolya's hands shot out.

Zoya watched, torn between lingering dread and fascination as the creature's legs buckled. It growled, then fell silent as Tolya slowed its heart and sent the monster into unconsciousness.

Zoya rose, cradling her dislocated arm, and looked down at the thing on the floorboards as its claws receded, the dark veins retracting and fading, its wings dissolving into shreds of shadow. The king of Ravka lay on the bell tower floor, golden hair disheveled, boyish and bleeding.

"Are you all right?" asked Tamar.

"Yes," Zoya lied.

Zoya. The sound of his voice in that moment, smooth as glass, neither human nor inhuman. Did that mean that whatever was inside him was not the mindless monster they'd assumed? It hadn't just been hungry; there had been something vengeful in its desire. Would Nikolai have woken with her blood on his lips?

"You know what this means," said Tamar.

They couldn't control him. The palace was no longer safe, and Nikolai was no longer safe in it. And right now, ambassadors, dignitaries, noblemen, and wealthy merchants were packing their best clothes and preparing to travel to Os Alta—to say nothing of the eligible princesses and hopeful noblewomen who accompanied them.

"We've invited emissaries from every country to witness this horror," said Tolya. To watch Nikolai descend into bloodlust, to play audience as a king became more monster than man.

Zoya had given her life to the Second Army, to a dream that they could build something better. She had believed that if her country was strong enough, the world might change for her kind. Now that dream was collapsing. Zoya thought of the stories Nina had told them of the prison at the Ice Court. She thought of the *khergud* emerging from the skies to steal Grisha from the safety of their lands. She remembered bodies littering the grounds of the Little Palace the night of the Darkling's attack. She would not let it happen again. She refused.

Zoya took a breath and slammed her shoulder back into place, ignoring the jolt of nausea that came with the pain.

"We find a cure," she said. "Or Ravka falls."

8
NINA

"I DON'T LIKE LEAVING LEONI BEHIND," said Adrik, his solemn voice like the tolling of a particularly forlorn bell. "They're hardly friendly at the convent, and she doesn't speak the language."

Nina and Adrik had made their way out of the valley, the sledge pulled behind their two mounts, a hard wind at their backs. Nina rode sidesaddle, her heavy skirts gathered behind her. She wasn't much of a rider to begin with, and this concession to Fjerdan sensibilities was one of the most challenging elements of her cover.

As they traveled farther from the town, the whispers rose in her head as if in protest. Now that she knew the dead had brought her to Gäfvalle, the sound seemed to have grown clearer, the high, sweet voices of the lost tugging at her thoughts. She hadn't told Adrik and

Leoni about the graves at the factory yet. The incident by the eastern gate had left her too shaken.

"Leoni will be fine," said Nina, turning her attention to Adrik. "She's resourceful and she knows how to lie low. Besides, we'll be back by midday tomorrow." Adrik said nothing, and Nina added, "Cosseting her isn't going to win you any points."

The chill had made Adrik's skin rosy beneath his freckles, and he looked a bit like a sulky actor whose cheeks had been rouged for a play. "She's a soldier under my command. I would never cross that line."

"She won't be under your command when this mission is over, Adrik, and it's obvious she likes you."

"She does?" He sounded disconsolate over the news. Nina wasn't fooled.

She adjusted the straps of her pack. "To my great astonishment."

"You like me too, Zenik. Must be my sunny outlook."

"Adrik, if the choice is between taking orders from you or Zoya Nazyalensky, you're always going to win."

His breath plumed in the cold air. "I used to be completely in love with her."

"Weren't we all? Even when she's slicing you in two with a few well-chosen words, it's hard to focus on anything but how good she looks doing it."

"Appalling," Adrik mused. "I once saw a student set fire to his own hair because he was so busy looking at Zoya. She didn't even spare him a second glance."

Nina fixed Adrik with a contemptuous stare, and in her most disdainful Zoya voice drawled, "Someone throw a bucket on that idiot before he burns down the palace."

He shuddered. "That was far too convincing." He consulted his map as they reached a crossroads. "Zoya was nice enough to look at," he said as he led them farther west. "But there was more to it. She was the only one who treated me the same after I lost my arm."

"Horribly?"

"She couldn't have shown me more contempt. Her insults were a lot easier to bear than Nadia constantly fussing over me."

"That's what sisters do. I assume. You were just as much of a mother hen when we all came back from the Fold." They'd both been children really. Nina had been a student at the Grisha school when they were all evacuated to the orphanage at Keramzin. But Adrik had begged to go with his sister, to fight beside the Sun Summoner. He hadn't been there when the Darkling took Nina and the other students hostage.

"I wasn't worried about *you*," said Adrik. "If you'd all died and I'd been the only one to leave school, can you imagine how tiring it would have been to live with the guilt?"

Nina made herself laugh, but she knew all about guilt. She often wondered why she'd survived so much—capture by the *drüskelle*, shipwreck, Kaz Brekker's mad heists, and the ordeal of *parem*. She was the only known Grisha to have lived through a dose of the drug. What had made that possible? Was it that particular strain of *jurda parem*? Was it her desire to spite Jarl Brum and his witchhunters by surviving? Chance, fortune, fate. She didn't know what name to give to it. Sometimes it felt like Matthias had kept her in this world through the sheer force of his will.

I failed you, Matthias. I wasn't strong enough to save you.

Little red bird, every day you choose the work of living. Every day you choose to go on. There is no failure here, Nina.

"Zoya's a better leader than I expected," admitted Adrik. "Even if I'd never tell her so."

"Can you imagine? You might as well ask her if she wants to snuggle. General Zoya Nazyalensky does not need or want our approval."

They fell into silence as the sun rose higher in the sky, the sledge rumbling over the ground. If it snowed, they would have to change the runners, but hopefully they would be back to Gäfvalle before the weather turned. It was a meager funeral procession, and Nina couldn't help but think Matthias deserved more. Something full of pomp and ceremony, a funeral fit for a hero even if his people believed he was a traitor.

I have been made to protect you. Even in death I will find a way.

His voice was too clear now, too strong. Because this was their final parting. Because once Matthias was in the ground, he would belong to Djel.

She wasn't sure she could do it. She couldn't bear the thought of abandoning his body to the cold earth, to the dark.

Let me go to my god.

She wished Inej were here beside her, that the Wraith were somewhere in all this silence. Nina longed for her stillness, her kindness. She was grateful to Adrik, but he hadn't known Matthias. And he didn't really know Nina either. Not anymore.

When at last they reached the fork of the river, they set up camp, a simple canvas tent lined with animal skins to keep the cold out. They made a fire, watered their horses, and sat down to a plain meal of tea and salt cod that Nina had to force herself to swallow. If anyone passed by, Adrik and Nina planned to say they were on their way to Malsk to show off their wares. The sledge was stocked with plenty of rifle loaders. But Nina doubted they'd have to offer any explanations. Like so much of Fjerda, this place was desolate and empty, the little towns like flowers, unlikely blooms in the snow.

Adrik took a flask from his pocket, poured a small amount of black fluid into a copper cup, and contemplated it skeptically.

"What is that exactly?"

"I just know it's distilled from pine tar. One of the fishermen said it was good for fighting the cold." He took a sip and instantly began coughing and pounding his chest. "Saints, that's disgusting."

"Maybe they just mean it kills you, so you don't have to worry about the cold anymore."

"Or maybe they just like selling overpriced misery to tourists." He offered her the flask, which Nina was quick to decline. For a while they sat staring at the waters of the river rushing past. At last he said, "You never told me how he died."

Nina wasn't certain what to say. Or if she wanted to say anything at all. The specifics of the Ketterdam auction were unknown to most in Ravka even among the Grisha, and Nina doubted Adrik would be thrilled to discover she'd been running with a gang of criminals. "I don't really know. We were . . . working together in Ketterdam. The worst of the mission was over. We thought we were all safe. But then Matthias showed up, bleeding. He'd been shot." He'd found his way to her, despite the fatal wound, despite the pain he was in. For one last kiss, for a final goodbye. "There were *drüskelle* in the city, and they certainly had their reasons for wanting Matthias dead. But we all had prices on our heads. People were hungry for our blood, and the streets were a holy mess."

She could still see his blood staining his shirt, feel the soft stubble of his nape beneath her fingertips. His hair had just begun to grow out properly, thick and golden. "He wouldn't tell me who was responsible," she said. Matthias hadn't wanted to burden her with that. He'd known she would strike out in her grief. But he should have understood that the mystery of his death would punish her. She'd thought her new mission working with the Hringsa in Fjerda, getting Grisha to freedom, would help ease her grief and her guilt, but she felt no better than she had at the start of it all. "It eats at me."

"I know that feeling." Adrik took another sip from his flask and winced at the taste. "Vengeance was all that drove me at the end of the war. I wanted the Darkling to pay for my arm, for the lives of my friends. I wanted him dead."

"And you got your wish."

"And yet my arm didn't grow back. None of my friends came back to life."

"I could help with that," Nina said, and was relieved when Adrik laughed his dry, reluctant chuckle. Some Grisha blanched at any mention of her new power. She'd been a Heartrender once, felt the pulse of the world beating along with her heart. *Parem* had changed her. Nina had felt like a fraud sitting beneath the golden dome in the Little Palace, wearing her red *kefta*. She could no longer manipulate the living, hear the flow of their blood or the song of their cells. But the dead did her bidding—and she supposed she did their bidding too. She'd come to Gäfvalle, after all.

Nina finished the last of her tea. She could sense Adrik waiting. She knew it was time. Maybe laying Matthias to rest would be the thing to help free her heart from this burden. She only knew she could not go on this way.

She rose. "I'm ready," she said, though she knew it wasn't true.

They rode out from camp, following the river.

Tell me a story, Matthias. She needed to hear him now, needed to know some part of him would remain with her. *Tell me about your family.*

Tell me about yours, Nina. Why did you never speak of them?

Because she'd never known them. She'd grown up in a foundling home not unlike the orphanage at Keramzin. There were no records of Nina's parents. She was one more child who had arrived without papers or history. *Keletchka*, as they called it—from the fruit crate. She'd been given the name of one of the home's patrons and had worn donated clothes that arrived tied up in big sacks and smelling of the chemicals they were boiled in to make sure they were free of lice.

Were you unhappy, Nina?

No, Matthias.

It wasn't in your nature, even then.

It is now, she thought. Whatever spark had burned in her was no match for this grief.

But back then, she hadn't been unhappy, despite the chores and the boring lessons and the meals that were mostly cabbage. There had always been noise and company and games to play. She had appointed herself the home's official greeter, welcoming new arrivals, helping to name the new babies, and offering up her rag doll, Feodora, to anyone who might need a friend on their first night in the dormitories.

Besides, the staff always treated her kindly. *Come, little Nina, tell us the news*, Baba Inessa would say and seat Nina on a stool in the kitchen, where she could suck on a bread crust and watch the women at their work.

Nina had been just seven years old when she'd met her first tyrant. His name was Tomek, and he changed everything at the foundling home. He wasn't the tallest or the strongest, he was simply the meanest, willing to strike and bite even the littlest orphans. If someone had a toy, he would break it. When a child was sleeping soundly, he would pinch them awake. He was all manners and dimples when the staff were near, but as soon as they were gone, cruel Tomek would return.

As if they'd just been waiting for a leader, a group of bullies coalesced around him—boys and girls who had always seemed nice enough until they developed a taste for others' tears. Nina did her best to avoid them, but it was as if Tomek could smell her happiness like smoke from a kitchen fire.

One morning just after the Feast of Sankt Nikolai, Baba Inessa gave Nina an orange to share with the other children. Nina warned them to be silent, but they'd giggled and whooped until of course Tomek had marched over to investigate and snatched it from her hands.

Give it back! she'd shouted as he'd dug his thumbs into the orange's waxy skin. *It's for everyone!*

But Tomek and his friends had just jeered. *You're fat enough already,* he'd said, and pushed her so hard she'd fallen on her backside.

Tomek had shoved the whole orange into his mouth and bitten down, laughing as pulp and juice dribbled over his chin. He laughed even harder when, to Nina's great shame, she started crying.

"Look how red you are," Tomek said, his mouth still full. "You look like a rotten apple."

He and his friends crowded around Nina, poking her belly, her arms, her legs. "Look how rotten she is!"

Nina had been scared, but more than anything, she'd been angry. Curled up on the floor, she'd felt something in her shift, a long, luxurious stretch, like a cat yearning toward a sunbeam. All her breathlessness and fear rushed out of her, and it was as if she could feel Tomek's lungs as they expanded, contracted. She squeezed her fists tight.

"Look how——" Tomek hiccuped. Then his friends hiccuped. It was funny. At first. They stopped poking Nina. They looked at one another and giggled, the sound broken by startled little huffs.

They kept hiccuping. "It hurts," said one, rubbing his chest.

"I can't stop," said another, bending double.

It went on that way, all of them hiccuping and moaning long into the night, like an assembly of discontented frogs.

Nina found she could do all kinds of things. She could soothe a crying infant. She could ease her own tummy ache. She could make Tomek's nose run and run and run until his whole shirt was wet with snot. Sometimes she had to stop herself from doing anything too terrible. She didn't want to be a tyrant too. Only a few months later, the Grisha Examiners had come to the foundling home and Nina had been taken to the Little Palace.

"Goodbye!" she'd called as she'd run through the halls, saying her farewells. "Goodbye! Write me lots of letters, please! And be nice," she'd warned Tomek.

"She's a merry child," Baba Inessa had told the Grisha woman in her red *kefta*. "Try not to break her of it."

No one has, Nina. No one ever will.

I'm not so sure, Matthias. War hadn't done it. Captivity. Torture. But loss was something different, because she saw no end to it, only the far horizon, stretching on and on.

Nina knew the spot as soon as she saw it—a copse of trees by the riverbank, a place where travelers might come to rest and where the water eddied as if the river were resting too. *Here*, she told herself as she dismounted and untied a shovel and pick from the sledge. *Here.*

It took her hours to dig. Adrik couldn't help with the task, but he used his power to keep the wind from tearing at her clothes and to shelter the lantern when the sky began to dim.

Nina wasn't certain how deep to dig, but she went on until she was sweating in her coat, until her hands blistered, and then until the blisters broke. When she stopped, panting, Adrik did not wait for her signal but began to untie the tarp on the sledge. Nina made herself help him, forced herself to move aside the boxes and gear that hid their true cargo. *Here.*

Matthias was wrapped in linen specially treated by the Fabrikators at the Little Palace to preserve him from decay, and reinforced by Leoni's craft. Nina thought of pulling the linen aside, of glimpsing his cherished face one more time. But she couldn't bear the idea of seeing his features still and cold, his skin gray. It was bad enough that she had the memory of his blood on her hands forever, the wound beneath her palms, his heart going still. Death was supposed to be her friend and ally, but death had taken him just the same. She could at least try to remember him as he'd been.

Awkwardly, Nina and Adrik rolled his body from the edge of the cart. It was huge and heavy. He tumbled into the tomb with a horrible thud.

Nina covered her face with her hands. She had never been more grateful for Adrik's silence.

Lying in the well of the grave, Matthias' body looked like a chrysalis, as if he were at the beginning of something, instead of the end. He and Nina had never exchanged gifts or rings; they'd had no possessions they shared. They had been wanderers and soldiers. Even so, she could not leave him with nothing. From her pocket, she drew a slender sprig of ash and let it drift down into the grave, followed by a smattering of withered red petals from the tulips their compatriots had placed on his chest when they bid him goodbye in Ketterdam.

"I know you never cared for sweets." Her voice wobbled as she let a handful of toffees fall from her hand. They made a hollow patter. "But this way I'm with you, and you can keep them for me when I see you next. I know you won't eat them yourself."

She knew what came now. A handful of earth. Another. *I love you*, she told him, trying not to think of the graceless sound of the soil, like the rattle of shrapnel, like sudden bursts of rain. *I loved you*.

Her eyes blurred from the tears. She couldn't see him any longer. The earth rose higher. There would be snow soon, maybe even tonight. It would cover her work, a burial shroud, white and unmarred. And when spring came, the snow would melt and find its way through the soil and carry Matthias' spirit to the river, to Djel. He would be with his god at last.

"Will you take the sledge back to camp?" she asked Adrik. There were still things she needed to say, but only to Matthias.

Adrik nodded and glanced up at the darkening sky. "Just don't be too long. A storm's coming." *Good*, she thought. *Let the snow come soon. Let it cover our work here.*

Nina knelt on the cold ground, listening to the hoofbeats of Adrik's horse fade. She could hear the rush of the river, feel the damp of the earth through the heavy wool of her skirts. *The water hears and understands. The ice does not forgive.* Fjerdan words. The words of Djel.

"Matthias," she whispered, then cleared her throat and tried again. "Matthias," she said more loudly. She wanted him to hear her, needed to believe he could. "Oh Saints, I don't want to leave you here. I don't want to leave you ever." But that was not the hero's eulogy he deserved. She could do this for him. Nina drew a long, shaky breath. "Matthias Helvar was a soldier and a hero. He saved me from drowning. He kept us both alive on the ice. He endured a year in the worst prison in the world for a crime he didn't commit. He forgave me for betraying him. He fought beside me, and when he could have abandoned me, he turned his back on the only country he'd ever known instead. For that, he was branded a traitor. But he wasn't. He believed his country could be more than it had been. He lived with honor and died with it too." Her voice broke and she forced the waver away from it. She wanted to be dignified in this moment. She wanted to give him that. "He wasn't always a good man, but he had a good heart. A great, strong heart that should have kept beating for years and years."

Little red bird, let me go.

She wiped the tears from her eyes. This was the first half of her debt paid. She'd brought him home to the land he loved. There should be something to mark this moment, a bell to toll, a choir to sing for him, something so she knew it was time to say her last goodbye.

But you're not done yet, my love.

"You and your sense of duty," she said on a bitter laugh.

The whispers rose inside her head. She didn't want to hear them now, not here.

Listen, Nina.

She did not want to, but she knew she could hide from them no longer—the voices of the dead, calling to her, down the mountain, through the town, over the ice. The voices of women, of girls, anguish in their hearts. Something had happened to them on that hilltop.

Help us, they cried. *Hear us at last.*

The words were clear now, and they were drowning out Matthias' voice. *Stop*, she told them. *Leave us alone. Leave me be.*

But the dead did not relent. *Justice*, they demanded, *justice.*

This was no hallucination. It wasn't madness either. The chorus was real, and they had brought her here for a reason. Nina had hoped her mission with Adrik and Leoni would be enough to start healing. It hadn't been. But the girls on the mountain would not be denied.

Justice. They had brought her this far—and they needed her to listen to them, not the echo of a love she could not hold on to.

Nina placed a hand to her heart then as the ache inside her broke, the ice giving way. There was only dark water beneath, the terrible pain of knowing he was truly gone, the awful understanding that she would never hear his voice again.

Because the chorus was real.

But Matthias' voice was not. It never had been.

"You were never here," she whispered, the tears coming hard now. "You were never here." All this time, she had wanted to believe that he was still with her, but it had been her voice all along, talking herself through the silence, forcing herself to do the work of living when all she wanted was to let go.

Goodbye, Matthias.

No one answered. She was alone in the silence.

9

NIKOLAI

"WE CAN CALL THEM BACK," said Genya, pacing before the fire. "It's not too late. We send messengers and just tell the girls and their families there's been a change in plans."

They'd gathered in the war room this morning, and Nikolai had called for coffee instead of tea. He'd developed a taste for it during his university days in Ketterdam. Though, between his exhaustion and the headache that had plagued him since the incident in Balakirev the previous night, he wouldn't have minded something stronger in his cup.

The incident. What a generous turn of phrase. Tolya had filled him in on every grim detail of his little display in the bell tower. He'd almost murdered one of his most valued generals, one of his only true friends, the person who had helped him to steer this cursed ship of a country for two years, who had kept his secrets and whom he had trusted to do so without question. He had almost killed *Zoya*.

"We'll tell them the king is unwell—" continued Genya.

"That is the last thing we tell them," said Tamar.

"Then we tell them there's been an outbreak of cholera or a massive sewage leak," said Tolya.

Tamar threw up her hands. "So our choices are looking indecisive, weak, or like the capital is swimming in excrement?"

Zoya had been silent through the meeting thus far, hovering by the samovar with crossed arms. Keeping her distance. He knew he needed to apologize to her, but for once in his ridiculous life, he was completely at a loss for words. And before he could wrestle with that particular failure, there was the problem of the party he had so cleverly planned—the one the demon within him seemed intent on crashing.

Nikolai took another sip of bitter coffee, hoping it would clear his head. "I think we may have a resource we didn't have before."

As if she could read his thoughts, Zoya's gaze snapped to his. "If you say that hideous flagpole of a monk, I will—"

"Marvel at my ingenuity? Plant a fond kiss upon my cheek? Put up a plaque to my genius?"

"I will put a plaque on the palace wall commemorating this date as the morning on which Nikolai Lantsov took leave of his senses. The boy is a lunatic, a zealot. He worships at the feet of the man who started a civil war and murdered half of the Second Army."

"He worships an ideal. It's something we've all been guilty of at one time or another."

Zoya turned away, but not before he saw the hurt on her face. Zoya Nazyalensky did not flinch, but the pain had been unmistakable. Nikolai wanted to stop the meeting and just . . . he didn't know what exactly, but he did know that the correct response to almost killing someone was not to try to score points off them the next day.

"Then by all means," said Zoya, "let's welcome a former member of the Priestguard into the war room and put our future in his grubby hands."

"Isn't she lovely when she agrees?" Nikolai asked, and savored Zoya's scowl. It was so much better than seeing that stark, wounded look and knowing he had caused it. But a moment later, he was kicking himself as Tolya escorted the monk into the war room and Zoya's grim expression turned to bemusement.

"Your Highness," said Yuri stiffly. He was so tall he had to duck entering the room, and so slender he looked as if he might turn sideways and get carried away by a draft. "I was warned of your glib tongue. You talk of breaking bread, but I spent last night confined to what amounts to a cell—"

"The Iris Suite? My aunt Ludmilla decorated it herself. Overly fond of the color puce, but *cell* seems a bit ungenerous."

"The *color* is fine. It is the armed guards that offend my sensibility. Is this how you treat all of your guests?"

"Tolya," whispered Nikolai, "I think he's calling you bad company." He leaned back and rested his elbows on the arms of his chair. "Yuri, you have enemies. Those guards were there for your protection."

Yuri sniffed. "My followers will not stand for this."

And that was why Nikolai had sent bread, smoked cod, and some very fine *kvas* to the people camped outside the city, compliments of the crown—men with full bellies complained less. In truth, Nikolai had meant to see to Yuri yesterday, but the afternoon's business had gotten the better of his time. And as for the night, well, that had certainly gotten the better of him too.

"Yuri, may I introduce—"

"No, you may not. I wish to speak on the matter of the Starless One and—" Abruptly Yuri straightened. His eyes widened and his jaw went slack as he looked around the room and seemed to finally register where he was. He clasped his hands like a soprano about to sing. "Oh," the monk gasped. "Oh. It's you. It's *all* of you. I . . ." He turned to the members of the Triumvirate and bowed deeply. "*Moi soverenye*, it's an honor." He bowed a second time. "An absolute honor." Down he went again. "A dream, really."

Nikolai suppressed a groan. Just what had he brought upon himself? Zoya and Genya exchanged a baffled glance, and even David looked up from his work long enough to frown in confusion.

"Do stop that," Zoya said. "You look like an oil derrick."

"Commander Zoya Nazyalensky," Yuri said on a strangled breath. "Yesterday . . . I didn't realize. I thought you were just—"

"One of the king's lackeys?" Zoya ignored Yuri's protests and said, "You do realize every member of this Triumvirate fought *against* your beloved Starless Saint in the civil war?"

"Yes, yes, of course." The monk pushed his wire-rimmed spectacles up the bridge of his long nose. "I do. But, well, David Kostyk, the great Fabrikator who forged the first amplifier worn by Sankta Alina herself." David looked at him blankly and returned to his reading. "Zoya Nazyalensky, who was one of the Darkling's most favored soldiers." Zoya's lip curled. "And then, of course, Genya Safin, the First Tailor, who bears the marks of the Darkling's blessing."

Genya flinched. "*Blessing?*"

"I beg your pardon?" said Zoya, already raising her hands either to summon a storm or to wring Yuri's neck. Tamar reached for her axes. Tolya actually growled.

Nikolai rapped his knuckles against the table. "That's *enough*. Everyone, stand down. Yuri, you are trespassing in territory you cannot begin to understand."

Despite his height, the monk looked like little more than a gawky child who had broken his mother's favorite vase. "I . . . Forgive me. I meant no offense."

Slowly, Genya stood, and silence fell around her. "How old are you, Yuri?"

"Eighteen, *moi soverenyi*."

"When I was a year older than you, the Darkling set his monsters on me, creatures born of the power you venerate so much. They had a taste for human flesh. He had to force them to stop."

"Then he was not so cruel—"

Genya held up a hand, and Nikolai was glad to see Yuri shut his mouth. "The Darkling didn't want me to die. He wanted me to live—like this."

"More fool him," said Nikolai quietly, "to let such a soldier survive."

Genya gave the barest nod. "Think twice before you use the word *blessing*, monk." She sat and folded her hands. "Proceed."

"Just a moment," David said, planting a finger on the page to mark his place in his book. "What was your name?"

"Yuri Vedenen, *moi soverenyi*."

"Yuri Vedenen, if you upset my wife again, I will kill you where you stand."

The monk swallowed. "Yes, *moi soverenyi*."

"Oh, David," Genya said, taking his hand. "You've never threatened to murder anyone for me before."

"Haven't I?" he murmured distractedly, placed a kiss on her knuckles, and continued reading.

"I am . . . Forgive me, I am overwhelmed." Yuri sat, then rose again, as if he couldn't help himself. "To think I'm in rooms built by the Starless One himself." He touched his fingers to the black seams that marked the Shadow Fold on the map. "It is . . . it is too glorious to contemplate. Is this cowhide?"

"Reindeer, I believe," said Nikolai.

"Remarkable!"

"Wait," said Zoya, blue eyes slitted. "You said the Starless One himself. Not his ancestors."

Yuri turned from the map with a smug smile on his lips. "Yes, I did. I know there was only one Darkling, one man of great power who faked his death many times. A precaution against small minds who might have feared his extraordinary power and his long life."

"And how did you arrive at this theory?" asked Nikolai.

Yuri blinked. "It's not a theory. I *know*. The Darkling revealed as much to me in a vision."

Zoya's brows rose, and Nikolai had to fight the urge to roll his eyes. Instead he tented his fingers and said, "I see."

But Yuri's smile just deepened. "I know you think me mad, but I have seen miracles."

And that was exactly why Nikolai had brought him here. "You said something the other day, that the Age of Saints was upon us. What did you mean?"

"How else do you account for the miracles taking place through-out Ravka?"

"So it begins," muttered Zoya.

"We've heard the stories," said Nikolai mildly. "But there are rational explanations for these occurrences. We live in difficult times, and people are bound to look for miracles."

To Nikolai's surprise, the young monk sat down at the table and leaned across it, his expression earnest. "Your Highness, I know you are not a man of faith. But the people believe these happenings are not just phenomena in search of explanation. They believe they are the work of Saints."

"They are the work of *Grisha*," said Zoya. "Possibly the Shu. Possibly your dear friend the Apparat."

"Ah," said Yuri. "But some people believe all of the old miracles were the work of Grisha."

"Then call it the Small Science and dispense with all of this superstition."

"Would that make it easier to accept the divine?" Yuri asked, his spectacles glinting. "If I call these works the 'making at the heart of the world,' would that help? I've studied Grisha theory too."

Zoya's eyes were hard as gems. "I'm not here to debate theology with a mop handle."

Yuri sat back, his expression beatific. "The Saints are returning to Ravka. And the Starless One will be among them."

"The Darkling is dead," Genya said, and Nikolai did not miss the white knuckles of her clasped hands. "I watched his body burn."

Yuri cast a nervous glance at David and said, "There are some who believe the Darkling did not die on the Fold and is simply awaiting his chance to return."

"I was there too, monk," said Zoya. "I saw him burn away to ash atop a funeral pyre fed by Inferni flame."

The monk closed his eyes briefly, pained. "Yes. Of course. That was his martyrdom, and his body was destroyed. But the Darkling's power was extraordinary, ancient. It *may* be gone, or it may still live on in the world and his spirit with it."

Zoya pressed her lips together, folding her arms tightly against her body, as if to keep away the cold.

Nikolai did not like what he was hearing. A scrap of that ancient power still resided within his own body—and if last night was any indication, it was growing stronger by the day.

"You think all of these separate incidents, these supposed miracles, are related to the Darkling?" he asked.

"No!" exclaimed the monk. He leaned even farther forward. In a moment, his chin was going to make contact with the table. "I *know* they are." He rose and gestured to the map behind them. "If I may?" He looked around, darting right and left, robes flapping like the wings of a deranged bird.

"*This* is what the Darkling's acolytes look like?" whispered Zoya. "If we'd left a body, he would be turning in his grave."

"Aha!" Yuri said, finding the small cloth flags that could be pinned to the hides. The maps were pocked with tiny holes where former leaders had planned military campaigns.

"The earthquake at Ryevost, the statue at Tsemna, the roof of myrrh at Arkesk, the bleeding walls in Udova, the roses in Adena." One after another he listed the supposed miracles as he put pins on the map. Then he stood back. "They began here, far along the coasts and mountains and borders, but day by day, the occurrences have become more frequent, and they've drawn closer to——"

"The Fold," said Nikolai. The pattern was clear, a radiant starburst with its heart dead center in the Unsea.

"Saints," breathed Zoya.

"Is that where——" Genya began.

"Yes," said Nikolai, though he didn't remember much of the final battle. He'd been infected with the monster already, fighting with it for control of his consciousness. And winning far more often than he was now. He'd been lucid in long flashes, even in his transformed state, and had sought out help from Alina. He had even tried to aid their forces in that last confrontation.

The miracle sites were closing in on the same central spot, the place where the Fold had once been, where the Darkling had made his last stand—where he had faced Alina Starkov and died by her hand. Victory. At least that was what it had looked like at the time—a country united, the possibility of peace, and Nikolai suddenly and swiftly purged of the demon that had battled him for control. He had believed the darkness within him had been vanquished at the moment of the Darkling's death. He had believed the war was over.

And yet the monster had risen up to take hold of him again. Had the demon always been there, troubling his dreams, his constant companion, awaiting its moment? Or had something woken it?

Nikolai looked at the pins splayed over the map. Was there a pattern, or was Yuri seeing what he wanted to? And was this seemingly guileless zealot playing a deeper game?

"Forgive me, Yuri," Nikolai said. "But your goal is to have the Darkling recognized as a Saint by the Ravkan church. You have every reason to try to tie these occurrences to the Starless One."

"I have no reason to lie," said Yuri. "Only days ago a sign appeared on the Fold, a lake of black rock, a sun in eclipse."

Zoya expelled an exasperated breath. "Or a geological anomaly."

Yuri poked his bony finger at the map. "This is not just where the Starless One passed from this life. It is a place of ancient power, the very place the Darkling first ruptured the world and created the Fold."

"You can't possibly know that," Zoya said with a dismissive wave.

"It was the subject of my studies in the Priestguard. It's all in the texts."

"Which texts?" she asked, and Nikolai wondered if she was deliberately trying to bait the monk.

"*The Book of Alyosha. The Sikurian Psalms.* You can see it illustrated in the *Istorii Sankt'ya.*"

"A children's book?"

"It was a holy site," insisted Yuri. "The place where Sankt Feliks was pierced by the apple boughs, an ancient place of healing and glorious power where men came to be purified."

Nikolai sat up straighter. "Purified of what exactly?"

Yuri opened his mouth, closed it. "I misspoke—"

"No, he didn't," said Tolya. "He's talking about the *obisbaya*. Aren't you, monk?"

"I . . . I . . ."

"I hate to admit my ignorance," said Nikolai. "It's so much more fun for people to discover it on their own. But what exactly is the *obis . . . bumpy?*"

"No idea," said Zoya. Genya shrugged, and even David shook his head.

To Nikolai's surprise, it was Tamar who spoke.

"The *obisbaya*," she said. "The Ritual of the Burning Thorn. Do you know how the Priestguard were first created?"

"Those are children's stories," said Zoya scornfully.

"Possibly," Tolya conceded.

"Tell me a story, then," said Nikolai.

Tamar folded her arms. "Why don't you do the honors, monk?"

Yuri hesitated, then said, "It begins with the first Lantsov king, Yaromir the Determined." He shut his eyes, his voice taking on a more confident, even cadence. "Before him, the territory that would become Ravka was little more than a collection of warring provinces led by squabbling kings. He subdued them and brought them together beneath his double-eagle banner. But the invasions from Fjerda to the north and Shu Han to the south were relentless and put the young kingdom in a constant state of war."

"Sounds familiar." Nikolai knew this story from his own childhood classrooms. He'd always found it disheartening that Ravka had been at war since its birth.

"There was no Second Army then," Yuri continued. "Ravka's soldiers fought and died just as other men did. But as the legend goes, Yaromir built an altar atop a hill in Os Alta—"

"The site of the first royal chapel," said Tolya.

Yuri nodded. "The young king prayed to all of the Saints who would hear him, and the next day, a group of monks arrived at his door and offered to fight by his side. They were not ordinary monks. When they went into battle they could take on the shapes of beasts. They fought not as men but as all manner of creature— wolf, dragon, hawk, bear. The king had heard stories of these monks but hardly believed they were true until he saw these miracles for himself."

"Always with the miracles," grumbled Zoya.

"Yes," said Yuri, opening his eyes, fervor burning in them like a brand. "*Always.* The monks agreed to fight for the king. They asked for neither gold nor land but only that one of them would always remain at the king's side so that Ravka would forever be devoted to the worship of the Saints. The monks plunged into battle and sent the enemies of Ravka scattering, pushing them back and forming the borders that would hold, more or less, for thousands of years." Yuri's voice rose, caught in the telling of his tale, all hesitation gone. "But the battle lasted so long that when it was over and it was time for them to return to their human forms, they could not. Their leader brought them to the site of an ancient thorn wood, and there they endured a dangerous ritual: the *obisbaya.* Those who survived became men once more and their leader took his place beside Yaromir. Eventually, the priest who held the office closest to the king was given the title of Apparat, and the holy soldiers that surrounded him became the Priestguard."

"Some people claim the first Priestguard were Grisha," said Tolya.

Tamar touched her fingers to the shark's tooth at her neck. "In that version, the animals they became were the first amplifiers. Their spirits made the monks' powers stronger."

Nikolai studied Yuri. The story was strange, no doubt, and likely more fiction than fact. Even so . . . "A ritual to purge beast from man. What exactly did it entail?"

Yuri pushed his spectacles up his nose, the confident scholar vanishing with a single gesture. "I'm not sure. There were . . . are conflicting texts."

"You're not really a firebrand, are you, Yuri?"

A smile touched the monk's lips. "I suppose not."

"And yet you ended up at my gates, calling me a traitor and a thief." Yuri at least had the manners to squirm. "What brought you there?"

"The Saints. I believe that."

Nikolai had his doubts. "Tell me about this ritual."

"Why?" Yuri asked, brow furrowing.

"I am a king. I long for entertainment."

The monk tugged on his scraggly beard. "I don't know the details. There are conflicting accounts in the texts, and I don't . . . I'm no longer permitted . . ."

"They're religious texts, aren't they?" Nikolai said. "From the Priestguards' library. You don't have access anymore."

"No." The ache in his voice was palpable. Nikolai thought he understood. There had been a time when words had been the only place he could find solace. No book ever lost patience with him or told him to sit still. When his tutors had thrown up their hands in frustration, it was the library that had taught Nikolai military history, strategy, chemistry, astronomy. Each spine had been an open doorway whispering, *Come in, come in. Here is a land you've never seen before. Here is a place to hide when you're frightened, to play when you're bored, to rest when the world seems unkind.* Yuri knew that solace. He had once been a scholar. Perhaps he'd like to be one again.

Nikolai stood. "Thank you, Yuri. You've been most helpful."

The monk rose slowly. "I have? Then will you lend your name to our plea, Your Highness? The Apparat cannot ignore the voice of the king. If you would petition him to—"

"I will think on it, Yuri. You've made an interesting argument. For now, I will have you escorted back to your rooms."

"Then I am a prisoner still?"

"You are a welcome guest whom I don't want to stray too far. And perhaps I can get you access to some reading materials."

Yuri paused as if uncertain he'd heard correctly. "My . . . books?"

"Perhaps."

"That would be . . . No, I must return to my fellow worshippers outside of the city. You cannot keep—"

"And you will. But we must ask that you enjoy our hospitality a short while longer. While we consider the merits of your case."

Yuri's chin lifted. "For the Starless One, I can wait an eternity. But do not play games with me, Your Highness. I did not come to the capital to be laughed at or to dillydally about."

"Dally, yes; dilly, no," said Nikolai. "Gave it up in my youth."

Zoya rolled her eyes, and Tolya shuffled Yuri out the door and into the care of two palace guards.

When Yuri was gone, Nikolai rose to look more closely at the pins on the map. In the wake of the monk's departure, the silence in the room felt heavy, as if another presence had entered the chamber, something old and nameless.

"The boy is mad," said Zoya.

"He's a believer," said Tolya. "Those aren't the same thing."

"And I'd rather a true believer than a man like the Apparat," Genya added.

"How can you say that?" said Zoya. "He worships a tyrant, a murderer, the man who tortured you."

Genya sighed. "Can we blame him for being drawn to the Darkling's strength? We all were."

"We didn't know what he was then."

"Didn't we?" Genya adjusted her eyepatch. "Yuri is a frightened boy looking for something bigger than himself to give his life meaning. There are people like him all over Ravka."

"That's what worries me."

Tolya sat down beside his sister, and Nikolai caught the look that passed between them. This was not the time to start keeping secrets. "What is it?"

Tolya heaved his great shoulders. "There may be something to Yuri's story. The Priestguard weren't always just lackeys for the Apparat. They were holy warriors who served the crown as well. When I was younger I wanted nothing more than to join them."

"What stopped you?" Nikolai asked. He wasn't surprised exactly. Both Tolya and Tamar had been raised in the church, and he was well aware that if Alina Starkov hadn't given Nikolai her blessing as king, the twins would never have pledged themselves as his guards.

"They wouldn't let me join," said Tamar. "No women allowed."

Tolya nodded. "I had to question a holy order that claimed to want warriors but would deny a fighter like Tamar."

Tamar rested her hands on her axes. "The Saints had a different plan for us."

"Ah," said Nikolai. "But what do the Saints have planned now? Zoya, when I got free from Duke Radimov's estate in Ivets, you found me where?"

"A goose farm on the road to Varena."

Nikolai touched his finger to the map. "A northeastern path. But every time I've gotten loose from the palace, I've headed northwest.

Each time I've taken the same route, just gone a little farther. What if the creature is trying to get to that spot on the Fold? What if it wants to be free of me as much as I want to be free of it?"

"Or what if these supposed miracles are a plan to lure you from the palace?" said Zoya.

"To the Fold? Why?"

Zoya cast up her hands. "I don't know."

"The 'miracles' began when the demon woke inside me. It may be connected to the Darkling's power or Yuri may be talking nonsense, but that pattern is real. Something is happening, and it's connected to this spot on the Shadow Fold."

"It's not safe to leave the palace—" Zoya protested.

"There are no safe places. Not anymore." He'd proven that himself last night. "Genya will mix me a stronger tonic. David will forge thicker chains. I'm going on a pilgrimage."

"To some mystical thorn wood?" said Zoya. "Even if it once existed, the Fold obliterated everything in its path. There's nothing there anymore."

Tolya spoke a long string of words, only a few of which Nikolai could pick out. Then he said, "*Lost faith is the roots of a forgotten wood, waiting to thrive once more.*"

Zoya narrowed her eyes. "We agreed no poetry during meetings."

"It's liturgical Ravkan," Tolya objected. "It's from the *Book of Alyosha*, which you might know if you ever went to church."

"It's a wonder I've survived this long without such knowledge."

"Tolya," Nikolai interrupted. "I'm going to need you to find any texts you can on the *obisbaya* and anything connected to it. I don't want Yuri to be the only scholar I can rely on."

"I'm not a scholar," protested Tolya.

"You might have been in another life," said Nikolai.

"What do you mean, *the only scholar?*" Zoya said. "You can't possibly mean to travel with the monk."

Genya shifted in her seat. "It will look like you're lending support to the Cult of the Starless. I don't like the message that sends."

"We'll make sure Yuri is disguised, and I don't intend to take a direct route to the Fold," said Nikolai. "There may be something we can learn at the other miracle sites, and visiting them will give me an opportunity to walk among my subjects before I choose a bride. We have armies massing at both borders, new Lantsov pretenders cropping up to make claims on the throne. Our coffers are empty and our allies are few. I cannot afford to lose the support of the common people. We're going to need it in the days to come."

"And what if it all leads to nothing?" asked Genya. "What if the Darkling left you with this curse and there are no answers to be found?"

Zoya laid her fingers flat on the table. "What if Yuri discovers the truth about the monster?"

"Then we pray I can silence him and keep this secret long enough to secure Ravka's future. Even without an heir, there may be a way to keep the throne safe and make sure the country isn't left vulnerable."

"And what exactly is that?" asked Zoya.

"Are you sure you don't want to try trusting me, Zoya? It's positively intoxicating." The idea had come to him the previous week, when they'd arrived from Count Kirigin's and had been greeted by Trukhin and Isaak.

Zoya pursed her lips. "I don't like any of this. There's too much room for disaster."

Nikolai knew that. They were running out of time, and this journey to the Fold smacked of desperation. He could not deny the fear that clung to him, the doubt it sowed in his heart. What if his mind unraveled and his will with it? What if he attacked one of his friends again and there was no one there to stop him? What damage might he unleash on the people he loved? On the world?

Nikolai could not deny those fears, but he refused to give in to them. He would not just hand the monster a victory.

He turned to the people assembled before him—his advisers, his soldiers, his family. He needed them to believe, if not in Yuri's tales, then in Nikolai himself, the person he had been before the Darkling and the war. He straightened the lapels of his velvet coat and winked.

"It's not exciting if nothing can go wrong."

He felt the monster recoil. Action. Decision. In moments like these, he felt almost like his old self. If this thing wanted to claim his soul, Nikolai intended to give it a damn good fight—and that battle began here, now, with a refusal to relinquish any bit of his spirit to the terror trying to drag him into the dark. He would do what he had always done: He would charge forward and pray that hope might be waiting like the roots of the thorn wood—just out of sight.

10
NINA

DUSK HAD FALLEN by the time she pushed to her feet.

The sky looked more gray than purple, wounded like a deep bruise, and the air felt moist against her cheeks. Snow had begun to fall in gentle drifts.

It didn't stay gentle for long.

Nina had never seen a storm come on so fast. The wind blew hard, and snow blurred the whole world white. *Gruzeburya*. Even the Ravkans had a name for this wind. *The Brute*. Not for the cold it brought but for the way it blinded you like a thug in a dirty fight. Nina was torn between trying to follow the sound of the river back to camp and being afraid she might stray too close to the banks and fall in.

She trudged on, squinting against the white. At one point she thought she heard Adrik's voice calling to her, glimpsed the bright yellow flag they'd raised above the tent, but a moment later it was gone.

Stupid, stupid, stupid. She had not been made for such places. Nina wouldn't survive a night without shelter in this weather. She had no choice but to continue on.

Then, like a miracle, the wind lifted, the curtains of snow seemed to part, and she saw a dark shape in the distance. *The camp.*

"Adrik!" she cried. But as she drew closer, she saw no flag, no tent, only the swaying bodies of a copse of trees—and in the snow before them, a slight indentation. She'd walked in a circle. She had returned to Matthias' grave.

"Well done, Zenik," she sighed. She was only eighteen years old, so why did she feel so tired? Why did everything behind her seem bright and everything before her look bleak? Maybe she hadn't come here to bury Matthias and claim her new purpose. Maybe she'd come out here to the ice, to this cold and unforgiving place, to die.

There would be no Saints to greet her on a brighter shore. Grisha didn't believe in an afterlife. When they died, they returned to the making at the heart of the world. It was a thought that brought her little comfort.

Nina turned back toward camp. There was nothing for it but to start marching again. But before she could take a step, she saw them—five hulking shapes in the snow. Wolves.

"Of course," she said. "Matthias, your country can kiss my fat Grisha ass."

The wolves prowled around her in a circle, surrounding her, cutting off any route of escape. Low growls rumbled from their chests. Wolves were sacred to the *drüskelle*. Maybe they'd sensed Matthias' presence. Or maybe they'd sensed Nina, a Grisha, an enemy. *Or maybe they sensed a nice juicy meal.*

"Just go," she said in Fjerdan. "I don't want to hurt you." *I don't want to die.*

Matthias had been forced to fight wolves during his year at Hellgate. Djel had a strange sense of humor. Nina flexed her fingers, felt her bone daggers ready to be called. They would work as well on an animal as a human. She hurled off her cloak, feeling the cold bite into her but freeing the bone shard armor at her back. She was a Saint surrounded by her relics.

Two wolves leapt. Nina's hands shot out and the bone shards flew true, piercing the animals' bodies in two clean, hard strikes. The wolves yelped and landed in the snow, motionless. The sound broke her heart. At least they were clean deaths. In the end, maybe that was all anyone could hope for.

But the others were closing in already. There was something odd about the way they moved. Their eyes glowed almost orange and they hunched and twitched as if animated by something more than hunger. What was wrong with them? There was no time to think.

They lunged. Nina struck out. This time her aim was less sure. One wolf fell, but the other pounced, landing on her with a weight that sent her tumbling into the snow.

Its jaws closed over her forearm, pain lancing through her. The wolf stank of something strange. She screamed.

Nina heard a loud snarl and knew she was about to die. *All those pretty words for Matthias. Who will speak for me?*

Then, in a blur, something smashed into the body of the wolf, freeing her from its weight. Nina rolled, clutching her bleeding arm to her chest, gasping for air. She plunged her arm into the snow, trying to get the wound clean. Her body started to shake. It was as if the wolf's bite had carried poison. Nina felt a heart-stopping rush go through her. She saw death all around—Matthias' body in the ground below, a graveyard to the north, an outbreak of plague farther on, the entropy of the earth, the decay in everything. The chorus screamed inside her head.

She pressed snow to her cheeks, trembling, trying to clear her thoughts, but when she opened her eyes, she wondered if the poison had fractured her mind. Two wolves were fighting in the snow—one gray, the other white and far larger. They rolled, and the white wolf clamped its jaws over the throat of the gray but did not bite down. At last, the gray slumped and whimpered. The white wolf released its hold and the smaller wolf recoiled, slinking away, tail tucked between its haunches.

The white wolf turned on Nina, blood on its muzzle. The animal was huge and rangy, but it didn't twist or shake the way the grays had. Something had been infecting them, something that had gotten into Nina's bloodstream, but this creature moved with the natural, unerring grace of wild things.

The white wolf stalked toward her. Nina pushed up onto her knees, holding out her hands to ward it off, reaching for another bone shard with her power.

Then she saw the scar that ran along its yellow eye.

"Trassel?"

The wolf's ears twitched.

Matthias' wolf? It couldn't be. He'd once told her that when a *drüskelle* died, his brothers gave his *isenulf* back to the wild. Had Trassel come to find the boy he'd loved, to be united with him even in death?

"Trassel," she said gently. The wolf cocked his big head to the side.

Nina heard hoofbeats. Before she could fathom what was happening, a girl rode into the clearing.

"Get back!" she cried, galloping her horse between Nina and the white wolf.

It took Nina a moment to understand what she was seeing—the tall girl from the convent. This time she wore leather trousers and furs, and the reddish-brown tumble of her hair streamed down her back, held away from her face by two long braids. She looked like a warrior queen—a sylph of the ice straight out of Fjerdan legend.

She raised her rifle.

Trassel backed away, snarling.

"No!" Nina screamed. She hurled a bone shard at the girl, striking her shoulder. The rifle shot went wide. "Run!" Nina yelled at Trassel in Fjerdan. The wolf snapped his jaws as if in argument. "*Djel commenden!*" Nina shouted. *Drüskelle* words. Trassel huffed once, then turned and loped into the storm, giving her a last betrayed look as if he couldn't believe she'd ask him to abandon a fight.

"What are you doing?" the tall girl demanded, yanking the bone dart from her shoulder and tossing it into the snow.

Nina howled her rage. Matthias' wolf, his troublemaker, his Trassel had somehow found his way to her, and this blundering podge had driven him off. She seized the girl's leg and yanked her from the saddle.

"Hey!" The girl tried to shove Nina away, clearly surprised by her strength. But Nina had been trained as a soldier. She might not be built like a Fjerdan warrior, but she was plenty strong.

"You scared him away!"

"That was a *wolf*," the girl shouted back in her face. "You know that, right? He already bit you once. Just because he follows some of your commands—"

"He didn't bite me, you ass. It was the other wolf!"

"The other . . . are you out of your mind? And how do you know *drüskelle* commands anyway?"

Nina found hot tears running down her cheeks. She might never

164

see Trassel again. What if Matthias had sent him to her? Called him here to help her? "You had no right!"

"I didn't mean to——"

"It doesn't matter what you meant!" Nina stalked toward her. "Careless, foolish, thoughtless." She didn't know if she was talking to this girl or herself anymore, and she didn't care. It was all too much.

She shoved the other girl hard, swept her leg behind her ankle.

"Stop it!" snarled the girl as she toppled.

But Nina could not stop. She wanted to get hit. She wanted to hit back. She grabbed the girl by her collar.

Nina grunted as sudden pain seized her chest. It felt like a fist around her heart. The girl had her hands up, something between terror and exultation in her copper eyes. Nina felt her body grow heavy; her vision blurred. She knew this feeling from her training as a Corporalnik. The other girl was slowing Nina's heartbeat.

"*Grisha*," Nina gasped.

"I didn't . . . I don't."

Nina pushed her own power against the other girl's, felt her living, vibrant force waver. With the last bit of her strength, Nina flicked her fingers and a bone shard flew from its sheath at her thigh. It struck the girl in the side, not hard—it bounced into the snow. But it was enough to break her concentration.

Nina stumbled backward, trying to regain her breath, fingers pressed to her sternum. She hadn't had Heartrender power used against her for years. She'd forgotten just how frightening it could be.

"You're Grisha," she said.

The girl leapt to her feet, knife drawn. "I'm not."

Interesting, thought Nina. *She has power but she can't control it. She trusts the blade more.*

Nina held up her palms to make peace. "I'm not going to hurt you."

Now the girl showed no sign of hesitation. Her body was loose, relaxed, as if she felt more herself with steel in her hand. "You sure seemed like you wanted to hurt me a second ago."

"Well, I did, but I've come to my senses."

"I was trying to save your life! Why do you care about a wolf anyway? You're worse than the *drüskelle*."

Now, that was something Nina had never expected to hear. "That wolf saved me from an attack. I don't know why. But I didn't want you to hurt him." This girl was Grisha, and Nina had almost killed her. "I . . . overreacted."

The tall girl shoved her knife back in its sheath. "Overreacting is throwing a tantrum when someone eats the last sweet roll." She pointed an accusatory finger at Nina. "You were out for blood."

"To be fair, I've considered killing over the last sweet roll."

"Where's your coat?"

"I think I took it off," Nina said, searching for an explanation for why she would tear off her coat that didn't involve disclosing her bone armor. "I guess I was going snow-mad."

"Is that a thing?"

Nina found the coat, already almost buried in wet white flakes. "Absolutely. At least in my village."

The other girl rubbed her muscled thigh. "And what did you hit me with?"

"A dart."

"You threw a *dart* at me?" she said incredulously. "That's ridiculous."

"It worked, didn't it?" A dart made of human bone, but some details were best avoided, and it was time to go on the offensive. Nina shrugged into her damp coat. "You put the guards to sleep at the convent. That's how you sneak out."

All the girl's confidence dissolved, fear dousing her fire like a rogue wave. "I didn't hurt anyone."

"But you could have. That's actually very delicate work. You could land someone in a coma."

The girl stilled as the wind howled around them. "How would you know?"

But Nina hadn't spoken without thinking. Grisha power was as good as a death sentence or worse in this country.

"My sister was Grisha," Nina lied.

"What . . . what happened to her?"

"That's not a story for the middle of a storm."

The girl clenched her fists. Saints, she was tall—but built like a dancer, a long coil of wiry muscle.

"You can't tell anyone what I am," she said. "They'll kill me."

"I'm not going to hurt you, and I'm not going to help anyone hurt you." The girl's face was wary. The wind rose, keening. "But none of that will matter if we both die out here."

The tall girl looked at Nina as if she really had gone snow-mad. "Don't be silly."

"You're saying you can find your way through this?"

"No," she said, patting her horse's flank. "But Helmut can. There's a hunting lodge not far from here." Again, she hesitated, and Nina could guess at the thoughts in her head.

"You're thinking of leaving me to the mercy of the snow," said Nina. The girl's eyes slid away guiltily. So she had a merciless streak. Somehow it made Nina like her more. "I might not survive. But I might. And then you can be sure I'll tell the first person I meet about the Grisha Heartrender living in secret among the Women of the Well."

"I'm *not* Grisha."

"You do a remarkable imitation."

The girl ran a gloved hand through her horse's mane. "Can you ride?"

"If I have to."

"It's that or go to sleep in the snow."

"I can ride."

The girl vaulted into the saddle in a single smooth movement. She offered Nina a hand, and Nina let herself be pulled onto the horse's back.

"You don't like to skip meals, do you?" said the girl with a grunt.

"Not if I can help it."

Nina settled her hands around the girl's waist, and soon they were moving through the growing drifts.

"You can be whipped for using those commands, you know," said the girl. "*Djel commenden.* That's considered blasphemy if a *drüskelle* isn't speaking."

"I'll say extra prayers tonight."

"You never told me how you know those commands."

More lies then. "A boy from our town served in the ranks."

"What's his name?"

Nina thought back to the fight at the Ice Court. "Lars. I believe he passed recently." *And no one wants him back.* He'd closed a whip over her and put her on her knees before Kaz Brekker had come calling.

The white world stretched on, frozen and featureless. Now that she wasn't walking, Nina felt the cold more deeply, the weight of it settling over her. Just as she began to wonder if the girl knew where she was going, Nina saw a dark shape through the snow, and the horse halted. The girl slid down.

Nina followed, her legs gone numb and aching, and they led Helmut to a sheltered space beside the lodge.

"Looks like we aren't the only ones who had this idea," she said. There were lights in the windows of the little lodge, and she could hear loud voices from within.

The other girl twisted the reins in her hands, removing her glove to stroke the horse's nose. "I didn't realize so many people knew about this place. There are probably men inside who came to wait out the storm. We won't be safe here."

Nina considered. "Do you have your skirts in your saddlebag?"

The girl pulled at a knotted belt around her waist, and the folds of her coat dropped into a skirt that fell into place over her trousers. Nina had to admit she was impressed. "What other tricks do you have up your sleeve? Or skirts, as the case may be?"

A smile flickered over her lips. "A few."

The door to the shelter flew open, a man with a gun silhouetted against the light. "Who's out there?"

"Follow my lead," Nina murmured, then cried, "Oh thank goodness. We were afraid no one would be here. Hurry, Inger!"

"*Inger?*" muttered the girl.

Nina stomped up to the door, ignoring the gun pointed at her, hoping the man holding it wasn't drunk or riled enough to shoot at an unarmed girl—or a girl who looked unarmed.

Nina climbed the steps and smiled sweetly at the big man as the other girl trailed her. "Thank Djel we've found shelter for the night." She glanced over his shoulder into the lodge. The room was crowded with men, ten at least, all gathered around a fire. Nina felt tension spike through her. This was a moment when she would have been glad to see *drüskelle*, who didn't drink and who were kept to a strict code regarding women. There was nothing to do but brazen it out. "And among gentlemen to protect us!"

"Who are you?" the man said suspiciously.

Nina pushed past him as if she owned the place. "Aren't we lucky, Inger? Let's get in front of that fire. And close the door . . ." She laid a hand on the man's chest. "I'm sorry, what was your name?"

He blinked. "Anders."

"Be a darling and shut the door, Anders."

They shuffled inside, and she met the stares of the men with a smile. "I knew Djel would guide our way, Inger. Surely your father will have a healthy reward in store for all of these fine fellows."

For a moment, the girl looked confused, and Nina thought they might be lost. But then her face cleared. "Yes! Yes, indeed! My father is *most* generous when it comes to my safety."

"And with you betrothed to the wealthiest man in Overüt." Nina winked at the men gathered by the fire. "Well, I suppose Djel has granted you gentlemen a bit of luck this night too. Now, which of you will stand guard for us?"

"Stand guard?" said a man with tufty orange brows by the fire.

"Through the night."

"Dumpling, I think you're in a muddle—"

"Lady Inger's father is most generous, but he cannot be expected to bestow ten thousand *krydda* on every one of you, so you must choose who is to be the beneficiary."

"Ten thousand *krydda*?"

"That was the price last time, was it not? When we were stranded in that amusing spot down south. Although, I suppose now that you are betrothed to the wealthiest man in Overüt, it may be twice the price."

"Who is this bridegroom you speak of?" the bearded man asked.

"You've heard of Bernhard Bolle, who made his fortune in smoked trout? And Ingvar Hals, who owns timberland from the Elbjen to the Isenvee? Well, Lennart Bjord towers above them all."

"Lennart Bjord?" the bearded man repeated.

"That does sound familiar," said someone by the hearth. Nina highly doubted that, since she'd made him up mere moments ago.

"I was the first to greet them," said the big man with the rifle. "It's only right I should get the reward."

"How is that fair? You happened to be by the door!"

"Now, don't get too riled," Nina said with a schoolmarm *tsk* in her voice as the men began debating who would take the watch. "Lennart Bjord will have a bit of something for everyone."

Nina and "Inger" settled in the corner, their backs to the wall as the men argued.

"That was pathetic," the girl seethed, resting her elbows on her knees and tugging her skirt over the toes of her boots.

"I beg your pardon?"

"You made us seem weak. Every time we behave that way, it just makes it easier for men to look at us and see nothing but softness."

"There is nothing wrong with softness," Nina said, her temper fraying. She was exhausted and cold, and she'd dug her lover's grave tonight. "Right now they're looking at us as two big bags of money instead of two vulnerable girls alone."

"We weren't vulnerable. I have my gun, my knife. You have those ridiculous darts."

"Do you also have twelve arms hidden in that coat? We're outnumbered." Nina actually suspected that she could have managed all of them, but only if she intended to reveal her true power, and that would mean putting this girl in the ground tonight too.

"They're drunk. We would have managed."

"You don't enter a fight you can't win," Nina replied, irritated. "I'm guessing you've had to train in secret, and that you've probably never had a real combat instructor. Being strong doesn't mean being sloppy."

The wiry girl drew her coat closer. "I hate it. I hate how they see us. My father is the same way. He thinks a woman wanting to fight or hunt or fend for herself is unnatural, that it denies men the chance to be protectors."

Nina snorted. "It really is a tragedy for them. What does your mother think?"

"My mother is the perfect wife, except she provided my father no sons. She does as he dictates." The girl sighed. She looked weary suddenly, the thrill of the fight and the storm gone. Her hair—that extraordinary color, like the woods in autumn, chestnut and red and gold—lay storm-damp and tangled against her brown cheeks. "I can't blame her. It's the way the world works. She's worried I'll become an outcast."

"So they sent you to a convent in the middle of nowhere?"

"Where I couldn't get into trouble or embarrass them in front of their friends. Don't pretend you think differently. I saw the way you looked at me when you helped us in the clearing."

"You were dressed as a soldier. I was entitled to a little surprise." And she'd been dedicated to maintaining her cover, not befriending a Grisha—one who might be able to get her closer to the factory. "In case you hadn't noticed, I travel on my own, make my own living."

"That's different. You're a widow."

"You needn't sound quite so envious."

The girl rubbed her hand over her brow. "I'm sorry. That was thoughtless."

Nina studied her. There was something relentless in her features—the cheekbones sharp, the nose rigorously straight. Only the full thrust of her lips gave any hint of softness. It was a challenging face, stubborn in its lines. Beautiful.

"We're not as different as you might think." Nina bobbed her head toward the men, who were now arm wrestling for the right to a generous reward that none of them would ever see. "It's fear that makes your father act as he does, that makes men write foolish rules that say you can't travel alone or ride as you wish to."

The other girl bit back a laugh. "Why should they be afraid? The world belongs to them."

"But think of all the things we might achieve if we were allowed to do the things that they do."

"If they were truly afraid, you wouldn't have to simper and preen."

Nina winked. "You've seen me simper. If I ever decide to preen, you'll need to sit down for it."

The girl stifled a snort. "I'm Hanne."

"Nice to meet you," Nina said. "I'm Mila." She'd told countless lies this night, but somehow it felt wrong to give this girl a false name.

"You don't really mean for us to sleep, do you, Mila?" Hanne's face was knowing.

"Not a chance. You're going to keep your hand on your dagger, and I'm going to keep first watch."

Nina touched her hand to her sleeve, felt the reassuring presence of the bones lining the fabric. She watched the flickering of the fire.

"Rest," she told Hanne, and realized she was smiling for the first time in months.

11

ZOYA

PREPARATIONS FOR NIKOLAI'S GRAND tour of the miracle sites required days of planning by the king's staff. Provisions had to be secured, vehicles made ready for the changing weather, appropriate clothing packed, and letters sent to noblemen and governors in the towns they intended to visit. Zoya found herself snapping at everyone even more than usual. She knew the talk was that she was in one of her moods, but the perks of ruling included permission not to slather her words in honey. She did her job. She did it well. If her students and servants and fellow Grisha couldn't endure a few curt replies in exchange, they were in the wrong damn country.

She might have been able to relax if everyone didn't move so *slowly*. But eventually the wagons were packed, the coach prepared, and outriders sent ahead to scout the condition of the roads for the royal procession. The specific itinerary for the trip would be kept secret, but soon Nikolai's people would know their king was traveling and they would come out in force to see their golden war hero.

Zoya wasn't sure what to think of the monk's stories of the thorn wood or the twins' talk of the Priestguard and the *obisbaya*. Part of her said that it was foolish to pin their hopes on such a mission, on the ramblings of a fanatic who clearly believed in Saints and all the pomp and nonsense that went with them.

She told herself the journey would be good for the crown and Nikolai's standing, regardless of what they found. She told herself that if it all came to nothing, they would find some other way to get through the next few months, to appease their allies and keep their enemies at bay. She told herself that the real Nikolai was still in control, not the monster she had seen that night in the bell tower.

But Zoya had survived by being honest with herself, and she had to acknowledge that there was another fear lurking inside her— beneath the anxieties that accompanied the preparations for this journey, beneath the ordeal of looking into the eyes of the demon and seeing its hunger. She was afraid of what they might find on the Fold. What if the genuflecting twits who worshipped the Starless One were actually right, and these bizarre occurrences heralded the Darkling's return? What if he somehow found a way back?

"This time I'll be ready for him." Zoya whispered the words in the dark, beneath the roof of the chambers the Darkling had once occupied, in the palace he had built from nothing. She wasn't a naive girl anymore, desperately trying to prove herself at every turn. She was a general with a long body count and an even longer memory.

Fear is a phoenix. Words Liliyana had spoken to her years ago and that Zoya had repeated to others many times. *You can watch it burn a thousand times and still it will return.* She would not be governed by her fear. She did not have that luxury. *Maybe so*, she thought, *but it hasn't kept you from avoiding Nikolai since that night in the bell tower.* She hated this frailty in herself, hated that she now kept Tolya or Tamar close when she was chaining the king to his bed at night, that even in meeting rooms she found herself on guard, as if expecting to look across a negotiating table and see his hazel eyes glimmer black. Her fear was useless, unproductive—and she suspected it was something the monster might enjoy.

When the morning of their departure finally arrived, she packed a small trunk. Unlike the luggage the servants had prepared for her *kefta* and traveling clothes, this one would be locked. It held Nikolai's shackles, reinforced twice over and with a new locking mechanism it had taken her hours to master. The weight of them was reassuring in her hands, but she still breathed easier when Genya and David arrived in her chambers.

Zoya peered at the tiny bottle Genya handed her. It was fitted with a glass stopper. "Is this enough?"

"More than enough," said Genya. "Give him one drop immediately before sleep, a second if you have any trouble. Any more than that and there's a good chance you'll kill him."

"Good to know. Regicide isn't on my list of preferred crimes."

Genya's lips twitched in a smile. "You're saying you've never wanted to kill Nikolai?"

"Oh, I have. I just don't want him to sleep through it."

Genya gave her another bottle, this one round and red. "Use this to wake him in the morning. Just uncork it and place it beneath his nose."

"What is it exactly?"

"A distillation of *jurda* and ammonia. Basically a very fast-acting stimulant."

"That isn't exact at all," said David. "It utilizes—"

Zoya held up a hand. "Exact enough."

Genya ran her fingers over the carved surface of the trunk. "The process won't be easy on him. It will be a bit like drowning every night and being revived every morning."

Zoya wrapped the bottles in cotton and placed them gently in the trunk, but as she moved to lock the lid, Genya laid a hand over hers.

"We've made the sedative as strong as possible," she said. "But we don't really understand what we're trying to control. Zoya, you may not be safe with him."

Zoya knew that better than anyone. She'd seen the horror that lurked inside Nikolai too closely to deny it. "What would you suggest I do?"

To Zoya's surprise, Genya said, "I could go."

David pressed his lips into a hard line, and Zoya knew that they'd discussed it, that Genya meant it. An unwelcome lump rose in her throat, but all she did was raise a brow. "Because you're so good in a fight? Nikolai needs warriors with him."

"The *nichevo'ya* left their mark on me too, Zoya. I understand the pull of this darkness."

Zoya shook her head and drew her hand away, pocketing the key. "You aren't prepared for this kind of fight."

A knock came and they turned to see Tolya's massive frame filling the doorway to the common room. "The coach is ready." He called back over his shoulder, "And Tamar is late!"

"I am not late," said Tamar from behind him. "My wife is just in a sulk."

Zoya peered past Tolya's shoulder and saw Tamar holding Nadia's hand, clearly trying to coax her out of her gloom.

"I have every right to a sulk," Nadia said. "You're leaving. My brother is somewhere in Fjerda, and I'm being asked to build a prototype of a submersible that doesn't work for a party I don't want to attend."

"I'll be back before you know it," said Tamar. "And I'll bring you a present."

"It had better be new goggles," said Nadia.

"I was thinking of something more romantic."

David frowned. "What's more romantic than goggles?"

"We're ready," said Zoya. She handed Tolya the trunk. "Genya, report to me frequently on the replies we receive from the hopefuls and the preparations for security. I'll send messages through our network on the road." She hesitated. She had the awful urge to hug Genya . . . and for once she indulged it.

She felt Tolya's disbelieving stare, felt Genya stiffen in surprise, then hug her back.

"Be safe," Zoya whispered. *Be safe.* As if those words could cast some kind of spell.

"The only danger to me will be an overabundance of menu planning," said Genya with a laugh. She drew back, and Zoya was both horrified and touched to see tears in Genya's amber eye. "Do you really believe a cure is possible?"

"I have to. Ravka can't endure another power grab, another coup, another war. Nikolai is insufferable, but he's the only option we have."

"He's a good king," Genya said. "I know the difference. Bring him back to us whole."

"I will," Zoya promised, though she didn't know if it was a promise she could keep.

"And be careful, Zoya. Ravka needs you too."

Zoya felt a suspicious prickling behind her eyes and hurried out the door before the situation became more maudlin than she could abide.

They traveled in luxury, surrounded by outriders and soldiers who carried the double-eagle flag. Yuri was kept in the coach, sequestered with Tolya as they scoured old scrolls and religious texts for information on the *obisbaya*. Another coach had been devoted to the books they'd gathered from the libraries at the Grand Palace and the Little Palace—and a few Tamar had obtained by stealth from the catacombs of the Priestguard—scholarly treatises bound in leather, crumbling hymnals, even old children's books, illustrations of what might have been a thorn wood curling at the borders of their yellowing pages.

Though Yuri had wrung his hands and protested in querulous tones, he had been convinced to set aside his black robes for the brown roughspun of an ordinary monk so he could travel with them anonymously. He'd given in readily enough. Yuri believed that the secret agenda of this trip—the visits to the miracle sites and the Fold—was to determine whether the Starless One should be made a Saint and a church built on the site of his martyrdom.

"But for that to happen," Nikolai had warned, "I need to know everything you can determine about the *obisbaya*—the ritual, the location of the thorn wood, this whole notion of purification."

Yuri's eyes had lit at that last word. "Purification," he'd repeated. "A return to true belief. The faith of the people restored."

Zoya knew Nikolai hoped the monk's research would lead them to a ritual that might purge him of the monster, but even if they were somehow successful, she had to wonder where all of it would end.

"What are you going to do with him when this is over?" she'd asked Nikolai. "The people will revolt outright if you actually try to make the Darkling a Saint. You could start a holy war and give the Apparat the perfect chance to challenge you outright—and he'll do it beneath Alina's banner."

"We'll find a way to compromise," Nikolai had said. "We'll set Yuri up in a nice snug hermitage to prepare a treatise on the Darkling's good works with all the books he wants. We'll tell him the matter has to be put before the people. We'll send him to the Wandering Isle to spread the gospel of the Starless One."

"That sounds suspiciously like exile."

"You say exile, I say extended holiday."

"We should send him to Ketterdam to preach to Kaz Brekker and the rest of those reprobates," suggested Zoya.

Nikolai winced. "He'd certainly get his martyrdom."

The king hadn't toured the country since immediately after the Darkling had been vanquished, when he'd stepped into the gap left by his exiled parents and onto the throne. Instead of remaining in the capital as the aristocracy had expected, Nikolai had taken to the roads and the skies, traveling without rest. Zoya had barely known the king then, and she certainly hadn't trusted him. She'd understood that he was their fractured country's best hope of survival, and she could admit that he'd shown ingenuity during the civil war, but he was also a Lantsov, and his father had brought nothing but misery to Ravka. For all Zoya knew at the time, the new king might be little more than a handsome, fast-talking catastrophe in the making.

But Nikolai had done what so many men had failed to do: He'd surprised her. He had shored up Ravka's borders, negotiated new loans with Kerch, reestablished their military outposts, and used the fleet he'd built in his secret life as the privateer Sturmhond to keep the Fjerdans stymied at sea. He had visited cities and towns, distributing food, talking to local leaders and nobility, marshaling every ounce of his appeal to win their support and cement public opinion in his favor after the destruction of the Fold. When he had finally returned to Os Alta, he had created a new flag with the sun in ascendance behind the Lantsov double eagle and been crowned by the Apparat in the newly built royal chapel. Zoya had felt the stirrings of what might have been hope.

She had been hard at work with the Triumvirate, trying to reassemble the Second Army and make a plan for its future. Some days Zoya had felt proud and full of excitement, but on others she'd felt like a child masquerading as a leader. It had been harrowing, thrilling to know that they were all standing at the precipice of something new.

But now, as they traveled from town to town, Zoya understood that the task of unifying Ravka and building a new foundation for the Second Army had been the easy part. Dragging the country into the future was proving harder. Nikolai had spent his life waiting to govern and learning how to do it, but while Nikolai craved change, Ravka fought it. His reforms to the tithing and land ownership laws had led to grumbling among the nobility. *Of course the serfs should have rights*, they protested, *eventually*. The king went too far and moved too fast.

Zoya knew Nikolai was aware of the resistance that had grown up against him, and he intended to use this trip to help defeat it. The days were given to travel and winning the commoners through spectacle and gifts of coin or food. In the evenings, their party took up lodging in the homes of noblemen and local governors and joined grand dinners that went late into the night. After the meals, Nikolai would sequester himself with the head of the house, talking through reforms, requesting aid, smoothing feathers ruffled by the peril of change. Sometimes Nikolai would ask Zoya to join them when all she wanted was to fall into bed.

"Why should I bother?" she grumbled at Baron Levkin's dacha in Kelink. "Your charm is enough to carry the day."

"They need to see my general," he said.

It was true enough. The nobles still thrilled to tales of warfare and the strength of the Second Army. But Zoya also knew that her presence—tart-tongued and sour as it might be—changed the atmosphere in the room, made the conversation seem less a negotiation than a friendly exchange. It was another reason Nikolai desperately needed a queen. So she did her best to paste a smile on her face and be pleasant, and occasionally offered a word regarding the Grisha forces if anyone thought to ask. It exhausted her.

"How do you do it?" she spat at Nikolai one night as they left a particularly productive session with a duke in Grevyakin. He'd begun the conversation determined to reject Nikolai's suggestion to use his fields for cotton farming, calling for a return to the old ways. His entire home was full of peasant woodcrafts and handwoven textiles, the props of a simpler time in which a serf might be counted upon to create pretty objects for his master and politely starve in silence. But two hours and several glasses of strong spirits later, the old duke was roaring with laughter at Nikolai's jokes and had agreed to convert two more of his farms to cotton. Another hour gone and he promised to allow a new mill and cotton gin to be built on his property. "How do you change their minds and make them thank you for the experience?"

Nikolai shrugged. "He has a noble's disdain for commerce but likes the idea of himself as a great benefactor. So I simply pointed out that, with all of the time and money his workers will save, they'll have more hours to devote to the ornament he loves so much. His estate might become a beacon for artists and craftsmen—the new world sustaining the old instead of replacing it."

"Do you really believe that?"

"Not at all. His serfs will get a taste of money and education and start thinking about building lives and businesses of their own instead of praying for their master's patronage. But by then it will be too late. Progress is a river. It cannot be called back once it leaps its banks."

"That wasn't what I meant anyway," Zoya said as Tolya led them to the chambers where Nikolai would be lodging. "How do you do *this*?" She waved a hand from the crown of his golden head to his perfectly polished boots. "Days on the road, bare hours of sleep." She dropped her voice to a whisper. "Being drugged every night and playing host to some kind of immortal evil inside you. But still you manage to look fresh and contented. I bet, if the duke had asked, you could have spent another hour playing cards and telling war stories."

"That's what the job requires, Zoya. Ruling is not just about military victories. It's not even about setting fair laws and seeing them enforced. It's about these moments, the men and women who choose to put their lives and livelihoods in our hands."

"Just admit that you need to be loved as much as they need to love you."

"Luckily, I'm very lovable."

"Less so by the moment. You don't look remotely fatigued. It's not normal."

"I think fatigue suits you, Zoya. The pallor. The shadows beneath your eyes. You look like a heroine in a novel."

"I look like a woman about to step on your foot."

"Now, now. You're managing remarkably well. And the smiling hasn't killed you yet."

"*Yet.*"

Tamar was waiting at the door to Nikolai's rooms. "Any trouble tonight?" Nikolai asked her. At their previous stop, Tamar had caught a servant skulking about the king's chambers and digging through his belongings, presumably on his master's orders.

"Nothing," she said. "But I'll do another search of the house just in case and have a look inside the duke's study later tonight."

The old duke seemed to have been won over, but if he'd had contact with Nikolai's opponents in West Ravka or with one of the Lantsov pretenders, they needed to know.

Once Nikolai had removed his boots and settled on the bed beneath a grotesque painting of Sankta Anastasia curing the wasting plague, Zoya pulled the tiny bottle from her pocket.

Nikolai shuddered. "Whatever David and Genya concocted, it feels less like sleep than being punched in the jaw."

Zoya said nothing. The sedatives they'd given him in the past had been simple potions that had made him softly blurry and often left him snoring before Zoya had departed the room. But with this new brew, Nikolai dropped into unconsciousness in the space of a breath—and he did not look like he was sleeping. His stillness was so complete she found herself pressing her fingers to the hollow beneath his jaw, seeking out the molasses-slow beat of his pulse. Dosing him was like watching him die every night.

"All I know is it's strong enough to shut you up," she said. She raised the bottle but kept it just out of reach. "Tell me how you manage it. How do you survive all of this glad-handing and unending performance?"

"You manage it every day at the Little Palace, Zoya. For all your bluster, I know you don't always feel clever or strong, but you make a good show of it."

Zoya tossed her hair over one shoulder. "Maybe. But I'm always me. You change like light over water. These moments, these inter-actions, they only seem to feed you. What's your secret?"

"The secret . . ." Nikolai mused. He held out his hand, and she dropped the silver vial into his palm. "I suppose the secret is that I cannot stand being alone." He uncorked the concoction. "But there are some places no one can go with us."

He touched the bottle to his tongue, and Zoya snatched it from his hand as he fell backward, plummeting into the dark before his head reached the pillow.

Zoya traveled with the outriders. Sometimes Nikolai rode in the coach with Tolya and Yuri, but mostly he stayed astride one of his white horses, bracketed by his guards, Tamar following a discreet distance away. He did not wear the full military regalia and sash that his father had favored but instead the olive drab coat that was standard-issue for soldiers of the First Army. He'd earned the respect of the military by serving in the infantry before becoming an officer, and the medals he wore pinned to his chest were not ceremonial but battle-won.

In every village and town, Zoya watched as the king worked his particular kind of magic. Even the way he sat his horse changed depending on the crowd he greeted. Sometimes he was relaxed, at ease in the saddle, the sun gilding his hair and gleaming off his perfectly polished boots as he smiled and waved to his beloved subjects. Sometimes he was somber and heroic, standing atop stages and on balconies to address crowds as they prayed in their churches and gathered in their town squares. Though he and Zoya took pains to hide the urgency of their mission, they rode hard each day and never spent more than a single night in any location. They had allotted three weeks for this journey. Whatever they did or didn't discover on the Fold, they'd be back in the capital to prepare for the festival with time to spare.

In Ryevost, where the great earthquake had struck, Nikolai stripped down to his shirtsleeves to work side by side with the men of the town, moving rubble and raising beams. He stood on the site where the great stone seal of Sankt Lubov had split, spewing forth a tide of tiny silver hummingbirds that had circled the town square in a whirring cloud for a fortnight before dispersing. He vowed to build a new church there, paid for with Lantsov gold.

"And where will all the money actually come from?" Zoya asked that night.

"The Kerch? My wealthy new bride? Maybe the Apparat can sell off a fancy altarpiece."

But she now saw what he had intended when he conceded to the Apparat's request for new churches. The Apparat would get these houses of worship, more places to lodge his spies and loyalists, but the people would not think of the priest when they said their prayers and heard the church bells chime. They would think of their golden king and whisper of the day he'd come to their village.

"I grew up in a place like this," Zoya said as they entered the next bleak backwater. "Hopeless. Hungry. Desperation makes people do ugly things, and it is always the girls who suffer first."

"Is that why you push so hard for the new factories we're building?"

Zoya gave the barest shrug. "A broad back is needed to lift an axe or move a stone, but it doesn't take strength to pull a lever or push a button."

She could sense Nikolai's scrutiny. "I've never known you to have much sympathy for the common people."

I was common enough once. Liliyana and Lada were common. "It has nothing to do with sympathy. For the Grisha to thrive, we need a strong Ravka."

"Ah, so you're just being practical, of course."

She could hear the skepticism in his voice, and she didn't appreciate it one bit. But it was hard not to look at these muddy streets, the gray houses with their warped roofs and slanting porches, the tilting spire of the church, and not think of Pachina, the town she'd left behind. She refused to call it home.

"Do you know what changed everything in my village?" She kept her eyes on the road, rutted with holes and broken rocks from the previous night's rain. "The draft. When the war was so dire that the crown was forced to start taking girls as well as boys to fight."

"I thought the draft was seen as a curse."

"For some," Zoya conceded. "But for others of us it offered an escape, a chance at something other than being someone's wife and dying in childbirth. When I was little, before my powers emerged, I dreamed of being a soldier."

"Little Zoya with her bayonet?"

Zoya sniffed. "I always had the makings of a general." But her mother had seen only the value in her daughter's beauty. Zoya's face had been her dowry at the tender age of nine. If not for Liliyana, she would have been bartered away like a new calf. But could she blame her mother? She remembered Sabina's raw hands, her tired eyes, the gaunt lines of her body—perpetually weary and without hope. And yet, after all these years, Zoya found no scrap of forgiveness for her desperate mother or her weak father. They could rot. She gave her reins a snap.

Zoya and the rest of Nikolai's party rode through the barley fields and inspected the new armaments factory, endured the singing of a children's choir, and then had tea with the local council and the choirmaster.

"You should poison the choirmaster for inflicting that atrocity on us," Zoya grumbled.

"They were adorable."

"They were flat."

Zoya was forced to put on a little demonstration of summoning for the local women's group and resisted the urge to blow the town magistrate's wig off his head.

At last they were permitted to ride out with the governor and see the great swath of forest that had supposedly been felled in a single night. It was an eerie sight. The smell of sap was heavy in the air, and the trees had fallen in perfect lines all the way to the crest of a hill that overlooked a tiny chapel dedicated to Sankt Ilya in Chains. The trees all lay in the same direction, like bodies laid to rest, as if pointing them west toward the Fold. They'd let Yuri emerge from the coach to stretch his legs and see the supposed miracle site, Tolya towering over him like the one tree that had refused to fall. According to Tolya, they'd begun to piece together a text that might well be the original description of the *obisbaya*.

"Has it ever occurred to you," Zoya said, watching the skinny monk talk animatedly to a beleaguered-looking Tolya, "that this is all contrivance? That the Apparat and the monk are not enemies at all? That they both wanted you away from the safety of the capital, and that they've gotten just that for their trouble?"

"Of course it has," said Nikolai. "But such displays are beyond even the Apparat's considerable reach. It pains my pride to say it, but there may be something at work here that's bigger than both of us."

"Speak for yourself," she said. But looking out at the felled trees, she felt as if an invisible hand were guiding them, and she did not like it. "I don't trust him," Zoya said. "Either of them."

"The Apparat is a man of ambition, and that means he can be managed."

"And our monk friend? Is Yuri easily managed as well?"

"Yuri is a true believer. Either that or he's the greatest actor who ever lived, which I know isn't possible."

"How can you be so sure?"

"Because I managed to smile through that choir concert, so clearly *I* am the greatest actor who ever lived." Nikolai nudged his horse with his heels. "On to the next town, Nazyalensky. We hope or we falter."

Zoya was grateful when they rode into Adena, their last stop before the Fold. Soon they would have answers or they would be headed home. At least she'd be free of the anticipation and the fear of what they might find when they reached the Unsea.

The village was like all the others except for the pretty lake it overlooked. This time they'd been greeted by an off-key band and a parade of livestock and giant vegetables.

"That squash is as wide as I am tall," Nikolai said beneath his breath as he smiled and waved.

"And twice as handsome."

"Half as handsome," he protested.

"Ah," said Zoya, "but the squash doesn't talk."

At last they rose from their seats on the bandstand and made their way to the church. For once, the locals did not follow. Zoya, Nikolai, Yuri, and the twins were left to walk the path out of town with only the local priest for company.

"Are there no pilgrims?" Tolya asked him as they left the outskirts of town.

"The pilgrims are kept to the confines of the village," said the priest. He was an older man with a tidy white beard and spectacles much like Yuri's. "Visitors are only permitted access to the site under supervision and at certain hours. The cathedral is being repaired, and we wish to preserve Sankta Lizabeta's work."

"Is it so very fragile?" asked Yuri.

"It is extraordinary and not something to be picked apart for souvenirs."

Zoya felt a chill creep over her. Something was different in the air here. The insects had gone silent. She heard no call of birds from the surrounding trees as they moved through the cool shadows of the wood and farther from the town. She met Tamar's gaze and they exchanged a nod. Even at a supposed holy site, the king could be at risk of assassination.

They emerged at the top of a high, mounded hill next to a cathedral surrounded by scaffolding, its golden domes gleaming in the late-afternoon sun. A statue of Sankta Lizabeta stood before the entrance. A riot of red roses had burst through the stone, cracking open her veiled skull. The flowers tumbled over the statue in wild profusion, surrounding its marble skirts in a wide circle like a pool of blood. Their sweet smell pulsed in a thick, syrupy wave that seemed to glow with summer heat.

Yuri's face was ecstatic. "I wanted to believe. I did believe, but this . . ."

Zoya realized he was weeping. "Be silent," she bit out. "Or I'll stuff you back into the coach myself."

"Look," said Tolya, and she heard new reverence in his voice.

Black tears ran from Lizabeta's eyes. They gleamed hard as obsidian, as if they'd frozen there or been cast in stone themselves.

In the valley below, Zoya could just glimpse the sprawl of Kribirsk in the distance and the glimmer of the dead white sands that had once been the Shadow Fold beyond. They were close.

Nikolai hissed in a breath, and Zoya looked at him sharply. The others' eyes were locked on the statue, but before Nikolai could yank the cuff of his glove back into place, Zoya glimpsed the dark veining at his wrist pulse black, as if . . . as if whatever was inside him had recognized something familiar here and woken. Part of her wanted to draw away, afraid that she would see the demon emerge, but she was a soldier and she would not waver.

"What was Lizabeta's story?" Nikolai asked. His voice was taut, but the others didn't seem to notice.

"It is both beautiful and tragic," Yuri said enthusiastically.

Zoya wanted to knock him into the roses. "Aren't all martyr-doms built to look that way?"

But Yuri ignored her or simply didn't hear. "She was only eighteen when raiders came to West Ravka's shore, pillaging and burning every village they encountered. While the men of her town cowered, Lizabeta faced the soldiers in a field of white roses and begged them to show mercy. When they charged her, she fell to her knees in prayer, and it was the bees that answered, rising from the blossoms to attack the soldiers in a swarm. Lizabeta's town was saved."

Zoya folded her arms. "Now tell our king how the people rewarded young Lizabeta for this miracle."

"Well," Yuri said, fiddling with a loose thread on his sleeve. "The villagers to the north demanded Lizabeta repeat this miracle and save their town too, but she could not." He cleared his throat. "They had her drawn and quartered. It was said the roses turned red with her blood."

"And this is the woman who is supposed to be answering the people's prayers." Zoya snapped a rose from its stem, ignoring the horrified gasp of the local priest. Its scent was cloying. Everything about this place set her teeth on edge. It felt as if something was watching her from the domes of the cathedral, from the shadows of the trees. "Why must all of your Saints be martyred?"

Yuri blinked. "Because . . . because it shows a willingness to sacrifice."

"Do you think Lizabeta was willing to be pulled apart? How about Demyan when he was stoned to death? Or Ilya, chained and thrown into a river to drown?" She was tired of these miracles, tired of the dread riding with her daily, and utterly sick of stories that ended in suffering for those who dared to be brave or strange or strong. "If I were Lizabeta, I wouldn't waste my time listening to the whining of—"

Movement on the roof of the cathedral caught Zoya's eye. She looked up in time to see something massive rushing toward her. It smashed through Lizabeta's statue, sending petals and shards of stone flying. Huge hands grasped Zoya's shoulders, digging into her flesh, lifting her from the ground. She kicked her feet, feeling the terrible sensation of nothing beneath her.

Zoya screamed as she was pulled skyward, the rose still clutched in her hand.

12
NIKOLAI

"ZOYA!"

Something had hold of her—something with wings, and for a moment Nikolai wondered if somehow the demon had leapt from his very skin. But no, her captor's wings were vast mechanical marvels of engineering that beat the sky as they rose higher.

Another winged soldier was wheeling toward Nikolai—this one female, black hair bound in a topknot, biceps armored in bands of gray metal. *Khergud*. The Shu had dared to attack the royal procession.

Tolya and Tamar stepped in front of Nikolai, but the soldier's target was not the king—she had come for the king's Heartrender guards. She had come to hunt Grisha. In a single movement the *khergud* released a metallic net that glittered in the air, then collapsed over the twins with enough weight to knock them to the ground. The *khergud* dragged them over the earth, gathering speed to lift them skyward.

Nikolai didn't hesitate. There were times for subtlety and times when there was nothing to do but charge. He ran straight for the *khergud*, clambering over the struggling bodies of Tolya and Tamar, who grunted as his boots connected. He opened fire with both pistols.

The *khergud* barely flinched, her skin reinforced with that marvelously effective alloy of Grisha steel and ruthenium. Nikolai would solve that problem later.

He cast his weapons aside but did not let his stride break. He drew his dagger and launched himself onto the *khergud*'s back. The soldier bucked with the force of a wild horse. Nikolai had read the files. He knew strength and gunpowder were no match for this kind of power. So precision it would have to be.

"I hope some part of you is still flesh and blood," Nikolai bit out. He seized the *khergud*'s collar and aimed the dagger into the notch between the soldier's jaw and throat, praying for accuracy as he drove the blade home.

The *khergud* stumbled, losing momentum, trying to dislodge the dagger. Nikolai did not relent, twisting the blade deeper, feeling hot blood spurt over his hand. At last the soldier collapsed.

Nikolai didn't wait to see Tolya and Tamar free themselves; he was already searching the skies for Zoya and her captor.

They were locked in a struggle high above the earth as Zoya kicked and fought the *khergud* who had hold of her. The soldier wrapped a massive arm around her throat. He was going to choke her into submission.

Abruptly, Zoya went still—but that was too fast for her to have lost consciousness. Nikolai felt the air around him crackle. The *khergud* had assumed Zoya was like other Grisha, who couldn't summon with their arms bound. But Zoya Nazyalensky was no ordinary Squaller.

Lightning crackled over the metal wings of the Shu soldier. He shuddered and shook. The *khergud*'s body went limp. He and Zoya plummeted to the ground. *No no no.* Nikolai raced toward them, his mind constructing and casting aside plans. Useless. Hopeless. There was no way to reach her in time. A snarl ripped from his chest. He leapt, the air rushing against his face, and then he had her in his arms. *Impossible. The physics wouldn't permit . . .*

Nikolai glimpsed his own shadow beneath him—too far beneath him, a dark blot bracketed by wings that curled from his own back. *The monster is me and I am the monster.* He flinched, as if he could somehow escape himself, and watched the monster's shadow twitch.

"Nikolai?" Zoya was looking at him, and all he saw on her face was terror.

"It's me," he tried to say, but only a growl emerged. In the next second a shock was traveling through his body—Zoya's power vibrating through his bones. He cried out, the sound a ragged growl, and felt his wings curl in on themselves, vanishing.

He was falling. They were both going to die.

Zoya thrust her free arm down, and a cushion of air pillowed beneath them, halting their momentum with a jolt. They rolled off it and hit the ground in a graceless heap. In a breath, she was scrambling away from him, arms raised, blue eyes wide.

He held up his hands in a gesture of surrender. "It's me," he repeated, and when he heard the words emerge from his lips, human and whole, he wanted to weep with gratitude. He'd never tasted anything so sweet as language returning to his tongue.

Zoya's nostrils flared. She turned her attention to the *khergud* soldier who had attacked her, looming over his body, looking for a place to unleash her fear. The fall should have killed him, but he was already pushing to his feet. Zoya flipped her palms up and thunder boomed, lightning sparking at her fingertips. The strands of her hair writhed like a halo of serpents around her face. She slammed her hands down on the soldier's chest. He convulsed as his flesh turned red and smoke rose from his torso, his body catching fire as it burned from within.

"Zoya!" shouted Nikolai. He lurched to his feet, but he didn't dare touch her, not with that kind of current running through her. "Zoya, look at me, damn it."

She raised her head. Her skin was pale, her eyes wild with rage. For a moment, she didn't seem to recognize him. Then her lips parted, her shoulders dropped. Zoya pulled her hands away, and the *khergud*'s charred body collapsed. She sat back on her knees and drew in a long breath.

The smell emanating from the *khergud*'s roasted corpse was sickly sweet. So much for an interrogation.

Tolya and Tamar had freed themselves from the net. They stood with Yuri, who was trembling so badly Nikolai thought he might be having some kind of seizure. Had the boy never seen combat? It had been a brutal exchange but a brief one, and it wasn't as if he'd been a target. Then Nikolai realized . . .

"You . . . he . . ." sputtered Yuri.

"Your Highness," said Tolya.

Nikolai looked down at his hands. His fingers were still stained black, curled into talons. They had torn through his gloves. Nikolai took a deep breath. A long moment passed, then another. At last, the claws receded.

"I know, Yuri," he said as steadily as he could manage. "Quite a party trick. Are you going to faint?"

"No. Possibly. I don't know."

"You'll be all right. We all will." The words were so patently untrue that Nikolai had to struggle not to laugh. "I need you to keep silent. Tolya, Tamar, you're uninjured?" They both nodded. Nikolai forced himself to look at Zoya. "You're not hurt?"

She drew in a shuddering breath. She nodded, flexed her fingers, and said, "A few bruises. But the priest . . ." She bobbed her chin toward where the man lay, blood trickling from his temple into his snowy beard. He'd been knocked unconscious by a piece of Lizabeta's stone veil.

Nikolai knelt beside him. The priest's pulse was steady, though he probably had a bad concussion.

"No outcry from the village," said Tamar as she used her power to check the priest's vitals. "No alarm. If someone spotted the *khergud*, they would have come running."

Hopefully the attack had been far enough from town to avoid drawing notice.

"I don't want to try to explain soldiers with mechanical wings," said Nikolai. "We'll have to hide the bodies."

"Give them to the roses," said Tamar. "I'll send two riders back to get them out after sunset."

When the corpses were hidden from view in the heaps of Lizabeta's red roses, they staged the area around the statue to their liking, and then Tamar brought the priest back to consciousness. As always, taking some kind of action helped to ease the tension thrumming through Nikolai. But he knew he couldn't rely on this illusion of control. It was a balm, not a cure. The monster had come calling in broad daylight. And it had allowed him to save Zoya. Nikolai didn't know what that meant. He hadn't commanded the demon. It had pushed to the fore. At least he thought it had. *What if it happens again?* His mind felt like enemy territory.

The priest came to with a start and then moaned, reaching up to touch his fingers to the growing bulge at his temple.

"You took quite a knock to the head," said Nikolai gently.

"There were soldiers!" the priest gasped. "In the sky!" Nikolai and Tamar exchanged a staged look of concern. "A man . . . he came out of the clouds. He had wings! Another came from the cathedral roof."

"I fear you may have a concussion," said Nikolai, helping the priest to his feet.

"I *saw* him! The statue . . . You see, he smashed the statue, *our* statue of Sankta Lizabeta!"

"No," said Nikolai, and pointed to the beam they'd managed to tear lose from the overhang of the cathedral. "Don't you see the broken beam? It gave way from the rafters and struck you and the statue. You're lucky you weren't killed."

"Miraculous," said Zoya dryly.

"Brother," the priest implored Yuri. "Tell me you did not see what I did!"

Yuri tugged at his straggly beard and Nikolai waited. The monk hadn't stopped staring at him since the *khergud* attack. At last, Yuri said, "I . . . I saw nothing without explanation."

The priest gave a helpless, baffled huff, and Nikolai felt a jab of guilt. "Come," he said. "If you don't have a headache, you will soon. Let's find you help."

They walked back along the forest path to the town, where many of the locals were still celebrating in the town square, and left the priest to their care.

"I don't like lying to a priest," said Tolya as they mounted their horses to ride out to the manse where they would spend the night.

"I agree," Yuri added quietly.

"The truth would have been harder for him to bear," said Tamar. "Think how unhappy he would be, constantly looking over his shoulder and thinking something was going to come out of the sky and pluck him from the ground like a hawk seizing a stoat."

"It's still a lie," said Tolya.

"Then you'll have to perform some kind of penance," said Nikolai, his exasperation growing. He was grateful to Tolya. He respected the twins' faith and its importance to them, but he couldn't worry over Tolya's conscience when his mind was trying to contend with a Shu attack on the royal procession and a demon that no longer wanted to wait until dark.

"You can start by rubbing my feet," Zoya told the monk.

"That's hardly an act of holy contrition," said Yuri.

"You've never seen her feet," said Nikolai.

Zoya tossed her hair over her shoulder. "A man once offered to sign over the deed to his summer home in Polvost if I would let him watch as I stepped on a pile of blueberries."

"And did you?" asked Tamar.

"Of course not. Polvost is a dump."

"The priest will be fine," Nikolai reassured Yuri. "And I appreciate your tact."

"I did what I thought was right," said the monk, more quiet and restrained than Nikolai had ever seen him, his jaw tilted at a stubborn angle. "But I expect an explanation, Your Highness."

"Well," Zoya said as they watched Yuri trot off ahead of the party, "now what?"

"You mean now that you've cooked an invaluable source of information from the inside out?" There was an edge to his voice that he wasn't entirely sorry for. It wasn't like Zoya to make that kind of mistake.

Zoya's back straightened. "It's possible I wasn't entirely in control. I suspect you're familiar with the sensation."

Because it wasn't just the *khergud* attack that had unsettled her. It was the memory of that night in the bell tower, of another winged monster. One that had shown its claws again today.

"Passingly," he murmured.

"And I wasn't talking about the *khergud*," said Zoya, pushing past the sudden chill between them. "What are you going to do about the monk?"

"I have a few hours to figure out what to tell him. I'll come up with something."

"You do have a gift for the preposterous," said Zoya, kicking her horse into a gallop. "And this whole cursed country seems to have a taste for it."

It was long past sunset when at last Nikolai was able to retire from dinner and join the others in the quarters the local governor had provided for them.

The room was clearly the best in the house, and everywhere Nikolai looked there were gestures toward Sankta Lizabeta—the honeycomb floor tiles, roses carved into the mantel, even the walls of the chamber itself had been hollowed into coffers to resemble a great hive. A fire burned in the grate, bathing the sandstone walls in golden light, the cheerful glow somehow inappropriate to the dire events of the day.

Tamar had returned to the cathedral as soon as night fell to retrieve the bodies of the *khergud* and arrange their transport to the capital for study. Tolya's reluctance to desecrate a fallen soldier's body had been considerably diminished by the ambush, and Nikolai felt no qualms at all. His guards had been attacked. Zoya had almost been taken. Besides, some part of him would always be a privateer.

If the Shu wanted to wage this kind of war, let them reap the consequences.

Tolya had been ordered to watch the monk and make sure he sent no messages to his followers about what he'd seen. Now Yuri sat before the fire, still looking shaken. Tolya and Tamar played chess at a low table, and Zoya perched on the sill of the window, framed by the casement, as if she were the one who might take flight.

Nikolai shut the door, unsure how to begin. He thought of the Shu soldier's body cut open on a table. He had seen dissection files, the detailed drawings rendered by Fabrikators and Corporalki. Was that what this problem required? For someone to cut him open and pull him apart? *I'd do it gladly*, he thought. *If this thing could be isolated and excised like a tumor, I'd lie down beneath the scalpel and guide the surgeon's hand myself.*

But the monster was wilier than that.

It was Yuri who spoke first from his place on the floor. "He did this to you, didn't he?"

"Yes," Nikolai said simply. He'd thought about what lies he might concoct to appease the monk's fear and curiosity. But in the end, he knew the truth—at least part of it—would work to best advantage. Yuri wanted to believe in Saints, and Saints required martyrdom.

Yet now that the time had come to speak, Nikolai did not want to tell this story. He did not want it to be *his* story. He'd thought the war was in the past, but it refused to remain there.

He plucked a bottle of brandy from the sideboard, chose a chair, and stretched his legs out in front of the fire. It was a pose of ease and confidence, one he had assumed many times. It felt false.

"During the war," he said, tugging the gloves from his hands, "I was captured by the Darkling. No doubt you've heard that I was tortured by your Starless Saint."

Yuri's eyes dropped to the tracery of black lines that spread over Nikolai's fingers and knuckles. "Korol Rezni," he said quietly. "King of Scars. I've heard the stories."

"And chalked them up to royal propaganda? A smear campaign against a fallen hero?"

Yuri coughed. "Well—"

"Hand me that brandy," said Zoya. "I can't tolerate this degree of stupidity on a clear head."

Nikolai poured himself a drink before turning over the bottle, but he knew mocking Yuri would do no good. Wasn't speaking the truth supposed to be freeing? Some kind of tonic for the soul? In Nikolai's experience, honesty was much like herbal tea—something well-meaning people recommended when they were out of better options.

"The Darkling had a gift for inflicting misery," he continued. "He knew pain or imprisonment would be too easy for me to bear. So he used his power to infect me with living darkness. It was my payment for helping the Sun Summoner escape his grasp. I became . . . I don't know what exactly I became. Part monster, part man. I hungered for human flesh. I was nearly mindless with the need. Nearly. Enough of my own consciousness still lived on in me that I continued to battle the monster's impulses and even rallied the volcra to face the Darkling on the Fold."

At the time, Nikolai hadn't known if there was any point to fighting on, if he would ever be himself again. He hadn't even known if the Darkling could be killed. But Alina had managed it, armed with a shadow blade wrapped in the Darkling's own power and wet with the blood of his own line.

"Before she died, the Sun Summoner slew the Darkling, and the darkness inside me perished with him." Nikolai took a long swig of his brandy. "Or so I thought." He'd plummeted to the earth and would have died had Zoya not used the wind to cushion his fall, much as she'd done today. "Several months ago, something began to seize my unconscious mind. Some nights I sleep as well as can be expected—only a lazy monarch rests easy. But on other nights, I become the monster. He controls me completely."

"Not completely," said Zoya. "You haven't taken a human life."

Nikolai felt a rush of gratitude that she would be the one to speak those words, but he forced himself to add, "That we know of. The attacks are getting worse. They come more frequently. The tonics and even the chains I've used to keep them at bay are temporary solutions. It may be only a matter of time before my mind gives itself up to the beast and its hungers. It is possible . . ." Now the words fought him, poison in his mouth. "It's possible the beast may overtake me completely and I'll never be able to return to my human form."

Silence filled the room, the quiet of a funeral. Why not throw a little more dirt on the coffin? "Today, the monster stepped forward in broad daylight, while I was still awake. That has never happened before."

"Was it deliberate?" asked Yuri. "Did you choose to—"

"I didn't choose anything. It simply happened. I think the shock Zoya sent through my body allowed me to come back to myself." He took a long sip from his glass. "I can't have this thing taking hold of me on a battlefield or in the middle of a state function. Ravka's position is precarious, and so is mine. The people have only just begun to recover from the war. They want stability and leadership, not a monster born of nightmares."

Peace. A chance to recover, to build their lives without the constant fear of battle, the threat of starvation. On this journey, Nikolai had seen the progress Ravka had made with his own eyes. His country could not afford to go to war again, and he'd done everything to make sure they wouldn't have to. But if the monster emerged, if Nikolai revealed this dark presence, he might be the very thing that set his country back down the path to violence.

"Perhaps you don't give the people enough credit," said Yuri.

"No?" said Zoya from her perch. "The people who still call Grisha witches despite the years they've kept this country safe? Who bar them from owning property in their towns—"

"That is illegal," said Nikolai.

Zoya raised her glass in a mock toast. "I'll be sure to inform them the next time a Grisha family is driven from their home in the middle of the night."

"People are always looking for someone to blame for their suffering," Yuri said earnestly. "Ravka has seen so much strife. It's only natural that—"

There was nothing natural about this.

"Yuri," said Nikolai. "We can debate Ravka's prejudices another time. I told you we came on this journey to investigate the miracle sites, to consider Sainthood for the Darkling."

"Was any of that true?"

Nikolai did not intend to answer that question directly.

"The Darkling may deserve to take his place among the Saints, but that can't happen until I'm rid of this affliction."

Yuri nodded, then nodded again. He looked down at his bony hands. "But is it something to be rid of?"

Zoya expelled a bitter laugh. "He thinks you've been blessed by the Starless Saint."

Yuri pushed his glasses higher on his long nose. "*Blessing* and *curse* are different words for the same thing."

"You may well be right," said Nikolai, forcing himself to find the diplomacy that had always served him well. If you listened to a man's words, you might learn his wants. The trick was to look into his heart and discover his needs. "But Yuri, the Darkling cannot possibly be considered a Saint until his martyrdom is complete." Zoya's eyes narrowed. Nikolai ignored her. He would say what he had to, do what he must to be rid of this sickness. "It was not coincidence that brought you to the palace gates. You were meant to bear witness to the last remnant of the Darkling's power. You were meant to bring us to the thorn wood. You were meant to free us both."

"Me?" said Yuri, his voice a bare breath, but Nikolai could see that he wanted to believe. *Don't we all?* Who didn't want to think fate had a plan for him, that his hurts and failures had just been the prologue to a grander tale? To a monk becoming a holy warrior. To a bastard becoming a king. "*Me,*" repeated Yuri.

Behind him, Zoya rolled her eyes. Neither Tolya nor Tamar looked happy.

"Only you can complete the Darkling's martyrdom," said Nikolai. "Will you help me? Will you help him?"

"I will," said Yuri. "Of course I will. I will take you to the thorn wood. I will build a holy pyre."

"Wait just a minute," Zoya said from her perch. "Are you saying you want to put the king of Ravka on a funeral pyre?"

Yuri blinked. "I mean, one hopes it would simply be a pyre?"

"A comforting and essential distinction," said Nikolai, though he couldn't say he was thrilled at the possibility. "Is that what the *obis-baya* requires?"

Tolya picked up a rook and turned it in his hand. "It isn't entirely clear, but that seems to be what most of the texts point to."

"Yes," said Yuri, intent now. "There's some suggestion that Sankt

Feliks may have in fact been a member of the Priestguard, and there is text for a ritual to be read during the process. Tolya and I have been trying to make sure the language is intact."

Nikolai's brows rose. "Sankt Feliks? Wasn't he spitted on a twig and cooked to death like a holy kebob?"

Tolya set the chess piece down. "Time and translation may have muddied the facts."

"Let's hope they were very muddied," said Nikolai. "Possibly sunk in a swamp."

But now Tamar picked up the rook. "Feliks' branches are always shown thick with thorns, not much like an apple bough. It could make a kind of sense," she said. "*If* we're right about the site of the thorn wood."

"*If* any part of it remains," added Zoya.

"*If* we can find enough of it to build the pyre," said Tolya.

"Then there's the small matter of surviving the flames," said Zoya.

"You will," said Yuri. "You will survive, and the Starless One will have his true martyrdom."

"We ride for the Fold tomorrow," Nikolai said.

"Come, Tolya," said Yuri, rising, his face lit with fervor. "I have some ideas about the translation of the third passage. We must be ready."

Tolya shrugged and unbent his massive body. "It's a kind of poetry."

Nikolai downed the last of his drink. "Isn't everything?"

Tamar made to follow them from the room, but before she left she turned to Nikolai. In the firelight, her bronze arms glowed umber, the black lines of her sun tattoos stark against her skin.

"I know you said those things because of the effect they would have on the monk, but Tolya and I have never believed in coincidence," she said. "Too much has happened in our lives for us to think that faith and fate didn't play their parts. They may be playing their parts now too." She bowed. "Good night, Your Highness."

Zoya hopped down from her perch, prepared to dose him for the night. He was pained to find that after the events of the day, he was looking forward to a little oblivion.

"Fate," Nikolai said as he opened the door to his bedchamber. "Faith. I fear we are in unknown territory, Nazyalensky. I thought you'd raise a louder protest to skewering me."

"What is there to object to?" Zoya asked, rearranging the chess pieces the twins had left in disarray. "If the thorn wood is gone, our hopes crumble to dust, we return to the palace empty-handed, and we get through this party or summit or whatever you want to call it to the best of our ability."

Nikolai sat down on the edge of his bed and pulled off his boots. "And if it is there? If fate has been guiding us all along?"

Zoya lifted a brow. "Then you'd best hope fate thinks you'll make a good king."

Nikolai had been told hope was dangerous, had been warned of it many times. But he'd never believed that. Hope was the wind that came from nowhere to fill your sails and carry you home. Whether it was destiny or sheer desperation guiding them onward, at least once they reached the Fold, he would have answers.

"We'll send a decoy coach to Keramzin," he said, "and travel in disguise. If we really do intend to dig a pit in the middle of the Fold, I don't want it done under the Lantsov flag."

"Do you think the Shu knew who we were? An attack on the king—"

"Is an act of war," finished Nikolai. "But they weren't after me. I don't think they had any idea who we were. They were hunting Grisha, and they found three of you."

"So far from the borders," said Zoya, lingering in the bedroom doorway. "I feel like they're taunting us."

Nikolai set his boots by the side of the bed. "I owe you an apology."

"You owe me an entire crop of them. Why start now?"

"I meant for the other night in Balakirev. For the bell tower." He should have said something before, but the shame of hurting her had been more profound than he could have imagined. "Zoya, I'm sorry. For what I did—"

"It wasn't you," she said with a dismissive wave of her hand. "Don't be daft." But she stayed in the doorway.

"We cannot work side by side if you fear me."

"I don't fear *you*, Nikolai."

But how much longer would he be himself?

Zoya crossed to the bed and sat down on the corner. Her elegant fingers made a smooth pleat in the blue silk of her *kefta*. "I asked how you do it all, but I've never asked you why."

Nikolai wedged himself against the headboard and stretched out his legs, studying her profile. "I suspect for the same reasons you do."

"I very much doubt that."

He rubbed his hands over his face, trying to will away his fatigue. It had been a day of too many revelations, but if Zoya was willing to sit here with him alone, in the quiet of this room, and if what he said might heal the breach between them, then he was not going to squander the opportunity.

But how to answer? Why did it matter to him what became of Ravka? Broken, needy, frustrating Ravka. The grand lady. The crying child. The drowning man who would drag you under rather than be saved. This country that took so much and gave nothing back. Maybe because he knew that he and his country were the same.

Nikolai had always wanted more. More attention, more affection, something new. He'd been too much for his tutors, his nannies, the servants, his mother. No one had quite known what to do with him. No matter how they cajoled or what punishments they devised, he could not be still. They gave him books and he read them in a night. He sat through a lesson in physics and then tried to drop a cannonball off the palace roof. He took apart a priceless ormolu clock and reassembled it into a ghastly contraption that whirred and dinged without surcease, and when his mother wept over the ruined heirloom, Nikolai had looked at her with confused hazel eyes and said, "But . . . but now it tells the date as well as the time!"

The only person who could get the young prince to behave was his older brother. Nikolai had worshipped Vasily, who could ride and wield a saber, and who was allowed to sit at state functions long after Nikolai was sent off to bed. Vasily was *important*. Vasily would be king one day.

Everything his brother did, Nikolai wanted to do too. If Vasily rode, Nikolai wanted to ride. When Vasily took fencing lessons, Nikolai begged and pleaded until he was allowed to join. Since Vasily was to study statecraft and geography and military histories, Nikolai insisted he was ready for those lessons too. Nikolai only wanted his brother's notice. But to Vasily, Nikolai was little more than a constantly gabbling, mop-headed barnacle that insisted on clinging to his royal hull. When Vasily favored Nikolai with a smile or a bit of attention, all was calm waters. But the more Vasily ignored his little brother, the more Nikolai misbehaved.

Tutors took jobs in the wilds of Tsibeya. *My nerves*, they said. *The quiet will be good for them.* Nannies gave up their posts to tend to their ailing mothers on the coast. *My lungs*, they explained. *The sea air will be a tonic.* Servants wept, the king raged, the queen took to her bed with her headache powders.

One morning, when he was nine, Nikolai arrived at his class-room feeling very excited about the mouse in a jar that he planned to release in his teacher's bag, only to discover another chair and desk had been set out, and another boy was sitting in them.

"Come meet Dominik," said his tutor as the dark-haired boy rose and bowed deeply. "He will be getting a bit of education with you."

Nikolai was surprised but delighted, as he had no companions his own age in the palace at all—though he grew increasingly frustrated as Dominik flinched every time Nikolai tried to speak with him.

"You needn't be so nervous," Nikolai whispered. "Mitkin is no fun, but he sometimes tells good stories about the old kings and doesn't leave out the bloody parts."

"Yes, *moi tsarevich*."

"You can call me Nikolai if you like. Or we could come up with new names. You could be Dominik the . . . I'm not sure. Have you done any heroic deeds?"

"No, *moi tsarevich*."

"Nikolai."

"Be silent, boys," said Mitkin, and Dominik jumped again.

But for once, Nikolai stayed quiet. He was busy devising how he might get Dominik to talk more.

When Mitkin stepped out of the room to retrieve a more detailed globe, Nikolai scurried to the front of the classroom and placed the mouse he'd found roaming the eastern wing beneath the fur hat Mitkin had left on his desk.

Dominik looked utterly terrified, but Nikolai was too excited to take much note.

"Wait until you hear the shriek that Mitkin makes," Nikolai said. "He sounds like a scandalized teakettle."

Tutor Mitkin did indeed scream, and Nikolai, who had meant to sit stone-faced, couldn't restrain his own laughter—until Mitkin told Dominik to come to the front of the room and hold out his hands.

The tutor took a slender birch rod from his desk, and as Nikolai looked on in horror, Mitkin slapped it down on Dominik's palms. Dominik released a small whimper.

"What are you doing?" Nikolai cried. "You must stop!"

Nikolai called for the guards, shouted down the hallway for help, but Mitkin did not stop. He smacked the rod against Dominik's hands and forearms ten times, until the boy's flesh was a mass of red welts, and his face was crumpled and wet with tears.

Mitkin set the rod aside. "Every time you act out or misbehave, Dominik will be beaten."

"That isn't right! It isn't fair—the punishment should be mine!" But no one would raise the rod to a royal prince.

Nikolai protested to his mother, his father, anyone who would listen. Nobody seemed to care. "If you do as Tutor Mitkin tells you, there will be no more trouble," said the king.

"I heard that little whelp mewling," said Vasily. "It's just a few lashes. I don't know why you're making such a fuss."

The next day, Nikolai sat quietly in his chair. He broke his silence only once, when Mitkin stepped out of the room.

"I'm sorry for what happened yesterday," he told Dominik. "I will never let it happen again."

"It's what I'm here for, *moi tsarevich*. Please do not feel badly."

"You're here to learn to read and write and add sums, and that is all," said Nikolai. "I'll do better. I vow it."

Nikolai held to his promise. He kept silent every day after that. He did not sneak into the kitchen to steal almond paste. He did not disassemble anything valuable, run through the portrait hall, set any fires. Everyone marveled at the changes wrought in the young prince and applauded Tutor Mitkin for his ingenuity.

What they didn't know was that, amidst all the quiet and calm, Nikolai and Dominik still somehow managed to become friends. They devised their own code to communicate in their lesson books and built toy boats with working sails that they launched in the abandoned water garden where no one ever ventured. They gave each other titles that changed with every day, some grand—Dominik the Bold, Nikolai the Just, and some less so—Dominik the Farter, Nikolai the Spider Squealer. They learned that as long as they didn't trouble the calm order of the palace, no one much cared what they did, and that if they appeared to be working hard at their studies, no one bothered to check whether they were memorizing dates or trying to figure out how to build a bomb.

When he was twelve, Nikolai asked for extra reading in chemistry and Kaelish history and retired to the library every afternoon for hours of quiet study. In fact, the reading and essays took him little time at all, and as soon as he'd sped through them, he would disguise himself in peasant roughspun and sneak out of the palace to visit Dominik's family in the countryside. He worked in the fields, learned to fix handcarts and farm equipment, to milk cows and gentle horses, and when he was thirteen, he took his first slug of home-brewed spirits from a beaten tin cup.

Each night, he fell into bed exhausted, happy to have occupation for the first time in his life, and in the mornings he presented his teachers with flawless work that made them wonder if perhaps Nikolai would become a great scholar. As it turned out, the prince was not a bad child; he just had no gift for remaining idle.

He was happy, but he was not blind. Dominik's family was

granted special privileges because of their son's status at the palace, and still they barely subsisted on the crops they harvested from their farm. He saw the way their neighbors suffered beneath the burdens of taxes from both their king and the dukes who owned their lands. He heard Dominik's mother weep when her eldest son was taken for the draft, and during a particularly bad winter, he heard them whisper about their neighbor Lusha's missing child.

"What happened to Lusha's baby?" Dominik asked.

"A *khitka* came for it," his mother replied. But Nikolai and Dominik were not children anymore, and they knew better than to listen to talk of evil forest spirits.

"She drowned it herself," Dominik told Nikolai the next day. "She had stopped making milk because her family is starving."

Even so, things might have continued on that way if Vasily hadn't discovered Nikolai sneaking back into the palace one night. He was fifteen by then, and years of getting away with deception had made him careless.

"Already tumbling peasant girls," Vasily had said with a sneer. "You're worse than Father."

"Please," Nikolai had begged. "Don't tell anyone. Dominik will be punished for it. He may be sent away."

But Vasily did not hold his tongue, and the next day, new guards had been posted at every door, and Dominik was gone, barred from the palace in disgrace.

Nikolai had cornered Vasily in the lapis drawing room. "Do you understand what you've done?" he'd asked furiously.

His brother shrugged. "Your friend won't get to study with his betters, and you won't get to keep rambling in the fields like a commoner. I've done you both a favor."

"His family will lose their stipend. They may not be able to feed themselves without it." He could see his own angry face reflected at him in gleaming blue panels veined with gold. "Dominik won't be exempt from the draft next year."

"Good. The crown needs soldiers. Maybe he'll learn his place."

Nikolai looked at the brother he had once so adored, whom he had tried to emulate in everything. "You should be ashamed."

Vasily was still taller than Nikolai, still outweighed him. He jabbed a finger into Nikolai's chest and said, "You do not tell *me* what I should or shouldn't do, Sobachka. I will be a king, and you will always be Nikolai Nothing."

But while Vasily had been sparring with instructors who never pushed him too hard and who always made sure to let the future king win, Nikolai had been spending his days roughhousing with peasants who didn't know whose nose they were bloodying.

Nikolai snatched Vasily's finger and twisted. His brother yelped and fell to the floor. He seemed impossibly small.

"A king never kneels, brother."

He left Vasily clutching his sprained finger and his wounded pride.

Again, Nikolai vowed he would make things right with Dominik, though this time it would be harder. He began by devising ways to funnel money to his friend's family. But to do more, he would need influence, something his brother possessed simply by virtue of being born first.

Since Nikolai could not be *important*, he turned his clever mind to the task of becoming charming. His mother was vain, so he paid her compliments. He dressed impeccably in colors that suited her tastes, and whenever he visited her, he made sure to bring her a small gift—a box of sweets, orchids from the hothouse. He pleased her friends with amusing gossip, recited bits of doggerel, and imitated his father's ministers with startling accuracy. He became a favorite at the queen's salons, and when he didn't make an appearance, her ladies were known to exclaim, "Where is that darling boy?"

With his father, Nikolai spoke of hunting and horseflesh, subjects about which he cared nothing but that he knew his father loved. He praised his father's witty conversation and astute observations and developed a gift for making the king feel both wise and worldly.

He did not stop with his parents. Nikolai introduced himself to the members of his father's cabinet and asked them flattering questions about statecraft and finance. He wrote to military commanders to commend them on victories and to inquire about the strategies they'd deployed. He corresponded with gunsmiths and shipwrights and applied himself to learning languages—the one thing at which he did not particularly excel—so that he could address them in their own tongues. When Dominik's other brother was sent to the front, Nikolai used every bit of sway he had to get him reassigned to a place where the fighting was light. And by then, he had considerable sway.

He did it because he liked learning the puzzle of each person. He did it because it felt good to feel his influence and understanding grow. But above all else, he did it because he knew he needed to rescue his country. Nikolai had to save Ravka from his own family.

As was tradition among noblemen, Vasily accepted his officer's commission and treated his military service as symbolic. Nikolai joined the infantry. He endured basic training with Dominik at Poliznaya, and they traveled together to their first assignment. Dominik was there when Nikolai took his first bullet, and Nikolai was there when Dominik fell at Halmhend, never to rise again.

On that battlefield, heavy with black smoke and the acrid scent of gunpowder, Nikolai had shouted for a medik, a Grisha healer, anyone to help them. But no one came. He was not a king's son then, just one more voice crying out in the carnage.

Dominik made Nikolai promise to take care of his family, to make sure his mother knew he'd died well, and then he said, "Do you know the story of Andrei Zhirov?"

"The revolutionary?"

Zhirov had been a radical in Nikolai's grandfather's time.

A grin ghosted over Dominik's blood-flecked lips. "When they tried to hang him for treason, the rope broke and he rolled into the ditch the soldiers had dug for his grave."

Nikolai tried to smile. "I never heard that story."

Dominik nodded. "*This country*, Zhirov shouted. *They can't even hang a man right.*"

Nikolai shook his head. "Is that true?"

"I don't know," said Dominik. A wet sound came from his chest as he struggled to breathe. "I just know they shot him anyway."

Soldiers did not cry. Princes did not weep. Nikolai knew this. But the tears fell anyway. "Dominik the Brave. Hold on a little longer."

Dominik squeezed Nikolai's hand. "This country gets you in the end, brother. Don't forget it."

"Not us," he said. But Dominik was already gone.

"I'll do better," Nikolai promised, just as he had so many years ago in Mitkin's classroom. "I'll find a way."

He had witnessed a thousand deaths since then. His nightmares had been plagued by countless other battlefields. And yet it was that promise to Dominik that haunted his waking hours. But how was he to explain any of this to Zoya, still sitting patiently at the corner of the bed, still keeping her distance?

215

He looked up at the honeycomb ceiling, blew out a long breath. "I think I can fix it," he said at last. "I've always known Ravka is broken, and I've seen the way it breaks people in return. The wars never cease. The trouble never stops. But I can't help believing that somehow, I'll find a way to outsmart all of the kings who came before and set this country right." He shook his head and laughed. "It is the height of arrogance."

"I'd expect no less of you," Zoya said, but her voice was not cruel. "Why did you send Nina away?"

"What?" The question took him by surprise—even more the rapid, breathless way Zoya had spoken the words, as if forcing them from her lips.

She did not look at him. "We almost lost her before. We barely had her back, and you sent her into danger again."

"She's a soldier," he said. "You made her one, Zoya. Sitting idle in the palace with nothing but her grief to occupy her mind was no good for her."

"But she was safe."

"And all of that safety was killing her." Nikolai watched Zoya carefully. "Can you forgive me for sending her away?"

"I don't know."

"I won't ask you to forgive me for what happened in the bell tower."

"You spoke," she said slowly. "That night in Balakirev. You said my name."

"But—" Nikolai sat up straighter. The beast had never had language before, not when he'd been infected during the war, and as far as he knew, not now that the monster had returned. When the Darkling had infected him, even in the moments when Nikolai was able to push his awareness to the fore, he hadn't been able to read, hadn't been able to communicate. It was one of the most painful elements of his transformation. "Maybe that's a good thing. Maybe my consciousness was trying to find a way through. Today—"

She shook her head. "You didn't sound like you."

"Well, in that form—"

"You sounded like *him*."

He paused. "I'm tempted to say it was fear or your imagination getting the best of you—" She glared at him. "But I'd prefer not to get slapped."

"I know it doesn't make sense. It might have been the fear or the fight, but I truly believed you wanted to kill me. You weren't just hungry. You were *eager*." Zoya clenched her fists against her thighs. "You liked frightening me."

He wanted to say that he wouldn't have hurt her, that he would have stopped the thing inside him before it could. But he refused to do either of them the dishonor of that lie.

"Is it possible?" he asked instead. "Could the Darkling's consciousness have somehow survived with his power?"

"I hope not." She unclenched her fists. "I hope there's a thorn wood waiting beneath the sands of the Fold. I hope all of this talk of magical rituals and warrior priests turns out to be more than just a fanciful tale. But if there is no cure and if this thing in you is more than just a curse the Darkling left behind, if he's trying to use you to find a way back to this world . . ." She looked at him, her blue eyes fierce in the lamplight. He sensed the deep well of loss inside her, the pain she worked so hard to hide. "I will put a bullet in your brain before I let that happen, Nikolai."

The men who had ruled Ravka had loved power more than they'd ever loved their people. It was a disease. Nikolai knew that, and he'd sworn he would not be that kind of leader, that he would not succumb. And yet, he'd never been sure that when the time came, he could step aside and give up the throne, the thing he'd fought so long and hard for. And if he let himself become more monster than man, it would mean he had failed. So he would put aside his doubt and his desires. He would try to be better. And the woman before him would make sure he protected Ravka. Even from himself.

He took her hand, pressed a kiss to her knuckles. "My ruthless Zoya, I'll load the gun myself."

13
NINA

NINA AND HANNE TOOK TURNS DOZING, shoulders pressed together, making a show of sleeping as their "guards" stood by. When both of them were in danger of giving in to exhaustion, they asked each other questions: favorite sweet, favorite book, favorite pastime. Nina learned that Hanne loved cream buns filled with vanilla custard; had a secret taste for the gruesome novels popular in Ketterdam, the gorier the better, though translations were hard to find; and that she was fond of . . . sewing.

"*Sewing?*" Nina had whispered incredulously, remembering the way Hanne had ridden into the clearing the previous night, rifle at the ready. "I thought you liked hunting and brawling and . . ." She wrinkled her nose. "Nature."

"It's a useful skill," Hanne said defensively. "Who darned your husband's socks?"

"I did, of course," Nina lied. Though soldiers were supposed to learn their way around a needle and thread, she'd never managed it. She'd always just gone with holes in her socks. "But I didn't enjoy it. The Wellmother must approve."

Hanne rested her head against the wall. Her hair had dried in thick, rosy brown waves. "You'd think that, wouldn't you? But apparently needlework is for ladies and sewing should be left to the servants. So should knitting and baking."

"You can bake?" said Nina. "You have my attention."

In the morning, Nina beamed at the men crowded into the room and insisted that they make sure to visit Lennart Bjord's house on their way through Overüt.

"Why can't we escort you now?" asked the bearded man.

"We'd be delighted, of course," Nina said through gritted teeth.

To Nina's surprise, Hanne chimed in, "We didn't think you'd want to stop over with us to do our penance with the Women of the Well. But how wonderful! I understand the sisters there are happy to perform the *skad* on any male visitors for only a small fee." Nina had read about the *skad*. Enduring it was a stamp of Fjerdan manhood but also occasionally a death sentence. It required a three-month vow of celibacy and ritual purging with lye to cleanse the spirit.

The bearded man blanched. "We'll take you to the outskirts of Gäfvalle, but then we have duties . . . uh . . . elsewhere."

"Yes," added the man with the tufty brows. "Many duties."

"Where exactly will we find Lennart Bjord's house?" another asked as he followed them outside. A thick layer of snow had covered the ground, though Nina could already see some of it melting away with the rising sun. The hard wind had dwindled to a soft breeze. The Brute must have tired himself out.

"Just head to the main square in Overüt," Nina said. "It's the grandest house on the boulevard."

"Look for the one with the biggest gables," added Hanne. "The pointiest in town."

"Is that your horse?" he said. "Where is your sidesaddle?"

"It must have been lost in the snow," said Nina, glad Hanne rode bareback and they didn't have a man's saddle to explain. "We'll just walk him to Gäfvalle."

When they were well out of view of the lodge, they mounted Hanne's horse.

"The *skad*?" Nina asked, resting her hands lightly at Hanne's lean waist as their thighs braced together.

Hanne glanced over her shoulder and cast Nina a surprisingly wicked smile. "My religious education should be good for something."

They circled back toward camp, and now that the snow had stopped they had no trouble spotting the yellow flag and Adrik's tent.

He waved to them, and Nina knew his relief that she had survived the storm was real, even as he made a great show of seeming incensed about Hanne's trousers.

"I thought the Zemeni didn't care about such things," Hanne grumbled.

"His wife is Zemeni. He's Kaelish, and he's concerned about why you were out on your own. Actually . . . what *were* you doing out here yesterday?"

Hanne tilted her face up to the sky, closing her eyes. "I needed to ride. When the weather is about to turn is the best time. The fields are empty then."

"Won't you be in trouble for spending a night away from the convent?"

"I volunteered to fetch fresh water. The Wellmother will just be glad she doesn't have to tell my father his daughter died of exposure in the middle of a storm."

"And your friends? They didn't come with you?"

Hanne kept her gaze on the white horizon. "It's a game to them. A childish bit of dress-up, a chance to be daring. For me . . ." She shrugged.

It was survival. There was something solitary in Hanne. Nina couldn't pretend to really understand it. She loved company, noise, the bustle of a crowded room. But for a girl like this? To be forever trapped in the convent, watched by the sisters, and constantly forced to perform pious Fjerdan womanhood? It was a dismal thought. Even so, Hanne's presence at the convent meant she might be a source of information about the factory. Though she was only a novitiate, she had to hear about the Springmaidens' visits up the mountain.

"Ride with us a little longer," Nina said to Hanne as she mounted her own horse.

Hanne looked like she wanted to bolt, but Nina knew the other girl didn't want to risk offense when she was still desperate to ensure Nina's silence.

"Come on," Nina urged gently. "I won't keep you long."

They set a moderate pace, Adrik trailing them with the sledge.

"How old are you anyway?" Nina asked.

Hanne's jaw set, her profile sharp against the silvery sky. "Nineteen. And yes, that's old for a novitiate."

So Nina was right; they were almost the same age. "You aren't ready to take vows." Hanne gave a curt shake of her head. "But you can't go home." Another shake of the head. "So what, then?"

Hanne said nothing, her gaze fixed on the snow. She didn't want to talk, or perhaps she felt she'd already said too much.

Nina cut her a sidelong look. "I can tell you're eager for a last chance to ride before you go back."

"Is it that obvious?"

"I can see it in the way your eyes stray to the horizon, the way you hold the reins." Nina hesitated, then added, "The trick of acting is to believe the lie yourself, at least a little. Acting begins in the body. If you want to convince anyone of anything, you start with the way the body moves. It tells a thousand stories before you ever open your mouth."

"And what stories am I telling?"

"Are you sure you want to know?" It was one thing to see the truth of someone. It was another to speak it back to them.

"Go on," said Hanne, but her hands were tight on the reins.

"You're strong, but you're afraid of anyone seeing it, so you hunch and try to make yourself smaller. You're only at ease when you think no one is watching. But then . . ." She reached out and tapped Hanne's thigh. "Then you're glorious."

Hanne shot her a wary glance. "I know what I look like."

Do you? Nina would have liked to tell Hanne that she could stroll into Os Alta, all six feet of her, with her chestnut-dipped-in-strawberry-syrup hair and her copper-coin eyes, and a thousand Ravkan courtiers would write songs to her beauty. Nina might be the first. But that would lead to a few questions.

At least she could offer Hanne something. "I won't tell anyone what you are."

Hanne's eyes turned hard. "Why? They'd reward you. Informing on Grisha carries a weight of silver. Why would you be that kind?"

I'm not being kind. I'm earning your trust. But I won't sentence you to death if I can help it.

"Because you dove in to save my life when you might have ridden by," Nina said, then took the leap. "And because I don't believe that Grisha power makes you evil."

"It's a sin," Hanne hissed. "It's poison. If I could rid myself of it, I would."

"I understand," said Nina, though every part of her wanted to protest. "But you can't. So the question is whether you want to hate what you are and put yourself at greater risk of discovery, or accept this thing inside you and learn to control it." *Or abandon this Saintsforsaken country altogether.*

"What if . . . what if I only make it stronger?"

"I don't think it works that way," said Nina. "But I know that if Grisha don't use their power, eventually they begin to sicken."

Hanne swallowed. "I like using it. I hate myself every time, but I just want to do it again."

"There are some," Nina said cautiously, "who believe that such power is a gift from Djel and not some kind of calamity."

"Those are the whisperings of heretics and heathens." When Nina didn't reply, Hanne said, "You never told me what happened to your sister."

"She learned to contain her power and found happiness. She's married now and lives on the Ravkan border with her handsome husband."

"Really?"

No, not really. Any sister of mine would be a Heartrender waging war on your ignorant, shortsighted government. "Yes," Nina lied. "I remember a great deal from the lessons she received. There was some concern that I might have a latent . . . corruption, and so I was taught alongside her. I may be able to help you learn to control your power too."

"Why would you ever take such a risk?"

Because I intend to pump you for information while I do it and knock some sense into you at the same time. After all, Nina had managed to get through to one thickheaded Fjerdan. Maybe she'd prove to have a talent for it.

"Because someone once did the same for my sister," she said.

"It's the least I can do. But we'll need a pretext for spending time together at the convent. How do you feel about learning Zemeni?"

"My parents would prefer I continue to work on my Kerch."

"I don't know Kerch," Nina lied.

"I don't wish to owe you a debt," Hanne protested.

She's afraid of her power, Nina thought. *But I can take away that fear.*

"We'll find a way for you to make it up to me," she said. "Promise. Now go, get a last ride in before the next snow comes."

Hanne looked startled, almost disbelieving. Then she dug her heels into her horse's flanks and took off at a hard gallop, body low, face turned to the wind, as if she and the animal were one, a hybrid creature born of the wild. How few people had been kind to Hanne that she would be so surprised by a small gesture of generosity?

Except you're not being generous, Nina reminded herself as she nudged her own mount forward. *You're not being kind.* She was going to use Hanne. If she could help her in the process, so be it. But Nina's duty was to the lost girls on the mountain, the women in their graves. *Justice.*

All Nina could do was throw this girl a rope. Hanne would have to be the one to seize it.

An hour later, Nina and Adrik entered the stables at the convent. They'd been gone one night, but to Nina it seemed as if a long season had passed. Her mind felt overburdened with emotion and new information. Matthias. Trassel. Hanne. The women buried at the factory. The puncture marks throbbing on her forearm. She'd been attacked by wolves, for Saints' sake. She needed a hot bath, a plate of waffles, and about twelve hours of sleep.

Leoni waved when she saw them. She was perched on a low stool in a shadowy corner of the stables, hidden from the curious eyes of passersby by a few of the crates Nina and Adrik had left behind. She'd set up a small camp stove, and the space around her was littered with the pots and glass vials she must have been using to test the water samples.

"I thought you'd be back sooner," she said with a smile.

Adrik led his horse to a stall. "Nina decided to have an adventure."

"A good one?" asked Leoni.

"An informative one," said Nina. "How long have you been at this?"

"All night," Leoni admitted. She didn't look well.

"Let's go to town for lunch," said Nina. "I can't handle another meal of convent mush."

Leoni stood, then braced her hand against the wall. "I—" Her eyes rolled back in her head and she swayed sharply.

"Leoni!" Nina cried as she and Adrik rushed to her side, just managing to reach her before she collapsed. They laid her gently back beside the camp stove. She was soaked in sweat and her skin felt like fire.

Leoni's eyes fluttered open. "That was unexpected," she said, and then she had the gall to smile.

"This is no time to be in a good mood," said Adrik. "Your pulse is racing and you're burning up."

"I'm not dead, though."

"Stop looking on the bright side and tell me when this started."

"I think I botched the testing," said Leoni, her voice thready. "I was trying to pull the pollutants from the samples, isolate them. I may have absorbed some into my body. I told you poisons are tricky work."

"I'll take you back to the dormitories," said Nina. "I can get clean water—"

"No. I don't want the Springmaidens getting suspicious."

"We can tend to her here," said Adrik. "Get her settled behind the sledge. I can make a fire and brew clean water for tea."

"There's a tincture of charcoal in my kit," said Leoni. "Add a few drops. It will absorb the toxins."

Nina arranged a bed of blankets for Leoni out of sight of the main courtyard and tried to make her comfortable there.

"There's something else," Leoni said as she lay back.

Nina did not like the gray tinge to her skin or the way her eyelids fluttered. "Just rest. It can wait."

"The Wellmother came to see me."

"What happened?" Adrik said, kneeling beside her with a steaming cup of tea. "Here, try to take a sip. Did one of the novitiates talk about seeing us in the woods?"

"No, one of them died."

Nina stilled. "The girl who fell from her horse?"

"I didn't realize her injuries were so serious," said Adrik.

"They weren't," said Leoni, sipping slowly. "I think it was the river. She was in the water for a while, and she had an open wound."

"All Saints," Adrik said. "What the hell are they doing up at that factory?"

"I don't know, but—" Nina hesitated, then plowed ahead. "But there are graves all over that mountain. Behind the reservoir, all over the factory yards. I felt them everywhere."

"What?" said Adrik. "Why didn't you tell us? How do you know?"

Leoni's eyes had closed. Her speeding pulse seemed to have slowed a bit—a good sign.

"Is there more clean water?" asked Nina. "We should try to ease the fever. And will you see if there's some carbolic in her kit?"

"Why?" Adrik asked as he fetched his canteen and the disinfectant. "Is she wounded?"

"No, I am. I got bitten by a wolf last night."

"Of course you did."

Nina shrugged off her coat, revealing her torn and bloodied sleeve.

"Wait," said Adrik. "You're serious?" He sat down beside Leoni and rubbed his temples with his fingers. "One soldier poisoned, another attacked by wolves. This mission is going swimmingly."

Nina pulled a length of cloth from the sledge and tore it in two. She used one half to make a compress for Leoni and the other to clean and bind the wound on her arm.

"Then that girl Hanne rescued you from a wolf attack?" Adrik asked.

"Something like that." Nina wasn't ready to talk about Trassel. The last thing she needed was Adrik's skepticism. "I think it's possible there was *parem* in the bite."

"*What?*"

Nina glanced at Leoni, whose eyelids fluttered. "I can't be sure, but the wolves weren't behaving normally. It *felt* like *parem*."

"Then your addiction—"

Nina shook her head. "I'm okay so far." That wasn't entirely true. Even the suggestion of *parem* was enough to make her feel the pull of that animal hunger. But the edge of need seemed duller than she would have expected.

"Saints," said Adrik, leaning forward. "If it's in the water and Leoni was dosed with it—"

"Leoni isn't acting like a Grisha exposed to *parem*. She would be clawing at the walls, desperate for another dose." Nina knew that all too well. "But her other symptoms are similar to exposure, and enough *parem* could kill someone without Grisha powers, like the novitiate."

"It wasn't *parem*," Leoni mumbled. "I don't think."

"I thought you were asleep."

"I am," said Leoni. "There's something corrosive in the water."

"Can you drink some more tea?" asked Adrik.

She nodded and managed to push up to her elbows. "I haven't isolated it yet. Why didn't you tell us about the graves when you found them, Nina?"

"You're sure you don't want to go back to sleep?" Nina asked, then sighed. She looked down at the folded compress in her hands. "I don't know why. I think . . . They led me to the eastern entrance."

"*Who* led you?"

Nina cleared her throat and patted Leoni's brow gently with the cloth. "I heard the dead . . . speak. I heard them all the way back in Elling."

"Okay," Leoni said cautiously. "What exactly did they say?"

"They need our help." *My* help.

"The dead," repeated Adrik. "Need our help."

"I realize I sound like I've gone loopy, but we need to get inside that factory. And I think I know someone who can help."

Nina brought Leoni back to the dormitories before nightfall and got her tucked into bed. Her fever had broken and she was already feeling better—further proof that whatever she'd found in the water was not *parem*. So what was wrong with those wolves, and what had been in their bite? And what had killed the novitiate?

She took a plate of kitchen scraps out to the woods and set them at the base of a tree in the silly hope that Trassel might find his way to her again. They'd probably be eaten by some ungrateful rodent.

Standing at the edge of the forest, Nina looked up at the factory, its lights glowing gold in the gathering dusk, the windows of the eastern wing dark. She thought of the twisting roots of Djel's ash, carved into the walls of the reservoir.

There's poison in this place. She could almost taste it, bitter on her tongue. *But just how deep does it go?*

The next morning, Nina was pleased to find a summons to the Wellmother's office had been slid beneath their door. Nina was to meet with her and Hanne after morning prayers to discuss the possibility of language lessons. So Hanne did want to learn more about her Grisha gifts—even if it was only to control them.

Of course, Adrik had been wary of her plan.

"We're better off using our time to gather intelligence here and in the neighboring towns," he complained. "Fjerda is gearing up for something. With the right information, our forces may be able to waylay a wagon or shipment or shut this place down entirely, but not if the Fjerdans catch wind of our activities and move their operations. You don't know how easy it is to ruin your cover, Nina. This is a dangerous game."

Nina wanted to scream. She'd been a spy for Zoya Nazyalensky on the Wandering Isle. She'd spent a year on her own in Ketterdam doing jobs for Kaz Brekker. She'd infiltrated the Ice Court as a girl from the Menagerie. She might be new to this particular game, but she'd played for high stakes plenty of times.

"I can manage this, Adrik," she said as calmly as she could. "You know she's our best possible asset. *We* can find out what's happening in that factory. We don't need someone else to do it."

"What do we really know about this girl?"

"She's Grisha and she's miserable. Aren't we here to save people exactly like her?"

"From what you've told me, she doesn't want rescue."

"Maybe I'll change her mind. And in the meantime, I can get access to the rest of the convent." Nina and Leoni were quartered in a room abutting the kitchens and locked off from the bulk of the building and the dormitories. "The Springmaidens are the only locals allowed into the factory. I may actually be able to figure out a way to get us inside."

"You'll take no action without my say-so," said Adrik. "And first you have to get past the Wellmother."

Nina left Adrik and Leoni in the stables and crossed the courtyard to the chapel, passing through the heavy door covered in its elaborate knots of ash bough. The sweet, loamy scent of the timber walls enveloped her, and she took a moment to let her eyes adjust to the gloom. The air was cold and still, the pews lit by the glow of lanterns and weak sunlight from a few slender windows set high above the transept. There was no altar, no painted scene of Saints—instead a massive tree sprawled across the apse of the chapel, its roots extending to the first row of pews. Djel's ash, fed by the Wellspring.

Whose prayers do you hear? Nina wondered. *Do you hear the words of soldiers? Of Fjerdan Grisha locked in Jarl Brum's cells?* The whispers in her head seemed to sigh—in regret? In longing? She didn't know. She smoothed her skirts and hurried down the side aisle to the Wellmother's office.

"Enke Jandersdat," the older woman said when Nina entered, addressing her by the title *widow*. "Hanne tells me you're willing to offer lessons in Zemeni. I hope you realize the convent cannot provide a tutor's fees."

Hanne remained silent, dressed in her pale blue pinafore and tidy white blouse, eyes on her impractical felt slippers. Her ruddy brown hair had been neatly braided and twisted into a tight corona on her head. The uniform didn't suit her. Nina had the urge to seize the pins from Hanne's braids and see all that glorious hair come down again.

"Of course," said Nina. "I would require no payment. All I ask is that you let us partake of your hospitality a bit longer and, if you have a copper cookpot, that my employers might have the loan of it." Leoni felt sure she could continue her experiments safely now that she knew what she was dealing with, but copper instruments would be a help.

"It seems a too-generous offer," said the Wellmother, her lips pressed into a suspicious line.

"You've caught me," said Nina, and saw Hanne's eyes widen. Saints, if Hanne intended to continue living in this wretched country, she was going to need an education in deception. Maybe an internship in Ketterdam. Nina hadn't been caught at anything, but she could tell the Wellmother thought she had some kind of angle, so she intended to give her one. "The truth is that I cannot continue my work as a guide much longer. The travel is a hardship, and at some point I need to seek a more permanent position to provide for myself."

"We do not hire outside of the order—"

"Oh no, of course, I understand. But a reference from the Wellmother of Gäfvalle would mean so much to other Fjerdans seeking a teacher for their children."

The Wellmother preened, her chin lifting. Piety was little defense against flattery. "Well. I can see how that might be a boon. We shall see what good you can do with our Hanne. It's a bit late for her to be taking up a new language. But to be frank, it's a relief to see her interested in anything that doesn't involve a muddy romp in the woods."

The Wellmother escorted them to an empty classroom and told them they were free to work until lunchtime. "I expect you to keep up with your other work, Hanne. Your father will not like it if you become a burden to this institution."

"Yes, Wellmother," she replied dutifully. But as the older woman departed, Hanne cast a black look at the door and slumped into one of the desks.

"She agreed to the lessons," said Nina. "It could be worse."

"She considers me one of her failures. Unmarried at nineteen, with no prospects and no signs of a true calling to Djel."

"Are all of the Springmaidens supposed to be called?" Nina asked as she picked up a piece of chalk and began to conjugate a Zemeni verb on the slate board that covered most of one wall.

"I don't know. Some say they are, claim to have visions. But I'm not sure Djel is interested in girls like me. Do you really mean to give up your life as a guide?"

"No," said Nina, trying to keep her chalk letters straight. "I'm not ready to live in one place just yet." Only when she said the words did she realize that might be true. She'd been restless in Ravka, and now she wondered if she might be restless anywhere she tried to settle.

Nina took a sheaf of papers from her pocket. "These are rudimentary Zemeni lessons. You'll need to copy them into your notebook so it looks like we're actually doing some work."

"You mean I'm really going to have to learn Zemeni?"

"A little. You don't have to be good at it." She gestured to the board. "We'll start with this verb: *bes adawa*." She raised her hands and planted her legs in the first stance each Grisha was taught. "To fight."

The lesson lasted two hours. Nina started just as her own education had begun at the Little Palace: by teaching Hanne to use her Heartrender power on herself.

"Have you ever tried it?" Nina asked.

"No . . . I'm not sure. Sometimes, when I can't sleep, I'll think of my heart slowing—"

Nina winced. "You're lucky you didn't put yourself into a coma."

Nina talked her through rudimentary breathing techniques and basic fighting stances. She had Hanne slow her own heart, then make it race. She touched only briefly on Grisha theory and how amplifiers worked, and she steered well clear of any talk of *jurda parem*.

"How do you know all of this?" Hanne said. Her cheeks were flushed from using her power, and her hair had escaped her braids to curl at her temples. "You really learned everything from your sister's teacher?"

Nina turned her back to erase the board and to hide her expression. It was possible she'd gotten carried away. *You don't know how easy it is to ruin your cover, Nina.* She could just imagine Adrik's singsong *What did I tell you?*

"Yes," she said. "I paid close attention. But you're also a natural. You're picking up on the work very quickly." That at least was true. Hanne had an ease with her power that was something special. But her face was troubled. "What is it?" Nina asked.

"That word. *Natural.*" Hanne ran her finger over one of the sheets where she'd scrawled the conjugation of another Zemeni verb. Her penmanship was tragic. "When I was younger, my father took me everywhere. To ride. To hunt. It was unorthodox, but he longed for a son, and I think he believed there was no harm in it. I loved it. Fighting, horsemanship, running free. But when I got older and it was time to present me at court . . . I couldn't shake it off."

And why should you have to? Nina thought. She didn't have any great love for horses and preferred not to run anywhere unless being chased, but at least she was allowed those opportunities.

Hanne folded her arms, her shoulders hunching, looking like she wanted to crumple into herself. "Unnatural, they called me. A woman's body is meant to be soft, but mine was hard. A lady is meant to take small, graceful steps, but I strode. I was a laughingstock." Hanne gazed up at the ceiling. "My father blamed himself for corrupting me. I couldn't sing or paint, but I could clean a deer and string a bow. I could build a shelter. All I wanted was to escape to the woods. Sleep beneath the stars."

"That sounds . . . well, that sounds horrible," admitted Nina. "But I think I can understand the appeal."

"I *tried* to change. I really did." Hanne shrugged. "I failed. If I fail again . . ."

Her gaze was bleak, and Nina wondered what grim future she was seeing. "What happens if you fail again?"

"The school was supposed to make me presentable. Good marriage material. If the Wellmother can't fix me, I'll never be allowed to go home, never be presented at court. It should have happened two years ago."

"Would it be so bad not to go back?"

"And never see my parents? Live like an exile?"

"Are those the choices?"

"I find a way to fit in, or I take vows and live the rest of my life out here, in service to Djel among Women of the Well." She scowled. "I wish I was an Inferni instead of a Heartrender."

"That's ridiculous," Nina said without thinking, her pride bristling. How could anyone want to be a Summoner instead of Corporalki? *Everyone knows we're the best Order.* "I mean . . . why would anyone *want* to be an Inferni?"

Hanne's bright eyes flashed as if in challenge. "So I could melt the Ice Court from the inside out. Wash the whole big mess into the sea."

Dangerous words. And maybe Nina should have pretended to be scandalized. Instead she grinned. "The grandest puddle in the world."

"Exactly," said Hanne, returning her smile, that wicked edge curling her lips

Suddenly, Nina wanted to tell Hanne all of it. *My friends and I blew a hole in the Ice Court wall! We stole a Fjerdan tank!* All Saints, did she want to *brag*? Nina gave her head a shake. *This is a chance to gain her confidence*, she told herself. *Take it.*

She sat down at the desk next to Hanne's and said, "If you could go anywhere, do anything, what would you choose for yourself?"

"Novyi Zem," Hanne said instantly. "I'd get a job, make my own money, hire myself out as a sharpshooter."

"You're that good?"

"I am," Hanne said without a hint of hesitation. "I think about it every time I ride out. Just disappearing. Making everyone believe I was lost in a storm or that I was carried away by the river."

Beastly idea. Come to Ravka. "Then why not do it? Why not just go?"

Hanne stared at her, shocked. "I couldn't do that to my parents. I couldn't shame them that way."

Nina narrowly avoided rolling her eyes. *Fjerdans and their honor.* "Of course not," she said swiftly. But she couldn't help but think of Hanne riding into the clearing, rifle raised, braids loose, a warrior born. There was gold in her, Nina could see it, the shine dimmed by years of being told there was something wrong in the way she was made. Those glimpses of the real Hanne, the Hanne who was meant to be, were driving her to distraction. *You're not here to make a new friend, Zenik*, she chastised herself. *You're here for information.*

"What if the Wellmother casts you out?" she asked.

"She won't. My father is a generous donor."

"And if she catches you flouncing about in men's trousers?" Nina prodded.

"She *won't.*"

"If my friends and I had been less generous, she might have."

Now Hanne leaned back and grinned with easy confidence. *There you are*, thought Nina. "It would have been your word against mine. I would have been dressed neatly in my pinafore and back behind the convent walls before you'd knocked on the Wellmother's door."

Interesting. Nina put all the condescension she could summon in her tone and said, "Of course you would have."

Hanne sat up straighter and jabbed her finger into the surface of the desk. "I know every step that creaks in this place. I know just where the cook stashes the key to the west kitchen door, and I have pinafores and changes of clothes stowed everywhere from the chapel to the roof. I don't get caught."

Nina held up her hands to make peace. "I just think you might consider more caution."

"Says the girl teaching me Grisha skills in the halls of Djel."

"Maybe I have less to lose than you do."

Hanne raised a brow. "Or maybe you just think you're better at being bold."

Try me, thought Nina. But all she said was, "Back to work. Let's see if you can make my heart race."

14

ZOYA

ZOYA HAD SPENT LITTLE TIME IN Kribirsk since the war. There wasn't much cause, and it held too many bad memories. In the days when Ravka had been split from its western coastline by the Shadow Fold, Kribirsk had served as the last place of safety, a town where merchants and bold travelers outfitted their journeys and where soldiers might spend a final night drinking away their terror or paying for comfort in a lover's arms before they boarded a sandskiff and were launched into the unnatural darkness of the Fold. Many never returned.

Kribirsk had been a port, but now the dark territory known as the Unsea was gone, and Kribirsk was just another small town with little to offer but a sad history.

Vestiges of the town's former glory remained—the jail and barracks, the building that had once housed officers of the First Army and where the Triumvirate had first met with Ravka's new king. But the sprawling encampment of tents and horses and soldiers was no more. It was said you could still find unspent bullets in the dust, and occasionally scraps of silk from the black pavilion where the Darkling had once held court.

Though the darkness of the Fold and the monsters that populated it were gone, the sands were not, and the shifting ground could be tricky for wagons to navigate. Merchants traversing Ravka still came to the drydocks to book passage on sandskiffs, but now guards were hired to protect cargo from marauders and thieves, not from the threat of the flesh-eating volcra that had once terrorized travelers. The monsters had vanished, and all that remained was a long, barren stretch of gray sand, eerie in its emptiness. Nothing could grow in the lifeless terrain that the Darkling's power had left behind.

The businesses of Kribirsk were the same as they'd always been— inns, brothels, outfitters—there were just fewer of them. Only the church had changed. The simple whitewashed building with its blue dome had once been dedicated to Sankt Vladimir. Now a blazing golden sun hung over the entry, a sign that the building had been reconsecrated to Sankta Alina of the Fold.

It had taken a long time for Zoya to think of Alina as anything other than a rival. She'd resented the orphan girl's gifts, envied her position with the Darkling. She hadn't understood what power meant then or the price that any of them would be forced to pay for it. After the war, Alina had chosen a life of peace and anonymity, bought with the charade of her death, but her name and her legend had only grown. Zoya was surprised to find she liked seeing Alina's name on churches, liked hearing it spoken in prayers. Ravka had given too much of its love to men like the Darkling, the Apparat, even the Lantsov kings. They owed a little of it to an orphan girl with no dress sense.

Though the symbol crowning the church's entry had changed, its outer walls remained the same. They were covered in the names of the dead, victims of the Darkling's slaughter of Novokribirsk, Kribirsk's sister city, the town that had once lain almost directly across the Shadow Fold. Sun and time had faded the painted script so that it would be nearly illegible to anyone who did not hold the names of the lost in their hearts.

One day those words will fade to nothing, Zoya thought. The people who mourned the dead would be gone too. *I'll be gone. Who will remember them then?* Zoya knew that if she walked to the southwest corner, she would find the names of Liliyana Garin and her ward. But she would not make that walk, would not trace those clumsy letters with her fingertips.

After all this time, she still had not found an end to her grief. It was a dark well, an echoing place into which she'd once cast a stone, sure that it would strike bottom and she would stop hurting. Instead, it just kept falling. She forgot about the stone, forgot about the well, sometimes for days or even weeks at a time. Then she would think Liliyana's name, or her eye would pause on the little boat painted on her bedroom wall, its two-starred flag frozen in the wind. She'd sit down to write a letter and realize she had no one to write to, and the quiet that surrounded her became the silence of the well, of the stone still falling.

No, she would not turn that corner of the church. She would not touch her fingers to those names. Not today. Zoya nudged her horse's flanks with her heels and turned her mount back toward town.

Zoya, Tamar, and Nikolai took up residence in a boardinghouse inauspiciously named the Wreck, which had been built to look like a large ship run aground. Zoya remembered it bustling with soldiers and merchants in its heyday and the terrible accordion player who had played from morning until night on the stoop to lure travelers from the road. At least he was long gone.

Tolya was billeted across the street with the monk. Together, the twins were too noticeable, and this particular stop on the royal itinerary was being kept a secret. They'd sent the great golden coach and its glittering outriders to Keramzin. There, the party would be welcomed by the couple who ran the orphanage and who they knew could be trusted with the secrets of the crown.

Zoya found her bath lukewarm and the meal of squirrel and stewed turnip unappetizing, but she was too tired to complain. She slept and dreamed of monsters.

In the morning, she woke Nikolai with the red bottle of stimulant, and they settled in his sitting room to tackle the business of the day. Later, they might find an ancient thorn wood buried in the sands, but Ravka required constant attention, and this morning that meant matters of state could not wait.

Zoya spent a few hours going over her correspondence. She sent Genya and David a coded missive with the essentials of the *khergud* attack and instructions to double the sorties patrolling the skies around Os Alta. The capital was exposed, and she hated to think what might happen if the *khergud* attacked the Grisha school. Any assault on the Little Palace would be considered an overt act of war, and she doubted the Shu would dare it, but Zoya didn't intend to take chances.

She sent similar missives to Grisha stationed throughout Ravka, with instructions to be vigilant night and day and requests that their First Army liaisons post additional soldiers in towers and high lookouts. It would have been more expedient to have the Grisha at the outposts make the requests directly, but protocol was protocol. Some part of her would always resent this dance, but these gestures existed to preserve the dignity of the people involved. The Grisha did not want to be vulnerable, and the First Army wanted to maintain their authority.

Once Nikolai had breakfasted, they worked side by side, largely in silence, only occasionally consulting each other.

"One of Tamar's sources claims there are rumors a member of the Shu royal guard wants to defect," said Zoya, reading through the file Tamar had left her.

"A member of the Tavgharad? That would be quite the coup."

Zoya nodded. "The party will be the perfect opportunity to make contact."

"Are you saying my Festival of Autumn Nonsense was a brilliant idea after all?"

"I said no such thing. But we'll make sure you have plenty of time to flirt with the Shu princess and that Tolya and Tamar have a chance to interact with the royal guard."

"For the prospect of that kind of intelligence, I can certainly develop a passion for the playing of the *khatuur.*"

"What if it's only twelve strings and not eighteen?"

"I'll endeavor to hide my disdain."

Zoya set the file aside and said, "Would you have Pensky requisition more soldiers at Arkesk for lookouts?" He was the First Army general Zoya dealt with most. "I think they could be particularly open to *khergud* attack."

"Why don't you write him yourself?"

"Because I've sent him two troop requests in the last month, so it would be better if this ask came from you."

Nikolai grunted, a pen between his teeth, then yanked it free and said, "I'll write to Pensky. But does that mean we should reassign the Grisha near Halmhend? And can you requisition me a napkin? I've spilled tea all over this note to the Kaelish ambassador."

Zoya sent two napkins fluttering over the side table and dropped them into a pile beside Nikolai's elbow. She was grateful for the quiet this morning, the easy return to routine.

There were times like this, when they worked side by side, when the rhythm between them was so easy that her mind would turn traitor. She would look at the tousle of Nikolai's gilded head bent over some correspondence or his long fingers tearing into a roll and she would wonder what it would be like when he finally married, when he belonged to someone else, and she lost these moments of peace.

Zoya would still be Nikolai's general, but she knew it would be different. He would have someone else to tease and lean on and argue over the herring with. She'd made men fall in love with her before, when she was young and cruel and liked to test her power. Zoya did not desire; she was desired. And that was the way she liked it. It was galling to admit that she wasn't at all sure she could make Nikolai want her, and more galling to think that a part of her longed to try, to know if he was as impervious to her beauty as he seemed, to know if someone like him, full of hope and light and optimistic endeavor, could love someone like her.

But even when her mind played these unkind games, Zoya knew better than to let them go too far. Her careful dealings with the First Army, her monitoring of Grisha matters all over Ravka, made it perfectly clear that—even if Nikolai had seen her as something more than an able commander—Ravka would never accept a Grisha queen. Alina had been different, a Saint, treasured by the people, a symbol of hope for the future. But to Ravka's common folk, Zoya would always be the raven-haired witch who ruled the storms. Dangerous. Untrustworthy. They would never give up their precious golden son to a girl born of lightning and thunder and common blood. *And I wouldn't have it any other way.* A crown was well and good, and sentiment made for moving melodramas, but Zoya had learned the power of fear long ago.

A sharp rap at the door drew Zoya from her reverie, and she found Tamar and Tolya in the hall—their uniforms concealed beneath heavy, nondescript coats—bracketing Yuri, his earnest face half hidden by a scarf. They would all travel to the Fold in disguise: high-collared coats and cloaks of peasant roughspun.

"Why can't we ever go undercover as wealthy people?" Zoya complained, taking the hideous cloak Tamar had brought her and fastening it over her *kefta*.

"A silk merchant and his glamorous model?" Nikolai asked.

"Yes. I'll even play the merchant. You can be my handsome muse."

"Zoya, did you just call me handsome?"

"All part of the act, Your Highness."

He clutched his heart in mock despair and turned to the others. "We'll take our first trip slowly. Do we know exactly where we're going? The Fold doesn't have many landmarks."

"The followers of the Starless Saint will be waiting," said the monk, practically dancing. "They know where he fell. They remember."

"Do they?" Zoya retorted. "I don't recall any of them being there. If they had been, they would remember all of the names of the dead, not just your precious Darkling."

"I was at the drydocks earlier," said Tamar quickly. "There's talk of a new encampment about ten miles due west."

"I told you," said Yuri.

Nikolai must have sensed Zoya's desire to snap every bone in the monk's body, because he stepped between them and said, "Then that's where we'll start. Yuri, you will remain with us and you will not interact with the pilgrims."

"But—"

"I do not want you recognized. I don't want any of us recognized. Keep in mind what's at stake here." He placed a hand on Yuri's shoulder and shamelessly added, "The very soul of a nation."

At least if Zoya vomited it would be on this awful cloak.

A skiff had been readied for them at the drydocks—a wide, flat craft on chubby sled rails designed to bear the weight of cargo over the sands. These old vehicles were built for silence since sound had risked drawing the attention of the volcra—and constructed cheaply since they were so frequently destroyed. The skiff was little more than a platform with a sail.

Two junior Squallers stood at the ready by the mast, looking eager and ludicrously young in their blue *kefta*. It was an easy assignment for students preparing to graduate—far from the fighting but where they could practice their languages and get the feel of following commands. Tolya stood at the prow. At the stern, Zoya and Yuri flanked Nikolai. Tamar stood guard at the monk's other side, in case he was compelled to try to commune with his fellow zealots.

Zoya kept her shawl up but watched the Squallers closely as they lifted their arms and summoned air currents to fill the sails. It was hard not to think of her early days in the Second Army, of the terror of her first crossing, surrounded by darkness, holding her breath and waiting to hear the shriek of the volcra, the flap of their wings as they came seeking prey.

"They're listing left," she muttered to Nikolai as the skiff surged forward over the sand.

"They're doing their best, Zoya."

Their best won't keep them alive, she wanted to bark. "I watched my friends die on these sands. The least these young dullards can do is learn to pilot a half-empty skiff across them."

Saints, she hated being here. Nearly three years had passed since the destruction of the Fold, but a strange quiet remained at its borders, the stillness of a battleground where good soldiers had fallen. The glass skiffs the Darkling had used to enter the Fold had long since been plundered and picked apart, but the wreckage of other vessels

245

lay scattered over the many miles of the Fold. Some people treated the snapped masts and broken hulls as shrines to the dead. But others had scavenged what they could from them—timber, canvas, whatever cargo the lost skiffs had carried.

And yet as they traveled deeper into the gray sands, Zoya wondered if the reverent quiet at the edges of the Unsea had been pure imagination, the ghosts of her past clouding her vision. Because as they journeyed farther west, the Fold came alive. Everywhere she looked, she saw altars dedicated to the Sun Saint. Ramshackle businesses had sprouted like pox over the sands: inns and restaurants, chapels, peddlers selling holy cures, pieces of Alina's bones, pearls from her *kokoshnik*, scraps of her *kefta*. It made Zoya's skin crawl.

"They've always liked us better dead," she said. "No one knows what to do with a living Saint."

But Nikolai's gaze was trained on the horizon. "What is that?"

Far ahead, Zoya could see a dark blot. It looked like a shadow cast by a bank of heavy cloud, but the sky above was clear. "A lake?"

"No," said Yuri. "A miracle."

Zoya considered pushing him over the railing. "If I pointed to a leaky faucet you'd say it was a miracle."

Yet as they drew closer, Zoya saw the shape on the horizon was not a body of water but a gleaming black disk of stone, at least a mile across, perfectly round and shiny as a mirror.

A rattletrap village of tents and makeshift shelters had grown up around the stone circle. There were no signs of the Sun Saint here, no golden icons or images of Alina with her white hair and antler collar. Zoya saw only black banners painted with the two circles representing the sun in eclipse. The Darkling's symbol.

"*This* is the place where the Starless One fell," said Yuri, reverence in his voice.

Was it? Zoya couldn't be sure. The battle was a memory of violet flames and fear. Harshaw bleeding on the ground, the skies full of volcra.

"Centuries before," Yuri continued, "the Starless One stood on this very spot and challenged the rules that bound the universe. Only he dared to try to re-create the experiments of the Bonesmith, Ilya Morozova. Only he looked to the stars and demanded more."

"He dared," said Zoya. "And the result of his failure was a tear in the world."

"The Shadow Fold," said Nikolai. "The one place where his power became meaningless. The Saints do love a bit of dramatic irony."

Zoya cut her hand through the air in irritation. "Not the Saints. This was no divine retribution."

Yuri turned pleading eyes upon her. "How can you be sure? How can you know that the Fold was not a challenge the Saints set before the Darkling?"

"You said it yourself. He defied the rules that bind the universe, that govern our power. He violated the natural order."

"But who created the natural order?" insisted Yuri. "Who is responsible for the making at the heart of the world?"

How she envied this boy's certainty, his visions, his ridiculous belief that pain had a purpose, that the Saints had some kind of plan.

"Why does it have to be a who?" demanded Zoya. "Maybe this is simply how the world functions, how it works. What matters is that when Grisha overreach their power, there is a price. The lesson is built into all our stories, even the tales told to little otkazat'sya children like you."

Yuri shook his head stubbornly. "The Black Heretic chose this place with care. There has to be a reason."

"Maybe he liked the view," she shot back.

"Still—" said Nikolai.

She planted her hands on her hips. "Not you too."

"There are places like this all over Ravka," he said, voice placating. "Places that have served old gods and new Saints, that have been built and ruined and rebuilt, because people returned to them again and again to worship." Nikolai shrugged. "Perhaps they're drawn to power."

"Or good weather or cheap building materials," Zoya said in exasperation. She'd had about enough. As soon as the skiff came to a halt, she leapt from the railing.

"Make sure Yuri stays here," she heard Nikolai instruct the twins as he jumped down after her.

"Welcome, fellow pilgrims!" said a man wearing black robes and a beatific smile.

"Why, thank you," said Zoya. Nikolai cast her a warning glance that she happily disregarded. "Are you in charge here?"

"I am just one more among the faithful."

"And you put your faith in the Darkling?"

"In the Saint without Stars." The pilgrim gestured to the gleaming disk of stone. It showed no imperfections, blacker than any night. "Behold the signs of his return."

Zoya ignored the shiver that slid up her spine. "And can you tell me why you worship him?"

The man smiled again, clearly elated at the opportunity. "He loved Ravka. He wanted only to make us strong and save us from weak kings."

"Weak kings," mused Nikolai. "Almost as vexing as weak tea."

But Zoya was in no mood for nonsense. "He loved Ravka," she repeated. "And what is Ravka? *Who* is Ravka?"

"All of us. Peasant and prince alike."

"Of course. Did the Darkling love my aunt who died beside

countless innocent civilians in Novokribirsk so that he could show the world his might?"

"Leave them be," Nikolai murmured, laying a hand on her arm.

She shook him off. "Did he love the girl he forced to commit those murders? What about the girl he tossed into the old king's bed for his own purposes, then mutilated when she dared to challenge him? Or the woman he blinded for failing to offer him unswerving devotion?" Who would speak for Liliyana, for Genya and Alina and Baghra if she did not? *Who will speak for me?*

But the pilgrim remained unshaken, his smile steady, gentle, maddening. "Great men are often the victims of the lies told by their enemies. What Saint has walked among us who did not face hardships in this life? We have been taught to fear darkness—"

"A lesson you failed to learn."

"But we are all alike in the dark," said the pilgrim. "Rich man, poor man."

"A rich man can afford to keep the lights on," Nikolai said mildly. He gave Zoya a hard yank on her arm, dragging her back to the skiff and away from the pilgrims.

"Let go of me," she seethed. "Where is the shrine to my aunt? To Saint Harshaw? To Sergei or Marie or Fedyor? Who will worship them and light candles in their names?" She felt the unwelcome prickle of tears in the back of her throat and swallowed them down. These people did not deserve her tears, only her anger.

"Zoya," Nikolai whispered. "If you keep drawing attention, we may be recognized."

He was right; she knew that. But this place, seeing that symbol on those banners . . . It was all too much. She whirled on Nikolai. "Why do they love him?"

"They love strength," he said. "Living in Ravka has meant living in fear for so long. He gave them hope."

"Then we have to give them something more."

"We will, Zoya." He cocked his head to the side. "I don't like it when you look at me that way. As if you've stopped believing."

"All those lives lost, all we've worked for, and these fools are so ready to rewrite history." She shook her head, wishing she could force out the memories, uproot them forever. "You don't know, Nikolai. The battle at the Spinning Wheel. Seeing Adrik's arm torn from his body. His blood . . . it soaked the deck. We couldn't get it clean. The people we lost here. On these sands. You don't remember. You were the demon then. But I remember it all."

"I remember enough," he said, and there was an edge to his voice she hadn't heard before. He laid his hands on her shoulders, his grip hard. "I remember, Zoya, and I promise I won't let the world forget. But I need you to come back to me. I need my general beside me now."

Zoya drew in a shaking breath, trying to find some calm, to stop the images from coming. *Don't look back. Don't look back at me.* She saw Liliyana's teacup sitting on the counter at her shop, smelled the warm orange scent of bergamot.

She couldn't breathe. Her head felt heavy and blurred as she let Nikolai pull her onto the skiff. The junior Squallers had already left their post to get a better look at the black stone. No discipline at all.

Nikolai signaled to the twins. "Tolya, Tamar, corral those Squallers and get them back here. Then take opposite sides of this big shiny eyesore and walk the perimeter. Find out what you can about when it appeared and how many people come to the site every day. We'll need to deal with them if we actually want to dig nearby. Zoya and I will take the skiff farther west with Yuri. We'll reconvene to decide next steps in an hour's time."

"I can help," Yuri protested, watching Tolya and Tamar leap down to the sands. "I can talk to the pilgrims——"

"You'll remain with us. We'll travel a little farther on and decide what to do. I don't know how we're going to dig here without these people getting involved."

Yuri pushed his spectacles up his long nose, and Zoya wanted to break them in two. "Perhaps we *should* get them involved," he said. "Or we could claim we're searching for relics from the battle for a museum—"

"That may only incense them," said Nikolai. "They'll claim the site is holy and can't be touched, or they'll want to dig themselves to locate objects for their altars."

Zoya didn't care what the pilgrims wanted. If she had to look at them and their black banners another minute, she thought she might well lose her mind.

She pushed up her sleeves, feeling the weight of the amplifier at her wrist. "Enough politicking. Enough diplomacy. They want darkness? I'll give it to them."

"Zoya—" warned Nikolai.

But her anger had slipped its leash, and she could feel the storm rise. All it took was the barest twist of her wrists and the sands shifted, forming ripples, then dunes, rising higher and higher. She saw Genya huddled in her black shawl, her arms thick with scars. She saw Harshaw dead in the sand, his red hair like a fallen flag. Zoya's nostrils were full of the scent of bergamot and blood. The wind howled, as if it were speaking her rage.

"Zoya, stop this," Nikolai hissed.

The pilgrims shouted to one another, taking shelter, huddling together. She liked their fear. She let the sand form shapes, a shining sun, the face of a woman—Liliyana's face, though no one there would know it. The wind screamed and the sands rose in a tidal wave, blocking out the sun and plunging the camp into darkness.

The pilgrims scattered and ran.

"There's your Saint," she said with grim satisfaction.

"*Enough*, Zoya," said Nikolai in the deep shadow her power had cast. "That is an order."

She let the sands drop. A wave of dizziness struck her, and for a moment the world seemed to flicker and warp. Her knees buckled and she fell hard to the deck of the skiff, frightened by the surge of nausea that had overcome her.

Nikolai seized her arm. "Are you——?" And then he seemed to stumble too, his eyes rolling back in his head.

"Nikolai?"

Yuri vomited over the railing.

"What just happened?" she said, pushing to her feet. "Why——" But the words died on her lips.

Zoya turned in a slow circle. The pilgrim camp was gone, the tents, the gleaming stone. The blue sky had bled away to a gray twilight.

"Where are Tolya and Tamar?" said Nikolai.

Tolya, Tamar, the Squallers, everyone who had been standing near the skiff was gone too.

"Where are they?" Yuri said. "What happened to them? What did you do?"

"I didn't do anything!" Zoya protested. "It was a little storm. No one was in any danger."

"Am I having some kind of episode?" said Nikolai, staring into the distance. "Or are you seeing this too?"

Zoya turned to the west. Above them loomed a palace wrought from the same bone-colored sand as the Fold. But it was less a palace than a city, a massive structure that rose in arches and peaks, clouds roiling around its highest spires. There was something in its construction, in its sweeping scale, that reminded her of the bridge at Ivets.

A shriek sounded from somewhere in the distance. *Volcra*, Zoya thought, though she knew that couldn't be.

"It's a miracle," said Yuri, falling to his knees.

Another shriek sounded, then another, and a rumble of thunder followed as dark shapes seemed to break from the palace, moving toward them at incredible speed.

"It's not a miracle," said Nikolai, reaching for his revolvers. "It's a trap."

THE WITCH
IN THE
WOOD

15
NIKOLAI

NIKOLAI HAD SEEN MANY ASTONISHING things—the fog ponies of the Zemeni frontier, said to be so fast that when they ran they became invisible; a sea serpent thrashing its way through the northern ice; the world unspooling before him as he rode the winds with the wings of a monster at his back—but his eyes could not make sense of what he saw swooping toward him in the sky.

Yuri was on his knees, praying. Zoya had her arms raised, and Nikolai could already feel the sand whipping around the skiff as she summoned the wind to their defense.

As soon as he'd heard that shriek in the air, Nikolai had drawn his revolvers and prepared to face the volcra. He had expected shadow monsters or some new embodiment of the Darkling's power. Hell, maybe some part of him had expected the Darkling himself, the Starless Saint resurrected, come to plague them all with charisma and ill intent.

Instead he saw . . . bees, a vast swath of them, moving through a sky the color of porridge, shifting and clustering into what might have been the shape of a woman. Behind the swarm, a grotesque loped over the sand, a massive body that kept forming and re-forming—two heads, then three; a thousand arms; a humped back with a spine that twisted in sinuous ridges; ten, twenty, thirty long, spindly legs moving in tandem. The forms were human one moment, animal the next—thick with fur and gnashing teeth. And there, circling high above, a third monstrosity, wings wide and scales gleaming . . .

"Zoya, say something spiteful."

"Why?" she asked faintly.

"Because I'm fairly certain I'm hallucinating, and in my dreams you're much nicer."

"You're an idiot, Nikolai."

"Not your best work."

"I'm sorry I can't deliver better wordplay right now. I seem to be paralyzed with fear."

Her voice was trembling—and if ruthless, unshakable Zoya was that frightened, then everything he was seeing was real: the bees, the grotesque, and yes, impossible but there nonetheless, the dragon, vast in size, its arching wings leathery, its scales glinting black, green, blue, gold in the flat gray light.

"Zoya, whatever you did to bring us here, this would be the time to undo it."

"If I could, I would," she growled, then hurled a wall of wind upward.

The bees struck it, like water parting around a rock in a stream, their loud buzz filling Nikolai's ears.

"Do something!" said Zoya.

"Like what?"

"You have guns!"

"I'm not going to shoot at bees."

"Then shoot at that thing."

Nikolai opened fire at the grotesque. His bullets struck its shifting body—a head, an arm, another arm, a distended chest. Now that the thing was closer, he glimpsed claws, jaws thick with canines, the dense brown pelt of what looked like a bear. All of his bullets were absorbed in the grotesque's body, then emerged a second later as if the writhing flesh had simply spat them out.

High above, the dragon roared and spread its enormous wings. A fountain of flame erupted from the beast's mouth and blasted toward them.

Zoya's hands shot upward, and a dome of air formed over their heads. The flames beat at the barrier. Nikolai could feel the heat singeing his brows.

The blast relented and the dragon shrieked again, wheeling above them.

"I think it's fair to say we're outgunned," said Nikolai.

"Lay down your arms," the grotesque said in a chorus of voices from a hundred mouths.

"In a moment," replied Nikolai. "I'm finding them very reassuring right now. Yuri, get off of your damned knees and at least try to look like you can fight."

"You don't understand," said Yuri, his eyes full of tears.

"That is entirely correct."

"I'm going to raise the sands again," said Zoya. "If I bring a big enough storm, we'll have cover to get . . . somewhere. You'll need to work the sails; I won't be able to control the storm and direct the skiff."

"Do it," said Nikolai, eyeing the lines. They were primitive at best, but he had managed rockier seas than these.

He opened fire, trying to lend Zoya cover as she swept her arms forward and the sands of the Fold—or wherever they were—rose with a whoosh. There was no subtlety now, no need to mask her actions to fool the pilgrims. Instead the storm came to life with a start like a man waking from a bad dream, a sudden wall of force that thrust the creatures back, the sands forming a whirling wall to hide the skiff's escape.

Nikolai holstered his revolvers and seized the lines, releasing the sail. The canvas snapped, filling with air, driving them east and back toward what he hoped were still the borders of the Fold. Whatever these creatures were, their power had to be tied to this place.

Suddenly the ground beneath them seemed to buckle. The skiff listed precariously starboard as one of its runners peeled away from the sand. Zoya and Yuri lost their footing, but Zoya did not falter. Even on her back, she kept the winds in motion. Nikolai held tight to the lines, trying to use the storm to help right the skiff. But the ground was bucking like a wild animal, as if the very sands beneath them had life.

The skiff tilted higher on its single runner. "We're going over!" Nikolai shouted. He had the uncanny sense that a giant hand was deliberately tipping them out onto the sands.

They landed in an unceremonious heap. Nikolai was on his feet in an instant, grabbing for Zoya and Yuri to roll all of them to safety. But the skiff thumped harmlessly down to its other side, and the sands instantly calmed.

Without Zoya's storm raging, the skies were clear again. A shape emerged out of the sand before them, then another, then another—a regiment of sand soldiers. They were faceless, but their uniforms were elaborately detailed. They looked like the paintings of ancient

Ravkan soldiers, the army of Yaromir the Determined, dressed in furs and bronze, but all of it wrought in sand. Zoya raised her hands and sent a fierce gust of wind slamming into the ranks of soldiers, but they stood solid and unmoving.

"What are they?" Zoya asked.

The soldiers continued to emerge in a rippling wave, an army that stretched to the horizon, where the castle still loomed.

"I think we're being shown just how overmatched we are," Nikolai said.

"By whom?"

The sand soldiers stepped forward as one, and the sound was like a shotgun blast. Zoya and Nikolai stood back-to-back, surrounded. Next to them, Yuri remained on his knees, his face filled with a kind of manic elation.

"I don't know how to fight this," Zoya said. She'd somehow steadied her voice, but he could hear the fear in it anyway. "Is this the part where we die well?"

The dragon was wheeling overhead. If these creatures wanted Nikolai dead, they'd chosen an elaborate means of making it happen, so something else had to be in play—hopefully something that would allow him to negotiate for Zoya's and Yuri's safety.

"No, this is the part where the king of Ravka surrenders himself, and the love we never had lives on in ballads and song."

"Nikolai," snapped Zoya, "don't you dare."

"Give me another option, Nazyalensky. One of us needs to survive this." Then he lowered his voice. "Get back to the capital and rally the Grisha." Assuming she could even get back to Os Alta from here.

He tossed his revolvers to the sand and raised his hands, scanning the rows of sand soldiers, the figures in the sky, the mountainous body of the grotesque hovering behind their ranks. "I'm not sure who I'm surrendering to—"

The dragon turned sharply in the air and dove for them. Maybe they did intend to kill him, after all.

"Zoya, get down!" Nikolai shouted, lunging for her.

"Like hell," she muttered, and knocked him into the sands, bracing before him with her feet planted and her arms raised.

The dragon unleashed its fire and Zoya let loose the storm. For a moment they seemed evenly matched—a golden cascade of flame buffeted by a wall of wind. Then Zoya swept her arms in a loop and cast them to the sides like a conductor concluding a symphony. For a moment Nikolai didn't understand, but then the flames collapsed. The dragon reared back, a choked wheeze emerging from its throat. Zoya had stolen its breath; she'd banished the air from the fire, depriving it of fuel, and left the dragon gasping.

Nikolai leapt for his guns, ready to seize the opportunity she'd offered, but before he could even aim, the dragon released a deafening roar. Its jaws opened and fire spurted forth. This time the flame burned blue, brighter and hotter than before, hot enough to melt stone—or sand.

"Zoya!" Nikolai shouted, but Zoya had already fisted her hands and raised them again, driving an icy wind against the dragon's onslaught.

Blue fire lit her face. Her hair rose like a black crown around her head, and her eyes blazed cobalt as if she too burned with the dragon's fire.

Zoya screamed as the dragon's flames pounded against the force of her power. She gritted her teeth, and Nikolai saw beads of sweat bloom on her brow. He opened fire on the dragon, but his bullets seemed to melt before they even came near the creature's scales. Ice crystalized on the fallen skiff, coated Nikolai's hands and the ranks of the sand soldiers surrounding them.

And then Zoya collapsed. She fell to her knees, and the winter storm evaporated, leaving nothing but a thin shell of melting frost in its wake.

Nikolai was on his feet, stumbling toward her, certain he was about to see her consumed by flame. But the dragon withdrew its fire. It hovered in the air, watching.

"Zoya," Nikolai said as he went to his knees beside her, catching her in his arms before she could topple. Her skin was aglow with the light of Grisha power, but her nose was bleeding and she was shaking.

The dragon landed before them, folding its vast wings. Perhaps it wanted to play with its food.

"Stay back," Nikolai said, though he had no way of preventing the beast's advance. His weapons were as good as toys. Yuri was still on his knees, swaying like a drunk who couldn't decide whether it was worth the effort to try to stand.

"The boy king," said the dragon, prowling forward, tail lashing the air. Its voice was a low rumble, like thunder on a distant peak. "The war hero. The prince with a demon curled inside his heart." Nikolai wasn't sure if he was more startled that the creature could speak or that it knew what had brought them on this cursed journey.

The dragon leaned forward. Its eyes were large and silver, its pupils black slits.

"If I wanted to harm her, she would be ashes, boy. So would you all."

"It sure looked like you wanted to harm her," Nikolai said. "Or is that how your kind says a friendly hello?"

The dragon rumbled what might have been a laugh. "I wanted to see what she could do."

Zoya released a howl of pure anguish. It was a sound so desperate, so raw, Nikolai could hardly believe it was coming from his general's mouth.

"What is it?" he pleaded, his arm tightening around her as he scanned her body for wounds, for blood.

But she cast him off, scrabbling in the sand, another wail of rage and pain tearing from her chest.

"For Saints' sake, Zoya, what's wrong?"

She snatched up something that glinted in her hand and clutched it to her chest, her sobs like nothing he had heard before. It took him a moment to force her fingers open. Cradled in her palm, he saw the broken halves of her silver cuff. Her amplifier had shattered.

"No," she sobbed. "No."

"Yes," hissed the dragon.

"Juris, stop this," said a woman, emerging from between the rows of soldiers. She wore a dress of blooming roses that blossomed and died in curling vines around her body. Her golden hair was a buzzing mass of bees that swarmed and clustered around her radiant face. "You got your battle. They know what they are facing."

"The first bit of excitement we've had in years, Elizaveta, and you seem determined to deny me my fun. Very well."

The dragon heaved its shoulders in a shrug, and then, before Nikolai's bewildered eyes, it seemed to shift and shrink, becoming a towering man in finely wrought chain mail that glittered like black scales. The sand soldiers parted to reveal the grotesque, his body still shifting and changing, now covered in eyes as if to better take in every inch of them.

"What is this?" Nikolai demanded. "Who are you?"

"Do the people not pray for Saints?" asked the man called Juris.

"At last," wept Yuri, still kneeling. "At last."

"Come," said Elizaveta, extending a hand, the bees buzzing gently around her in a hum that was almost soothing. "We will explain all."

But Nikolai's mind had already leapt a chasm into preposterous territory. Sankta Lizabeta, who had been martyred in a field of roses. Sankt Juris, who . . .

"You slew the dragon," said Nikolai. "It's . . . it's in all of the stories."

"Sometimes the stories are rough on the details," said Juris with a gleaming smile. "Come, boy king. It's time we talked."

16

ISAAK

ISAAK WAS TRYING VERY HARD not to sweat through his uniform, and the effort was only making him sweat more. It was not so much the pain of transformation that bothered him but the proximity of Genya Safin as she moved her fingers over the lines of his nose and brow. He'd been sequestered with her for nearly two days in a practice room usually occupied by the Corporalki. It had no windows, and its single door was always guarded by one of the Bataar twins. The light for Genya's careful work came from the vast skylight above, the glass so clear it could only be Grisha made.

Isaak had little to do but stay as still as possible, stare at Genya, and let his mind wander down the path that had brought him to this incomprehensible situation. Had it begun with his father's passing? With the draft? Had it begun during the northern campaign, when he'd served under Nikolai Lantsov? His prince had been just past eighteen, only a few months older than Isaak himself. Isaak had come to admire his commander, not just for his bravery but for the way he could think himself out of a tight situation. He never forgot a name, never failed to ask after an ailing relative or the progress of a healing wound.

After the battle of Halmhend, the prince had visited the infirmary to speak to the wounded. He had spent hours there, chatting by each soldier's bedside, charming every nurse, raising spirits. When he'd sat down beside Isaak's cot, filled Isaak's water glass, and gone so far as to lift the glass to Isaak's lips so he could drink, Isaak had been so overwhelmed he'd had to remind himself how exactly one swallowed water.

They'd talked about Isaak's childhood, his sisters, and Isaak found himself telling the prince all about his father, who had been a tutor in the house of Baron Velchik. Isaak hadn't spoken of his father's death in years and had never told anyone about how his life had changed in the wake of that tragedy, how his family had been forced to leave the baron's estate and take up residence in a tiny rented room above a dressmaker's shop, where his mother had done her best to feed and clothe Isaak and his sisters by taking in piecework.

The prince had praised Isaak's gift for languages and suggested he cultivate the talent now that it was time for Isaak to leave the front.

"I'm not sure that's something my family can afford," Isaak had admitted with some shame. "But I will certainly consider it, Your Highness."

He'd returned home and begun looking for work as soon as he was able. Months passed as Isaak took on odd jobs and waited for his body to heal so that he could return to active duty and the pay his family so desperately needed. Then, one evening, he arrived home to find his mother waiting for him with a letter. He'd spent a long day shoveling manure, for which he'd earned all of six eggs, which he'd carried home gently cradled in the folds of his shirt. He nearly dropped them all when he saw that the letter in his mother's hand was stamped with the pale blue wax of the prince's double-eagle seal.

> *Dear Isaak,*
>
> *Delighted to see we both survived my leadership. If you'd like to leave your village and make the arduous journey to Os Alta, there's a job waiting for you in the royal guard at the Grand Palace. It will require a great deal of standing up straight, not looking bored through the most tiresome events man can conceive, opening doors, and keeping your buttons shiny, so I would not blame you if you'd prefer literally any other occupation. But if you've the courage to face such horrors, you will also find my own tutors happy to school you in the languages of your choosing. I hope you will select Shu, Kerch, and Zemeni, as they are the languages that might best serve a prince or a king, but you are certainly welcome to indulge your taste for Kaelish poetry. I did, and my stomach's been aching since.*
>
> *With fondest regards,*
> *Nikolai Lantsov,*
> *Grand Duke of Udova,*
> *Prince of Ravka, etc.*

Isaak's mother and sisters had gathered round to touch the fine, heavy paper and press their fingers to the tracery of the wax seal. His mother had wept both because her son was leaving and because the prince had done them this great honor. Positions in the palace guard were usually reserved for war heroes and the sons of lesser noblemen.

As for Isaak, he had spent the rest of the week patching holes in the roof that their landlord refused to repair, and when the work was done, he'd kissed his mother and his baby sisters and promised that he would write to them as often as he was able. He'd put on his army boots and his much-darned coat and set out for the capital.

Isaak had enjoyed his work at the palace, the quiet of Os Alta after the chaos of war and the hardships of home, the pleasure of learning languages in his off-hours. With the wages he sent home every month, his family was able to move into a snug cottage with a garden large enough to grow vegetables, and a north-facing window where his mother could do her sewing in the sun.

It was not always easy. He had known little more than the confines of his small town and the routine of the army, and he was not sure what he found more intimidating: the dishes with their golden filigree, the ladies in their jewels, or simply the sight of Second Army soldiers in their red, blue, and purple *kefta* moving about the grounds. But in time he'd found his place and adapted to the rhythms and requirements of palace life. When the Darkling had staged his attack on the throne, Isaak had taken up arms to support the Lantsov name. And when Prince Nikolai had become King Nikolai, he'd stood at attention in the newly rebuilt chapel and watched his king crowned with pride in his heart.

Life had gone on. Isaak had become fluent in Shu, Zemeni, Kerch, and Suli. He earned extra pay working as a translator for the crown, and despite his king's warnings, Isaak developed a taste for poetry of all kinds.

Then the summons had come. Isaak had been on duty at the entrance to the southern wing when Tamar Kir-Bataar had sought him out. Isaak had been confused and more than a little frightened. It was not every day one was called before the Grisha Triumvirate—though he was relieved to find that Zoya Nazyalensky was still traveling with the king, so he could at least avoid her scathing look of disdain. She could wither a man's balls just by raising a brow.

He'd spent scant time in the Little Palace and had never ventured past the Hall of the Golden Dome, but Tamar escorted him through the vast double doors emblazoned with the Triumvirate's bunched arrows and down winding hallways to a small room lined in elaborate maps of Ravka and the world.

Genya Safin and David Kostyk were there, along with Tamar's twin, Tolya, who was so tall his head nearly brushed the ceiling and whom Isaak occasionally traded volumes of verse with. He was surprised to see both of the twins—at least one could usually be counted upon to be in the company of the king.

"Captain Andreyev, won't you sit?" Genya Safin had asked. To his astonishment, she'd served him tea and asked after his health, and only then had she said the words that would change the course of his life: "The king is missing."

The story that followed had been strange indeed, and Isaak knew he was being told only the barest details: King Nikolai and Commander Nazyalensky had been traveling with the Bataars when they'd vanished from the sands of the Unsea. Though the twins had searched as extensively as discretion would allow, they'd found no sign of them.

"We do not yet know if the king is in need of rescue or beyond it," Genya said. "But we do know that if our enemies learn of the king's disappearance, they're sure to take advantage of our vulnerability. There is no clear line of succession for the Ravkan throne, and it is essential that no one discover we are without a ruler until the king can be found or a strategy put into play."

"Of course," Isaak murmured, thinking of the panic it would create among the people.

Genya took a deep breath. "But in two weeks' time, seventeen princesses, noblewomen, and ladies of worth will arrive in Os Alta, surrounded by their servants and retainers, all of them hoping to meet Nikolai Lantsov and become Ravka's queen. Unfortunately, we are short one monarch. That is why we need you."

"Me?"

"To play the role of the king."

Isaak smiled because he could think of no other way to respond. Though he didn't understand the joke, he was willing to play along. But Genya Safin did not return his smile.

"It was a contingency plan the king himself conceived in case he was injured or . . . incapacitated," she said gently, "though we had no reason to think we would need to act on it so soon or with so little preparation. You were on his list of candidates. You are of approximately the right height. You can speak multiple languages. I believe I can tailor you to look enough like the king that you will be able to fool even the guards who have watched over him for years."

"Sitting still at least," said Tolya.

"Correct," said Genya. "Looking like Nikolai will only be the first challenge. Talking like him, walking like him, and all the rest . . . well, that would be up to you."

"I . . . you can't mean for me to pretend to be him," said Isaak. It was unthinkable. Absurd.

"We can," said Tolya, his massive arms crossed. "We do."

"Surely the proceedings could be delayed. If the king is meant to choose a queen—"

"The brides could be put off," said Tamar. "But there are matters of national security that cannot. We have intelligence suggesting that a member of the Tavgharad may be ready to defect. This may be our only chance to make contact with her and learn the locations of valued Shu military assets."

Tavgharad. The strict translation was "stone fisted," but Isaak knew the word referred to the elite soldiers who guarded and served the Shu royal family. If one of them was willing to turn traitor, there was no telling what information might be gleaned.

Tamar Kir-Bataar had looked at him with hard golden eyes and said, "Your country needs you."

But it had been Genya with her scarred mouth who had swayed him when she'd added, "And so does your king."

Isaak said yes. Of course he had said yes. It was his duty as a soldier and the least he could do for the king who had done so much for him and his family.

So it had begun—the lessons in deportment, in elocution, in how to sit and stand correctly. It was not just that Isaak had to pretend to be a man of wealth and means; he had to pretend to be a *king*. And not just a king, but a boy king who had become a legend. Nikolai was everything that Isaak was not. Confident, assured, cosmopolitan. Isaak's only gift was a facility with language—and even that had become something of a liability, since he spoke Shu better than the king and had a cleaner Zemeni accent.

But the strangest of all these processes was the time he'd spent here, beneath this glass dome, sweating through his clothes in the presence of Genya Safin with her single amber-colored eye and her sunset hair. Though Isaak knew she was only performing a task, it was hard not to feel that she was studying him, lavishing her attention upon him, and he'd found himself falling a bit in love with her. It was a silly infatuation. She was clearly in love with David Kostyk, the brilliant Fabrikator who sat silently through many of their sessions, reading from stacks of documents and scribbling on a giant tablet of drafting paper. But her apparent taste for unassuming men made him like her all the more. One of her scars tugged the left corner of her mouth down slightly, and he would catch himself daydreaming about kissing her there. He was rapidly brought back to reality by the sharp poke of her finger to his shoulder. "Sit up straight, Isaak," she would say, or, "You're blocking my light, Isaak."

Sometimes the others came to read to him from a book on Kerch history or quiz him on trade routes while Genya worked. Other times they talked strategy, and he was expected to do nothing but sit there like a lump of clay.

"We can sneak him out of the palace through the tunnels after dark," Tamar said, twirling one of her axes in a way that made Isaak sweat even more, "then stage the king's return from his pilgrimage the next morning. It will look like he just made a stop at Count Kirigin's estate."

"How do we account for Zoya's absence?" Tolya asked.

Genya leaned back to examine the work she was doing on Isaak's chin. "We'll say she stayed behind to journey to Os Kervo." She rubbed her eyes and reached for her teacup. "I don't understand it. No one just vanishes."

"Leave it to Nikolai to do the impossible," said Tolya.

"Maybe he just wanted a vacation," said Tamar.

Tolya grunted. "Maybe Zoya finally got sick of him and buried him beneath a pile of sand."

But Genya did not laugh. "Or maybe this was the Apparat's doing and he's back in the business of staging coups."

"If that's the case," said David, "he'll come for us next."

"Thank you, my love. That's very encouraging."

Tamar slowed the twirling of her axe. "If the Apparat orchestrated this, I'd have expected him to make a move to expose the king's disappearance by now."

"Either way," said Tolya, "we'll have to keep him away from Isaak. The priest is too canny not to realize the king . . . isn't himself."

Genya slumped down in a chair and rested her head in her hands.

Isaak had never seen her look so defeated, and it hurt his heart. "Who are we kidding? This isn't going to work."

"It will," said Tamar. "It has to."

"He's already almost identical to the king," said David, peering at Isaak's face. "I'd say it's your best work."

Genya cast away the compliment with a wave of her hand. "It's not just the features. It's the way Nikolai inhabits them, the tilt of his mouth, the cant of his head. We might fool the guests, maybe even a few of the courtiers, but the servants? The royal ministers? People who see him every day, who have dined with him and danced with him? Forget it. This is hopeless."

"I'm sorry," Isaak said. He hated to think he was failing his country and his king as well as the talented girl before him.

Genya threw up her hands. "That's what I mean. Nikolai would never lower his head that way or apologize with such sincerity."

"I'm sorry," Isaak said again without thinking, and then winced.

"We're out of options," said Tamar. "We cancel the party and risk Nikolai's absence being discovered, or we take this risk."

"And if we're found out?" Tolya asked.

"I'm not even sure what we'd be guilty of," considered David. "Is impersonating a king treasonous if you're doing it for the king's benefit?"

Isaak swallowed. Treason. He hadn't even thought of that.

"We could be handing the Apparat an easy way to eliminate all of the Grisha leadership in a single move," said Tamar.

Genya released a sigh. "Isaak, I know you're doing your best, but we've asked too much of you. This was madness from the start."

Isaak hated to see these brave people lose hope. He remembered Nikolai Lantsov perched beside his infirmary bed, thought of his mother's smile and his sisters' plump cheeks the last time he'd returned home.

He leaned back, draped an arm over the top of his chair, and said with all the easy, drawling arrogance he could summon, "Genya, my love, ring for brandy. I can't be expected to tolerate certain doom when I'm this sober."

They stared at him.

David tapped an ink-stained finger to his lips. "Better."

"*Better?*" cried Genya, clapping her hands with glee. "It was perfect! Do it again."

Isaak felt a moment's panic, then arched a brow. "Are you giving the orders now? I hope this means I can indulge in a kingly nap."

Tamar grinned. Tolya whooped. Genya leaned down and pressed a huge kiss to Isaak's cheek—and Isaak did what Nikolai Lantsov never would have done.

He blushed.

17
NIKOLAI

THE SKIFF WAS ABANDONED, and the sands carried Nikolai, Zoya, and Yuri to the giant palace, the dunes sliding beneath their feet in a way that made Nikolai's stomach lurch. He prided himself on adapting easily, but it was one thing to implement a new technology, adopt a new fuel, or dare to wear shirtsleeves at dinner without a waistcoat. It was quite another to see your understanding of the natural world smashed to bits in an afternoon.

"You look unwell, boy king," rumbled Juris, who had resumed his dragon form.

"A novel means of transport. I don't suppose you'd consider carrying us on your back."

The dragon huffed. "Only if you'd like to return the favor."

Nikolai had to crane his neck to take in the palace as they approached. He'd never seen a structure so vast. It would have taken a regiment of engineers working for a thousand years to imagine such a creation, let alone see it built. The palaces and towers were clustered around three major spires: one of black stone, one of what looked like glowing amber, and one of what could only be bone. But there was something wrong about the place. He saw no signs of life, no birds circling, no movement at the many windows, no figures crossing the countless bridges. It had the shape of a city, but it felt like a tomb.

"Is there no one else here?" he asked.

"No one," said the shifting grotesque in a chorus of baritone voices punctuated by the growl of a bear. "Not for almost four hundred years."

Four hundred years? Nikolai looked to Zoya, but her gaze was distant, her hand clasped around her bare left wrist.

The sand rose, lifting them higher, and Nikolai saw that the three spires surrounded a domed structure, a mass of terraces and palaces and waterfalls of cascading sand that shimmered in the gray twilight.

They passed beneath a large arch and into a wide, circular chamber, its walls glinting with mica. The sand beneath their feet became stone, and a round table swelled up from the floor, its center a milky geode. Elizaveta gestured for them to sit in the stone chairs that emerged beside it.

"I fear we can offer you no food or drink," she said.

"We'll settle for answers," said Nikolai.

Yuri knelt on the stone floor, his head bowed, nattering in what Nikolai thought was liturgical Ravkan, since he could only pick out an occasional word—*promised, foretold, darkness.*

"Please stop that," Elizaveta said, her bees humming in distress. "And please, sit."

"Leave him be. He's abasing himself and enjoying it," said Juris.

He folded his wings and settled onto the floor a good distance from Yuri. "Where to begin?"

"Custom dictates we start with who the hell are you?"

"I thought we'd already covered that, boy king."

"Yes. But Sainthood requires martyrdom. You all look very much alive. Unless this is the afterlife, in which case I am sorely underdressed. Or overdressed. I suppose it depends on your idea of heaven."

"Does he always talk this much?" Juris asked Zoya, but she said nothing, just gazed up at the flat expanse of colorless sky above them.

"We all died at one time or another and were reborn," said Elizaveta. "Sometimes not quite as we were. You can call us what you like, Grisha, Saints—"

"Relics," said Juris.

Elizaveta pursed her lips. "I don't care for that term at all."

Yuri released a small, ecstatic sob. "All is as was promised," he babbled. "All I was told to hope for—"

Elizaveta sent a vine curling over his shoulder like a comforting arm. "That's enough," she said gently. "You're here now and must calm yourself."

Yuri grasped the vine, pressing his face into the leaves, weeping. So much for the great scholar.

"Where are we exactly?" Nikolai asked.

"In the Shadow Fold," said one of the mouths of the grotesque who had introduced himself as Grigori. Sankt Grigori. If Nikolai recalled correctly, he'd been torn apart by bears, though that hardly explained his current condition. "A version of it. One we cannot escape."

"Does any of this matter?" Zoya said dully. "Why bring us here? What do you want?"

Juris turned his slitted eyes on her, his tail moving in a long sinu-

278

ous rasp over the floor. "Look how the little witch mourns. As if she knew what she had lost or what she stands to gain."

Nikolai expected to see Zoya's eyes light with anger, but she just continued to stare listlessly at the sky. Seeing her this way, devoid of the spiky, dangerous energy that always animated her, was more disturbing than any of the bizarre sights they'd encountered. What was wrong with her? Had the amplifier meant so much? She was still strong without it. She'd be strong with both arms tied behind her back and a satchel of lead ball bearings weighing her down.

"I wish we could have brought you elsewhere, young Zoya," said Elizaveta. "We had power before the word Grisha was ever whispered, when the extraordinary was still called *miracle* and *magic*. We have lived lives so long they would dwarf the history of Ravka. But this place, this particular spot on the Fold, has always been holy, a sacred site where our power was at its greatest and where we were most deeply connected to the making at the heart of the world. Here, anything was possible. And here we were bound when the Darkling created the Fold."

"What?" Zoya asked, a spark of interest at last entering her eyes.

"We are woven into the fabric of the world in a way that no other Grisha are, the threads tightened by years and the use of our power. When the Darkling tampered with the natural order of the world, we were drawn here, and when his experiment with *merzost* failed, we were trapped within the boundaries of the Fold."

"We cannot leave this place," said Grigori. "We cannot assume physical form anywhere but here."

"Physical form," Juris sneered, and thumped his tail. "We don't eat. We don't sleep. I don't remember what it is to sweat or hunger or dream. I'd chop off my left wing just to hear my stomach growl or taste wine again or take a piss out a window."

"Must you be so vulgar?" Elizaveta said wearily.

"I must," said Juris. "Making you miserable is my sole entertainment."

Grigori settled into the shape of what looked like three bear heads topping the body of a single enormous man and folded two sets of arms. "We endured this endless twilight because we believed our purgatory would end with the Darkling's death. He had many enemies, and we hoped he might have a short life. But he lived on."

"And on," grumbled Juris.

"He survived and became nearly as powerful as one of us," said Grigori.

The dragon snorted. "Don't flatter him."

"Well, as one of us in our youth," amended Elizaveta. "Then at last the time came when the Fold was destroyed and the Darkling was slain. And yet our bonds did not break. We remained prisoners. Because the Darkling's power lives on. In you."

Nikolai's brows rose. "So naturally I must die. This is all very civilized, but if you wanted to murder me, why not get on with it during the battle?"

Juris snorted again, steam billowing from his huge nostrils. "That was hardly a battle."

"Then during that delightful cocktail party where you chased us down and tried to set fire to my hair."

"We cannot kill you, boy king. For one thing, we know the unrest it would cause your country, and we do not wish to see more people die if it is not necessary. Besides, even in your death, the power might well survive. No, the Darkling's curse must be burned out of you."

"*Obisbaya*," said Nikolai. "The Burning Thorn."

Elizaveta nodded. "Then you know the old ritual."

"It is true, then," cried Yuri. "All of it. This is the site of the thorn wood where the first Priestguard came."

"Congratulations, Yuri," Nikolai said. "Looks like you do get to put me on a pyre."

"Pyre?" asked Grigori.

"No pyre," said Elizaveta. "The thorn wood is older than all of us, older than the first magic. It is the wood from which the first altars were made and from which the walls of the Little Palace were constructed. I can raise it from the roots that survive beneath the Fold to begin the ritual, but then it will be up to you to summon the monster from inside and slay it."

"*You* created those miracles," said Zoya. "The bridge, the roses, the earthquake, the bleeding statues, the black disk, all of them, to bring us here."

"The Age of Saints," Yuri declared. "Just as he promised."

Elizaveta's vine curled a bit more tightly around the monk's shoulders. "Our power can still reach beyond the limits of the Fold, but only in the places where we are still worshipped."

"A Grisha's power doesn't rely on faith," Zoya said angrily.

"Are you so sure, little witch?" asked Juris.

Zoya looked directly at him, her gaze unflinching, and Nikolai knew she was planning a thousand punishments for the dragon. He felt a rush of relief at the promise of retribution in her eyes.

But he couldn't afford to get caught up in the mechanics of Grisha power. "You say you want me to summon the monster, but the thing inside me doesn't follow orders."

"Then you must teach it to," said Juris.

Elizaveta clasped her hands and roses bloomed over her wrists, enveloping her fingers. "Once the thorns rise, they will pierce your body. If you don't vanquish the shadow inside you, they will burn you from the inside out."

Quite a bit like Sankt Feliks of the Apple Boughs after all.

Suddenly, the pyre didn't sound so bad. "Thank goodness I'm not ticklish."

"What are the chances he'll survive?" Zoya asked.

Roses flowered over Elizaveta's shoulders. "As Juris said, we have no wish to destabilize Ravka."

"That isn't an answer."

"It is . . . perilous," Elizaveta conceded. "There are means we can use to prepare you for the trial, but I cannot promise you will emerge unscathed."

"Or that you will emerge at all," said Juris.

Elizaveta sighed. "Is it necessary to cast this in the least favorable light?"

"It's best they know."

Nikolai shifted on the stone chair. It had not been made for comfort. "So after you skewer and roast me and I wrestle with my actual demons, what happens?"

"The Darkling's power will be eradicated once and for all. The boundaries of the Unsea will break. Life will return to the Fold, and we will be free."

"Free to do what exactly?" Zoya asked. It was the right question. She might be mourning her lost amplifier, but she was always a general. And perhaps Nikolai was too desperate for a cure to think like a king. Maybe power of the kind they'd just witnessed should be contained.

"Don't you know, little witch?" said Juris. "Great power always has a price."

Elizaveta gave a single nod of her head. "When we leave the bounds of the Fold, we will be mortal once more."

"Mortal?" Zoya asked.

"Otkazat'sya, you would say. Without Grisha power. Humans who will live brief lives and die permanent deaths."

Zoya's eyes narrowed. "Why would you give up such power?"

"Do not think it is an easy choice," said Elizaveta, some bitterness in her voice. "We have spent hundreds of years in debate over it. But we cannot go on in such a way. This is what the universe demands for freedom from this half life."

"One eternity is enough," said Juris. "I want to walk the world once more. Return to the shores of my homeland. Maybe fall in love again. I want to swim in the sea and lie in the sun. I want to age and die and pass into realms I have never explored."

"You should understand," said Grigori. "It is not just your life at risk, but your country as well. If we fail, if you cannot endure the ritual, we might create another tear in the world and cause this blighted place to overspill its shores."

"But that may happen anyway," said Elizaveta. "Everything is connected, tied to the making at the heart of the world. As the power within you grows stronger, there's no way to tell what kind of chain reaction it might trigger."

"You will want to discuss it," said Grigori. "But make your choices quickly. *Merzost* is unpredictable, and every day the monster inside you takes firmer hold."

"There's nothing to discuss," Nikolai said. They had their answers, and time was short. "When do we begin?"

18

NINA

THAT NIGHT, NINA STAYED AWAKE as Leoni's breathing turned deep and even. Sleep tugged at her, but she plaited her hair in the dark and waited, hoping to hear sounds of activity drift through the narrow window above her bed. Sure enough, just after midnight, she heard low voices and a cart being loaded. Nina stood on tiptoe and saw lanterns lit in the laundry and the Springmaidens carrying stacks of what she assumed was clothing wrapped in paper and string.

Nina hurried to the convent dining hall—a place with a strict schedule that she knew Hanne could always count upon to be empty at specific times. If an unhappy novitiate was looking for a safe spot to stash clothing, this would be an obvious place for it. She got on her knees and made her way around the perimeter of the hall, lightly rapping her knuckles against the slate tiles of the floor. She'd nearly given up hope when her knock returned an odd, echoing *thunk*. Hollow.

She wedged her fingers under the tile and pulled it up. Boots, military-issue trousers, two hats, a gun belt, and—thank the Saints— a long pale blue pinafore and white blouse. Nina yanked them over her clothes, pinned her braids into a messy crown, and slipped into the kitchens, where a long search revealed the cook's key beneath a flour tin. By the time she'd unlocked the kitchen door and made it out to the yard, the Springmaidens were shutting the doors to the wagon and on their way.

Nina knew where they were headed, so she didn't bother with the road, cutting through the trees and taking a more direct route to the main entrance of the old fort instead. She also knew she was being reckless. She should have included Adrik and Leoni in her plans. She should have waited to perform more reconnaissance. But here was the reality: They couldn't stay in Gäfvalle much longer without drawing suspicion. The Women of the Well could lose their access to the fort at any time. And, if Nina was honest with herself, she needed to act. She needed to know why those whispers had brought her to this place and what had happened up on that hill. The dead hadn't spoken to Adrik or Leoni. They had called to Nina—and she intended to answer.

She set a fast pace, picking her way through the trees, checking her direction against the lights of the factory in the distance.

Despite the sadness and anger she'd carried with her to Fjerda, she could admit that she liked traveling in this country. She liked see- ing the ordinary business of Fjerdan lives, remembering that they were people and not monsters, that most of them longed for pros- perity and peace, a good meal, a warm bed to sleep in at night. But she also knew the prejudices so many of them carried, that they still believed Grisha deserved to be burned on a pyre. And she could never forget what the Fjerdan government was capable of, the suffering she'd endured at the hands of the *drüskelle* who had starved her in the hold of a ship, the nightmare of the Grisha cells at the Ice Court, where Jarl Brum had tried to turn her kind into weapons against themselves.

Nina reached the rocks overlooking the main entrance in time to see the convent cart arrive and the gates open. She stumbled down the slope to the road, sliding on her heels and nearly losing her balance completely. The shape of the body Genya had given her still felt strange, and she'd never had a talent for stealth.

Moving through the shadows of the trees that lined the road, she saw the last of the Springmaidens pass through the doors, burdened with their stacks of clothing. Only then did she step onto the road and scurry up to the doors, breathless.

"I'm so sorry," she said. "I fell behind."

"That's your problem," said the guard. "Do you know how heavy these doors are? You can wait out here for your sisters."

"But . . . but . . . you don't understand . . . I had to . . . I had to use the necessary," Nina whispered in tones of great agony.

"The what?"

"I had to . . . to relieve myself." The guard looked instantly distressed. Bless the Fjerdans and their peculiar prudishness. "I had to *urinate*." Nina lingered on the word. "In the trees."

"That . . . that's no concern of mine," he sputtered.

Nina forced tears to her eyes. "But I had to gooooo," she wailed. "And they're going to be so muh-mad."

"Oh, in Djel's good name, don't cry!"

"I'm so so-sorry," Nina sobbed. "I just don't want to get yuh-yuh-yelled at again."

"In, in!" said the guard hurriedly, unlocking the bolts and dragging the door open to usher her inside. "Just stop that!"

"Thank you, thank you," Nina said, bowing and sniveling until the door shut behind her. She wiped her nose and took a good look around. The factory was quiet, already closed down for the night. Somewhere, she knew men would be playing cards or settling in to sleep. Others would be keeping the watch.

Nina hurried through the entryway that led to a vast central chamber full of heavy machinery, hulking and silent in the watery moonlight from the windows. The next room revealed massive vats, but it was impossible to tell what they might contain. She laid her hand against the side of one of them. Still warm. Were they smelting metals here? Mixing dyes?

The next room held the answer: tidy, endless stacks of stubby, bullet-shaped cylinders the size of pumpkins—row after row of ammunition for tanks. Were they really just making munitions up here? Were the poisons in the river some corrosive by-product from the assembly lines? But if so, why had the wolf's bite sent a bolt of lightning through her blood? It didn't add up.

Nina wasn't sure where to go next. The factory felt much larger now that she was inside it. She wished she had Inej's gift for spywork or Kaz's gift for scheming, but she only seemed to have Jesper's gift for bad decisions. She knew the eastern wing was unoccupied and in disrepair, so the Springmaidens had probably headed toward the western wing, the domestic heart of the fort, where the soldiers would eat, be billeted, and train when they were not operating the factory. If she were Inej, she could climb into the eaves and probably glean some excellent intelligence. But she was not a tiny soundless shadow with a gift for knifework.

It wasn't too late to go back. She'd confirmed this was a munitions factory, a military target for Ravka's bombers if war came. But the whispers had not ceased their rustling, and they did not want her to leave. She closed her eyes and listened, letting them guide her footsteps to the right, into the dark quiet of the abandoned eastern wing.

Every part of her protested that she was wasting her time as she made her way down the corridor. This wing of the factory was deserted. She'd seen no lanterns lit in the windows at dusk, and the roof of the far corner was slumped in where it had given way to snow or time and never been repaired. But the voices drew her on. *Closer*, they whispered, young voices and old. They had a different quality now—clearer, louder, the memory of their pain vibrating through every word.

The dark was so complete she had to edge along the walls, fingers trailing over uneven brick, hoping she wouldn't stumble into some neglected piece of machinery and land on her rump. She thought of that ruined roof. Had there been some kind of accident at the factory that had led to the wing being abandoned? Were those the graves she'd sensed? Had women worked the line here and been buried on the mountain? If so, she'd find nothing but old misery in this place.

Then she heard it—a high, thin wail that raised the hair on her arms. For a moment, she wasn't sure if the sound was in her head or had come from somewhere deeper in the eastern wing. She was too well acquainted with the dead to believe in ghosts.

Does it matter where it's coming from? she thought, heart racing. What would an infant be doing in the ruined wing of an old factory? She forced herself to continue moving along the wall, listening, ignoring the ragged sound of her own breathing.

At last she saw a dim slice of light beneath a door up ahead. She paused. If there were soldiers on the other side of the door, she had no way to justify her presence there. She was too far from the main body of the building to pretend she'd simply gotten lost.

She heard a noise behind her and saw the swaying circle of a lantern approaching. Nina pressed herself against the wall, expecting to see a uniformed soldier. Instead, the lamplight caught the profile of a woman dressed in a Springmaiden's pinafore, braids piled atop her head. What was she doing so far from the others?

As the Springmaiden pushed through the door, Nina glimpsed another dark hallway, the gloom of it heavy between lanterns set at distant intervals. Nina gathered her courage and trailed the Springmaiden inside. She followed as closely as she dared, her heart thumping hard in her chest as sounds began to float back to her from the darkness ahead—the low murmurs of women's voices, someone singing what sounded like a lullaby, and then a sweet, high-pitched sound of delight. A baby laughing.

The whispers in Nina's head rose again, less angry than longing. *Hush now*, they said, *hush*.

The Springmaiden passed through an archway into . . . a dormitory. Nina sank into the shadows by the arch, not quite believing what she saw before her.

Women and girls lay in narrow beds as the Springmaidens moved among them. Beyond them, Nina glimpsed a row of bassinets. The room was otherwise bare, the dusty ruin of the factory wing cleared of equipment. The windows had been papered over in black—to prevent any lamplight from leaking outside and raising questions.

A girl who couldn't be more than sixteen was being walked up and down the length of the corridor by a Springmaiden. Her feet were bare and she wore a light gray gown that stretched over her jutting belly.

"I can't," she moaned. She looked unspeakably frail, the thrust of her stomach at odds with the sharp knobs and angles of her bones.

"You can," said the Springmaiden, her voice firm as she led the girl by her elbow.

"She needs to eat," said another of the women from the convent. "Skipped her breakfast."

The Springmaiden *tsk*ed. "You know you aren't to do that."

"I'm not hungry," panted the girl between heavy breaths.

"We can either walk to help the baby come or I can sit you down for some *semla*. The sugar will give you energy during the birth."

The girl began to cry. "I don't need sugar. You know what I need."

A tremor passed through Nina as understanding came. She recognized that desperation, that deep hunger that sank its teeth into you until all you were was wanting. She knew the need that turned everything you'd ever cared for—friends, food, love—to ash, until all you could remember of yourself was the desire for the drug. The wasted body, the dark hollows beneath her eyes—this girl was addicted to *parem*. And that meant she must be Grisha.

Nina peered down the row of beds at the women and girls. The youngest looked to be about fifteen, the oldest might have been in her thirties, but the ravages of the drug made it hard to tell. Some cradled small bumps beneath their thin blankets, others hunched over high, protruding stomachs. A few might not have been pregnant—or might not have been showing yet.

Nina felt her body tremble, heard the thunder of her heartbeat in her ears. What was this place? Who were these women?

Help us. Could these be the voices she had heard? But none of the women were looking at Nina. It was the dead who had summoned her. *Justice.*

The door behind Nina opened again, and as one, the patients in their beds turned their heads like flowers seeking the sun.

"She's here!" cried one of them as the Wellmother swept in. She was pushing a cart. The women began to rise from their beds, but the Wellmother gave a short, sharp "Be still!" They sank back obediently against their pillows. "There will be no rushing or shoving. You will get your injection when we come to you."

Nina eyed the rows of syringes on the cart and the ruddy liquid inside them. She wasn't even sure if it was *parem*, but she felt the pull of the drug, could swear she smelled it on the air. A year ago she would have clawed her way to those syringes without a second thought for revealing herself. She'd fought hard to break free from the addiction and had learned that using her new power helped. Now she focused on that power, on the current of that cold and silent river. She needed all the sense and calm she could summon because none of what she was seeing made sense.

Grisha under the influence of *parem* were beyond powerful. They could accomplish things that were otherwise unimaginable even with the most extraordinary amplifier. Jarl Brum had attempted to experiment on Grisha with the drug in the hope of turning them into weapons to be used against Ravka—but always under carefully controlled conditions. His Grisha captives had been confined to specially built cells that prohibited them from using their power, and the *parem* had been mixed with a sedative to try to make the prisoners more compliant.

These women weren't even in restraints.

The Wellmother moved down the line, handing syringes to the sisters, who injected the orange concoction into waiting arms. Nina heard a few sobs, a low, contented groan, a grumbled "She always starts on that end. It isn't fair."

The pregnant girl being walked along the aisle said, "Please. Just a little."

"Not so soon before the baby comes. It could put you both at risk."

The girl began to cry. "But you never give it to the mothers after the babies come."

291

"Then you'll just have to get pregnant again, won't you?"

The girl cried harder, and Nina didn't know if it was hunger for the drug or dread at what the Springmaiden was suggesting that made the girl cover her face and weep.

The women fell back in their beds, fingers flexing at their sides. The fire in the lanterns leapt. A gust of wind shifted a stack of bedsheets. Mist gathered over one girl's bed—she must be a Tidemaker. But they were all docile, gave not a single sign of defiance. Grisha on *parem* didn't behave this way. It was a stimulant. Had the drug been combined with another substance? Was this what had poisoned the wolves? If Nina somehow managed to steal a syringe, would Leoni be able to discern what new atrocity the Fjerdans had concocted? And how had the girls survived long enough on the drug to bear children, maybe multiple children?

A baby began to cry in one of the tiny cribs. A Springmaiden snatched a bottle from the bottom of the cart and picked up the infant, quieting it. "There you go, sweetheart," she crooned.

Nina pushed back against the wall, afraid her legs might give way. This could not be. But if the mothers were ingesting *parem* . . . then the babies would be too. They would be born addicted to the stuff. Perfect Grisha slaves.

Nina shuddered. Was this Brum's work? Someone else's? Were there other bases that had been given over to these experiments? *Why did I think these nightmares stopped at the Ice Court? How could I have been so naive?*

Her gaze fell on a woman lying in a daze, face nearly as pale as her pillow. A young girl lay in the bed next to her. Nina gripped the wall to steady herself. She recognized them. The mother and daughter from the Elling docks. Birgir had sent them here. Nina wished she'd killed him more slowly.

Was this what had become of the Grisha women who hadn't

made it to the safe house in Elling? Were they in this room right now? *Girls go missing from Kejerut.* Not just any girls. Grisha.

A bell sounded somewhere in the factory. The Wellmother clapped her hands, and several of the Springmaidens gathered to follow her.

"Have a good night, Marit," she said to one of the uniformed women as she left. "We'll have a shift in to relieve you tomorrow night."

Nina slipped in behind them as they left the dormitory. She kept to the gloom, trying to steady herself and think of the task ahead—getting out of the factory. But her mind felt fractured and wild, crowded with the images of that room.

Help us. The voices of the dead. The pain of the living.

Ahead she could see the Springmaidens approaching the guards at the main door.

"Did your straggler find you?" she heard one of the guards ask the Wellmother.

"What straggler?"

"I don't know, braids, pinafore. Looked the same as the rest of you."

"What are you talking about? We're all very tired and—"

"Line up for a head count."

"Is that strictly necessary?"

"Line up."

Nina did not wait to hear the rest. She set off at a sprint, back down the hall toward the eastern wing, trying to keep her footsteps light. The main entrance wasn't an option anymore. If the guards discovered an extra Springmaiden had—

A bell began to sound, different from the last, high and shrill. An alarm.

Lights came on all around her, the sudden glare blinding.

She wasn't going to make it back through the dormitory to the eastern gate.

Nina slid behind a dusty hunk of machinery as two guards stormed past, guns at the ready.

She looked up. Several of the windows here were broken, but how to reach them? And what was on the other side?

No time to debate the issue. By now the guards and the Wellmother knew that a rogue Springmaiden or someone dressed in a convent pinafore had infiltrated the factory. Nina had to get down the mountain and back to the convent before anybody found her bed empty. She scrambled atop the old piece of equipment and reached for the window ledge, struggling to haul herself up. She managed to wedge her foot between two bricks and shove her body onto the stone ledge.

Through the broken glass, she could see the twinkling lights of the town in the distance, patches of snow on the forest floor far below.

She heard footsteps and saw another squad of armed soldiers charging through the eastern wing on heavy boots.

"Lock down the perimeter," one was saying. "We'll search in a grid and work our way back toward the central hall."

"How do we even know someone is here?" another complained.

If they looked up—

But they continued on, conversation fading.

Nina took one last glance out the window.

"No mourners," she whispered, and launched herself through the broken glass.

She fell fast and hit the ground hard. Her shoulder and hip screamed at the force of the impact, but Nina stifled any sound as she rolled down the slope, unable to stop her momentum. She tumbled into the tree line, struck the base of a pine, and forced herself to shove to her feet.

She made herself take a moment to get oriented, then ran, dodging through the trees, keeping her hands up to try to stave off the slicing branches, trying to ignore the pain in her side. She had to get back to the convent and inside before the Wellmother returned. If she didn't, Leoni and Adrik would be taken unawares, and all their covers would be blown.

She came to a stream and charged through, shoes squelching in the shallows, then plunged down the next hill.

There, the convent—its windows still dark, though she could see lanterns in the stables, the chapel yard, the dish of scraps she had left out for Trassel.

Nina ran, lost her footing, righted herself, half falling now, trying to get down the mountain. When she reached the edge of the trees, she slowed, angling to the south so she could avoid the stables.

She heard the sound of hoofbeats and peered along the road. She saw the wagon, the driver whipping his horses hard. The Wellmother was returning from the factory, and Nina knew they would be searching the rooms within minutes.

Nina pulled off her muddy shoes, slid inside the kitchen, locked the door, and shoved the key beneath the flour tin. She hurried to her bedroom, already dragging her ruined clothes over her head.

"What's going on?" Leoni asked groggily as Nina stumbled into the room and hurriedly shut the door behind her.

"Nothing," whispered Nina. "Pretend to be asleep."

"Why?"

Nina heard doors slamming and voices in the convent entry. She yanked off her clothes, wiped her face and hands clean with the inside of her blouse, and stuffed the whole sodden mess into the trunk at the foot of her bed. "I was here all night."

"Oh, Nina," groaned Leoni. "Please tell me you were just getting a midnight snack."

"Yes," said Nina, wiggling into a night rail. "A very muddy one."

Nina threw herself under the covers just as the door sprang open and light from the hall flooded the room.

Nina made a pretense of startling awake. "What is it?"

Two Springmaidens stormed inside, pinafores rustling. Nina could hear voices in the dormitories above them, the clatter of doors opening and girls being woken from their sleep. *At least we're not the only ones under suspicion*, thought Nina. *Maybe they think a student snuck out to visit a soldier in the factory barracks.*

"What's going on?" asked Leoni.

"Be silent," snapped one of the Springmaidens. She held up her lantern, casting her gaze around the room.

Nina saw it in the same moment the Springmaiden did—a smudge of mud on the floor near the base of her bed.

The Springmaiden handed her companion her lantern and threw open the trunk, rummaging inside. She pulled out the filthy pinafore and blouse.

"Why do you have a novitiate's uniform?" the Springmaiden demanded. "And why is it covered in mud? I'm going to get the Wellmother."

"There's no need." The Wellmother stood in the doorway, round face stern, hands folded over the dark blue wool of her pinafore. "Explain yourself, Enke Jandersdat."

Nina opened her mouth, but before she could say a word, Hanne appeared behind the Wellmother. "The clothes are mine."

"What?"

"They're mine," repeated Hanne, looking ashen and lost, her hair flowing in thick, ruddy waves over her shoulders. "I went riding when I was not supposed to and took a fall from my horse."

The Wellmother narrowed her eyes. "Why would you hide them here?"

"I knew my dirty clothes would be discovered in my room, so I planned to wash them myself."

"And somehow the widow Jandersdat didn't notice a heap of muddy clothing in her trunk?"

"Mila said she would hide them for me until I could see to them."

The Wellmother eyed the soiled pinafore. "The mud seems fresh."

"I went riding only this morning. You'll see the clothes are my size, far too long for Mila. It is my fault, not hers."

"Is this true?" the Wellmother asked Nina.

Nina looked at Hanne.

"*Is it?*" the Wellmother demanded.

Nina nodded.

The Wellmother huffed a frustrated breath. "Finish the search," she instructed the Springmaidens. "Hanne, I cannot begin to express my disappointment. I will have to write to your father immediately."

"I understand, Wellmother," Hanne said, her misery clear. It was no performance. She had risked her future at the convent to save Nina.

"And you, Enke Jandersdat," said the Wellmother. "Your role here is to instruct Hanne in the Zemeni language, not to enable her disruptive behaviors. I will have to reconsider this whole arrangement."

"Yes, Wellmother," said Nina contritely, and watched as the woman shuffled Hanne down the hallway, closing the door behind her.

Leoni flopped back on the pillows. "Please tell me whatever you learned inside the factory was worth it."

Nina lay back, adrenaline still flooding her body. "It was worth it." But she'd seen the look in Hanne's eyes as the Wellmother led her away—she was going to want answers.

Nina thought of the punishment Hanne would take, what a letter home to her father might mean. She owed Hanne—maybe her life. She most certainly owed her the truth.

Help us.

But there was no way Nina could give it to her.

19

ZOYA

ZOYA HAD THOUGHT THEY would be led to new rooms that would serve as their living quarters. Instead, Juris and Grigori departed, and with a wave of Elizaveta's hand, the table and chairs dropped into the floor. A moment later, new walls rose around them. The sand twisted and arched, forming three doorways around a central chamber—all of it the lifeless, sun-leached color of old bone.

Zoya was not sure how much more of this she could stand. The world felt like it had been torn open.

"I wish we could offer more comfortable accommodations," said Elizaveta. "But this is a place of few comforts. Rest if you can."

Zoya's room looked like a bedchamber in a castle of old: pointed windows, heavy leather-backed chairs that sat before a vast fireplace, a huge canopied bed hung with velvet curtains. And yet there was no glass in the windows. There was no leather, no velvet. It was all that fine-grained sand, every item, every surface wrought in the same driftwood hue. The fire that burned in the grate flickered blue like that horrid dragon's flames. It was a phantom room. Zoya's hand went to her wrist. She needed to talk to Nikolai.

She opened the door—though it was hard to even think of it as a door when it hadn't existed moments before.

Nikolai stood in the archway of a chamber identical to hers.

"It's like looking at a sketch of something grand," he said, turning slowly to take in his new quarters. He ran a hand over the gray sand mantel. "Luxurious in its details but devoid of anything that would actually make you want to stay here."

"This is a mistake," said Zoya. Her head hurt. Her heart hurt. She had to keep her fingers from wandering continuously to her wrist. But she needed to think clearly. There were larger things at stake than what she'd lost. There always were.

"Where's Yuri?" he asked.

"Probably genuflecting somewhere. Nikolai, is this a bargain we want to make?"

"We came here for a cure, and now we've been offered one."

"You could die."

"A risk we've long been willing to take. In fact, I believe you offered to put a bullet in my head not so long ago."

"We have less than three weeks before the party in Os Alta," she protested.

"Then I will have to master the monster in that time."

"You saw what they can do. What if we shatter the bounds of the Unsea and unleash them on Ravka? Are you willing to make that gamble?"

Nikolai ran his hands through his hair. "I don't know."

"And yet you agreed to dance at the first asking like a boy at a country ball."

"I did."

And he didn't sound remotely sorry about it. "We can't trust them. We don't really even know who they are."

"I understand that. Just as you understand that is the choice we must make. Why are you fighting it, Zoya?"

Zoya leaned her head against the edge of the window and looked out at the nothing beyond. Had the Saints been staring at this same empty view for hundreds of years?

"If these are the Saints," she said, "then who have we been praying to all this time?"

"Do you pray?" Nikolai couldn't conceal his surprise.

"I did. When I was young. They never answered."

"We'll get you another."

"Another . . . ?" It took her a moment to understand what he meant. Without realizing it, Zoya had let her hand return to the place where her amplifier had been. She forced herself to release her wrist. "You can't get me *another*," she said, her voice thick with scorn. *Good.* Better that than self-pity. "It doesn't work that way. I've worn that cuff, those bones, since I was thirteen years old."

"Zoya, I don't believe in miracles. I don't know who these Saints really are. All I know is that they're the last hope we have."

She squeezed her eyes shut. Elizaveta could be as gracious as she liked. It didn't change the fact that they'd been abducted. "We're prisoners here, Nikolai. We don't know what they may ask of us."

"The first thing will be to banish your pride."

Nikolai and Zoya jumped. Juris stood in the doorway. He was in human form, but the shape of the dragon seemed to linger over him.

"Come, Zoya Nazyalensky, little storm witch. It's time."

"For what?" Zoya bit out, feeling anger ignite inside her—familiar, welcome, so much more useful than grief.

"For your first lesson," he said. "The boy king isn't the only one with something to learn."

Zoya did not want to go with the dragon, but she made herself follow him down the twisting halls of the mad palace. She told herself she'd be able to learn more about the ritual Nikolai was expected to endure and determine the Saints' true motives. The stronger voice inside her said that if she got to know Juris, she could find a way to punish him for what he'd taken from her. She was too aware of her pulse beating beneath the skin of her bare wrist. It felt naked, vulnerable, and utterly wrong.

Still, as much as she would have liked to give her thoughts over to revenge, the path they were taking required all her attention. The palace was vast, and though some individual rooms seemed to have specific characteristics, most of the hallways, stairs, and passages were wrought of the same glittering, colorless sand. It didn't help that no matter where you were inside the massive structure, you always had the same view: a wide gray expanse of nothing.

"I can feel your anger, storm witch," Juris said. "It makes the air crackle."

"That word is offensive," she said to his back, soothed by the thought of shoving him down the long flight of stairs.

"I can call you whatever you like. In my time, *witch* was the word men used for women they should steer clear of. I think that describes you very well."

"Then perhaps you should take your own advice and avoid me."

"I think not," said Juris. "One of the only joys left to me is courting danger, and the Fold offers few opportunities for it."

Would he even tumble if she pushed him, or just sprout wings and float gently to the bottom of the stairway? "How old are you anyway?"

"I've long since forgotten."

Juris looked to be a man of about forty. He was as big as Tolya, maybe larger, and Zoya could imagine he must have cut a daunting figure with a broadsword in his hand. She could see a tracery of scales over his shaven scalp, as if his dragon features had crept into his human body.

Her curiosity got the better of her. "Do you prefer your human form?"

"I have no preference. I am both human and dragon always. When I wish to read, to argue, to drink wine, I take the form of a man. When I wish to fly and be free of human bother, I am a dragon."

"And when you fight?"

He glanced over his shoulder and his eyes flashed silver, the pupils slitting as he smiled, his teeth slightly too long and predatory for his human mouth. "I could best you in either form."

"I doubt that," she said with more confidence than she felt. If she'd still had her amplifier, there would have been no hesitation.

"Do not forget I was a warrior in my first life."

Zoya raised an unimpressed brow. "Sankt Juris who slew the dragon was really a Grisha who made it his amplifier?" She knew the story well; every Ravkan child did—the warrior who had gone to best a beast and fought it three times before finally vanquishing it. But now she had to wonder how much was legend and how much was fact.

Juris scowled and continued down the stairs. "*Amplifier.* Like that pathetic bauble you clung to so desperately? When I slew the dragon, I took his form and he took mine. We became one. In the old times, that was how it was. What you practice now is a corruption, the weakest form of the making at the heart of the world."

In the old times. Was there truth, then, in the stories of the Burning Thorn? Had those monks not been ordinary men but Grisha who had taken the shapes of beasts to better wage war against Ravka's enemies? Had both the Grisha theorists and the religious scholars gotten it so wrong? Zoya didn't know. Her tired, battered mind couldn't make sense of it.

They entered an enormous chamber that looked at once like a cavern and the great hall of an ancient castle keep wrought in black stone. A crest hung on one high wall above a fireplace tall enough for Zoya to stand in. The crest showed three six-pointed stars and was of the type Kaelish families used, though Zoya did not know their iconography well enough to identify which name Juris might have once claimed. One wall had been left entirely open to the elements, the wide horizon of dead sand visible beyond. The jagged overhang made Zoya feel a bit like she was looking out at the world through the opening of a cave. Or the mouth of a beast whose belly she had made the mistake of wandering into.

"What is it you want from me?" she asked.

"When I pass into the mortal world, my magic will go with me, but my knowledge need not. You will carry it."

"What an honor," she said without enthusiasm.

"All of the rules the Grisha have created, that you live by, the colors you wear. You think you've been training to make yourself stronger, when really you've been training to limit your power."

Zoya shook her head. First this oversized lizard had robbed her of the amplifier she'd earned with her own blood, and now he was insulting the training she'd dedicated her life to. She'd taken her education at the Little Palace seriously, the theory she'd read in the library, the poses and techniques she'd learned in Baghra's hut by the lake. She'd practiced and honed her abilities, forged her raw talent into something more. There had been other Etherealki who had started with more natural ability, but none had worked as hard. "You can say that, but I know that training made me a better Squaller."

"Yes, but did it make you a better Grisha?"

"Isn't that what I just said?"

"Not quite. But I began in ignorance as deep as yours and—just like you—with nothing but the wild wind at my fingertips."

"You were a Squaller?" Zoya asked, surprised.

"There was no name for what I was."

"But you could summon?" she pushed.

"I could. I did. It was one more weapon in my arsenal."

"In what war?"

"In countless wars. I was hero to some. Others would have called me an invader, a barbarian, a sacker of temples. I tried to be a good man. At least, that's what I remember."

How men liked to recount their deeds.

"Not all of us take to nobility as well as your king."

Zoya strolled the perimeter of the room. There was little to look at. Other than the weapons collected on the wall, everything was black stone—the mantel of the great fireplace where blue flame leapt and danced, the decorations atop it, the crest upon the wall. "If you expect me to damn Nikolai for his goodness, you'll have to wait awhile."

"And if I tell you Ravka needs a more ruthless ruler?"

"I'd say that sounds like the excuse of a ruthless man."

"Who said anything about men?"

Was that this creature's game? "You wish me to steal my king's throne? You mistake my ambitions."

Juris rumbled a laugh. "I mistake nothing. Do you really believe you were meant to spend your life in service? You cannot tell me you have not contemplated what it would mean to be a queen."

Zoya picked up a tiny agate horse on the mantel, one of a herd of what might be hundreds that flowed over the stone. Was this how Juris spent his eternity? Using fire to fashion tiny reminders of another life? "As if a queen does not live her life in service too. I serve the Grisha. I serve Ravka."

"Ravka." He rolled the *R* in a growl. "You serve a nation of ghosts. All those you failed. All those you will continue to fail until you become what you were meant to be."

All those you failed. What did he know about anything? Zoya set down the horse and rubbed her arms. She didn't like the way the dragon talked. His words rattled around inside her, made her think of that falling stone, that empty well, that endless hollow. *Do not look back*, Liliyana had warned her once. *Do not look back at me.* Zoya hadn't listened then, but she'd learned to heed those words.

"Finish your story, old man, or set me free to go find a glass of wine and a nap."

"You'll find no wine here, little witch. No sleep either. No respite from oblivion."

Zoya gave a dismissive wave. "Then set me free to find more interesting company."

Juris shrugged. "There is little more to tell. A ravening beast came to our land, burning everything in its path, devouring all those who dared oppose it."

Idly, Zoya touched her finger to the ball of a mace on the wall. Juris must have had the weapons with him when they were trapped on the Fold. "I always thought the dragon was a metaphor."

Juris looked almost affronted. "For what?"

"Heathen religion, foreign invaders, the perils of the modern world."

"Sometimes a dragon is just a dragon, Zoya Nazyalensky, and I can assure you no metaphor has ever murdered so many."

"You've never heard Tolya recite poetry. So the great warrior went to meet the dragon in his lair?"

"Just so. Can you imagine my terror?"

"I have an inkling." She would never forget her first sight of Juris with his vast wings spread—and she wanted to know how he'd bested the beast. "What did you do?"

"What all frightened men do. The night before I was to meet the dragon, I went down on my knees and prayed."

"Who does a Saint pray to?"

"I never claimed to be a Saint, Zoya. That is just the name a desperate world gave me. That night I was nothing more than a scared man, a boy really, barely eighteen. I prayed to the god of the sky who had watched over my family, the god of storms who watered the fields and fed on careless sailors. Maybe it is that god who watches over me still. All I know is something answered. When I faced the dragon and he breathed fire, the winds rose to my command. I was able to snatch his breath away, just as you tried to do with me. Twice we clashed and twice we retreated to see to our wounds. But on the third meeting, I dealt him a fatal blow."

"Juris in triumph." She would not do him the courtesy of sounding impressed.

But he surprised her by saying, "Perhaps I should have felt triumphant. It's what I expected. But when the dragon fell, I knew nothing but regret."

"Why?" she asked, though she had always felt sorry for the dragon in Juris' story, a beast who could not help his nature.

Juris leaned his big body against the basalt wall. "The dragon was the first true challenge I'd ever known as a warrior, the only creature able to meet me as an equal in the field. I could not help but respect him. As he sank his jaws into me, I knew he felt just as I did. The dragon and I were the same, connected to the heart of creation, born of the elements, and unlike any other."

"Like calls to like," she said softly. She knew that feeling of kinship, of ferocity. If she closed her eyes, she would feel the ice on her cheeks, see the blood in the snow. "But in the end, you killed him."

"We both died that day, Zoya. I have his memories and he has mine. We have lived a thousand lives together. It was the same with Grigori and the great bear, with Elizaveta and her bees. Have you never stopped to wonder how it's possible that some Grisha are themselves amplifiers?"

Zoya hadn't really. Grisha who were born amplifiers were rare and often served as Examiners, using their abilities to test for the presence of Grisha power in children. The Darkling had himself been an amplifier, as had his mother. It was one of the theories for why he had been so powerful. "No," she admitted.

"They are connected to the making at the heart of the world. In the time before the word *Grisha* had ever been spoken, the lines that divided us from other creatures were less firm. We did not just take an animal's life, we gave up a part of ourselves in return. But somewhere along the way, Grisha began killing, claiming a piece of the power of creation without giving anything of ourselves. This is the pathetic tradition of your amplifiers."

"Should I feel shame for claiming an amplifier?" Zoya said. He had no right to these judgments. How often had Zoya cried? How many futile prayers had she spoken, unable to rid herself of that stubborn, stupid belief that someone would answer? "It must be easy to ponder the universe, safe in your palace, away from the petty, brutal dealings of man. Maybe you don't remember what it is to be powerless. I do."

"Maybe so," said Juris. "But you still wept for the tiger."

Zoya froze. He couldn't know. No one knew what she had done that night, what she had seen. "What do you mean?"

"When you are tied to all things, there is no limit to what you may know. The moment that bracelet dropped from your wrist, I saw it all. Young Zoya bleeding in the snow, heart full of valor. Zoya of the lost city. Zoya of the garden. You could not protect them then, and you cannot protect them now, not you and not your monster king."

Do not look back at me. The well within her had no bottom. She tossed a stone into the darkness and she fell with it, on and on. She needed to get out of this room, to get away from Juris. "Are we done here?"

"We haven't yet begun. Tell me, storm witch, when you slew the tiger, did you not feel its spirit moving through you, feel it take the shape of your anger?"

Zoya did not want to speak of that night. The dragon knew things he could not know. She forced herself to laugh. "You're saying I might have become a tiger?"

"Maybe. But you are weak, so who can be certain?"

Zoya curled her lip. She kept herself still though the rage inside her leapt. "Do you mean to goad me? It will take more than the slights of an old man."

"You showed courage when we fought—ingenuity, nerve. And still you lost. You will continue to lose until you open the door."

He turned suddenly and lunged toward her, his body growing larger, blotting out the light as his wings spread. His vast jaws parted and flame bloomed from somewhere inside him.

Zoya threw her arms over her head, cowering.

Abruptly the flames banked and Juris stood looking at her in his human form. "Have I chosen a weakling?" he said in disgust.

But now it was Zoya's turn to smile. "Or maybe just a girl who knows how to look like one."

Zoya stood and thrust her hands forward. The storm thundered toward him, a straight shot of wind and ire that knocked Juris from his feet and sent him tumbling, skating along the smooth stone floor and right out of the cave mouth. *Weak.* A fraction of the strength she had commanded with her amplifier. But he rolled over the edge and vanished, the surprise on his face like a balm to Zoya's heart.

A moment later the dragon rose on giant wings. "Did I break your will when I broke your silly bauble?"

Had he? Without her amplifier, summoning her power was like reaching for something and misjudging the distance, feeling your fingers close over nothing but air. She had always been powerful, but it was the tiger's life that had given her true strength. And now it was gone. What was she—*who* was she without it? If they ever got free of this place, how was she supposed to return to her command?

"Choose a weapon," said Juris.

"I'm too tired for this."

"Give me a worthy fight and you can go hide wherever you like. Choose a weapon."

"I *am* the weapon." Or she had been. "I don't need a cudgel or a blade."

"Very well," said Juris, shifting smoothly into his human form. "I'll choose one for you." He grabbed a sword from the wall and tossed it to her.

She caught it awkwardly with both hands. It was far too heavy. But she had no time to think. He was already springing toward her, a massive broadsword in his hands.

"What is the point of this?" she asked as he struck her blade with a blow that reverberated up her arms. "I've never been any good at swordplay."

"You've spent your life only choosing the paths at which you knew you could excel. It's made you lazy."

Zoya grimaced and parried, trying to remember her long-ago education with Botkin Yul-Erdene. They'd used knives and rapiers and even taken target practice with pistols. Zoya had enjoyed all of it, particularly the hand-to-hand combat, but she'd had little cause to practice her skills since. What was the point of using her fists when she could command a storm?

"Not bad," he said as she succeeded in dodging one of his thrusts. "Using your power has become too easy for you. When you fight this way, you have to focus so entirely on surviving that you stop thinking about everything else. You cannot worry about what came before or what happens next, what has been lost or what you might gain. There is only this moment."

"What possible advantage is that?" Zoya said. "Isn't it better to be able to predict what comes next?"

"When your mind is free, the door opens."

"What *door*?"

"The door to the making at the heart of the world."

Zoya feinted right and stepped close to deny Juris the advantage of his longer reach. "That is already what I do when I summon," she said, sweat beginning to drip from her brow. "That's what *all* Grisha do when we use our power."

"Is it?" he asked, bringing his sword down again. The clash of metal filled her ears. "The storm is still outside you, something you welcome and guard against all at once. It howls outside the door. It rattles the windows. It wants to be let in."

"That makes no sense."

"Let the storm in, Zoya. Do not summon. Do not reach for it. Let it come to you. Let it guide your movements. Give me a proper fight."

Zoya grunted as his blade struck hers. She was already breathless, her arms aching from the weight of her weapon. "I'm not strong enough to beat you without using my power."

"You do not *use* it. You *are* it. The storm is in your bones."

"Stop. Talking. Nonsense," she snarled. It wasn't fair. He was forcing her to play a game she couldn't win. And Zoya always won.

Very well. If he wanted her to fight without summoning, she would, and she would best him at it too. Then Juris could hang his big ugly head in shame. She charged him, giving in to the thrill of the fight, the challenge of it, ignoring the pain that shivered up her arms as his blade met hers again and again. She was smaller and lighter, so she kept to the balls of her feet and stayed well within his guard.

His blade hissed against the flesh of her arm, and she felt the pain like a burn. Zoya knew she was bleeding, but she didn't care. She only wanted to know he could bleed too.

Lunge. Parry. Attack. React. React. React. Her heart pounded like thunder. In her blood she felt the roaring of the wind. She could feel her body move before she told it to, the air whistling past her, through her. Her blood was charged with lightning. She brought her sword down, and in it she felt the strength of the hurricane, tearing trees up by their roots, unstoppable.

Juris' blade shattered.

"There she is," he said with his dragon's smile.

Zoya stood quaking, eyes wide. She had felt her strength double, treble, the strength of a whirlwind in her limbs. It shouldn't have been possible, but she couldn't deny what she'd felt—or what she'd done. The proof was in the broken weapon that lay at her feet. She flexed her hand around the grip of her sword. *The storm is in your bones.*

"I see I finally have your attention," said the dragon.

She looked up at him. He'd stolen her amplifier, broken some part of her. She would repay him for that—and he would help her learn to do it.

"Is there more?" she asked.

"So much more," said Juris.

Zoya dropped back into fighting stance and lifted her blade—light as air in her hands. "Then you'd better get yourself a new sword."

20

NINA

ADRIK WAS FURIOUS—still glum, but furious. It was like being yelled at by a damp towel.

"What were you thinking?" he demanded the next morning. They'd walked out to the southern part of town, with Leoni and the sledge in tow, ostensibly to try to make sales to local hunters and trappers. But they'd stopped near an old tanning shed so that Adrik would have privacy to let Nina know just how disastrously she'd behaved. "I gave you direct orders. You were not to engage, certainly not on your own. What if you'd been captured?"

"I wasn't."

Leoni leaned against the cart. "If Hanne hadn't stepped in to help, you would have been. Now you're in that girl's debt."

"I was already in her debt. And have you forgotten she's Grisha? She won't talk. Not unless she wants to put herself in danger."

Adrik glanced up at the factory looming over the valley. "We should destroy this place. It would be a mercy."

"No," Nina said. "There has to be a way to get the girls out."

Adrik looked at her with his moping, melting-candle expression. "You know what *parem* does. They won't come back from this. They're as good as dead."

"Stop being such a head cold," Nina retorted. "I came back from it."

"From *one* dose. You're telling us these girls have been dosed for months."

"Not with ordinary *parem*. The Fjerdans are trying something new, something different. It's why Leoni got sick but didn't get a real reaction. It's why my own addiction didn't get triggered again."

"Nina—"

She seized his arm. "The Second Army knows more now than we did when I took *parem*, Adrik. They've made progress on an antidote. It's possible the Fabrikators and Healers at the Little Palace could help them."

Adrik shook off her grip. "Do you understand what you've done, Nina? Even if they decided last night was nothing more than a bit of miscommunication, they're going to increase security in that factory. They may report the breach to their superiors. We need to leave this town while we still can, or we risk compromising the entire Hringsa network and any chance Ravka has of acting on the information you learned. You didn't even get a sample of the drug they've developed."

She hadn't had the chance—and she'd been too shaken to think clearly. But she wasn't going to make the girls on the mountain pay for her mistake.

"I won't do it, Adrik. You can leave me here. Tell the king I deserted."

"Those women are going to die. You can make up any happy

ending you want, but you know it's true. Don't ask me to sacrifice the hope of the living for the comfort of the dead."

"We aren't just here to recruit soldiers—"

Adrik's blue gaze sharpened. "We are here on orders from the king. We are here to salvage the future of our people. Ravka won't survive without more soldiers, and the Grisha won't survive without Ravka. I saw the Second Army decimated by the Darkling. I know what we've lost and how much more we stand to lose. We have to preserve the network. We owe it to every Grisha living in fear."

"I can't leave them behind, Adrik. I won't." *They brought me here.* They were the reason she'd finally been able to lay Matthias to rest. The voices of the dead had called her back to life with their need. She would not fail them. "Leoni," she pleaded. "If it were you up there, someone you loved . . ."

Leoni sat down on a fallen tree trunk and looked up at the fort.

"Leoni," said Adrik, "we have a mission. We can't compromise it."

"Both of you be quiet," Leoni said. "I won't be pulled this way or that because you say so." She closed her eyes, turned her face to the winter sun. After a long while, she said, "I told you I almost died as a child, but I never told you it was from drinking poisoned well water. The zowa healer who helped me perished in order to save my life. She died pulling the poison from my body." Leoni opened her eyes, a sad smile on her lips. "Like I told you, poisons are tricky work. So now I wear two jewels." She touched her hands to the golden stones woven into the twists of her hair on the left. "Topaz for strength, for my mother who gave me life and raised me to be a fighter." She turned her head slightly and light caught on the three purple gems in her twists on the right. "Amethyst for Aditi Hilli, the Fabrikator who returned my life to me when I was careless and might have lost it."

"Hilli?" said Adrik. "You were related?"

"No. I took her family name, and I swore I would honor her sacrifice, that I would make something of the life she gave to me." She bobbed her chin toward the factory. "If we're not here for the girls on that ward, then what are we doing here?"

Adrik sighed. "You do know this is my command. We don't put things to a vote."

Leoni smiled, that brilliant, thousand-sunrise smile. Adrik sucked in a breath as if he'd taken a blow to the gut. "I know," she said. "But I also know you fought beside Alina Starkov. You got your arm torn off by a shadow demon and kept fighting. You didn't come to this country to play it safe, Adrik."

"Leoni," Nina said. "Have you ever had Kerch waffles?"

Leoni's brows rose. "I have not."

"Well, I'm going to make you a stack so tall you have to climb over it."

"I didn't know you could cook."

"I can't. Not even a little bit. But I'm very good at convincing people to cook *for* me."

Adrik yanked his pinned sleeve into place. "The two of you are impossible. And guilty of insubordination."

Leoni only smiled wider. "We're splendid, and you know it."

"Fine," Adrik huffed. "Since you're both so determined to compromise our mission, just how are we going to transport a bunch of infants and pregnant women out of this tragedy of a town and get them to a port in the middle of the night?"

Nina looked up at the mountain, at the factory road lolling like a long, greedy tongue, at the guardhouse at its base—the first line of security for the soldiers working above. She remembered the lessons she'd learned in Ketterdam, when she'd run not with soldiers bound by honor but with liars, thugs, and thieves. *Always hit where the mark isn't looking.*

"Easy," she said. "We do it in the middle of the day. And we make sure they see us coming."

Nina wasn't at all sure that Hanne would show up to their next lesson—either because the Wellmother might forbid it or because she didn't want to speak to Nina again. But she decided to go to the classroom anyway.

On the way, she stopped by the kitchens for fresh scraps and went to the woods to set out another plate for Trassel. Nina took a moment to gather her thoughts, grateful for the quiet of the trees, breathing in the scent of sap, the cold air still fresh with fallen snow. She could admit her foray into the factory had been a catastrophe, but that didn't change what was happening on the mountain or the opportunity she'd been given. She felt like she was at the start of something bigger than the horrors on that hilltop, that there was more she was meant to do.

"But what?" she murmured.

"Enke Jandersdat?"

Nina nearly leapt into the nearest branch. A young woman was standing at the edge of the trees, hands tugging nervously at the skirts of her pale blue pinafore. It took Nina a long moment to realize she'd seen the novitiate before—dressed as a Fjerdan soldier on the banks of the river. Had she heard Nina speak Ravkan?

"Yes?" Nina said.

"I didn't mean to startle you."

"A bit of excitement is good for me," Nina said, as if she hadn't recently jumped out of a window and fled down a mountain for her life. The girl had blond hair and skin the color of a new peach. She didn't seem wary at all, just nervous.

"I wanted to thank you and the Zemeni traders for not saying

318

anything about . . . what you saw by the river. Even after what happened to Grette."

Grette . . . She must mean the girl who had died from exposure to the water.

"It was enough of a tragedy," Nina said.

The girl shivered, as if death had come too close. "Her mother came to collect her body. It was terrible. But if her family knew how she got those injuries? The shame—"

"I understand," said Nina, then ventured, "Will you ride out again?"

"Of course not," said the girl earnestly, almost pleadingly. "*Never* again."

Nina believed her.

"Tell me," Nina said, "was it Hanne's idea to steal the uniforms?" Hanne was essential to Nina's plan. The more she understood her, the better. And she could admit she was curious too.

The girl worried her lower lip. "I . . . She . . ."

"I won't tell the Wellmother. If I spoke up now, she would wonder why I'd held my tongue for so long. It would do no one any good."

The thought seemed to put the girl at ease. "Hanne . . . Hanne takes risks she shouldn't." A small smile tugged at her lips. "But it can be hard not to want to follow."

"Do you ride out with her often?"

"Only when she lets us."

"A great deal to chance for a bit of freedom."

"It's not just that," said the girl. "Hanne . . . Sometimes people send to the convent for help, and the Wellmother will not grant them aid—for good and proper reasons, of course."

"Of course. What kind of people?"

"Families who can't afford an extra pair of hands when someone falls sick." The girl's cheeks flushed. "Unmarried women who have . . . gotten themselves into trouble."

"And Hanne goes to them?" Nina asked, surprised. That wild, wiry girl with a rifle on her back and a dagger at her hip? It was hard to imagine.

"Oh yes," said the girl. "She has a gift for it. She's nursed more than one hopeless case back from the brink and even helped deliver babies—one that got all turned around in her mother's belly."

She's a Healer, Nina realized. *She's using her power and she doesn't even know it.* She remembered Hanne saying of the other novitiates, *It's a game to them. A childish bit of dress-up, a chance to be daring.* Nina had thought she understood, but she hadn't really.

"If you'd told on us," the girl said, "Hanne would have had to stop. The Wellmother—"

"I won't say a word," said Nina. "I don't believe Djel could frown upon such kindness."

"No," said the girl thoughtfully. "I don't either."

"I'm sorry about your friend Grette."

"Me too." The girl plucked a cluster of pine needles from a branch. "Sometimes . . . I think Gäfvalle doesn't want us here."

"The convent?"

She shook her head, eyes distant. "Girls . . . any of us."

Nina wanted to push further, but a bell began to clang inside the chapel.

The girl curtsied quickly. "May Djel keep you, Enke Jandersdat," she said, and rushed off to her classes.

Nina hurried after. If Hanne did decide to come to class, Nina didn't want to be late. Adrik had already sent word to the Hringsa network in Hjar to make sure a ship would be waiting—assuming they somehow managed to get the women out of the factory. But if Hanne didn't come today, Nina would have to seek her out and find a way back into her good graces. She needed Hanne for the plan she had in mind, and, if she was honest with herself, she didn't much like the idea of Hanne being mad at her.

She had written out half of the day's lesson in Zemeni vocabulary on the board and was starting to feel like the whole endeavor was futile, when Hanne appeared at the classroom door. Nina wasn't quite prepared for the anger radiating off of her. She stood in silent fury as Nina clutched the chalk in her hands and tried to think of something conciliatory to say. Hanne's copper eyes looked like vivid sparks against her cheeks, but Nina knew from experience that *You're beautiful when you're angry* was never a great place to start.

"I didn't think you'd come," she began.

"The Wellmother says I may continue my lessons, since she doesn't want me left idle."

"That's won——"

"I didn't say *I* wanted to continue," Hanne whispered furiously. "What were you doing at the factory? I want the truth."

And I wish I could give it to you. All of it. But despite what she'd learned from the girl in the woods, she didn't trust Hanne that much. Not yet.

Nina gestured her inside and shut the door. She leaned against it. She'd spent last night thinking about how to answer Hanne's questions. "Do you remember the sister I told you about?" Nina asked. "The one who married and lives in the south?" Hanne nodded. "She was caught."

Hanne's fists bunched. "But you said——"

"I don't know how it happened, but she was caught using her Grisha power, and she was taken by the *drüskelle*."

"What became of her husband?"

"He was taken too. And put to death for harboring her secrets. I think they brought Thyra here."

"They brought your sister to a munitions factory?"

321

"The factory is only part of the story. Soldiers are keeping Grisha girls in the abandoned wing of the fort. They're experimenting on them. The Wellmother is helping, along with some of the Springmaidens."

Hanne folded her arms. "They wouldn't do that. Discovered Grisha are taken to the Ice Court for trial."

Trials at which they were never found innocent, at which they were always sentenced to death. But the sentences were rarely carried out. Instead, Jarl Brum had secretly imprisoned those Grisha and subjected them to doses of *parem*.

"Don't cover your ears and pretend you don't know what men are capable of, Hanne. Tell me something: Have girls and women gone missing from Kejerut? From Gäfvalle? From all of the river cities?"

"*Gone missing?*" Hanne scoffed.

"How have they explained the disappearances?" Nina persisted. "Sickness? A sudden decision to take a trip? Wild animals? Brigands?"

"All of those things happen. That's what living out here is like. Fjerda has hard ways." Her voice was defensive but also proud.

Still, Nina didn't think she'd imagined the slight hesitation, the quick flash of fear on Hanne's face.

"You've seen the Ice Court, Hanne."

"What does that have to do with anything?"

"Do you really believe it was built by human hands? What if it was Grisha craft? What if Fjerda needs Grisha as much as it hates them?" And as Nina said it, she thought of the new weapons the Fjerdan military had been developing, the sudden leap in their progress. As if they were working with Fabrikators. Maybe they hadn't managed to weaponize *parem*, but they'd certainly found new ways to exploit Grisha slaves.

Hanne bit her lip and gazed out the classroom window. She had a smattering of freckles over the bridge of her nose, not golden like

Adrik's, but rosy, the color of ripe persimmon. "There was a girl here," she said hesitantly, "Ellinor, a novitiate. She always kept to herself. One morning she was just gone. The sisters told us that she'd secured an offer of marriage and gone to Djerholm. But when I snuck into the woods to ride that day, I saw the Wellmother. She was burning Ellinor's things."

Nina shivered. Was Ellinor in that ward? Or was she already in a grave on the mountain?

"And a woman who lived between here and Kejerut," Hanne said slowly, as if fighting the words. "Sylvi Winther. She . . . she had just come through a bad illness. She was faring well. She and her husband just packed up and left."

Had this been one of the women Hanne had tended to in secret? Had she ridden out one cold afternoon and knocked on their door, only to find Sylvi and her husband gone?

"I know you've been taught to hate Grisha, Hanne . . . to hate yourself. But what the Wellmother and those soldiers are doing to those women is unforgivable."

Hanne didn't look angry anymore. She looked sick and frightened. "And what are we supposed to do about it?"

Nina thought of Matthias lying bleeding in her arms. She thought of girls lined up like misshapen dolls in the gloom of the old fort. She thought of the way Hanne hunched her shoulders as if she could somehow make herself invisible.

"Save them," said Nina. "Save them all."

21

ISAAK

ISAAK SAT ON THE RAVKAN throne—crafted by the legendary Fabrikator Eldeni Duda from Tsibeyan gold, crowned by a looming double eagle, and host to the backsides of countless generations of Lantsovs. All he could think of was how badly he needed to go to the bathroom.

They were two hours into the presentations, speeches, and gifts of the arriving delegations. He could tell that many of those present in the overheated throne room were flagging, weak from standing on their feet and bored by the proceedings. But Isaak would have been wide awake even without the menacing presence of Tolya Yul-Bataar to his left and Tamar Kir-Bataar to his right.

He wasn't expected to do much more than say "thank you" when handed an elegant pair of new revolvers from Novyi Zem or a lapis chest full of gemstone birds from Kerch. But despite the pretense of gifts and courtship, Isaak knew enemies lurked among this roomful of allies. Who was a potential asset to the king? Who wished to do him harm?

Isaak smiled into the faces of the Fjerdan delegation—all tall, blond, and regal, their slim bodies arrayed in sparkling white and pale gray, as if they'd drifted in off the ice. He accepted their gifts of sea pearls and remembered the two Fjerdan bullets that had been taken from his thigh after Halmhend. The Fjerdans had backed the Darkling in the civil war. They'd been at least partially responsible for the death of the king's older brother, Vasily. Each member of each delegation had been vetted, but they were still risks. At least Isaak's work as a guard had prepared him for such threats.

The Shu party was entirely female. Princess Ehri Kir-Taban wore emerald silks embroidered with silver leaves, her long dark hair caught up in jeweled combs. She was known as the least beautiful but the most beloved of the five royal sisters. The Tavgharad marched behind their charge, expressions fixed in the hard, empty gaze Isaak had mastered during his own tenure as a palace guard. But these were no ordinary soldiers. They were elite fighters, trained from childhood to serve the Taban dynasty. They wore black uniforms, the screaming beak of a falcon carved from garnet on the left epaulet, square black caps set at a sharp angle over their tightly bound hair. Tamar had said one of them intended to defect. *But which?* Isaak wondered, scanning their faces. They *looked* like falcons with their stern mouths and gleaming golden eyes. Why would one of them turn her back on her country and betray the women she'd been trained to protect? Did one of them really intend to defect, or was this some kind of trap for the king? The princess wobbled slightly in her curtsy, a light sheen of sweat on her upper lip, and Isaak saw the face of the guard directly behind her harden even further. He knew he shouldn't, but he felt for the princess as she rose from her curtsy and gave him a tremulous smile. He had gotten the barest taste of what it meant to be royal, and he didn't like it at all.

Isaak hadn't really understood what it would mean to wear the king's face, to walk in his shoes. Tolya and Tamar had spirited Isaak out of the palace the previous night to the estate of the notorious Count Kirigin. He would have liked to see the grounds of the infamous Gilded Bog, but at dawn, with Isaak now dressed in the olive drab coat King Nikolai favored, they'd set him atop an exquisite white gelding, and the party had turned back to the city for a staged ride to the capital. They'd been joined by a group of guards and soldiers in military dress—the king's retinue—and that had been Isaak's first test. But no one had done more than bow to him or salute. He'd been safely tucked between the Bataar twins and a crew of Grisha soldiers, including Tamar's wife, Nadia, as they rode through the countryside and then back through the lower town.

He'd been reminded of the first time he had glimpsed Os Alta, how awed he'd been by its bustle and size. It looked no different now that he was seeing it through the eyes of a king.

"Stop that," whispered Tolya.

"What?"

"Gawking at everything like some kind of wide-eyed yokel," said Tamar. "You must look at the world as if you own it."

"Because you are the king, and *you do*," added Tolya.

"As if I own it," Isaak repeated.

"You could order this city and every building in it burned to the ground."

Was that supposed to make him feel better? "I should hope someone would stop me?"

"Someone might try," said Tamar. "And he'd probably be hanged for it."

Isaak shuddered.

"At least he can seat a horse well," grumbled Tolya.

But Isaak managed to get that wrong too, because a king did not leap from his horse and take his mount to the stables; he waited for the groom. A king tossed the reins to him with a smile and a bob of the head and a "Many thanks, Klimint" or a "How's your cough, Lyov?" Because of course Nikolai Lantsov knew the names of every servant in the palace. If he'd been a lazier sovereign this might have been easier.

The way everyone gazed at Isaak frightened him. Isaak had been a nobody, a First Army grunt and then a palace guard. In the lower town, people had addressed him with respect or resentment when they saw his uniform. He remembered the pride of putting on the white and gold for the first time, the bizarre experience of people stepping out of his way or offering him a free glass of kvas, while others spat in the street and swore beneath their breath when they saw him and his comrades pass. It had been nothing like this. Had he looked at the king the way these people did—full of open gratitude and admiration? And what about the others, who looked on the king with suspicion and, sometimes, outright fear?

"Why do they stare so?" he whispered. "What do they expect to see?"

"You are no longer one man," said Tamar. "You are an army. You are the double eagle. You are all of Ravka. Of course people stare."

"And them?" Isaak said, bobbing his head toward one of the windows where girls had perched themselves, arrayed in their best dresses, hair curled, cheeks and lips pinked. "The king is not . . . he's not one for dallying with commoners, is he?"

"No," said Tolya. "Nikolai is not a man to take advantage of his position."

"Then what do they hope to accomplish?"

Tamar laughed. "You've read the old tales of princes falling in love with commoners and kings taking peasant queens. Nikolai is without a bride. Can you blame them for hoping one of them might catch his eye? That he might not fall instantly and unequivocally in love with a girl's beauty or the curve of her neck or her auburn hair, as kings in stories are wont to do?"

"You needn't be quite so good a study of all the lower town has on offer," said Nadia tartly.

Tamar gave no apology, only flashed a knowing smile that sent the blood rushing to Nadia's cheeks. "I may peruse the gaudy wares, but I recognize true quality when I see it."

Now Isaak looked out at the crowded throne room and wondered if he could just run back to the stables, get on that fine white horse, and ride until he was captured or shot at.

Tolya gave the throne the lightest nudge of his toe, and Isaak realized it was his time to speak.

He rose. "My friends——" His voice cracked, and he saw Genya close her eyes as if in pain. He cleared his throat and tried again. "My friends," he began in Ravkan, repeating himself in Shu, Zemeni, and Fjerdan. "I welcome you to Ravka and thank you for taking this small step toward a peace that I hope will be profitable and fruitful for us all. In this moment, we are not nations; we are friends who will eat together——" Here Isaak paused just as he'd been instructed and let a bit of Nikolai's rakish grin touch his lips. "And drink together. Let this night mark the start of a new age." *And let me get through dinner without choking on a lamb chop or causing a war.*

Isaak nodded, the doors on either side of the throne opened, and the crowd parted to let him pass.

He hadn't even made it inside the dining room before disaster struck. The footmen threw open the doors, and Isaak, focused on how sweaty his hands had become in his gloves, did what he had been trained to do and had done for years—he stepped aside, slipping into attention, eyes in the middle-focus stare that had been taught to him by his elders along with the method of shining his boots and the proper technique for sewing on a button, since "no servant need be troubled by the likes of us."

Guards always gave way for those of higher status, and in a palace, almost everyone was of higher status—including many of the more valued servants. But no one was of higher status than the king of Ravka.

Isaak felt the gasp as much as he heard it and had the sudden lurching sensation that the floor had dissolved beneath him, that he would fall and keep falling until he struck hard ground. At which point, Genya would stand above him and kick him with her slippered toe.

"Your Highness?" asked the Shu princess, who would enter the dining room first since her delegation had given their presentations last. She looked almost as panicked as he felt.

Isaak's first impulse was to search the room for someone, *anyone,* to help him, to tell him what to do. *Don't panic. Kings don't panic. But you're not a king. There's still time to leap out a window.*

He sketched a shallow bow and used the seconds he gained to fix a confident smile on his face. "Tonight, I am first a host and then a king."

"Of course," said the princess, though she appeared utterly flummoxed.

The rest of the guests filed past, some of them looking amused, others pleased, others disapproving. Isaak stood there and kept his smile pasted on, his chin lifted as if this were all a test for Ravka's next queen.

When the last of the foreign dignitaries had filled the hall, Genya and David entered. Genya looked serene, but he could see the strain around the corners of her mouth. David seemed distracted as always.

"No need to worry," said Genya. "You're doing marvelously."

David frowned, his face thoughtful. "So when you said *This is a fiasco*—"

"It's a figure of speech."

"But—"

"Be silent, David."

"That bad?" whispered Isaak miserably.

Genya offered him a brittle approximation of a smile. "At best, our visitors think Nikolai is eccentric, and at worst insane."

All over one tiny breach of etiquette? Isaak did his best not to show his distress as he took his seat and the meal began. There were a thousand rules to remember when it came to formal dining, but they'd sidestepped many of them this first night by serving their guests a Ravkan peasant feast, complete with fiddles and dancing.

The evening passed uneventfully, and Isaak thanked all his Saints for it, though there was another tense moment when the Fjerdan ambassador asked after the extradition of Nina Zenik.

Genya was quick to reply that the Grisha girl had been on a trade mission to Kerch for nearly two years.

"An unlikely story," the ambassador said mulishly.

Genya poked Isaak under the table, and he smiled amiably at the ambassador. "My stomach is too full to digest diplomacy. At least wait for the sorbet."

At one point Tolya bent his head to Isaak's ear and muttered, "Eat, Your Highness."

"Everything tastes like doom," he whispered.

"Then add salt."

Isaak managed to chew and swallow a few bites, and soon, to his great amazement, the dinner was over.

The guests dispersed to their chambers, and Tolya and Tamar

whisked him down the hall, through the back passages reserved for the king, to the royal quarters.

But just as they were about to enter, Tolya put his huge hand on Isaak's chest. "Wait." He scented the air. "Do you smell that?"

Tamar lifted her nose, cautiously approaching the door. "Garlic," she said. "Arsine gas." She signaled a guard. "Get a Squaller and David Kostyk. The door is rigged."

"Poison gas?" asked Isaak as the twins shepherded him away from the king's chambers.

Tolya clapped him on the back. "Congratulations," he said with a grim smile. "You must have been convincing if someone's already trying to kill you."

22
NIKOLAI

NIKOLAI WAS STRUGGLING to acclimate himself to his chambers, to the strange mix of sand and stone. They might have been a well-appointed if antiquated set of rooms in his own palace if not for the lack of color, the uniform texture. It was a place seen distantly through fog. The exception was his bed: an absurdly romantic bower of red roses that he assumed was Elizaveta's work. He lay down on it, determined to rest, but could not find sleep. If he did, would the monster emerge? Would it try to hunt in this barren place?

Nikolai was deeply tired, and yet it was as if his body had lost any sense of time. It had been late morning when they'd set out for the Fold, but in this permanent twilight, he wasn't sure if days or hours had passed. He had the sense of time slipping away from him. *We don't eat. We don't sleep. I don't remember what it is to sweat or hunger or dream.*

The Saints—or whatever they were—had been trapped here for hundreds of years. How had they not lost their minds?

Nikolai shut his eyes. Even if he couldn't sleep, he could attempt to order his mind. The demon gnawed constantly at his sense of control, and the bizarre experience of being plucked out of his reality and thrust into this one wasn't helping. But he was a king, and he had the future of a country to consider.

Tolya and Tamar had seen Nikolai and Zoya vanish with Yuri in the sandstorm. What would they do? Conduct a search, then create a cover story, stick those junior Squallers somewhere they couldn't tell tales. The twins would carry word of his disappearance back to Genya and David. . . . After that, his imagination failed him. What course of action would they choose? If he'd only had the chance to work with Isaak or one of the other candidates for his stand-in, they might have had an option. But to attempt such a thing with so little time to prepare? Well, Nikolai might have been daft enough to attempt it, but Genya and the others were far too sensible to court that kind of disaster.

There was still time to salvage the festival, their leverage with the Kerch, all of it—if the Saints made good on their promises. And if Nikolai survived the Burning Thorn. Then he could at least give Ravka a fighting chance. He'd be himself again. His mind would belong to him alone.

He would have to find a bride immediately, make the alliance Zoya had pushed so hard for. Marriage to a stranger. A performance of civility without true companionship. He would be acting for the rest of his life. He sighed. This place was making him morose.

Nikolai sat up straight. He'd heard a noise outside, a soft snuffling. When he opened the door, he saw nothing—until he looked down: A bear cub was tugging gently at his trousers with shiny little claws. His fur was thick and glossy, and where his back legs should have been, he had two wheels, the spokes of which looked distinctly like finger bones. The effect was both enchanting and bizarre.

The cub tugged again, and Nikolai followed, stepping into the central chamber. It was only then that he saw Grigori, his massive, shifting body huddled against the wall.

"Forgive me," Grigori said, three mouths talking this time, appearing in vague faces and then dissolving. "We have been alone a long time here, and I cannot be comfortable in enclosed spaces."

Nikolai gestured to the gray sand walls. "Couldn't you just change them?"

"They are your rooms now. That seems . . . rude."

The snuffling bear wheeled around the perimeter, bumping against the doors to Zoya's and Yuri's chambers.

"Your minion is charming."

"I find creation soothing, and I know how much easier it is for otkazat'sya to witness the monstrous in particular forms."

Nikolai paused, unsure of what protocol was expected around a Saint. "Is that why you're huddling in the corner?"

"Yes."

"Please don't do so on my account. Rumor has it I have a gift for the monstrous myself."

Grigori's many heads chuckled softly, a jury of laughing Grigoris. "I can no longer control the form I take. I was once just myself and the bear, but now a thought enters my mind and my body races ahead to meet it. It is exhausting."

Grigori shrank, and for a moment, Nikolai glimpsed the shape of a man with gentle eyes and dark curly hair. He wore the skins of a bear around his shoulders, and the bear's head as a mantle . . . but then the bear moved, and it was as if man and animal were one, standing together.

"I don't know whether I should mention this," said Nikolai. "But

I've been told the pelt of the bear that killed you is in the vault of the royal chapel in Os Alta. I wore it at my coronation."

"I'm afraid your priests have been sold a counterfeit," said Grigori, the image of the mantle flickering over his shoulders again. "That bear never died, much as I never truly died."

"It became your amplifier?"

"It's more complicated than that," said Grigori as he split once again into a larger body, a tide of legs and arms.

"I think I remember your story. You were a healer." A young healer, renowned for his cures of the most hopeless cases. He had healed the son of a nobleman afflicted with some plague, and the nobleman's doctor, most likely afraid he was about to be out of a job, had accused Grigori of trafficking in dark magic. Grigori had been sent into the woods to be torn apart by beasts, but he had fashioned a lyre from the bones of those who had trespassed in the wood before and played a song so soothing, the bears of the forest had lain down at his feet. The next day, when Grigori emerged from the woods unharmed, the nobleman's soldiers bound his hands and sent him back into the forest. Unable to play his lyre, Grigori was savaged by the very bears who had slept at his feet the night before. Bloody reading for a young prince. It was a wonder Nikolai had slept at all as a child.

"I was a healer," Grigori said, and his many legs bent at the knee as if he might rest many chins on them. "But I did things that perhaps I should not have. I made babies for mothers who had none. I made brides for men who desired them. I made a great soldier, twelve feet tall with fists like boulders, to protect a count's castle."

"The stuff of children's stories," Nikolai said, remembering his nannies' tales of witches and gingerbread golems.

"Now, yes. Then . . . I had no care for the boundaries that governed my power. *Merzost* was too great a lure. I thought little of whether I should do a thing but only if I could."

"That kind of power is unpredictable," said Nikolai, quoting David.

Grigori chuckled again, the sound rueful and murmuring as a crop of new heads clustered together, their expressions mournful.

"Death is easy. But birth? Resurrection? The work of creation belongs to the First Maker alone. I trafficked in *merzost* and lost control of my own form. So I became a hermit, at least for a time. Eventually, of course, people sought me out, eager to learn my secrets regardless of how disturbed they were by the way I looked. We are always drawn to the lure of power, no matter the cost. They called me the Bodymaker, and I took on hundreds of students over time. I taught them how to use their gifts for healing and for combat. They went out into the world and they all bore my name, or a form of it."

"Grisha," Nikolai said in surprise. Grigori had trained the first Healers and Heartrenders, the first Corporalki. "That was where it all began?"

"Maybe," said Grigori. "Or maybe that's just another story. It was all so long ago." His entire form seemed to slump, a sleeping bear, a weary man, the burden of his imprisonment settling over him. "You will not see much of me in your tenure here. I do not like to be looked at, and I find it hard to bend my hermit's ways. But if there is anything you need, please do not hesitate to come to my tower. I know it is not a welcoming place, but I assure you, you are welcome."

"Thank you," Nikolai said, though he could concede that he had little desire to enter a tower made of bone and gristle.

"Elizaveta can be a harsh teacher, but I hope you will not be swayed from your goal. There is a great deal at stake in your success. For all of us."

"What will you do when you are free of the Fold?"

"You're so certain you will endure the trial?"

"I like to bet on myself whenever I can. But usually with other people's money."

Grigori's dejected form seemed to regain some of its structure, sprouting into a curved spine and a series of folded arms. He looked like a strange tree, tilting toward the sun. "When my power is gone, when I become mortal, I will once again take on a steady form. Or perhaps I will die. Either way, I will be free."

"Then I will do my best for all of us."

Now Grigori leaned forward, a chorus of human heads with dark eyes, jaws like muzzles full of pointed animal teeth. Nikolai had to force himself not to step back.

"You must, my friend. Everything is connected. The world is changing, and so is Grisha power. If the Fold continues to exist, it will not remain the same either."

Nikolai had felt it too, this rush toward change. Borders were shifting; weapons were evolving. It was impossible to know what might come next. "Yuri claims we're about to enter an Age of Saints."

Grigori sighed, and the sound gusted through the chamber. "Do you know why the monster inside you woke? Why the Darkling's power was able to emerge after all of this time? It began with the drug *parem*. It made things possible that never should be. It altered the bounds of Grisha power."

"*Parem*?"

"If the drug had been eradicated—"

"We tried."

The teeth in Grigori's many mouths grew longer. "You did not. You tried to alter it, bend it to your will. That is the lure of power."

Nikolai could not deny it. He had known that if they did not find a way to harness the power of *parem*, in time some other country would, even without Kuwei's knowledge to guide them. But then Ravka's experiments . . . "I helped to wake the demon."

Grigori's heads nodded. "We are all connected, King Nikolai. The Grisha, the Fold, the power inside you. The Fold is a wound that may never heal. But perhaps it was not meant to. Remember that when you face your trial."

Nikolai felt he was supposed to say something profound, place his hand over his heart, make a solemn vow. He was saved from such displays by Yuri, who entered the chamber from the hallway. So the monk had not been quietly muttering psalms in his room.

"Sankt Grigori," he said with a deep bow, his glasses glinting like coins. "Forgive me. I did not mean to interrupt."

"Not at all," said the Bodymaker, but Nikolai could already see him shrinking, hands emerging from his own torso to pull him down the corridor, as if herding himself away from the interest of curious eyes. "Best of luck to you, King Nikolai," he said, and was gone.

"I . . . I meant no offense," stammered Yuri.

"I fear he thinks he's the one giving offense."

"His form is disconcerting, yes, but he is a Saint, a divine being."

"We're trained to understand the ordinary, to fear difference, even if that difference is divine." Nikolai clapped his hands together. "Now, are we ready to figure out how to kill me?"

"Oh, Your Highness, no, no. Certainly not. But I do have some thoughts on the ritual, and *Elizaveta*—" He hesitated over her name as if even the speaking of it was a holy rite. "Elizaveta wishes to begin your training."

"She sent word to you?"

"I am to accompany you," Yuri said proudly.

"Very well," said Nikolai, straightening his cuffs. "Let's go get Zoya."

Yuri cleared his throat. "Commander Nazyalensky was not asked for."

"She rarely is, but I'd like her there just the same." Yuri frowned, but Nikolai knew he was not going to contradict his king in this. "Now we just have to find her."

He felt a tug at his trouser leg and looked down. The bear cub on its bone wheels was there. Yuri released a little yelp.

"He's friendly," said Nikolai. "I hope."

Nikolai and Yuri followed the bear down the hall, and as they moved, the walls seemed to ripple, as if in response to their passing. Again Nikolai had the sense of something that was lifelike but lifeless. There was nothing to do but continue on. His world had slid into the strange, and he could adapt or go mad.

They traveled through winding passages and out onto a long, narrow bridge that led them to another of the huge spires—Juris' domain. The spire was hewn from jagged black rock and gave the impression of old castle ruins he'd seen on the Wandering Isle. Its bulk was pocked with caves and caverns, and its peak looked like a talon, clawing its way toward the sky.

He could see Yuri was ill at ease as they crossed the bridge. "Is it that you don't like heights or that you don't approve of Commander Nazyalensky?"

"Your Highness, I would never say I don't *approve*."

"Answer enough. Why don't you like her?" Zoya didn't aspire to likability. It was one of her most endearing qualities. Still, he wanted to know.

"Those things she said to the pilgrims . . ." Yuri shook his head. "I don't understand her anger. The Darkling's crimes are many, but she was one of his favorites."

It wasn't something Zoya liked to discuss. She liked to burn her past like the fuse on a stick of dynamite.

"What do you suppose fuels her anger?" said Nikolai.

"Hate?"

"Of a kind. All fuels burn differently. Some faster, some hotter.

Hate is one kind of fuel. But hate that began as devotion? That makes for another kind of flame."

Yuri ran a bony hand over the roughspun of his robes. "I've read the histories. I know he did wicked things, but—"

"The books do not tell the whole story."

"I know, of course, yes. Yes. But I find . . . I find I don't entirely disagree with his motives."

"And his methods?"

"They were extreme," Yuri conceded. "But perhaps . . . perhaps in some cases necessary?"

"Yuri, if you wish to keep your head attached to your body, I recommend never saying that within Commander Nazyalensky's hearing. But you're not entirely wrong."

Yuri blinked. "I'm not?"

"The Darkling wanted peace. A stronger Ravka. A haven for the Grisha. Those are all things that I'd like to see in my rule."

"Yes," said Yuri. "Exactly! He was not a good man, but he was a man of vision—"

Nikolai held up a hand. He doubted Yuri's mind could be changed, but if he worshipped the Darkling, he should at least do so with open eyes—and there were limits to how equitable Nikolai could be. "There is a difference between vision and delusion. The Darkling claimed to serve Ravka, but that ceased to be true when Ravka failed to serve him. He claimed to love the Grisha, but that love dissolved when they did not choose him as their master. He broke his own rules, and he nearly broke a nation in the process."

Yuri worried his lip.

"Go on," said Nikolai. "I can see you have more to say."

Yuri pushed at his spectacles. "If your father . . . If the former king had not been so . . ."

"Weak? Venal? Incompetent?"

"Well—"

"I take no pleasure in admitting my father's mistakes. Or his father's. Or his father before him. There have been good Lantsov kings and bad. King Anastas gave Ravka its roads but put nearly two thousand men to death for heresy. Ivan the Golden built schools and museums but failed to hold the Sikurzoi against the Shu. My father . . . I wish I could be proud of my father. The Lantsov line is said to be descended from the firebird, but we are just men and often very weak men. I can't change what my ancestors did. I can only hope to repair some of the damage and set us on a different course."

"And what of your son?"

Nikolai grinned. "I may have had a wild youth, but I also had a cautious one."

Yuri flushed. "I meant your future sons and daughters. Are you so sure they will be suited to rule?"

Nikolai laughed as they passed beneath an arch and into Juris' spire. "So you're not only a heretic but a radical?"

"Of course not, Your Highness!"

"It's all right, Yuri," he said. "There's a reason I've strengthened the local governors and put more power in the hands of their assemblies. Ravka may not always need a monarch. But change takes time."

And it may not be possible. He'd meant what he said to Zoya. Ravkans were drawn to figures of power, to strength. They had never been allowed to learn the ways of ruling for themselves because decisions had always been taken from them by kings, Darklings, generals, priests. Over time that might shift. *Or maybe I'll die in this ritual and the country will be plunged into chaos.*

He'd left Ravka unforgivably vulnerable. There were ministers who could rule in his stead, but he hadn't made any order of succession clear. He had no heir. He had no wife to step forward as a rallying symbol. And who would protect her anyway, this imaginary girl he was to wed? The answer was obvious: Zoya Nazyalensky could do the job—assuming she could get free of this purgatory.

He would make her his First Minister and Protector of the Realm, not just the commander of the Grisha forces. If Nikolai died before his heir came of age, she would be there to watch over Ravka and the line of succession. The people had come to trust her—as much as they could trust a Grisha. And despite her dark moods and vindictive heart, *he* had come to trust her. She was maturing into a steady, confident leader.

Or not, he thought as the bear cub led them into Juris' inner sanctum and the presence of two fighters locked in combat. Zoya's teeth were bared, and she wielded twin axes of the type Tamar favored, though these looked older and less refined. Juris was bearing down on her with a huge broadsword.

Yuri tugged nervously at his scrap of beard. "That doesn't seem at all safe."

"For either of them," Nikolai said.

Storm clouds gathered around the fighters, and thunder shook the floor. The bear rolled away, little paws held over its ears as if fleeing the sound.

For a moment, as unlikely as it seemed, they appeared evenly matched. But Nikolai knew Zoya's talents didn't lie in this type of warfare, and sure enough, when Juris feinted left, Zoya made the mistake of trying to move with him.

"Guard your flank!" Nikolai shouted.

Juris turned sharply and brought his broadsword down in a sweeping arc. Zoya brought her axes up, and they seemed to glow with blue fire. As the blades met the thrust of Juris' sword, lightning crackled from the axe blades, and the big warrior roared, smoke rising from his black scale armor.

What had Zoya just done? And how had she withstood the power of Juris' strike?

"Good!" Juris said as they drew apart. He rolled his shoulders as if nearly being cooked alive was a commonplace experience. Maybe for an ancient dragon it was.

Zoya's hair was damp with perspiration, her shirt clung to her skin, and her grin was pure exhilaration—a smile he'd never seen from her before. Nikolai found his mood souring.

He cleared his throat. "If you're done trying to cleave my general in two, I have need of her."

Zoya whirled, wiping the sweat from her brow with her sleeve. "What is it?" Her eyes were so blue they seemed to glow.

"We've been summoned to Elizaveta. I want you there to learn about the ritual."

The dragon huffed. "Her time is better spent with me. The thorn wood is a path you walk alone, boy king."

"But it's a very arduous path," Nikolai said. "Who will carry my snacks?"

Juris shook his head and turned to Zoya, who had already hung her axes on the wall. "You waste your time with trifles."

"My country's future is not a trifle."

"King and country are not the same."

Zoya unrolled her sleeves, fastening the buttons at the wrist. "Close enough."

Juris' wings spread as his body swelled to its dragon form. Nikolai forced himself to maintain a calm demeanor despite the primal terror the sight created in him. Was that what he looked like when the monster rose?

Again Juris huffed, this time from his huge snout and with enough force to send a whirlwind through the entire chamber. "You will see in time. When he grows old and you grow only more powerful."

Zoya lifted her shoulder in a disinterested shrug. "And you'll long be dust in the ground, so you won't even be here to gloat about it."

The dragon flew off in a sulk. Nikolai gave him a cheerful wave, but Juris' words chased Nikolai's thoughts as he backtracked through the halls with Zoya and Yuri. He was concerned they might lose their way, but the rippling of the walls seemed to be directing them, and they soon found themselves on another bridge, one Nikolai hoped would lead to Elizaveta's spire.

Nikolai knew that Grisha lived long lives and that the greater their power, the longer they survived. How many years might Zoya live to protect Ravka and the Lantsov line? Could she shepherd Ravka wisely, or would she succumb to the madness of eternity the way the Darkling had? And would Ravka's people accept her? Or in time, would they deem her unnatural? He'd be dead by then, these problems well beyond his care or control, but that was not a cheerful thought.

Yuri stopped walking so abruptly that Nikolai almost ran into him. "Oh . . ." he said. "Oh."

Elizaveta's spire loomed before them, its amber panels glowing golden in the strange, flat light of the Fold. Nikolai could see the shapes of giant insects frozen within each panel, and the whole structure seemed to hum like a great hive.

"*Sankta*," Yuri whispered exultantly.

He hadn't shown such veneration for the dragon, Nikolai noted, but Juris' spire had given the impression of a beast's lair. This place felt like a temple, terrifying and holy.

"You were wrong about the pyre," Zoya said to Yuri. "Do we really know anything about what this ritual requires?"

"Only that it's dangerous," said Yuri.

"And here I thought the king would just have to eat candy and perform a monologue."

"I've already prepared some selections," said Nikolai.

As they approached, the panels of the spire shifted and arranged themselves to create an entrance. Inside, the air smelled of roses and honey, and everything shimmered with the buttery light of the gilded hour before sunset. And yet there was no sunset here.

Elizaveta herself seemed cast in gold, surrounded by bees and dragonflies, the roses of her gown blooming and dying and blooming again.

"Welcome," she said warmly. If she was surprised or displeased to see Zoya, she showed no sign of it. Instead, she smiled at all of them. "My king, shall we see if we can make the monster come when we call?"

Nikolai bowed, and Elizaveta gestured to a table where a small clay pot sat. "When the time comes for the ritual, I will raise the thorn wood from the sands of the Fold." As she spoke, she fluttered her fingers, and a prickly, iron-colored branch emerged from the pot's soil. "When it is mature, its thorns will be as long as a cutlass. You will call to the monster, and when it emerges, you will drive a thorn through both of your hearts."

"Just how is he supposed to survive that?" asked Zoya.

The little thorn tree seemed to swell, its spikes lengthening.

"It is up to the king. We can practice helping him summon and control the monster, but the fight will be his alone. If his will is strong enough, he will survive. If not, the monster will claim him."

Nikolai found he was rubbing his hand over his chest and forced himself to stop. "My will?"

"The trial is both physical and mental. It is meant to separate man from beast and beast from man. The pain will be unlike anything you've ever known, but worse will be facing the monster."

"What exactly is it?" asked Nikolai.

This time Elizaveta's smile was pitying, as if she could sense the fear that Nikolai carried inside him, the anger and confusion that had plagued him since the demon had taken hold. "A remnant of the Darkling's power. A sliver of his own intent and ambition. Beyond that, I cannot be sure. The monster does not want to be driven out. It will try to confuse you to keep you from completing the ritual and using the thorn. If that happens, it will take you over completely. Do you think you can win?" she asked gently.

"We beat the Darkling once before."

"Alina beat him," corrected Zoya.

An expression of distaste crossed Elizaveta's face. "The Sun Saint," she sneered. "How desperate the people are for miracles. How low they will stoop." Nikolai saw Zoya's eyes narrow and laid a hand on her arm. They weren't here to champion Alina's legacy.

"But it is not the Darkling you will face," Elizaveta continued. The thorn tree shot upward. The pot cracked as the tree's roots burst through the clay in questing tendrils. "Not exactly. This is a creature animated by the Darkling's will, just as it animated his shadow soldiers, the *nichevo'ya*. But it has lived inside you for over three years. It has shared your thoughts and desires, and it will marshal them against you. It will be fighting for its life just as surely as you are fighting for yours."

Nikolai supposed he was meant to be cowed. A wise man probably would think twice about being impaled on a giant thorn, but he felt nothing but anticipation. The idea that this was a thing he could face and conquer, or even be destroyed by, was so much easier to accept than the notion of a nightmare he would have to endure forever. He'd begun to believe this thing would be with him always. There were parts of himself he despised—the endless ambition, the self-serving streak Alina had noted so accurately—and if Elizaveta was right, the monster would bring those weapons and worse to bear in the fight against him. So let it. He knew his desire for life would prove greater in the end.

"When the time comes," Nikolai vowed, "I'll be ready."

The tree suddenly leapt from the table, its stalk thick and pulsing, its thorns like iron daggers. It shot over the floor and stopped a bare breath from Nikolai's chest, the lethally pointed tip of a long thorn poised directly above his heart.

"I hope so," said Elizaveta. "We have waited an eternity for you, Nikolai Lantsov. It would be a shame if you failed us now."

Nikolai exchanged a glance with Zoya. Yuri was gazing at Elizaveta with naked adoration. Helpful as always.

"I'm fairly sure you're trying to frighten me," said Nikolai, reaching out a finger to touch the tip of the thorn. "I'm not sure why, but may I suggest a spider wearing a suit?"

"Why a suit?" asked Zoya, frowning. "Why not just a spider?"

"Where did he get the suit? How did he fasten the buttons? Why does he feel the need to dress for the occasion?"

Elizaveta was studying them. She flicked her fingers and the thorn tree receded. "I had intended to torture the monk to force your darkness to the fore," she said contemplatively. "But best to cut to the chase."

She lifted a hand and the floor rose around Zoya, encasing her in glistening panels of amber.

Zoya shouted, her face startled and frightened before her instincts took hold. She threw her hands out, buffeting the luminous walls with the force of her power. A golden substance began to rise from her feet, filling the chamber.

Nikolai reached for Zoya, but the thorn wood grew up between them in a wild, impenetrable tangle. There were thorns all around him, a wall of deadly gray spikes.

"Stop this, Elizaveta," he shouted, though he could no longer see the Saint.

He heard Zoya scream.

"I know you're not going to kill her," he said, though he knew no such thing. "Juris needs her."

Elizaveta appeared from the thicket surrounded by a bloom of roses. "Do you think I care what Juris needs? It's freedom I require. And if losing her will drive you to act, that seems a small price."

Nikolai lunged at her, but Elizaveta vanished into the thorn wood. He leapt onto the brambles, ignoring the pain as the thorns jabbed at him through his clothes. They were wickedly sharp, sinking into his flesh like teeth.

"You will have to fly, my king," said Elizaveta's voice. "Or you will never be free, and neither will we."

Zoya's screams rose.

From somewhere in the thicket, Yuri cried, "Oh no! Please, you must not. I beg you."

Nikolai forced his eyes shut. *Come on, you bastard*, he implored the monster. *You want to spread your wings? This is your chance. I'll even let you gnaw on that so-called Saint as a thank-you.*

But if the monster was listening, it must be laughing too. Whatever dark thing resided within him had no interest in playing this game.

The Saint will not harm her, Nikolai told himself. *It's a ploy.*

And then Zoya's screams stopped.

Yuri was sobbing.

"Zoya?" Nikolai shouted. "Zoya!"

He hurled himself against the barbed thicket. "Zoya!" he yelled, but it emerged as a snarl.

This time he felt the creature inside him drag its way to the surface as if its talons were scraping against his chest cavity.

No. He did not want this, did not want to give the monster control.

But another voice within him hissed, *Yes.*

Remember, he told himself, *remember who you are.*

He felt his claws emerge, felt his teeth grow long.

I am Nikolai Lantsov, privateer and king.

He screamed as the wings burst through his back and he rose up over the thorn wood, into the high cavern of the tower. *Remember who you are.*

Elizaveta gazed up at him, her face triumphant. Yuri wept. Beside them Zoya floated in a golden sarcophagus, like an angel caught in amber, her eyes closed, her body still.

He did not recognize the sound that tore from his throat as he hurled his body at Zoya's prison. He struck it with a bone-crunching thud, but it did not budge.

He turned on Elizaveta, snarling. *I am the monster and the monster is me.* He could feel the demon fighting for control even as it lent him its strength. But Elizaveta only smiled, gentle, beneficent. With a wave of her hand, the amber walls containing Zoya collapsed and the thorn wood wilted into the floor.

He seized Zoya's limp body before it could fall. She was covered in golden sap. Elizaveta closed her fist and Zoya began to cough. She opened her eyes, lashes thick with resin, blinked in confusion, then her face flooded with terror and she began to thrash in his arms.

He wanted to soothe her. He wanted to . . . The smell of her fear mingled with the sap. It made him feel drunk. It made him feel *hungry.*

All he wanted was to dig his claws into her flesh. All he wanted was to consume her.

Remember, he demanded. *Remember who you are.*

Nikolai Lantsov. Ruler of Ravka. Privateer. Soldier. Second son of a disgraced king.

A growl of pure appetite rumbled through him as Zoya tried to scramble away, her movements stunted by the weight of the sap.

Remember who she *is.* Zoya sitting beside him writing correspondence. Zoya glowering at a new crop of students. Zoya holding him in the confines of a coach as he shook and shook and waited for the monster to leave him.

He clung tightly to the recollection of that sensation, that terrible trembling. *Go*, he demanded. *Go.*

Grudgingly, haltingly, the monster sank back into whatever dark place it resided, leaving the acrid taste of something burning in Nikolai's mouth.

He collapsed, shaking, to his knees.

He couldn't bear to look at Zoya's face and see the disgust there. There would be no coming back from this. He felt her hands on his shoulders and forced himself to meet her gaze.

She was beaming.

"You did it," she said. "You called him up and then you sent him packing."

"You were almost killed," he said in disbelief.

She grinned wider. "But I wasn't."

Elizaveta tapped the table. "So I am forgiven, Squaller?"

"That depends on how hard it is to get this stuff out of my hair."

Elizaveta raised her hands, and the sap slid from Zoya in golden rivulets, returning to the floor, where it solidified.

Yuri wiped the tears from his face. "Will . . . will Commander Nazyalensky have to endure this ordeal every time?"

"I'll do it if I have to."

Elizaveta shrugged. "Let us hope not."

Zoya offered him her hand. "You opened the door."

Nikolai let her help him to his feet, forced himself to celebrate with the others. But he'd felt the will of the monster, and he wondered, when the time came, if he'd be able to match its ferocity.

He'd opened the door.

He doubted it would be so easy to close the next time.

23

ISAAK

HE'D MADE IT THROUGH three days of parties, din-
ners, and meetings, and no one had attempted to murder him again.
It was a bit like being on the front. You survived for an hour, then
another hour. You hoped to make it through the day. At night, Isaak
fell into bed and lay staring at the ceiling, heart pounding, thinking
of the many things he'd done wrong and the many more things he
was bound to do wrong tomorrow.

Today, they were to enjoy the morning boating on the lake beside
the Little Palace, and then they would picnic on its shores.

"We've arranged for you to spend time with the Shu princess
before lunch," Tamar had told him.

"And I . . . do what with her?"

"Be charming. Ask her about her guards and how long she's
known them. Get us any information you can."

"Can't you and Tolya just bond with the Tavgharad over your Shu childhoods or something?"

The twins had exchanged a glance. "We're worse than Ravkans to them," said Tamar. "We had a Shu father, but we wear the tattoos of the Sun Saint and serve a foreign king."

"Why *did* you choose service to Ravka?"

"We didn't," said Tamar.

Tolya put his hand to his heart. "We chose Alina. We chose Nikolai. All of this"—he gestured to the palace grounds—"means nothing."

Isaak didn't know what to say to that. He considered himself a patriot, but he could admit that, unlike the king, Ravka had never been particularly kind to him.

"Chat with Princess Ehri," said Tamar. "Get her talking."

"Hypothetically, if I weren't possessed of natural charisma and a gift for witty conversation, just how would I do that?"

Tamar rolled her eyes, but Tolya said, "Compliment her. Express your admiration for Shu culture. You might consider reciting—"

"Oh, for Saints' sake, Tolya, that's the last thing he should do." Tamar knelt in front of Isaak. "Just listen to her. Ask her questions. Women don't want to be seduced. They want to be seen and listened to. You can't do either of those things if you're thinking up strategies on how to win her over—or reciting the *Fourth Epic of Kregi*."

"There *is* no *Fourth Epic of Kregi*," growled Tolya. "The third was unfinished by the poet Elaan."

"Then that's definitely the one he should recite."

Why did the thought of a simple conversation make Isaak's heart rattle? Possibly because he'd never been good at talking to girls—other than his sisters. But arguing with Belka and Petya over the price of ribbon was a far cry from making small talk with royals. And he was supposed to somehow wheedle information from a princess? He tried to remind himself that he was handsome now—a fact that took him by surprise every time he caught a glimpse of himself in a mirror. He hadn't been ugly before, just unremarkable—tidy brown hair that curled if he left it too long, regular enough features, slightly crooked bottom teeth. His mother had told him he was nice looking, but she'd also told his sister she had a lovely singing voice, and that was definitely not the case.

Now Isaak tried to look at ease as he reclined on a cushioned divan on the royal barge, attempting his best approximation of Nikolai's relaxed slouch. He'd spent too many years standing at attention. Before him, elegantly decorated sloops and barges dotted the lake like water lilies, banners snapping, awnings striped in Ravkan blue and gold.

The lake was too cold for swimming, but the Tidemakers had heated its surface so that mist rose from the water in dense clouds, which Squallers manipulated into symbols of various countries and families of standing. Isaak had permitted himself a few sips from a tiny bell-shaped glass of apricot wine to try to soothe his nerves but still remained alert, listening to the conversation as one of the Fjerdan ambassadors asked if they might have a tour of the Grisha school.

"Of course you may," said Genya. "It would be our great pleasure."

Isaak did not think he imagined the current of excitement that passed between the ambassador and another member of his delegation.

Genya smoothed her skirts and added, "But I fear you may find it boring. The students are currently traveling with their teachers as part of their instruction."

"All of them?"

"Yes," said Genya. "We find work in the field is so beneficial for a child's education. And I must say I'm not sorry for the peace and quiet. Young Grisha can be quite high-spirited, as I'm sure you can imagine. We didn't want them getting underfoot with such important new friends visiting."

Isaak had never known the Grisha students to be underfoot. They were kept busy, and the school was isolated enough from the rest of the palace that they would have had trouble getting anywhere without notice. No, they'd been moved for their safety. And the Fjerdans knew it.

"You evacuated all of them?" the ambassador asked coldly.

"*Evacuated?*" said Genya with an amused laugh. "That would imply there was some kind of threat." She tapped the ambassador on the knee playfully. "A threat! To a group of children who could set fire to this barge and stop the hearts of everyone on it with the sweep of a hand." She dabbed at her eyes. "It is *too* droll."

Isaak turned to Genya as the Fjerdans walked to the sloop's railing to enjoy the view and possibly to seethe. "You sent the students away to protect them?"

"Of course," said Genya, all mirth gone. "You think we would keep one of Ravka's greatest assets here when a bomb or poison gas could eliminate an entire new generation of Grisha in moments? But a fearful Fjerdan is one less likely to act, and I just relish the idea of them having bad dreams about a bunch of schoolchildren."

Isaak gave a slight shake of his head. "Listening to you talk is like watching a sailor who knows the secret shape of a bay, all of the places where storms strike, and the rocky spots where ships run aground. You navigate these waters with such surety."

Genya was quiet for a long time. "I was thrown into the water early," she said. "The Darkling gave me to the queen of Ravka as a gift when I was just a little girl, a pretty thing who could be of service to her."

"Then you knew the king as a boy?"

"I saw him and his brother in passing. I was a cherished servant, but a servant all the same. They were very *loud*." She toyed with one of her topaz earrings. "The household staff used to call them the Two Headaches. How I envied them, the way they were free to run and play and make trouble."

"But to be a favorite of the queen," said Isaak. "That must have been a great honor?"

Genya popped a slice of plum into her mouth. "For a time, I was the queen's doll. She would dress me in lovely clothes and brush my hair and let me sleep at the foot of her bed and sit beside her at meals. I watched the sharks and learned. When I grew older, and I had the misfortune of catching the old king's eye . . ." Genya wiped her fingers slowly on a linen napkin, the leavings of the plum staining the cloth. "I convinced myself that the suffering I endured was an honor because I was the Darkling's soldier and his spy. He trusted me above all others, and one day all would know the good I'd done him. He could not have managed his coup so easily without the information I fed him."

Isaak stared at her. "You are confessing to treason," he whispered.

"Sweet Isaak," she said with a smile. "Nikolai Lantsov pardoned me long ago, and in that moment he earned my loyalty forever. The Darkling threw me into the water, then watched me drown to serve his own purposes."

"So he was as cruel as the stories say?"

"Cruel? Oh yes. But he didn't leave me to the king's predations to punish me. He just never even considered my misery. What was the anguish of one girl if it might help to earn him an empire? He was playing a long and complicated game. It was only when I dared to think for myself, when I interfered with his grand plan, that he set his monsters on me and—"

A loud splash sounded from somewhere on the lake. They stood in time to see a billow of yellow silk sinking beneath the surface near a barge crowded with members of the Kerch delegation. One of the merchant's daughters had fallen into the water and was sinking fast.

"Jump in," whispered Genya furiously. "Go save her."

"There are Grisha—"

"Nikolai wouldn't wait for the Grisha."

She was right, but . . . "I can't swim."

"Please tell me you mean that metaphorically."

"Afraid not," he said, panic rising.

"Why didn't you tell me?"

"It never came up!"

"Just *jump*," said Genya. "And don't you dare flail. Sink as fast as you can and we'll do the rest."

Isaak couldn't believe she was serious, but one look at her expression made it clear this was no joke. *Well,* he thought as he leapt onto the railing and launched himself into the water with what he hoped was a modicum of grace, *at least if I drown, I won't have to sit through dinner.*

The water was bitterly cold, and as he sank, everything in Isaak's body demanded that he move, fight, do *something* to get back to warmth and air. *Do not flail.* He remained still, the ache building in his lungs as panic began to set in. He looked up, up, to the dim glow of light at the surface. It seemed impossibly far away, the lake dark and silent around him, an endless, starless sky. A rotten place to die. *Is this it?* he wondered. *Am I really going to drown to preserve the king's reputation as a hero?*

Then Nadia had hold of his arm. She was surrounded by a bubble of air that she had created and that two Tidemakers beside her were propelling forward. She yanked him into the circle of air and he took a long, gasping breath.

"Come on," she said. He felt the current around him moving, dragging them along like a fast-running river.

A bundle of yellow silk billowed in the water ahead of them. The girl—Birgitta Schenck—wasn't moving. Her eyes were closed and her hair was splayed around her face like a corona. *Oh Saints*, was she dead?

"Grab her," said Nadia, and as soon as his hand closed over her wrist, they were shooting through the water again.

They emerged on the opposite side of the tiny island at the lake's center, away from the pleasure crafts. Tolya and Tamar were waiting. They pulled Birgitta onto the steps of one of the practice pavilions and began the work of trying to revive her.

"Please tell me she's alive," said Isaak.

"There's a pulse," replied Tolya. "But there's water in her lungs."

A moment later, Birgitta coughed, lake water spewing from her lips.

"Scatter," commanded Tolya.

"Be charming," Tamar said as she disappeared with the others into the mist. "You're a hero."

Isaak bent over the girl, trying to remember that it would be the king's face she would see. "Miss Schenck?" he said. "Birgitta? Are you quite well?"

Her long lashes fluttered. She looked up at him with dazed green eyes and burst out crying.

Well. Perhaps being handsome wasn't a cure for everything.

"You almost drowned," he said. "You've cause to be emotional. Come, we must get you warm."

Isaak felt frozen and exhausted too, but he forced himself to do what he thought would look best. He slipped his arm beneath the girl's legs and lifted her into his arms. All Saints, she was heavy. Was so much silk really necessary?

She leaned her head against his chest, and Isaak strode across the island, his teeth chattering, his boots squelching wetly, until they emerged from the trees onto the island's opposite bank.

Everyone was peering at the water as would-be rescuers paddled around the Kerch boat and Grisha Tidemakers pulled back the lake in sheaves of water that hovered above the surface.

Someone caught sight of Isaak and Birgitta and shouted, "There they are!"

"She's right as rain!" Isaak called. "But twice as damp. We could both use some dry clothes and some hot tea."

The crowd burst into applause. Isaak set down Birgitta before his arms gave out, depositing her on the sand like a pile of wet laundry. He bowed and managed to stop his teeth chattering long enough to kiss her hand.

He'd graduated from minor breaches of etiquette to nearly getting himself and someone else drowned. Perhaps tomorrow he'd manage to burn down the palace.

Birgitta Schenck and Isaak were hustled onto the royal barge, wrapped in blankets, and dosed with hot brandy as servants chafed their hands. But it wasn't until he was back in Nikolai's quarters and submerged in a steaming bath in the king's vast tub that Isaak finally started to feel warm again.

Genya and the others had remained in intense conversation in the sitting room while Isaak had been left to soak in peace. He was going to miss this tub when the king returned. The rest he could do without.

He stayed in the bath until the water turned cold and he'd started to prune. He didn't particularly want to face the people waiting next door, but he forced himself out of the tub and dried himself off with one of the long linen bath sheets.

Nikolai employed no valet, which had been a relief to Isaak; he hadn't had anyone help him dress since he was a child. He put on the king's soft breeches and boots, the shirt and suspenders, the fitted coat embroidered with the Lantsov eagle. He could admit the clothes weren't a bad part of the deal either. They had been constructed meticulously and were as comfortable as they were elegant. As Isaak adjusted his coat, his fingers touched on something in the right pocket. He was always finding things tucked away in the pockets of the king's clothes—a note the king had scrawled to himself or a sketch of what might be a new invention, a small silver bead. This time he pulled a tiny knot of wire from his coat. It had been fashioned into the shape of a sailing ship. He set it on the king's vanity.

"We think this may actually be a good thing," said Tamar as Isaak entered the sitting room.

He joined them by the fire, glad for the warmth. "So I should try to drown more often?"

"It wasn't *ideal*," Genya said, pouring him a cup of tea. "You missed your chance to chat with Princess Ehri. But we made the best of it, and the king looked like a hero."

"The carry was a nice touch," said Tamar.

"Very heroic," said Tolya, "like a prince out of the epic poems. *And so Ivan the Gilded Hair bore her across the—*"

"Keep reciting poetry and I will personally drown you in the lake," said Tamar.

Tolya scowled and muttered "It's a classic" into his tea.

Isaak didn't agree, but he doubted this was the time to debate poetry.

Genya nudged David, and he looked up from the treatise he was reading. "We traced the trigger device used to rig the king's door with arsine gas. It's most likely Fjerdan."

"Will they be arrested?" asked Isaak.

Tamar looked almost bemused. "Of course not. It's not something we can actually prove, and, in a way, this is good news."

"Of course," said Isaak. He scratched his ear. "Exactly how is it good news?"

"We already suspected the Fjerdans didn't come to play. If it had been the Kerch or the Shu, we would have had real cause to worry. This means the Shu are still open to an alliance. We were curious to see who might attempt the king's life."

"Without risking the king?" Isaak asked, surprised at the bitter edge in his voice.

Tolya rested a giant hand on his shoulder. "We would never let harm come to you, Isaak."

"I know," said Isaak. But did he? And could he really complain? It was a soldier's lot to be expendable. A guard's job to put himself between his ruler and harm. Wasn't that exactly what he was doing now?

Tamar leaned back in her chair and crossed her long legs. "I've searched the chambers of the Shu guards."

"They're our guests," protested Tolya.

"They're our enemies," said Tamar.

"And potential allies," said Genya. "It wouldn't do to make them mad."

"We were cautious. But there was little to learn. The few journals I found were kept in code, and I doubt any member of the Tavgharad would be foolish enough to put damning details to paper."

"And the Kerch made an attempt on our labs," said Tolya.

David looked up from his reading, startled. "Did they get in?"

"We let them make it all the way to the Fabrikator workshops."

"Oh," said David, losing interest.

"We're not concerned about that?" asked Isaak.

"The real work happens elsewhere," said Tamar. "We even planted some fake blueprints for them to find. All of it should help set the stage for our performance at the Gilded Bog."

"We're going to the Gilded Bog?" asked Isaak, unable to hide his excitement.

"Unfortunately," said Tolya.

Genya tucked her slippered feet beneath her. "We'll be using Count Kirigin's lake to show the Kerch our prototype of the *izmars'ya*." A look passed between the others that Isaak didn't understand, but that was nothing new. He assumed someone would tell him what exactly an *izmars'ya* was so he could nod sagely about the subject when the time came.

"You will be working," added Tamar. "Not sampling Kirigin's entertainments."

"Of course," said Isaak. But he could at least get a *glimpse* of what all the fuss was about.

Genya pushed a sheaf of papers over to him. "Here are notes for the dinner tonight. You won't be expected to make a speech, but this will be a more formal affair, so you'll need to do your best to seem at ease. Tomorrow is the hunt."

"I can hunt at least," said Isaak with relief.

"Not like a gentleman hunts. But Nikolai was never much for the sport anyway. He has a fondness for foxes. The hunt is just an excuse to ride and get to know the hopefuls. Remember to spread your conversation evenly amongst them. We'll go over the particulars tonight after dinner."

They filed out and Isaak let his head flop back, staring at the gilded ceiling. He felt both tired and restless. He glanced at the notes on place settings and how to eat oysters and tossed them aside. He needed to clear his head.

As soon as he opened the door, Tolya was there. "Is something wrong?"

"I just want to take a walk."

Tolya fell back a few steps as Isaak made his way down the hall, but it was still unsettling to know he was being watched. There were rumors Nikolai had run away from university to pursue a life of adventure on the high seas as the privateer Sturmhond. A ridiculous story, but Isaak could understand the impulse. Who wouldn't choose that kind of freedom over this constant performance? He passed through the portrait gallery, ignoring the paintings of countless Lantsov kings and queens, and entered the conservatory.

It was Isaak's favorite place in the Grand Palace. The high-ceilinged room ran half the length of the southern wing. Sunlight streamed through walls made entirely of glass panels, and steam pipes heated the red tile floor. The conservatory's winding paths were lined with potted fruit trees and tall palms, flowering shrubs that overflowed the walkways, and hedges trimmed into tiered arches and lattices. An artificial stream flowed through the room's center, narrowing and widening to form lily ponds and reflecting pools.

A girl was seated by one of the ponds—no, not a girl, a princess. Ehri Kir-Taban. Daughter of Heaven. The Shu usually carried the names of one or both of their parents, but the royal family all took the name of the first Shu queen and founder of the Taban dynasty. There were Ravkan guards and Shu Tavgharad stationed at the room's perimeter. He should have noticed them sooner, but he'd been too preoccupied. Distraction was something neither a guard nor a king could afford.

So this was his chance. He could make up for his missed meeting with the princess and try to gather the information Genya and the others required. *Be charming.* Right. Charming.

But before he could decide on a good opening line, the princess lifted her head.

She rose hurriedly and curtsied. "Your Highness."

"I didn't mean to intrude on your peace," he said in Shu.

"I am a guest here. There can be no intrusion." She glanced at the guards. "Would you . . . would you care to sit and talk awhile?"

There. I didn't even have to ask. And yet he still wanted to turn and scurry right back through the door. But to say no now would be seen as a snub. Besides, Tolya might well block the door and refuse to let him through.

Isaak took a seat beside her on the wide rock next to the pond. The air smelled of sweet orange blossom, and the low splash of fish at play in the water was soothing. It might have been a pleasant place to rest if not for the guards glowering in the doorways. Isaak vowed that when he had his face back and returned to duty, he'd try to look a little friendlier.

"Thank you for joining me," Ehri said.

"It's my pleasure."

"Hardly that," she murmured with a small smile. "No doubt you came here to be alone—as alone as we ever can be—just as I did."

"But if you wish to be alone, why invite me to join you?"

"I must be seen to be making an effort or the guards will report back to my sister, and then I will never hear the end of it."

"Your sister?"

"Makhi Kir-Taban, Born of Heaven, our most celestial princess who will inherit the crown and rule wisely and justly for many years."

"And what will you do?" asked Isaak. *A woman wants to be listened to.*

"Marry you, of course."

"Of course," Isaak said, willing himself not to squirm. "But if you were not to marry me?"

At this, she looked almost panicked, as if the question was not one that had been scripted for her, and she wasn't at all sure how honest she should be. Isaak could sympathize. "Please," he said gently, both to put her at ease and because he found he was genuinely curious. "I'd like to know."

She brushed her thumb over the silk of her gown. "I suppose that, if I hadn't been born Taban, I would like to be a soldier . . . maybe even a member of the Tavgharad."

"Truly?" He couldn't help but laugh. It was too absurd to contemplate a guard pretending to be a prince talking to a princess who wanted to be a royal guard.

She frowned slightly. "It isn't kind to laugh."

Instantly Isaak sobered. "I didn't mean to insult you. I was just surprised. Serving in the royal guard is a very noble calling. And it would allow some measure of freedom, though even guards have duties."

"Yes, but they're not forced to pose and preen just to be sold off like chattel." She paled, realizing what she'd said. "Forgive me, I didn't mean . . . It would be my greatest honor—"

"Don't apologize. Please. I asked for your honesty. I don't expect every woman I meet to be eager to wed me."

A crease appeared between her brows. "You don't?"

Damn it. Another misstep. Isaak winked. "Not at first." That was a far more Nikolai answer—though the princess looked slightly disappointed.

"You can make it up to me," said Ehri. "I have been honest with you; now perhaps you will share a secret with me. It's only fair."

I'm not the king of Ravka, just a lowly grunt trying not to perspire in his fancy clothes. No, that was definitely not the right reply. Isaak supposed he should say something flirtatious, but he wasn't sure which secrets belonged to him and which belonged to the king.

"Very well. My secret is that I did wish to be alone, but that I'm still enjoying your company. It's been a hard morning."

"Has it?"

"A girl almost drowned."

Ehri released an unprincess-like snort. "It's her own fault for throwing herself in the lake."

"Pardon?"

"I would wager my best axe there was nothing accidental about her plunge into the water."

"Your best *axe*?"

Ehri tucked a strand of dark hair behind her ear. "I am an avid collector."

A princess who wanted to be a palace guard and who liked weapons. She was at least interesting.

"How can you be so sure the Schenck girl jumped?" he asked.

"Because my own advisers suggested I do the same thing last night."

Isaak stared. "You're saying she risked her own life just to——"

"Gain the notice of a king and give him the chance to play hero?" Ehri sniffed, and smoothed the silk of her gown. "A reasonable gambit, but not one I was prepared to make."

He studied her. "Not when you could simply wait for a pensive king to amble by and find you looking like a painting in green silk with flowers in your hair?" Her golden eyes shifted away guiltily. "How long were you waiting, hoping I might stroll by?"

She bit her lip. "Two hours and twelve minutes. Give or take."

He was both annoyed and pleased that she'd actually been frank. "That stone ledge can't be very comfortable."

"I regret to say, I can no longer feel my buttocks."

At that Isaak burst out laughing, then caught himself. That was *not* Nikolai's laugh. He saw one of the palace guards cock his head to

366

the side. *Trukhin*. Isaak had worked countless shifts with him around the palace. He had every reason to recognize Isaak's laugh.

All Saints, Isaak was tired of this charade already. But the princess had provided him an opening.

"If you can't manage a short stint sitting on a rock, I don't see how you could hope to fill the role of guard standing at attention for hours."

"Then thank goodness I was born royal."

"I confess I know little of the Tavgharad," said Isaak, hoping his voice sounded natural. "Are they drawn from noble families?"

"They aren't *drawn* from anywhere," Ehri said, a surprising bite to her voice. "They come from every town and every village where they test and train and hope to be chosen. There is no greater honor."

"Than defending you?" He couldn't keep the smile from his voice.

Ehri bit her lip. "The Taban line. I'm one of the lesser jewels in the crown."

Isaak found that hard to believe. She was awfully pretty. He couldn't imagine what her sisters looked like if she was the plain one.

He pressed on. "It must be a hard life, even if it is rewarding. Do they leave their families behind as the Grisha do?"

She stiffened slightly. "They're happy to do so." She trailed a hand over the water. "I think it's hardest for the twins."

"Twins?"

"They're very common among our people." She bobbed her head toward Tolya. "Like the Keb-Bataar."

"It's an interesting word, *kebben*. We don't have one like it in Ravkan." It could mean close kin or twin, but also someone bound to your heart.

Ehri closed her eyes and recited, *"Everyone mourns the first blossom. Who will weep for the rest that fall?"*

Isaak couldn't help but smile. It seemed Tolya's advice would come in handy after all. "*I will remain to sing for you, long after the spring has gone.*"

"You know it?" Ehri said in surprise.

"I learned it when I was first studying Shu." It was a poem simply titled "Kebben'a," and there was considerable debate over whether the title should be translated as *My Dear* or *My Kin* or *My Only.*

"It's an old poem, long out of fashion, but it describes the spirit of *kebben* well."

"I believe it was set to music," Isaak said. "I've been told you play the *khatuur?*"

She bunched her hands in her silks, her expression tightening again. "Yes," she said curtly. What had he done wrong?

"I've found . . ." he fumbled, afraid he might be about to botch everything horribly. "I've found that this position, this life of display, can take the savor from many things I once enjoyed."

For a moment Ehri looked startled, even frightened, then something sparked in her eyes and she leaned forward. "I know," she whispered. "At least if we were guards, we could spend the day doing something more exciting."

"We could go riding."

"Eat with our fingers."

Ehri lowered her chin and whispered, "Belch."

"With fervor."

"We could—oh dear," said Ehri. "I think we have company."

And sure enough down both garden paths he saw the hopefuls and their chaperones approaching like a flock of beautifully dressed birds of prey. "Someone must have reported we were in private conversation."

"Perhaps they'll all throw themselves into the pond to get your attention," whispered Ehri, and Isaak had to resist the urge to laugh again.

"What amuses the king so?" asked the Fjerdan princess as she approached, her fan fashioned to resemble an elegant spray of frost.

"Many things, I must confess," said Isaak. "The king is a simple man."

It wasn't true, but so little was these days.

24

NINA

NINA KNEW GETTING THE WOMEN out of the fort would be no small challenge. Security would be tighter thanks to her little stunt, but they could at least hope that the soldiers might think the breach had been the result of a novitiate out to pull a prank or attempting a meeting with a soldier, not the work of a Ravkan spy.

When Nina met with Leoni and Adrik to plan, they kept their discussions in Zemeni and made sure to talk well away from the convent, under the cover of one of their excursions to sell the loading devices. They'd actually made sales to a few of the local fishermen who were attempting to hunt game for hides and meat now that the fish seemed to be dying off. They would have to restock soon.

That morning, Nina had seen a flash of white fur appearing and disappearing through the trees as they trekked out of town. She'd strayed away from Adrik and Leoni and wended her way into the woods as silently as she could. There, she'd seen Trassel, prowling the far banks of the river. Her heart had caught in her throat when she'd glimpsed the other shapes in the woods. Gray wolves. But these animals did not seem to have the orange eyes and rangy bodies of those she'd encountered on the ice. Every time one of them moved toward the water, Trassel would snap his jaws and the gray wolves would edge farther back into the trees.

He's herding them, she realized. *He's keeping them away from the poisoned river.*

She wanted to stay and watch, to see if he might let her approach— even if he continued to turn his nose up at her kitchen scraps. But Adrik and Leoni were waiting. And so were the girls on the mountaintop. Reluctantly, she left Trassel behind and returned to the sledge.

The plan seemed simple enough: Get the women and their babies out and make it through the checkpoint at the base of the hill before anyone knew the prisoners were missing.

Leoni hadn't been thrilled to learn they'd need explosives. "I have barely any training in blasting powders," she said as they repacked their wares, "and long fuses are almost always trouble."

"We need a distraction," said Nina. "Once we get clear, the bombs will start a fire in the active portion of the factory that will spread to the maternity ward. By the time it's extinguished and they realize there are no bodies to find, the girls will be well on their way to Hjar." There, a whaler commissioned by members of the Hringsa would be waiting to take them to Ravka. Actually, the crew would be expecting Grisha fugitives, not a tide of young women and infants addicted to what Leoni suspected was synthetic *parem* or something very much like it. But Nina would find some way to explain. "We can't tell the girls who we are. Not if we want them docile."

Leoni looked uneasy. "Shouldn't they have a choice in this?"

"*Parem* takes away choice. All they'll be thinking of is when the next fix will come. If we want them to go with us quietly, they can't know we're taking them away from their supply. We should try to acquire some ordinary *jurda* for them too. It may help with the withdrawal."

Adrik squinted down the road. "What happens when they realize that next fix isn't coming?"

"Leoni, could you create a sedative mild enough to keep them manageable but safe enough for the mothers who are still carrying?"

"Are we really talking about sedating pregnant women?" Adrik asked. "What if we get the dose wrong?"

"I don't like it either, but I know what it's like to be in the grips of that longing."

"I can do it," said Leoni. "I think. But . . ." She looked down at the knot she was tying. "What if they *don't* come back from this? We could be dooming them to a horrific journey, maybe even death."

Nina remembered the agony of her battle with *parem* too well. She'd begged for death, prayed for it. Without Matthias, she wasn't sure she could have held on. And that had just been the first struggle. What would she have done without Inej to give her purpose? Or Jesper to make her laugh? Even that little bastard Kaz had done his part, ruthless to the last. She'd needed all of them to keep her going in those long, merciless days as she fought her way back to herself. These women would be without family or friends in a foreign land. They would have to learn to lean on one another. If they survived.

Nina looked at Leoni, at Adrik. "I won't pretend I'm thinking straight. Seeing those women, those girls that way . . . I understand what *parem* does. I've been through that war. I know what I would choose."

"And you're willing to make that choice for them?" said Adrik.

"We *all* have to be willing."

Leoni took a deep breath. "I wouldn't want to live under another's control. I wouldn't want to doom my child to a life of that."

"Adrik?" Nina asked.

"I told you what I think, Nina. We're risking our lives and the lives of other Grisha to deliver what I suspect will be a ship full of corpses to Ravka. But I won't turn my back on them. If nothing else, I'll have something new to complain about for the rest of my days."

"You're welcome," said Nina.

Adrik gave her a dour little bow. "But how are we supposed to convince the mothers or the guards that a one-armed man and two women have any business being there?"

"We can get you a uniform and stuff your sleeve. Leoni and I can wear Springmaiden pinafores."

"You think they won't notice that I can barely speak Fjerdan and that I'm trying to drive a team of horses with one hand?"

"Hanne will help."

"Are you sure?" Leoni asked. "I saw her face the other night. She's been under the Wellmother's thumb a long time."

Not just the Wellmother. Her parents. All of Fjerda. But Hanne had still lied for Nina. She'd defied the dictates of the convent to help people who needed her. She'd still managed to keep the fierce part of her heart alive in this wretched place.

Adrik leaned back against the cart. "If she finds out we're Grisha—"

"*She's* Grisha."

"And she hates herself. Don't think she won't turn that hatred on us. Even if we get through this without revealing who we really are, she'll be the one left to face the consequences when we're gone." Nina shifted uneasily and Adrik's brows rose. "You think she'll go with us. Oh, Zenik. I thought Leoni was the hopeless optimist."

"Hanne doesn't belong here." Even if she managed to keep her powers a secret, Fjerda would break Hanne's spirit eventually. Nina didn't think she could bear that particular casualty in this war.

Adrik studied her. "Don't make us the only option, Nina. It's not something Hanne will forgive."

She might not forgive me, Nina thought, *but at least she'll survive.*

When Nina arrived in the classroom the next day, she was startled to find not just Hanne waiting but one of the Springmaidens.

"Kori of the Well would like to learn too," Hanne said dully.

Nina tried to look delighted. "Another student! Excellent. Do you have any knowledge of Zemeni?"

"No," Kori said sulkily. Clearly she wasn't thrilled to be stuck with this duty. And clearly the Wellmother thought Nina and Hanne shouldn't be left alone.

"Then we'll begin at the beginning. Let's start with the verb *to pray*."

Hanne rolled her eyes, and Nina found it hard not to laugh. If this was the worst challenge they faced over the next few days, Nina would count them very lucky indeed.

But as she was walking Hanne and Kori through some basic vocabulary—*chair, desk, window, sky, girl, cloud*—a knock came and a novitiate poked her head through the door. It was the peach-cheeked girl who'd approached Nina in the woods, one of the same novitiates who had ridden with Hanne as a Fjerdan soldier.

The girl curtsied to Kori, who asked, "What is it?"

"The Wellmother sent me to fetch you, Hanne," said the novitiate. "Your father is here."

Hanne's whole body seemed to crumple like a flower wilting in a sudden frost. Nina had seen her scared, angry, but this was something new and unwelcome, as if all the fire that animated her had suddenly and abruptly banked.

Even Kori looked worried as she said, "Go on, then," to Hanne.

Hanne closed her workbook and rose. Nina knew she shouldn't, but as Hanne walked past, she grabbed her hand and squeezed it tightly. Hanne glanced at the Springmaiden, who was watching them with narrowed eyes, then squeezed back.

"It will be all right," whispered Nina. "*Adawe.*" The first verb she'd taught Hanne. *Fight.*

Hanne's spine straightened slightly. She released Nina's hand, but the novitiate added, "He wishes to meet you too, Enke Jandersdat."

Good. If Hanne's father wanted to meet his daughter's teacher, she would do her best to handle and pacify him. Maybe she could help Hanne weather this storm. She rose.

"*Adawesi,*" Hanne said, full lips quirking in a smile. *We fight.*

When they reached the chapel, the novitiate led them down a long hall, and Nina realized they were headed to the same office where she and Hanne had met with the Wellmother to discuss language classes.

The Wellmother waited at her desk, just as she had before, and a tall man of military bearing stood by the window, hands clasped behind his back. A thick red scar ran along the base of his pale skull. Nina felt something cold unfurl in her belly.

"Wellmother," said Hanne, curtsying deeply. "*Min fadder.*"

Nina knew who it would be before he turned. But there was nothing she could do to stop the terror that seized her as she looked once more into Jarl Brum's cold blue eyes.

The last time Nina had encountered Jarl Brum, he'd tried to imprison and enslave her. She'd been deep in the grips of her first and only dose of *jurda parem* when she'd faced him and his *drüskelle* in the

Djerholm harbor. She'd wanted to murder him, and she could have with barely a thought. But Matthias had begged her to show mercy, and she had. She'd left Brum and his men alive, though in a last petty act, she'd torn the scalp from his head. Someone had apparently sewn it back on.

Nina sank into a low curtsy, training her eyes on the floor, trying to steal a moment to gather her wits and hide her fear. *Get yourself together, Zenik*, she ordered herself. Brum had seen through her clumsy disguise when she'd met him in the Ice Court, but now she'd been tailored by the master, Genya Safin. Her very bones and body had been altered, and she knew her command of the Fjerdan language was pristine. She remembered what she'd said to Hanne, that performance began in the body, and right now Nina needed to give the performance of her life. Instead of hiding her fear, she would use it. It was her loathing she needed to bury.

When she rose from her curtsy, she was not Nina Zenik; she was Mila Jandersdat, a girl whose livelihood might very well depend on the favor of Jarl Brum.

But Brum's focus was on Hanne. His face softened when he looked at his daughter.

"Hanne," he said, stepping forward and embracing her. "You're looking . . . hearty."

Hanne hunched a little more. "Thank you, Papa."

"Your form would soften if you would leave off riding so much."

"I'm sorry, Papa."

He sighed. "I know you are." His gaze shifted to Nina, who bowed her head and turned her eyes to the floor demurely. "And this is your new teacher? She's young enough to be a student here."

"She's serving as a guide to the Zemeni tradesmen who arrived last week," said Hanne.

"So the Wellmother tells me," said Brum, stalking toward Nina.

"A stranger arrives with two foreigners, and only days later the security at the factory is breached. An unlikely coincidence."

Nina looked at him with what she hoped was bewildered dismay. Brum snatched the tip of her chin and tilted her face up.

Whoever had sewn the skin back onto his head had done so with considerable skill, but his golden hair was gone and there was no hiding the scar that circled his skull like the fat pink tail of a rat. A Grisha Healer or Tailor could have faded it, but of course then he'd have had to let one of them near his head. Nina wanted to meet his incisive gaze with a glare of her own. Instead she allowed her eyes to fill with tears.

Brum frowned. "How old are you?"

"Eighteen, sir."

"You were widowed young."

"I have been unlucky."

His lip curled slightly. "Why do you tremble so?"

"I have had little cause to be in the presence of great men."

Brum's brows rose, but she didn't miss the flash of satisfaction in his eyes. So this was what Commander Brum liked—flattery, timidity, fear. When she'd met him last, she'd been bold and flirtatious. Now she understood her mistake.

"Where did you learn Zemeni?" he asked.

"My husband ran a small business shipping frozen goods and fish. He traded frequently with the Zemeni. I had a talent for it and took over the communications."

"And how did he die?"

"Lost to the waters." A tear rolled down her cheek. Nina could not have asked for better timing.

Brum's eyes tracked its progress almost hungrily. "A shame." He released Nina's chin and stepped back. "I'll want to question the Zemeni traders," he told the Wellmother.

"What about my lessons, Papa?" Hanne asked.

"Your lessons," Brum said thoughtfully. "Yes, I think the influence of a girl with country manners might be good for you, Hanne. You may continue."

Nina sank into another curtsy. "Thank you, sir," she said, looking up at him through wet lashes. "It is an honor."

As Brum and Hanne left the room to chat privately, Nina curtsied to the Wellmother and turned to go.

"I know what you're up to," said the Wellmother.

Nina froze with her hand on the doorknob. "What do you mean?"

"Commander Brum is happily married to a woman of noble birth."

Nina blinked and almost burst out laughing. "Why would that concern me?"

The Wellmother's eyes slitted. "I doubt it would *concern* you at all. I knew there was more to your motives than a simple teaching position."

"I only wish to make a living."

The Wellmother clucked in disbelief. "You aim to land a wealthy provider. You may have the good commander fooled with your wide eyes and wobbly lip, but you are no honest woman."

And you are the worst kind of hypocrite, Nina thought, anger flaring. This woman had dosed young girls and women with *parem*—or some equivalent. She'd put on her pious little pinafore and walked the halls of that factory with her cursed drug, helping soldiers make slaves. *When those girls go missing, I'm going to make sure Jarl Brum blames you. Then we'll see how you enjoy the good commander's attentions.*

But all she said was "Commander Brum is old enough to be my father."

"And wise enough to resist your clumsy allure, I'll warrant. But I will be watching."

Nina shook her head with false concern. "You have been cloistered here too long, Wellmother, if your thoughts turn so readily to sin."

"How dare you—"

Nina fluffed her skirts primly over her toes. "I'm not sure it's an entirely wholesome atmosphere for a girl like Hanne. A shame," Nina said as she turned to go. "But I will pray for you."

She left the Wellmother red-cheeked and sputtering.

As much as Nina enjoyed baiting the Wellmother, she was glad of the woman's suspicions. *What's the easiest way to steal a man's wallet?* Kaz Brekker had once explained. *Tell him you're going to steal his watch.* If that sour-mouthed crone thought Nina's goal was to become a rich man's mistress, then she'd be distracted from their real plan.

And what if Brum is bluffing? What if he knows exactly who I am? Nina had been fooled by Brum once before and had nearly lost her life in the process. This time, she would be more cautious. When she tangled with Jarl Brum again, she did not intend to leave him standing.

But she wasn't prepared for the storm awaiting her in the classroom.

"What was that?" Hanne railed. Kori was nowhere to be found, and Hanne paced back and forth, her pinafore billowing behind her. "Quivering like a leaf in a storm. *Crying* like some kind of frightened child. That wasn't you."

Nina felt a sudden surge of anger. What she'd seen at the fort, the shock of meeting Brum again, the crimes of the Wellmother, it was all too much. "You barely know me," she snapped.

"I know you're brave enough to want to help your sister and reckless enough to break into a military stronghold to do it. I know you're clever enough to dupe a roomful of drunk hunters and generous enough to help a desperate friend. Or is that all an act too?"

Nina clenched her fists. "I'm trying to make sure I survive, that both of us survive. Your father . . . I know his reputation. He's a ruthless man."

"He's had to be."

Nina wanted to scream. How could fierce, spirited Hanne be Brum's daughter? And why couldn't she see what he was? "If he knew you were Grisha, what would he do?"

Hanne turned toward the window. "I don't know."

"What if he knew I was trying to help you?"

Hanne shrugged. "I don't know," she repeated.

You know, Nina thought. *You know what that bigoted bastard would do, but you're too afraid to admit it.*

Nina wanted to take her by the shoulders and shake her. She wanted to pull Hanne onto a horse and ride until they reached the shore. But she couldn't think about any of that, not if they were going to free the girls in the fort. *Adawesi.* We fight. And Nina knew fighting meant using all the tools at her disposal—even Hanne's guilt.

"You owe it to your father to keep this secret." Nina felt sick saying those words, aware of the effect they would have. Hanne owed Brum nothing, but Nina forced herself to continue. "If he knew you were Grisha, it would put him in an impossible position. His reputation and his career would be at tremendous risk."

Hanne slumped at the desk and put her head in her hands. "You think I don't realize that?"

Nina crouched down before her. "Hanne, look at me." Nina waited, and at last Hanne looked up. Her vibrant eyes were dry but anguished, and Nina knew that pain was not for herself but for the embarrassment she'd cause her father. "This country . . . this country does terrible things to its women and to its men. Your father thinks the way he does because he was raised to. But I can't help him. I can't fix him. I can help my sister. I can help you. And I'll do what I have to in order to make that possible. If that means batting my lashes at your father and convincing him I'm a model of Fjerdan womanhood, I'll do it."

"It's disgusting. You looked at my father as if he were an incarnation of Djel."

"I looked at your father the way he wants to be looked at—like a hero."

Hanne ran her calloused thumb down the length of the old wooden desk. "Is that what you do with me?"

"No," said Nina, and that, at least, was the truth. She had told Hanne countless lies, but she'd never flattered, never manipulated her in that way. "When I said you were talented, I meant it. When I said you were glorious, I meant that too." Hanne met her gaze, and for a moment, Nina felt as if they weren't stuck in this classroom or even this country. They were someplace better. They were someplace free. "Our first job is always to survive," she said. "I won't apologize for it."

Hanne's lips twitched. "Have you always been this sure of yourself?"

Nina shrugged. "Yes."

"And your husband didn't complain?"

"He complained," Nina said—and suddenly she had to look away, because it was not some fictional merchant who had come to mind but Matthias with his strict propriety and his disapproving glower and his loving, generous heart. "He complained all the time."

"Was he quick to anger?" Hanne asked.

Nina shook her head and pressed her palms to her eyes, unable to stop the tears that came, not wanting to. Saints, she was tired. "No. We didn't always agree." She smiled, tasting salt on her lips. "In fact, we almost never agreed. But he loved me. And I loved him."

Hanne reached across the desk and let her fingers brush Nina's hand. "I had no right to ask."

"It's okay," said Nina. "The hurt just still catches me by surprise. It's a sneaky little podge."

Hanne leaned back, studying her. "I've never met anyone like you."

Nina knew she should lower her head, make some comment about reining in her boldness of spirit, demonstrate that she gave a damn about Fjerdan ways. Instead, she sniffled and said, "Of course you haven't. I'm spectacular."

Hanne laughed. "I would cut off a thumb for a thimbleful of your confidence."

Nina brushed her tears away and squeezed Hanne's hand, felt the warm press of her palm, the calluses of her fingers. Hands that could sew. String a bow. Soothe a sick child. It felt good to take this small bit of comfort—even if it also felt like she was stealing.

"I'm glad I met you, Hanne," Nina said.

"Do you mean that?"

She nodded, surprised at how much she did. Hanne might not be loud or reckless with her words, she might bow her head to her father and the Wellmother, but she had never let Fjerda break her. Despite her curtsies and her talk of family honor, she had remained defiant.

Hanne sighed. "Good. Because my father wants you to join us for dinner tonight after he tours the factory."

"When does he return to the capital?"

"Tomorrow morning." Hanne's gaze was steady, knowing. "You're planning something."

"Yes," said Nina. "You knew I would. I won't act until he's gone. But I'm going to need your help."

"What do you want me to do?"

A great deal. And none of it will be easy. "I want you to become who your father always hoped you'd be."

25

ZOYA

NIKOLAI WAS GETTING BETTER AT calling the monster, but his mood seemed to be growing darker. He was quieter and more distant at the end of each visit with Elizaveta, though it was Zoya who had to face drowning. By now they didn't think Elizaveta had any real intention of killing her, but the monster still seemed to believe the threat was real—a fact that didn't sit well with Zoya. Thanks to her lessons with Juris, she suspected she could break through the amber walls the Saint erected around her, and when the sap began to rise around her legs, it was hard not to try. But she wasn't there to prove her strength, only to help Nikolai make the monster rise.

From general of the Grisha army to bait for a monster. It was not a position she enjoyed, and only the progress she'd made in Juris' lair kept her temper from getting the best of her.

Today, she'd arrived at Elizaveta's spire early. Yuri and Nikolai hadn't yet shown up, and the Saint herself was nowhere to be found. Or was she? The great golden chamber hummed with the sound of insects. If Juris was to be believed, they were all her.

Six sides to the chamber. Six sides to each amber panel that comprised its soaring walls. Was this why the Little Palace had been built on a hexagonal plan? Zoya had seen the shape repeated in Grisha buildings, their tombs, their training places. Had it all begun with Elizaveta's hive? There were tunnels leading from each of the six walls. Zoya wondered where they led.

"You were one of his students, weren't you?"

Zoya jumped at the sound of Elizaveta's voice. The Saint stood by the table where the thorn tree she'd grown still sprawled over the surface.

Zoya knew Elizaveta meant the Darkling, though *student* was not the right word. *Worshipper* or *acolyte* would have been more accurate. "I was a soldier in the Second Army and under his command."

Elizaveta slanted her a glance. "You needn't play coy with me, Zoya. I knew him too." Zoya's surprise must have shown, because Elizaveta said, "Oh yes, all of us crossed paths with him at one time or another. I met him when he had only just begun his service to the Ravkan kings. When I was still in my youth."

Zoya felt a shiver at the thought of just how ancient Elizaveta must be. Her connection to the making at the heart of the world had granted her eternity. Was she really ready to reject it?

"Did he know what you were?" Zoya asked instead. "What you could do?"

"No," said Elizaveta. "I barely did. But he knew I had great power, and he was drawn to that."

He always was. The Darkling prized power above every other trait. Zoya sometimes worried if she might be very much the same.

"Count yourself lucky," she said. "If he had known the extent of your gifts, he would have pursued you until he could use them for himself."

Elizaveta laughed. "You underestimate me, young Zoya."

"Or you underestimated him."

The Saint gave a skeptical bob of her head. "Perhaps."

"What was he like then?" Zoya could not resist asking.

"Arrogant. Idealistic. Beautiful." Elizaveta smiled ruefully, her fingers trailing the spine of the thorn tree. It curled to meet her like a cat arching its back. "I met him many times throughout the years, and he adopted many guises to hide his true self. But the faces he chose were always lovely. He was vain."

"Or smart. People value beauty. They can't help but respond to it."

"You would know," said Elizaveta. "The fairy stories really aren't true, are they? They promise that goodness or kindness will make you lovely, but you are neither good nor kind."

Zoya shrugged. "Should I aspire to be?"

"Your king values such things."

And should Zoya seek his approval? Pretend to be something other than she was? "My king values my loyalty and my ability to lead an army. He will have his wife to smile and simper and cuddle orphans."

"You'd give him up so readily?"

Now Zoya's brows rose in surprise. "He isn't mine to keep."

"There is a reason I use you and not the monk to provoke his demon."

"The king would fight to save anyone—princess or peasant in the field."

"And that's all there is to it? I see the way his eyes follow you."

Was something in Zoya pleased at that? Something foolish and proud? "Men have been watching me my whole life. It's not worth taking note of."

"Careful, young Zoya. It is one thing to be looked at by a mere man, quite another thing to garner the attention of a king."

Attention was easy to come by. Men looked at her and wanted to believe they saw goodness beneath her armor, a kind girl, a gentle girl who would emerge if only given the chance. But the world was cruel to kind girls, and she'd always appreciated that Nikolai didn't ask that of her. Why would he? Nikolai spoke of partnerships and allies, but he was a romantic. He wanted love of a kind Zoya could not give and would never receive. Maybe the thought stung, but that prick of pain, the uneasy sense that something had been lost, belonged to a girl, not a soldier.

Zoya glanced down one of the tunnels. It seemed darker than the others. The smell of honey and sap that emanated from it was not quite right, sweetness punctured by the taint of rot. It might have been her imagination, but the bees even sounded different here, less the buzz of busy insects than the lazy, glutted hum of battlefield flies sated on the dead.

"What's down there?" Zoya asked. "What's wrong with them?"

"The bees are every part of me," said Elizaveta. "Every triumph, every sadness. This part of the hive is weary. It is tired of life. That bitterness will spread to the rest of the hive until all existence will lose its savor. That is why I must leave the Fold, why I will take on a mortal life."

"Are you really ready to give up your power?" Zoya asked. She couldn't quite fathom it.

Elizaveta nodded at the dark chamber. "Most of us can hide our greatest hurts and longings. It's how we survive each day. We pretend the pain isn't there, that we are made of scars instead of wounds. The hive does not grant me the luxury of that lie. I cannot go on this way. None of us can."

The thorny vine curling beneath Elizaveta's hand suddenly

sprouted with white blossoms that turned pink and then blood red before Zoya's eyes.

"Quince?" she asked, thinking of the tales of beasts and maidens she had heard as a child, of Sankt Feliks and his apple boughs. What had Juris said? *Sometimes the stories are rough on the details.*

Elizaveta nodded. "Most women suffer thorns for the sake of the flowers. But we who would wield power adorn ourselves in flowers to hide the sting of our thorns."

Be sweeter. Be gentler. Smile when you are suffering. Zoya had ignored these lessons, often to her detriment. She was all thorns.

"Your king is late," said Elizaveta.

Zoya found she wasn't sorry. She did not want to drown today.

Juris sensed Zoya's mood when she entered the cavern.

"You've been to see Elizaveta," he said, setting aside the tiny obsidian horse he had been carving to add to his herd. "I can smell it on you."

Zoya nodded, reaching for the axes she had come to favor. She liked the weight and balance of them, and they reminded her of Tamar. Was she homesick? She'd lost track of time here. No food. No rest. Hours bled into days. "Everyone is so concerned with the naming of their wounds and the tending of them," she said. "It's tiresome."

Juris gave a noncommittal grunt. "No weapons today."

Zoya scowled. She'd been looking forward to working through her melancholy with a little combat. "Then what?"

"I had hoped by now you would be further along."

Zoya planted her fists on her hips. "I'm doing brilliantly."

"You can still only summon wind. Water and fire should also be at your command."

"Grisha power doesn't work that way."

"You think a dragon cannot control fire?"

So Juris was claiming to be an Inferni as well as a Squaller? "And I suppose you are a Tidemaker too?"

"Water is my weakest element, I confess. I come from a very wet island. I've never been fond of rain."

"You're saying I could summon from all orders?"

"What have we been playing at, if that is not our aim?"

It didn't seem possible, but in only a short time, Juris had shown her that the boundaries of Grisha power were more flexible than she'd ever have believed. *Are we not all things?* They were words she remembered from long ago, from the writings of Ilya Morozova, one of the most powerful Grisha ever known. He had theorized that there should be no Grisha orders, no divisions between powers— if the science was small enough. If all matter could be broken down to the same small parts, then a talented enough Grisha should be able to manipulate those parts. Morozova had hoped that creating and combining amplifiers was the way to greater Grisha power. But what if there was another way?

"Show me."

Juris shifted, his bones cracking and re-forming as he took on his dragon form. "Climb on." Zoya hesitated, staring up at the massive beast before her. "It is not an offer I make to just anyone, storm witch."

"And if a foul mood strikes you and you decide to cast me from your back?" Zoya asked as she laid her hands on the scales at his neck. They were sharp and cool to the touch.

"Then I have made you strong enough to survive the fall."

"Reassuring." She pressed her boot into his flank and hitched herself onto the ridge of his neck. It wasn't comfortable. Dragons had not been made for riding.

"Hold on," he said.

"Oh, is that what I'm supposed to—" Zoya gasped and clung tight as Juris' wings flapped once, twice, and he launched himself into the colorless sky.

The wind rushed against her face, lifting her hair, making her eyes water. She had flown before, had traveled on Nikolai's flying contraptions. This was nothing like that. She could feel every shift Juris made with the currents as he rode the wind, the movement of the muscles beneath his scales, even the way his lungs expanded with each breath. She could feel the force of a stampede in the body beneath her, the heaving power of a storm-tossed sea.

There was nothing to see in the Saints' Fold. It was all barren earth and flat horizon. Maybe that was maddening for Juris—to fly for miles and yet go nowhere. But Zoya didn't care. She could stay this way forever with nothing but sky and sand surrounding her. She laughed, her heart leaping. This was the magic she'd been promised as a child, the dream that all those fairy stories had offered and never delivered. She wished the girl she'd been could have lived this.

"Open the door, Zoya." The dragon's words rumbled through his body. "Open your eyes."

"There's nothing to see!" But that wasn't entirely true. Up ahead, she glimpsed a jagged blot on the landscape. She knew instantly what it was. "Turn around," she demanded. "I want to go back."

"You know you cannot."

"*Turn around.*" The strength of the storm filled her bones, and she tried to move the dragon's head.

"Zoya of the lost city," he said. "Open the door."

The dragon swooped and dove for the ruins of Novokribirsk.

It felt like falling. Zoya was the stone, and there was no bottom to the well, no end to the emptiness inside her. *Do not look back at me.*

The past came rushing at her. Why now? Because of Elizaveta's talk of wounds? Juris' taunts? The torment of being drowned each day as Nikolai grew more distant? She did not want to think of Liliyana or all that she'd lost. There was only the wind and the darkness before her, the dead gray sky above her, the ruins of a lost city below.

And yet it was the memory of her mother's face that filled Zoya's mind.

Sabina's beauty had been astonishing, the kind that stopped men and women alike on the street. But she had made a bad bargain. She had married for love—a handsome Suli boy with broad shoulders and few prospects. For a time, they were poor but happy, and then they were just poor. As they starved and scraped by, the affection between them wasted away too. Long days of work and long months of winter wore at Sabina's beauty and her spirit. She had little love to give to the daughter she bore.

Zoya worked hard for her mother's affection. She was always first in her lessons, always made sure to eat only half of her supper and give Sabina the rest. She was silent when her mother complained of headaches, and she stole peaches for Sabina from the duke's orchards.

"You could be whipped for that," her mother said disapprovingly. But she ate the peaches one after another, sighing contentedly, until her stomach turned and she vomited them all beside the woodpile.

Everything changed when Zoya caught the eye of Valentin Grankin, a wealthy carriage maker from Stelt. He was the richest man for a hundred miles, a widower twice over, and sixty-three years old.

Zoya was nine. She did not want to be a bride, but she did not want to displease her mother, who petted her and cooed at her as she had never done before. For the first time, Sabina seemed *happy*. She sang in the kitchen and cooked elaborate meals with the gifts of meat and vegetables that Valentin Grankin sent.

The night before the wedding, Sabina made orange cakes and laid out the elaborate pearl *kokoshnik* and little gold lace wedding gown Zoya's bridegroom had provided. Zoya hadn't meant to cry, but she hadn't been able to stop.

Aunt Liliyana had come all the way from Novokribirsk for the ceremony—or so Zoya had thought until she heard her aunt pleading with Sabina to reconsider.

Liliyana was younger than Sabina and rarely spoken of. She had left home with scant fanfare and braved the deadly journey across the Shadow Fold to make a life for herself in the hardscrabble town of Novokribirsk. It was a good place for a woman alone, where cheap property could be had and employers were so desperate for workers they gladly offered positions to women that would otherwise be reserved for men.

"He won't hurt her, Liliyana," Sabina said sharply as Zoya sat at the kitchen table, her bare feet brushing the wooden slats of the floor, the perfect circle of her untouched orange cake uneaten on the plate before her. "He said he would wait for her to bleed."

"Am I to applaud him?" Liliyana had demanded. "How will you protect her if he changes his mind? You are selling your own child."

"We are all bought and sold. At least Zoya will fetch a price that will give her an easy life."

"Soon she will be old enough to be a soldier—"

"And then what? We'll live off her meager pay? She'll serve until she's killed or injured so that she can go on to live alone and poor like you?"

"I do well enough."

"Do you think I don't see your shoes tied together with string?"

"Better to be a woman alone than a woman beholden to some old man who can't manage a wife his own age. And it was my choice to make. In a few years Zoya will be old enough to make her own decisions."

"In a few years Valentin Grankin will have found some other pretty girl to occupy his interests."

"Good!" retorted Liliyana.

"Get out of my house," Sabina had seethed. "I don't want to see you anywhere near the church tomorrow. Go back to your lonely rooms and your empty tea tins and leave my daughter alone."

Liliyana had gone, and Zoya had run to her room and buried her face in her blankets, trying not to think of the words her mother had said or the images they'd conjured, praying with all the fervor in her heart that Liliyana would come back, that the Saints would save her, even as she soaked her pillow with tears.

The next morning Sabina had muttered angrily about Zoya's blotchy face as she dressed her in the little gold gown and the attendants came to walk the bride to church.

But Aunt Liliyana was waiting at the altar beside a flummoxed priest. She refused to budge.

"Someone do something about this madwoman!" Sabina had screamed. "She is no sister of mine!"

Valentin Grankin's men had seized Liliyana, dragging her down the aisle. "Lecher!" Liliyana had shouted at Grankin. "Procurer!" she yelled at Sabina. Then she'd turned her damning eyes on the gathered townspeople. "You are all witness to this! She is a child!"

"Be silent," snarled Valentin Grankin, and when Liliyana would not, he took up his heavy walking stick and cracked it against her skull.

Liliyana spat in his face.

He hit her again. This time her eyes rolled back in her head.

"Stop it!" cried Zoya, struggling in her mother's arms. "Stop!"

"Criminal," gasped Liliyana. "Filth."

Grankin lifted his stick again. Zoya understood then that her aunt was going to be murdered before the church altar and no one was going to prevent it. Because Valentin Grankin was a rich, respected man. Because Liliyana Garin was no one at all.

Zoya screamed, the sound tearing from her, an animal cry. A wild gust of wind slammed into Valentin Grankin, knocking him to the ground. His walking stick went clattering. Zoya fisted her hands, her fear and rage pouring from her in a flood. A churning wall of wind erupted around her and exploded into the eaves of the church, blowing the roof from its moorings with an earsplitting *crack*. Thunder rumbled through a cloudless sky.

The wedding guests bellowed their terror. Zoya's mother gazed at her daughter with frightened eyes, clutching the pew behind her as if she might collapse without its support.

Liliyana, one hand pressed to her bleeding head, cried, "You cannot sell her off now! She's Grisha. It's against the law. She is the property of the king and will go to school to train."

But no one was looking at Liliyana. They were all staring at Zoya.

Zoya ran to her aunt. She wasn't sure what she'd done or what it meant, only that she wanted to be as far away from this church and these people and the hateful man on the floor as she could get.

"You leave us alone!" she shouted at no one, at everyone. "You let us go!"

Valentin Grankin whimpered as Zoya and Liliyana hurried past him down the aisle. Zoya looked down at him and hissed.

It was Liliyana who took Zoya, still dressed in her wedding finery, to Os Alta. They had no money for inns, so they slept in ditches and tucked into copses, shivering in the cold. "Imagine we are on a ship," Liliyana would say, "and the waves are rocking us to sleep. Can you hear the masts creaking? We can use the stars to navigate."

"Where are we sailing to?" Zoya had asked, sure she could hear something rustling in the woods.

"To an island covered in flowers, where the water in the streams tastes sweet as honey. Follow those two stars and steer us into port."

Every night, they traveled somewhere new: a coastline where silver seals barked on the shores, a jeweled grotto where they were greeted by the green-gilled lord of the deep—until at last they arrived at the capital and made the long walk to the palace gates.

They were filthy by then, their hair tangled, Zoya's golden wedding dress torn and covered in dust. Liliyana had ignored the guards' sneers as she made her requests, and she'd kept her back straight as she stood with Zoya outside the gates. They'd waited, and waited, and waited some more, shivering in the cold, until at last a young man in a purple *kefta* and an older woman dressed in red had come down to the gates.

"What village are you from?" the woman had asked.

"Pachina," Liliyana replied.

The strangers murmured to each other for a moment, about tests and when the last Examiners had traveled through those parts. Then the woman had pushed up Zoya's sleeve and laid her palm on the bare skin of her arm. Zoya had felt a surge of power race through her. Wind rattled the palace gates and whipped through the trees.

"Ah," the woman had said on a long breath. "What gift has arrived at our doorstep looking so bedraggled? Come, we'll get you fed and warmed up."

Zoya had grabbed Liliyana's hand, ready to begin their new adventure together, but her aunt had knelt and said gently, "I can go no further with you, little Zoya."

"Why not?"

"I need to go home to tend to my chickens. You don't want them to get cold, do you? Besides," she said, smoothing the hair away from

Zoya's face, "this is where you belong. Here they will see the jewel you are inside, not just your pretty eyes."

"For your troubles," the young man said, and dropped a coin into Liliyana's palm.

"Will you be all right?" Zoya asked her.

"I will be fine. I will be better than fine knowing you are safe. Go now, I can hear the chickens clucking. They're very cross with me." Liliyana kissed both of Zoya's cheeks. "Do not look back, Zoya. Do not look back at me or your mother or Pachina. Your future is waiting."

But Zoya looked back anyway, hoping for one last glimpse of her aunt waving through those towering gates. The trees had crowded the path. If Liliyana was still there, Zoya could not see her.

That very day, her training had begun. She'd been given a room at the Little Palace, started classes in language and reading, started to learn Shu, studied with the miserable wretch of a woman known only as Baghra in the hut by the lake. She'd written every week to her aunt and every week received a long, newsy letter back with drawings of chickens in the corners and tales of the interesting traders who came through Novokribirsk.

By law, the parents of Grisha students were paid a stipend, a rich fee to keep them in comfort. When Zoya learned this, she petitioned the bursar to send the money to her aunt in Novokribirsk instead.

"Liliyana Garin is my guardian," she'd told him.

"Are your parents dead, then?"

Zoya had cast him a long look and said, "Not yet."

Even at ten she'd had such cold command in her eyes that he'd simply put his pen to paper and said, "I will need an address and her full name."

It would be six years before Zoya made her first crossing of the Shadow Fold, as a junior Squaller in the Second Army. The Grisha around her had been trembling, some even weeping as they'd entered the darkness, but Zoya had shown no fear, not even in the dark where no one would see her shake. When they'd arrived at Novokribirsk, she'd stepped down from the skiff, tossed her hair over her shoulder, and said, "I'm going to go find a hot bath and a proper meal."

It was only once she'd cleared the docks and left her companions behind that she'd broken into a run, her heart lifting, carrying her on light feet over the cobblestones to Liliyana's small corner shop.

She'd burst through the door, alarming Liliyana's one customer, and Liliyana had emerged from the back room, wiping her hands on her apron and saying, "What is causing such fuss—?"

When she saw Zoya, she'd pressed her hands to her heart as if it might leap from her chest. "My girl," she said. "My brilliant girl." And then Zoya was hugging her aunt tight.

They'd closed up the shop, and Liliyana had cooked them dinner and introduced Zoya to the child she'd taken in whose parents hadn't made it back from their last crossing—a scrawny snub-nosed girl named Lada, who demanded Zoya help her draw the Little Palace in extensive detail. They'd shelled hazelnuts by the fire and discussed the personalities of the chickens and all the gossip of the neighborhood. Zoya had told her aunt about her teachers, her friends, her chambers. She'd given Liliyana gifts of calfskin boots, fur-lined gloves, and an expensive gilded mirror.

"What will I do with this? Look at my old face?" said Liliyana. "Send it to your mother as a peace offering."

"It's a gift for *you*," Zoya replied. "So you can look into it each morning and see the most beautiful person I've ever known."

When the Darkling had used Alina to gain control of the Fold and expand it, he'd destroyed Novokribirsk to show his enemies his power. The darkness had consumed the city, turning its buildings to dust and its people to prey for the unnatural monsters that roamed its depths.

In the wake of the disaster, all crossings had ceased, and it had taken weeks for news of the casualties to reach Kribirsk. The Second Army was in chaos, the Sun Summoner had disappeared or been killed, and the Darkling was said to have emerged somewhere in West Ravka. But Zoya did not care. She could only think of Liliyana. *She'll be sitting in her little shop with Lada and the chickens*, she told herself. *All will be well.* Zoya waited and prayed to every Saint, returning to the Kribirsk drydocks day after day, begging for news. And finally, when no one would help her, she'd commandeered a small skiff on her own and entered the Fold with no one to protect her.

She knew that if the volcra found her, she would die. She had no light or fire with which to fight them. She had no weapons but her power. But she'd taken the tiny craft and entered the dark alone, in silence. She had traveled long miles to the broken remnants of Novokribirsk. Half the town was gone, swallowed by the darkness that reached all the way to the fountain in the main square.

Zoya had run to her aunt's shop and found no one there. The door was unlocked. The chickens squawked in the yard. A cup of bergamot tea, Liliyana's favorite, sat on the counter, long since gone cold.

The rest of the town was quiet. A dog barked somewhere, a child cried. She could find no word of Liliyana or her ward until at last she spotted the same customer she'd seen that long ago day in her aunt's shop.

"Liliyana Garin? Have you seen her? Is she alive?"

The old customer's face paled. "I . . . She tried to help me when the darkness came. She pushed me out of the way so that I could run. If not for her—"

Zoya had released a sob, not wanting to hear any more. Brave Liliyana. Of course she had run toward the docks when the screaming began, ready to help. *Why couldn't you be a coward this one time?* Zoya could not help imagining the dark stain of the Fold bleeding over the town, the monsters descending from the air with their teeth and claws, shrieking as they tore her aunt apart. All her kindness had meant nothing, her generosity, her loving heart. She'd been nothing but meat to them. She'd meant even less to the Darkling, the man who had unleashed his horrors just to make a point, the man she had as good as worshipped.

"She should have let you die," Zoya spat at the old customer, and turned her back on him. She found a quiet street, curled up against a low stone wall, and wept as she had not done since she was a child.

"Smile, beautiful girl," said a stranger passing. "We are still alive! There is still hope!"

She snatched the air from his lungs and drove him to his knees. "Smile," she commanded as his eyes watered and his face turned red. "Smile for me. Tell me again about hope."

Zoya left him on the ground, gasping.

She'd made the crossing once more, silent and unnoticed in her craft, back to Kribirsk and the remnants of the Grisha camp. There she'd learned that the Darkling had raised his banner and called his loyal Grisha to him. Members of the Second Army were deserting, flocking to the Darkling's side or returning to Os Alta to try to mount a campaign against him.

Zoya had stolen a horse and ridden through the night to the capital. She would find the Darkling. She would destroy him. She would take away his dream of ruling Ravka even if she had to lead the Second Army herself.

Zoya never told Alina the details of why she had chosen to fight beside her, why she'd turned against the man she'd once revered. It didn't matter. She'd stood shoulder to shoulder with the Sun Saint. They'd fought and they'd won. They'd watched the Darkling burn.

"And still the wound bleeds," said the dragon. "You will never be truly strong until it closes."

"I don't want it to heal," Zoya said angrily, her cheeks wet with tears. Below, she saw the version of Novokribirsk that existed in this twilight world, a black scar across the sands. "I need it."

The wound was a reminder of her stupidity, of how readily she'd been willing to put her faith in the Darkling's promise of strength and safety, of how easily she'd given up her power to him—and no one had needed to force her down the aisle to make her do it. She'd done it gladly. *You and I are going to change the world*, he'd told her. And she'd been fool enough to believe him.

"Zoya of the lost city. Zoya of the broken heart. You could be so much more."

"Why didn't you come?" she sobbed, surprised at the fresh tears that rose in her. She'd believed them long since shed. "Why didn't you save her? All of them?"

"We didn't know what he intended."

"You should have tried!"

She would always be that girl weeping into her pillow, whispering prayers no one would answer. She would always be that child dressed in gold being led like an animal to slaughter. It was power that had saved her that day in the church, and that was what she had learned to rely on, to cultivate. But it had not been enough to save Liliyana. After the war, she'd gone in search of Lada, hoping the child might have survived. She found no trace. Zoya would never know what had become of that bright-eyed, pug-faced girl.

"Can you forgive us?" Juris asked. "For being foolish? For being frail? For being fallible despite our great powers? Can you forgive yourself?"

For loving the Darkling. For following him. For failing to save Liliyana. For failing to protect the Second Army. The list of her crimes was too long.

Zoya, the dragon rumbled. It was less a spoken word than a thought that entered her head, a sense of eternity. *Open the door. Connect your past to your future.*

Zoya rested her head on the dragon's neck and felt strength flow through her. She heard her heart beating in time with his, slow and relentless, and beneath it, a deeper sound, lower, one that touched everything, the sound of the universe, the making at the heart of the world. She wished she could be strong enough for this, but whatever Juris wanted from her, she could not find her way to it.

You are the conduit, Zoya. You will bring the Grisha back to what they were meant to be before time and tragedy corrupted their power. But only if you can open the door.

Why me? she wondered.

Because you chose this path. Because your king trusts you. Juris tipped his wing and wheeled back to the palace. *Because you are strong enough to survive the fall.*

26
ISAAK

ISAAK HAD PASSED ON THE INFORMATION
he'd gleaned from his conversation with Ehri, though some part of
him had felt a little dirty doing it. He'd shared every detail about the
Tavgharad, and sure enough, Tamar's sources had been able to learn
that one of them, a young recruit named Mayu Kir-Kaat, had a twin
brother who also served in the Shu military.

"He was stationed with a regiment in Koba," Tamar said. "But no
one seems to be able to find him."

"Is that bad or good?" Isaak wanted to know.

"Good for us. Bad for our Tavgharad guard," said Tamar. "We've
tracked shipments of ruthenium to Koba. If her brother has been
drafted into the *khergud* program, she may not be happy about it.
Many candidates don't survive, and those that do are much changed."

Isaak didn't know a lot about the *khergud* soldiers, only that they were rumored to be somewhere between man and killing machine. "So if this guard Mayu is the defector," he said, "you'll initiate contact?"

"It won't be easy," said Tolya. "The Shu guards are rarely alone. But let us focus on that."

Tamar agreed. "We need you at your best for your meeting with the Kerch."

And yet no amount of preparation could have readied Isaak for his disastrous encounter with Hiram Schenck.

Isaak started the evening thrilled to be visiting the Gilded Bog, wondering what mad debauchery he might witness and if he'd get a glimpse of Count Kirigin's wine cellars. They rode out with only a few soldiers, the twins, and Hiram Schenck and his guards. Despite the chill of the evening, Schenck had been giddy.

"This is most exciting, Your Highness," he said. "A fortuitous moment for both our countries." He had the same ruddy coloring and auburn hair as his daughters.

"Indeed," said Isaak. It was a very useful word.

The count greeted them in the gardens of his sparkling mansion, dressed in a vibrant crimson coat, the lapels studded with rubies the size of pullet eggs.

"Delighted to have you!" he said in Ravkan. "Welcome to my little hideaway."

"Thank you for your hospitality," Isaak said, as instructed. "We knew we could count on your discretion."

"Always," said Kirigin. "A necessity of statecraft and seduction alike. I have sent all of my houseguests away, and the grounds are yours. When you finish with your revels, I hope you'll come restore yourselves by my humble hearth and share a cup of something warming." Then he cleared his throat and lowered his voice. "I sent

Commander Nazyalensky an invitation to my autumn revels next week. I wonder if Your Highness might consider encouraging her to come?"

"Of course," said Isaak. "She isn't currently in the capital, but I'm sure she'd be happy to join the fun."

Kirigin blinked. "She would?"

"Perhaps we should be on our way, Your Highness," interjected Tolya, shepherding Isaak away from the count, who was looking at him strangely. "They'll be waiting for us at the lake."

"Did I say something wrong?" he whispered to Tolya as they rode down a gravel path lit by torches.

"Zoya Nazyalensky isn't happy to join Count Kirigin for anything," said Tolya.

Tamar gave her reins a snap. "Least of all fun."

Genya and David were waiting at the shores of an utterly dreary lake. They boarded a small sailing craft, a member of the Ravkan royal navy at the wheel. The night was still, and so a Squaller stood at the mast, raised his hands, and filled the sail with wind. Above them, the night sky was lit by fireworks launched from somewhere on Kirigin's grounds. Isaak wondered who they were for if all his guests were gone, but they created a lovely atmosphere.

The boat came to a halt, bobbing gently. He could see a variety of other vessels moored not too far away, their sails lit by lanterns. No one seemed to be aboard.

"As you know," said Isaak in Kerch, reciting the speech Genya and Tolya had prepared for him, "I've never been content with being confined to land. I have traveled the skies. I have ridden the sea. But then I began to wonder, why should the frontier that lies beneath the waves I love so well be closed to us? And so was born"—he swept his arm dramatically to port—"the *izmars'ya!*"

The water beside the sailboat began to foam and surge. What

looked like the back of a silver beast breached the surface. Isaak stifled a gasp. He wished the others had prepared him for the size of the thing. It dwarfed the sailboat.

Schenck grasped the railing, trying to take it all in. "Incredible," he said. "To think it was beneath us the whole time. Now let's see what it can do."

"Of course," said Isaak, and lifted his hand to give the signal.

The *izmars'ya* descended again, vanishing beneath the surface. All was quiet, the only sound the pop and whine of fireworks dotting the sky with cascades of light.

Then a loud *boom* sounded from too close by. The water next to the boat nearest them exploded in a massive plume. The sleek-looking schooner listed starboard and collapsed, the lights from the lanterns catching in its sails and setting them ablaze. The craft began to sink, taking on water at an alarming rate, as if someone had ripped its hull wide open.

Boom. Another boat collapsed—this one a huge old galleon. Another—a tidy clipper. Even if these craft had been manned and had attempted to mount some kind of defense, there was nothing to shoot at. There was no sign of the *izmars'ya*, only the calm surface of the lake.

A chill traveled through Isaak that had nothing to do with the cool night or the gloomy fog around the lakeshore. So this was why the Kerch were so eager for these underwater ships. They could strike at any time without risk to themselves—an invisible enemy. It was a frightening thought.

Schenck was clapping his hands and whooping. "Stupendous! Better than I could have imagined. The Council will be thrilled. How long is the range? Can the missiles rupture a steel hull? What kind of fuel will we need?"

Isaak didn't know how to answer. No one had prepared him for this kind of interrogation. He'd thought they would just offer a demonstration and then retire to Count Kirigin's home to warm up.

"All in due time," Isaak said—or would have said. But he had not gotten the first word out when the *izmars'ya* breached the waters next to the sailboat with an earsplitting roar. Its metal flank slammed into the sailboat, knocking Isaak and the others to the deck. Hiram Schenck screamed.

The hull of the *izmars'ya* had cracked open, and the interior body of the ship was visible. It was filling with water as the crewmembers shouted and tried to pull themselves up the metal walls. There was another loud boom as its fuel tanks exploded into giant clouds of flame. Isaak heard a high whine, followed by another and then another, as the *izmars'ya*'s missiles shot into the night sky, joining Kirigin's fireworks.

A stray missile grazed one of the sailboat's masts, snapping it in two. Isaak shoved Hiram Schenck aside before it could collapse on the merchant.

"Get us out of here!" shouted the captain, and the Squaller filled the remaining sails with wind, driving them swiftly to shore.

The rest of the disaster was a blur: soaked soldiers, Hiram Schenck's hysterics, Count Kirigin calling, "Then you *won't* be staying for dinner?" from the steps of his house as their party beat a hasty retreat to the palace.

When they finally entered the king's sitting room and Isaak stripped off his wet coat, he was prepared for a long night of strategizing and recriminations. Instead Tamar threw herself down on the couch and burst out laughing. Tolya picked up David in one arm and Genya in the other and spun them both around.

"Brilliant," gasped Genya, thumping on Tolya's shoulder so he would set her down. "A performance worthy of the too-clever fox himself."

"The way Schenck squealed," crowed Tamar. "I think he may have wet himself."

"I almost did the same," said Tolya. "Was the missile supposed to hit the mast?"

"Of course it was," David said sternly. "You said you wanted a spectacle."

Genya planted a kiss on his cheek and repeated, *"Brilliant."*

Isaak stared at them. "Then . . . that wasn't a disaster?"

"It was a *triumph*," said Tamar.

"I see," said Isaak.

"Oh, Isaak," said Genya. "I'm so sorry. We just weren't sure you could feign real surprise."

"We needed your reaction to be natural," Tamar said.

Tolya's face was contrite. "We only had one chance to get this right."

Isaak sat down on the couch. "Damn it."

"We're sorry," Genya said, crouching at his knee and looking up at him imploringly. "Truly."

"Can you forgive us?" asked Tolya.

"I was just so excited," Isaak said. He pulled off his left boot and watched it spill what looked like half a lake onto the carpet. "Finally something went wrong and I had nothing to do with it."

27

NIKOLAI

THE NIGHT BEFORE THE RITUAL, Nikolai sat with Zoya in front of the fire in his chambers. Yuri had retired early to pray.

The fire in the grate was wholly unnecessary. The Fold was neither hot nor cold—weather would have required some kind of change in the punishing monotony of this place. But the flames were all they had for entertainment, and Nikolai was in desperate need of distraction.

He had insisted he was ready for the ritual. Elizaveta had wanted to delay for a few more days so he could solidify his control, but Nikolai was unwilling to risk it. He needed to get back to the capital. But it was more than that. He could sense the monster getting stronger with every day, and he suspected that it had become easier to make his demon rise because it wanted to stretch its wings. It could taste the possibility of freedom.

"Just a little longer," Elizaveta had said.

But Nikolai had held firm. "Tomorrow," he'd told her. Or whatever passed for tomorrow in this cursed place.

He had never wished for sleep more, for some relief from thoughts of the challenge to come. He could sense the monster waiting. Somehow it knew that tomorrow they would face each other, and it was ready. Its anticipation was more frightening than the fact that he would have to drive a thorn through his chest in a matter of hours. Nikolai craved a glass of wine desperately. No, skip the glass. He'd go straight to the bottle.

But there was no wine to be had. No food to fill a plate. He was hungry and yet his stomach never growled. He was thirsty and yet his mouth was never dry.

Nikolai watched Zoya watching the flames. She flexed her fingers, and the sparks leapt. He still could not quite fathom what Juris had taught her in this short time. She wore the same clothes she'd worn the morning they'd disappeared, though the roughspun cloak had long since been discarded. He was grateful for the familiarity of the deep blue silk of her *kefta*.

She sat with a knee tucked up, one cheek resting against it. Nikolai realized he'd never seen her look so at ease. At court, Zoya always moved with grace, her steps smooth, her gaze sharp and unforgiving as the blade of a knife. But he realized now it was the grace of an actress on the stage. She was always performing, always on guard. Even with him.

Nikolai released a startled laugh, and she glanced over at him. "What is it?"

He shook his head. "I think I'm jealous."

"Of what?"

"A dragon."

"Don't let Juris hear that. He thinks enough of himself as it is."

"He should. He can fly and breathe fire, and he's probably got piles of gold stashed somewhere."

"That's an unfair cliché. It could very well be jewels."

"And he made you look like that."

Zoya raised a brow. "Like what precisely?"

"Comfortable."

Zoya's back straightened, and he felt tremendous regret at seeing her armor lock back into place.

After a minute she asked, "What do you think will happen when we leave this place?"

"Hopefully not too many things will be on fire."

Zoya sighed. "David and Kuwei have been left unattended too long. For all we know they've blown up half the capital."

"That is worryingly plausible," admitted Nikolai. He scrubbed a hand over his head. Red wine. White wine. That drink made with fermented cherries he'd tried at the Crow Club. Anything for a little respite, a night of real rest. Not even Genya's sleeping concoction worked here. It just made his mind sluggish. "I don't know what we'll find. I don't even know who I'll be tomorrow."

"You will be who you were always meant to be. Ravka's king."

Maybe, he thought. *Or maybe it will be left to you to set Ravka to rights.*

He removed a folded document from his pocket and placed it beside her hand.

She picked it up and turned it over, frowning at the wax seal he'd impressed with his signet ring. "What is this?"

"Don't worry, I haven't written you a love letter." She turned her face to the fire. Was even the mention of love too much for Zoya's ruthless sensibilities? "This is a royal order declaring you Ravka's protector and making you commander of both the First and Second Armies."

She stared at him. "Have you lost your wits entirely?"

"I'm trying to do the responsible thing. I think it's giving me indigestion."

Zoya tossed the letter to the floor as if the paper had singed her fingers. "You don't think you're going to survive tomorrow."

"Ravka's hopes shouldn't live and die with me."

"So you're pinning them on me instead?"

"You are one of the most powerful Grisha the world has ever known, Zoya. If anyone can protect Ravka, it's you."

"And if I tell you I don't want the job?"

"We both know better. And did I mention the position comes with some truly spectacular sapphires?" Nikolai rested his hands on his knees. "If the twins and the Triumvirate weren't able to hide our disappearance, Ravka may already be in turmoil. We both know it's possible I won't survive the ritual and someone will have to restore order. Every man and woman who claims to have a drop of Lantsov blood will make a bid for the throne, and our enemies will seize the chance to tear the country apart. Pick one of the pretenders to back, the smartest or the most charming or—"

"The most easily controlled?"

"You see? You were made for this. Rally the Grisha. Try to save our people."

Zoya gazed into the fire, her expression troubled. "Why is it so easy for you to contemplate your death?"

"I'd rather look at a thing squarely than let it catch me by surprise." He grinned. "Don't tell me you'd miss me."

Zoya looked away again. "I suppose the world would be less interesting without you in it. I wouldn't let myself be drowned in amber for just anyone, you know."

"I'm touched," he said. And he was. It was the closest thing to a compliment she'd ever given him.

She drew a slender chain from the neck of her *kefta* and pulled it over her head. The key she had used for his shackles. She dangled it from her finger. "We won't ever need this again after tomorrow."

He took it from her, feeling the weight of it in his palm. The metal was warm from her skin. He hadn't missed their nightly ceremony, but he'd missed having an excuse to talk to her each evening and each morning. He supposed that would be at an end now too.

Nikolai hesitated. He wasn't anxious to spoil her goodwill. "Your amplifier . . ." Zoya's hand twitched, and he knew she was resisting the urge to touch her bare wrist. "Will you tell me how you got it?"

"Why does it matter?"

"I don't know that it does." But he wanted to know. He wanted to sit here and listen to her talk. For all the time they'd spent together, Zoya was still a mystery to him. This might be his last chance to unravel her.

She smoothed the silk of her *kefta* over her knees. He thought she might not speak, just sit there, silent as a stone until he gave up waiting. Zoya was perfectly capable of it. But at last she said, "I was thirteen. I had been at the Little Palace for almost five years. The Darkling took a group of Grisha to Tsibeya. There were rumors the white tigers of Ilmisk had returned, and he suspected at least one of them was an amplifier."

"Near the permafrost?"

"A little farther south. I was the youngest of the group and so proud to be chosen to go. I was half in love with him already. I lived for the rare moments he appeared at the school." She shook her head.

"I was the best, and I wanted him to see that . . . The older Grisha were all in contention for the amplifier. It was up to them to track the tigers and see who would earn the right to the kill. They followed a female for nearly a week and cornered her in the woods near Chernast, but she somehow escaped their grasp."

Zoya wrapped her arms around her legs. "She left her cubs. Abandoned the three of them. The Darkling's men penned them in a cage so the Grisha could squabble over who deserved their teeth the most. All night we could hear the mother prowling the perimeter of the camp, snarling and yowling. My friends talked about going into the dark to pursue her. I knew they were all bluster, but I couldn't stop thinking about the cubs. So when the camp was asleep, I created a distraction for the guards by knocking over one of the tents with a gust of wind, and I chased the cubs out of the cage. They were so little," she said with the smallest smile. "They couldn't really run, only roll a bit, stumble, right themselves. I just kept them moving away from the camp. Saints, I was scared." Her eyes were far away now, as if looking into that long-ago night. "We were still in sight of the torches when I realized I wasn't alone."

"The mother?"

She shook her head. "A male. I don't know why, but he went straight for the cubs. I panicked. I should have fought, used my power, but all I could think to do was cover their bodies with mine. When the male attacked, his claws tore clean through my coat and my *kefta* all the way to the skin of my back." Zoya's fists clenched. "But I protected those cubs. I remember . . . I remember I had my eyes squeezed shut, and when I opened them the snow looked black in the moonlight." She turned her face to the fire. "It was stained with my blood. I could feel the cubs wriggling against me, yowling their terror, their little claws sharp as needles. That was what brought me back to sense—those tiny, vicious little pinpricks. I gathered the last of my strength and summoned the most powerful gust I could. I threw open my arms and sent the male flying. That was when the Darkling and his guards came running. I guess I'd been screaming."

"Did they kill the tiger?"

"He was already dead. He'd struck a tree when I threw him. It snapped his neck. The cubs escaped."

Zoya rose. She turned her back to him and, to his astonishment, shrugged the silk of her *kefta* from her shoulders, letting it pool at her hips. An unwelcome bolt of desire shot through him, and then he saw—along the smooth skin of her back lay eight long, furrowed scars.

"The other Grisha were furious," she said, "but I had killed the white tiger. The amplifier could only belong to me. So they bandaged my wounds, and I claimed the tiger's teeth for my wrist. He left me with these."

The firelight caught the pearly surface of the scars. It was a miracle that she'd survived.

"You never had them healed? Tailored?"

She drew the *kefta* back up to her shoulders and fastened the clasps. "He left his mark on me and I on him. We did each other damage. It deserves to be remembered."

"And the Darkling didn't deny you the amplifier, despite what you'd done?"

"It would have been a fair punishment, but no. An amplifier that powerful was too rare to waste. They put the fetter on me, bound the old cat's teeth in silver so that I could never remove it. That's how all of the most powerful amplifiers are fashioned."

She gazed out the open frame of the window to the flat gray expanse of the sky. "When it was all over, the Darkling had me brought to his tent and said, 'So, Zoya, you freed the tiger cubs. You did the selfless thing. And yet somehow you are the one who has finished the day with greater power. More than any of your betters who have patiently waited their turn. What do you say to that?'

"His disapproval was more painful than any wound from a tiger's claws. Some part of me always feared that he would send me away, banish me forever from the Little Palace. I told him I was sorry.

"But the Darkling saw me clearly even then. 'Is that really what you wish to say?' he asked."

Zoya pushed a dark strand of her hair behind her ear. "So I told him the truth. I put my chin up and said, 'They can all hang. It was my blood in the snow.'"

Nikolai stifled a laugh and a smile played over Zoya's lips. It dwindled almost instantly, replaced by a troubled frown. "That pleased him. He told me it was a job well done. And then he said . . . 'Beware of power, Zoya. There is no amount of it that can make them love you.'"

The weight of the words settled over Nikolai. *Is that what we're all searching for?* Was that what he'd hunted in all those library books? In his restless travels? In his endless pursuit to seize and then keep the throne? "Was it love you wanted, Zoya?"

She shook her head slowly. "I don't think so. I wanted . . . strength. Safety. I never wanted to feel helpless again."

"Again?" It was impossible to conceive of Zoya as anything less than mighty.

But all she said was, "When Juris broke that fetter, it was like he'd torn a limb from my body. You cannot imagine it."

He couldn't. And he couldn't imagine what words might bring her comfort. "What became of the cubs?"

Zoya ran her finger over the window ledge, sand trailing from it in a glittering fall. "He told me . . . The Darkling said that because they had my scent on them, their mother wouldn't raise them." Her voice wobbled slightly. "He said that I'd doomed them as surely as if

I'd taken a knife to their throats myself. That she'd leave them to die in the snow. But I don't believe that, do you?"

Her face was composed, but her eyes were imploring. Nikolai felt as if he were looking at the young girl she'd been on that cold and bloody night.

"No," he said. "I don't believe that at all."

"Good," she said. "Good . . ." She gave her cuffs a firm tug, seeming to return to herself. "Every lover I've taken has asked about those scars. I make up a new story for each of them."

He found he did not want to think of Zoya's lovers. "And what did I do to earn the truth?"

"Offered me a country and faced imminent death?"

"It's important to have standards, Nazyalensky."

Zoya bobbed her chin toward the sealed order that still lay on the floor. "It's not too late to burn that."

Nikolai thought of the smooth planes of her back striped by those furrowed scars. He thought of the stubborn tilt of her chin. He imagined her huddled in the snow, risking her position with the mentor she worshipped, risking her very life to save those cubs.

"The more I know of you," he said, "the more I am sure you are exactly what Ravka needs."

In that moment, he wished things might have been different. That he might not die tomorrow. That he could be led by his heart instead of duty.

Because Zoya was not kind and she was not easy.

But she was already a queen.

28

NINA

NINA HAD NEVER SAT THROUGH such a long, strange dinner. One of the prettier rooms off the chapel had been set with a private meal for Brum, his daughter, and her new language teacher. The food was a marked improvement on the simple fare of the convent: seared perch served with mussels, cabbage shoots and cream, smoked eel, pickled mushrooms, and braised leeks. Nina tucked two tiny quail eggs into her skirts in case Trassel had a taste for the finer things, and found herself wondering if they might finish with sugared almond cookies. One could plot violent espionage and still hope for dessert.

Brum had questioned Adrik and Leoni that afternoon, and apparently their answers had satisfied him. Nina had expected Adrik to refuse to continue on with their plan now that they were facing the *drüskelle* commander's scrutiny, but he'd surprised her.

"I always figured I'd die young," Adrik said, gloomy as ever. "Why not do it shoving my boot up that murderer's ass?"

Tonight, she was Nina Zenik, seated across from her greatest enemy—Matthias' former mentor and the architect of some of the worst crimes against her people. But she was also Mila Jandersdat, a poor girl dining with those high above her station, all while watching her friend suffer.

And Hanne was her friend. She thought of Hanne sneaking away from the convent to deliver an unwanted child. She thought of her crouched over the neck of her horse, racing through the fields, of her standing in the classroom, hands raised in fighting stance, cheeks flushed. A warrior born. She had a wild, generous streak that could bloom into something magical if it was only allowed to flourish. That might happen in Ravka. It was definitely not going to happen at this table.

Brum subjected Hanne to endless questions about her comportment classes and her plans for the next year.

"Your mother and I miss you, Hanne. You've been gone too long from Djerholm."

"I miss you too, Papa."

"If you would only set aside these unseemly pursuits and apply yourself, I know you would be welcome back at court. Just think of how good it would be to all be together again."

"Yes, Papa."

"I don't like the idea of you remaining out here, especially with the foreign influences encroaching in these small towns. The Wellmother tells me a novitiate was caught with an icon of some heathen Saint tucked beneath her pillow. You belong at the Ice Court."

"Yes, Papa."

Hanne's attempts to discuss her studies were dismissed with the wave of a hand. "You've always been smart, Hanne. But that will not garner you a powerful husband."

"Would he not wish for a wife with whom he can discuss politics and matters of state?"

Brum sighed. "A man who spends all day handling the country's business does not want to converse about such things with his wife. He wishes to be soothed, entertained, reminded of the gentler things in this world, the things we fight so hard to protect."

Nina stifled a gag. She wasn't sure she was going to be able to keep her excellent dinner down.

As the argument between Hanne and her father became heated, she discreetly excused herself. Brum was staying at the factory, and they would hold their attack until he left in the morning.

Nina used the washroom, then checked the pockets of the coat Brum had left neatly folded on the chair in the sitting room. She found a letter full of talk of "the little Lantsov" and someone named Vadik Demidov. She did her best to commit the rest of the information to memory, but she couldn't afford to be gone from the table long.

Nina snuffed the candle and slipped out of the sitting room. Jarl Brum was standing in the dimly lit hall.

"Oh!" she cried, letting her hand flutter to the neckline of her dress. "You startled me."

"Did you get lost on your way back from the washroom?"

"No, sir," she said, adding a hint of breathlessness to her voice. "I saw the candles were burning low and stopped to extinguish them."

"Is that not servants' work, Enke Jandersdat?"

"Please, call me Mila."

Brum peered down at her in the gloom. "That would not be entirely proper."

How the Fjerdans loved their propriety, but she had started to wonder if they loved to make their rules simply for the thrill of breaking them.

"Forgive me," she said, dropping into an unnecessarily deep curtsy. "I meant no offense. I'm afraid my country manners have displeased you."

Brum placed his finger beneath her chin, but he was gentle this time as he bid her stand and tilted her face upward. "Not at all. I find them refreshing. You'll learn to navigate the company of your betters in time."

Nina lowered her eyes. "If I am lucky enough to have cause to."

Brum studied her. "I leave tomorrow morning, but I often pass back through Gäfvalle to make sure the munitions factory is running smoothly." *And to oversee your experiments*, Nina thought with a flash of rage. "I look forward to seeing how Hanne's lessons progress."

"I do not have a permanent position here," Nina said, wringing her hands. "I'm not sure how long the Wellmother will tolerate my presence."

Brum placed his hand over hers, and she stilled. "Such a nervous little thing. The Wellmother will always have a place for you if I say so."

Nina looked up at him with every bit of awe she could muster. She clasped his hand tightly. "Thank you, sir," she said fervently. "Thank you."

They rejoined Hanne in the dining room to say their goodbyes.

As soon as her father was gone, Hanne sagged against the wall in relief. "Thank Djel that's over. Did you get what you needed?"

Nina held up the blob of warm candle wax she'd pressed against Brum's signet ring to form a perfect impression of his seal. "I did. The rest is up to you."

Adrik had been right about the problem of entering the factory. Even with Brum's seal on a military order, there was no way the guards at the eastern entrance would ever release the women and girls without a convincing Fjerdan soldier in charge.

Hanne did not get out of bed the next morning, claiming that the rich food of the previous night's dinner hadn't agreed with her.

The Wellmother had little patience for it. "Our duties do not include seeing to a pampered girl with a fragile stomach."

"Of course, Wellmother," Hanne agreed. "Enke Jandersdat can look after me." Then she'd bent over the side of the bed and vomited.

The Wellmother pressed her sleeve to her nose to ward against the smell. "Fine. Let her empty your sick bucket and clean up your mess."

"Perhaps Leoni's emetic worked a little too well," Nina said as soon as they were alone together, the door firmly closed.

Hanne moaned and flopped back on her pillows, looking distinctly green. Nina sat down on the bed and held a fizzing glass vial to Hanne's lips. "Here, this will help. Leoni is just as good at tonics as emetics."

"I hope so," said Hanne.

Nina cleaned up the sickroom while Hanne rested, then made her eat some plain bread and an egg. "You'll need your strength."

Hanne propped herself up in bed, shoving a pillow behind her back. She'd left her hair unbraided in a rosy brown tumble around her shoulders, and Nina had the urge to twine one of the thick curls around her finger.

"I don't know if I can do this," said Hanne. "I've never tried to tailor anything before."

Nina parted the curtains to let in as much sunlight as possible. Hanne's room was on the second story, so they didn't have to worry about prying eyes. "It's just another way to manipulate the body."

"You've seen it done?"

"Just once," lied Nina. Her entire face and body had been tailored to be totally unrecognizable. She'd even tried her hand at it a few times.

"What if I can't put it back once I've done it?"

"Then we'll find someone who can," she promised. *Even if I have to drag you to Ravka to manage it.* "But I really don't think it will be a problem. You're only going to make very small changes." Nina sat down in front of Hanne and held up a mirror she'd polished to perfection.

Hanne gazed at herself in the glass. "Where do I start?"

"Let's try the jaw. We'll mess with the nose once you get the hang of it. I don't want you accidentally sealing off a breathing passage." Hanne's eyes widened. "I'm kidding!" said Nina. *Mostly.*

Hanne steadied her breathing and pressed her fingers gently to the left side of her own jaw.

"Focus on the cells of the skin," said Nina. "Think of the direction you want them to move."

"This is terrifying," whispered Hanne as the line of her jaw slowly began to shift.

"More terrifying than the Wellmother when she catches someone having a good time?"

A scrap of a smile curled Hanne's lips, and she seemed to relax a bit. "Not even close."

The work took hours as Hanne strengthened her jawline, giving it a squarer shape, then added weight to her brow, and finally broadened her nose. Nina sat curled beside Hanne in the narrow bed, watching her progress in the mirror, offering suggestions and encouragement. Periodically, she would leave the room to retrieve cups of broth and pretend to empty basins, maintaining the illusion that Hanne was still ill.

At last it was time for the final touch.

"Are you sure?" Nina said, holding the thick, ruddy tresses of Hanne's hair. They were shot through with gold and felt cool and silken in her hands, like fast-running water. "We could just tuck it under your cap."

"I'm not going to jeopardize this whole plan for the sake of my vanity." She squeezed her eyes shut. "Do it."

It felt like a crime to cut such magnificent hair, but Nina took up the shears and sliced through the thick strands. She finished the job with the razor, cropping Hanne's hair close to the skull in the way of the Fjerdan military. Only *drüskelle* kept their hair long. When Hanne had tailored her face back to its original state, she could claim that shaving her hair had been a penance to Djel.

Nina tidied up the hair, gathering it all in a basin, and then tossed it into the garbage, making sure it was well buried. When she returned, she found Hanne sitting on her bed, staring into the mirror, tears in her eyes.

"Don't cry," Nina said, shutting the door behind her and rushing to Hanne's side. "It will grow back. I promise."

"It's not that," Hanne said, gazing at her face. A boy was looking back at her. The jaw, the brow, the nose, a roughening of the skin of her cheeks to make it look as if she'd shaved. They were small changes, but the effect was startling. "If I had just been a boy. If I had been the son my father wanted . . ."

Nina gripped Hanne's shoulders. "You are perfect, Hanne. That your father can't value your strength speaks only to his weakness."

Hanne looked back at the mirror, blinking her tears away. "The lips are still too full."

"Leave the lips," said Nina sharply, then rose to hide her blush. "They're just right."

29

ISAAK

AFTER THE CHAOS OF THE demonstration at the
Gilded Bog, Isaak shouldn't have felt nervous walking into a
trade meeting the following day. But there was no reason for the
Triumvirate to be in attendance, so he was left to face the Kerch,
Kaelish, and Zemeni with no one but Nikolai's finance ministers. He
was afraid he'd be found out. He was afraid he'd make the king look
like a fool. He was afraid he'd send the Ravkan economy into a tail-
spin just by scratching his nose wrong.

Before the meeting began, he did as Genya and the others had
suggested and met privately with his ministers. "I'd prefer you took
the lead on this, Ulyashin," he said. "I trust you to get this right."

The trade minister had beamed and happily spent the meeting
debating tariffs and import taxes, all while gracefully dodging the

looming specter of Ravka's loans. Isaak felt an overwhelming rush of gratitude toward Ulyashin. Perhaps he could gift him with a boat or a title or whatever kings did to say thank you.

The meeting closed on what seemed to be a positive note, and Isaak was already heaving a sigh of relief as he rose and shook hands with the attendees. But just when he thought he was going to make his escape, Hiram Schenck cornered him and whispered furiously, "Do you think you can continue to play games with us?"

Genya had told him that if he got caught unawares in any situation, his best approach was to say, "I beg your pardon?" with as much haughty grandeur as possible.

Isaak deployed that strategy now, looking down his nose with ferocious disdain. "I beg your pardon? Didn't I recently drag your sodden daughter from a pond?"

Schenck was not deterred. "Did you really think we would be fooled by that bit of theater last night? You were close to completing the submersibles and the missile system when we received our information months ago, and we all know that you do not rest until your inventions are perfected. You cannot continue to flirt like a debutante at a ball. We will have our prototype or you will be treated like the pauper state you are."

Nikolai Lantsov would never have stood for such an insult. He would have replied with the perfect words to make Schenck quake with fear and wish he'd never opened his mouth.

"*I beg your pardon,*" Isaak said firmly, and stepped past Schenck to the safety of the open door.

He hurried out of the room, gut churning, and found the twins waiting in the hall to escort him over the next dismaying hurdle.

"The Kerch didn't buy last night's performance," he said as they strode down the corridor.

"We know," said Tamar. "We were listening."

424

"Maybe the wayward missiles were too much," Tolya said.

Isaak straightened his plum-colored coat. "What do we do now?"

"I don't know," admitted Tamar. "Let's just get through the afternoon."

A few more days, Isaak told himself. *A few more parties. I can do this.*

But where was the king?

The previous night, after he'd gone to change into dry clothes, he'd overheard the others talking in the sitting room.

"We just have to get past the closing ball," Tamar had said as she put her arm around Genya. "Then we'll make a decision."

"How can there be no sign of them at all?" Genya asked with a soft sniffle. "It's been nearly three weeks. People don't just disappear. I never thought I would say this, but I *miss* Zoya."

"Me too," said Tolya. "Even though I know she'd kick me for wasting time worrying about her."

"I think the Apparat knows something," Tamar said. "He sent a request for an audience with the king to hear about his pilgrimage and demanding information on Yuri. The priest won't be put off forever and he's been gone from the city too much for my liking. He has his own warren of tunnels leading in and out of the capital. There are too many places for him to hide."

"We could get him more involved with the guests," said Tolya. "Ask him to perform a service—"

But Tamar had cut him off. "We can't afford to let the priest near Isaak. He's too canny for that."

"Perhaps we should have him killed," said David.

Genya had burst into fresh tears. "When you say that, it just makes me miss Zoya more."

What comes next? Isaak wondered. He might make it through the afternoon, he might well make it through this whole series of parties and pomp without inciting any more disasters. But that didn't mean he was capable of governing a country or even serving as some kind of figurehead while Genya and the others did the real ruling.

He rounded a corner into the portrait gallery and came upon Princess Ehri and several of her guards—just as the twins' lookout had said he would. Isaak did his best to feign surprise as he greeted the princess and made small talk about the morning's entertainments.

"We found the weather too brisk for the garden party," said Ehri. "So we thought we might stroll through the portrait gallery."

"How are you finding the paintings?"

"They're all very stern."

Just don't look too closely, thought Isaak. "Perhaps I can offer you a tour of this wing of the palace?" He could have sworn he felt the approval of her guards. They really must report Ehri's successes and failures back to her sister.

They passed through the blue splendor of the lapis drawing room and the concert hall and then through some of the humbler parts of the palace: the musty trophy room, its walls crowded with stags' antlers and the heads of various big game; the armory with its old-fashioned saddles and swords; and, at last, the training rooms.

"Come, let's step inside," he suggested. The words sounded awkward and staged to his ears, but at least he knew she had a fondness for axes.

"Is this where your guards train?"

"Yes," said Isaak. He himself had trained here and practiced with the king. "Tamar, perhaps you could give us a demonstration?"

Tamar took two dulled axes from the wall. "You," she said, pointing at one of the Tavgharad. She was young, her face serious, the chin sharply pointed. This had to be Mayu Kir-Kaat, whose twin brother had gone missing and who, perhaps, had tired of service to the Shu crown.

One of the older women stepped forward. "I will gladly spar with you." She had a long scar across her elegant nose.

Tamar cocked her head. "Is there only one lioness in this pride?"

"I will fight her," said the pointy-chinned girl.

"Mayu," said another of the guards softly.

But Mayu stepped forward, undeterred—or perhaps anticipating the invitation.

An uncomfortable current passed through the room.

"Perhaps we should spar too," said Isaak. The twins wanted the Tavgharad watching Ehri, not Tamar and Mayu. He plucked a wooden sword from the wall.

"I have little talent for combat," said Ehri nervously.

"I thought all of the Taban family were trained to defend themselves."

"Of course. But my sisters are the better warriors."

"Maybe I can teach you a thing or two." Isaak didn't want to push her, but he also knew Tamar was relying on him to create a distraction while she attempted to speak to Mayu. A friendly chat while sparring wasn't ideal, but there was no other way to get one of the Tavgharad alone.

Isaak tossed Ehri a practice sword, and she snatched it from the air with ease. He heard a murmur of disapproval from the Tavgharad.

"Princess—" the older woman began.

But Ehri was already on the attack.

She had radically understated her talents. She was a gifted swordswoman and moved without a hint of hesitation. Distantly he heard the grunts of the other fighters and dared a glance at them. He saw Tamar handily knock Mayu on her behind. She leaned low when she helped the girl up, and he could only hope they were exchanging the words they needed to—assuming Mayu was the guard who wished to defect.

Then the flat of Ehri's sword struck him in the gut and his breath left him with an audible *oof*.

Ehri raised a brow. "Ravka's king lacks focus."

"How could anyone not be distracted by your beauty?" A weak riposte at best.

Ehri just laughed. She seemed more relaxed than he had ever seen her.

"You have a different fighting style than I expected," she said. *Probably because you expected a king raised from birth to wield a sword*, thought Isaak. Instead she was getting a tutor's son who hadn't touched a blade until he had been drafted.

"I might say the same of you," he replied honestly. He had the sense that she was holding back, though he couldn't be sure. Were all the Shu princesses trained to wield a blade so well? He would be teaching her nothing.

Isaak heard a cry from over his shoulder, and both he and Ehri turned to see Mayu doubled over and gasping for breath.

"Enough!" said the older Shu guard harshly.

"My apologies," Tamar said with a deep bow.

"And mine as well," added Isaak. What had happened? Had Tamar gotten the information she sought? Was this all part of the plan? "I can take you to our infirmary. We—"

"No," gasped Mayu Kir-Kaat. "I'll be fine."

"Please," said Isaak. "I would hate to think one of my guests was harmed in what should have been a bit of good fun."

"It was an accident," said Princess Ehri. "We all know this."

For a moment, the room bristled with tension as if trouble were racing from mind to mind, looking for a place to take hold.

"If I may, Princess," said Mayu, straightening. "Among the Shu, amends would have to be made."

Tamar frowned. "What did you have in mind?"

The guard exchanged a glance with Ehri. "Perhaps a private dinner?"

Tamar shook her head. "That would be seen as a sign of favoritism among the other hopefuls."

Ehri looked uneasy. "We don't want to cause problems for the king."

"Surely the others wouldn't need to know," said Isaak before he thought better of it.

Tamar's frown deepened, but she said, "Of course, Your Highness."

When Ehri and her guards had gone, Tamar's frown vanished. She punched him on the arm. "Well done. Another opportunity to chase information." But his expression must have shown his disappointment, because Tamar drew back. "Oh no. Isaak, you witless podge. You like her, don't you?"

"Don't be ridiculous," he said, feeling his cheeks heat. "I know the game we're playing. What did you learn from Mayu?"

"Nothing." Tamar's gaze grew thoughtful. "I told her I had heard she was *keb* and asked after her twin brother, but she gave me very little, only that they were from the Bol province."

"Maybe she's not the one."

"Possible. She was scared of something though, and she doesn't fight as well as I'd expect. I didn't mean to hurt her, but I misjudged her reaction times. She's young and new to the ranks, so it's natural for her to be a lesser fighter than the other Tavgharad. But if she's failing in her training, she might be looking to get out before they throw her out."

"Would she just go into the regular military?"

"After witnessing the Taban at their most vulnerable? Absolutely not. She would be exiled for her failure. She'd never see her brother or the rest of her family again." Tamar returned her sword to the wall. "It could be someone else. Or no one else. Our intelligence networks

429

in Shu aren't what they should be. I'll try to make sure I have time alone with each of the Tavgharad during your romantic interlude with the princess. Just make it a nice long meal."

"If I must."

"*Yuyeh sesh*, Isaak," Tamar said as she gestured for a servant to put the practice room back in order.

Despise your heart. A Shu saying. Do what has to be done. He knew how he was supposed to reply, the way a Shu soldier would reply, maybe the way a king would reply: *Niweh sesh. I have no heart.* But the words that came to mind instead were of the "Kebben'a" and the first blossom's fall.

He was not a Shu warrior, and he was not a Ravkan king. He was just a peasant boy who wanted to have dinner with a girl who had been kind to him.

Isaak left the room in silence.

When Isaak met with Genya and David and the twins that night in his sitting room, he expected them to be excited over the prospect of his secret dinner with Ehri. Instead, it was as if he'd walked into a wake.

"What is it?" he asked. "Is it the king?"

Tolya looked grim, Tamar's expression was murderous, and Genya looked like she'd aged twenty years. Even David had put aside his reading and looked, if not like the world was ending, at least mildly concerned.

"We've had news from Fjerda," said Tamar. "They're preparing to march on Ravka. It could be a week or a month, but war is coming."

Isaak sat down hard. War. They'd barely had three years of peace.

"It gets worse," said Tolya. "They're marching under the Lantsov banner."

Isaak looked up at him. "I don't understand."

"Their rulers have declared for Vadik Demidov."

"Who?"

"He says he is a Lantsov cousin and the rightful heir to Ravka's throne."

"But that's nonsense. Even if he is a Lantsov——"

"His claim is supported by a man named Magnus Opjer," said Genya, "a Fjerdan shipping magnate."

"He was once an emissary to Ravka," Tamar continued. "Opjer says he had an affair with the Ravkan queen. He claims he is Nikolai's true father."

"That can't be," protested Isaak. "It's just Fjerdan propaganda."

"He has her letters," Genya said quietly. "If they can be authenticated——"

"Even if they can't," said Tamar. "It's enough pretext for the Fjerdans."

"No," Isaak said, and stood, though he wasn't sure why. "Ravka loves their king. They will rally to his side."

"Maybe," said Tolya. "I'd feel better if we could locate the Apparat. He and most of the Priestguard have gone to ground somewhere. If he backs the pretender's cause——"

David shifted the book in his lap. "We probably should have had him killed."

Tamar rubbed her hands over her face. "We're going to have to make a deal with the Kerch."

"We need the Zemeni at sea," said Tolya. "Our navy is no match for the Fjerdans."

"Not without Kerch money," argued Tamar.

"Even then we'll need time to build."

Isaak couldn't believe what he was hearing. He opened his mouth to talk and was horrified when a slightly hysterical laugh escaped his lips. "Have you all gone mad?" They stared at him. "I'm not Nikolai Lantsov. I can't lead a nation at war. This charade has to end."

For a long moment there was quiet.

At last, Genya asked, "Is the Fjerdan delegation still here?"

"Yes," said Tamar. "I have spies at the Ice Court, but none of this is common knowledge, even among most of their government officials."

"Very well. We will see this out to the end of the week and the final ball. When the guests are gone, we'll make a plan." She looked up at Isaak. "One we can all live with."

The initial anticipation Isaak had felt for his dinner with Ehri had been thoroughly clubbed to death by the news from Fjerda. If the king never returned, could they really ask him to live as Nikolai forever? Perhaps he should be happy at the prospect of being rich and well cared for. Wasn't this what the storybooks promised humble boys with good hearts? But Isaak knew he was no hero from a story. He was a shy boy and an average soldier who had been lucky enough to garner the king's attention—a stroke of good fortune he might pay for with his very identity.

A table had been set in the woods on the island at the center of the lake, far from the Grand Palace and curious eyes. The surrounding trees were hung with lanterns, and somewhere in the shadows he could hear the gentle music of a balalaika. A very romantic setting—and it would provide plenty of opportunity for Tamar to approach the Tavgharad guards who would be stationed in the woods.

Isaak had been rowed out to the island under cover of darkness. He was dressed in a teal velvet coat, one he thought suited the king's coloring particularly well. He'd found another cluster of silver beads in the pocket.

He grew increasingly nervous as he waited. He was tired of luxury and fine clothes. He'd continued writing letters home, pretending that everything was as it should be at the palace, but all Isaak wanted was to sit in his mother's tiny kitchen and look out at the garden and play cards with his little sisters. He wanted to be with people who truly knew him.

Would they know him? They certainly wouldn't recognize him. Every day he passed by his fellow palace guards, men he'd known for years, and there were moments when he wanted to shout, *It's me! Isaak Andreyev!* His captain had been told that he was needed in Os Kervo for translation work, and that was the end of it. It had been that easy to simply make him disappear.

At last, Tolya said, "She's coming."

Ehri moved slowly into the clearing. She had been robed in embroidered grass-green silk and an elaborate gold headdress studded with emeralds as large as his thumbnail.

"How much does it weigh?" he whispered when they were seated and the first course was served.

"I'm not sure," said Ehri. "But it feels like a team of pack animals is sitting on my head, so somewhere between two and twelve oxen?"

"Do they make you train your neck muscles?"

"Of course not. The women of the Taban line are born with strong necks, a gift of divine purpose."

"Silly me." He felt himself relax. Ehri was simply easier to talk to than . . . everyone. The twins, Genya, David, certainly the other hopefuls. The other prospective brides seemed to carefully pick and choose their words, saying the things that Isaak—or rather Nikolai—would want to hear. But Ehri didn't seem to care very much about being chosen as his bride. It was a thought that both comforted and distressed him. He had no doubt she would have been smitten with the real Nikolai, and that made him jealous of a man she'd never met.

Ehri glanced down at her plate. "What has your cook served us tonight?"

"Something in jelly. He seems to believe that if you can put it in aspic, you absolutely should."

"What's your favorite thing to eat?"

"My mother's cabbage rolls."

"The queen cooked?"

Damn it. "Well, the servants made it, but my mother would serve it to me when I was sick." He had no idea if such a thing was likely, but it sounded all right. "What about you?" he asked hurriedly.

She thought for a long moment. "There is a dish we only eat once a year during the spring festivals. Milk pudding molded to look like the moon and flavored with rosewater. I know it doesn't sound very good, but it's the tradition of the way it's eaten. You sit with all of your family and you tell stories and watch fireworks, and you try to make the pudding last the whole night."

"Even the royal family does this?"

She nodded slowly. "Yes, though it's been a long time since we were all together. I sometimes wonder if we ever will be again."

"You mean if you wed and come to live in Ravka?"

She blinked away the shine of tears. "Yes."

Isaak found himself panicking at the sight of her unhappiness. "I would . . . I would gladly let you visit whenever you liked." He had no idea if that was a promise a king could keep.

"Let's not think on it," Ehri said, dabbing the tears from her eyes with her napkin. "We are here now, and we should try to enjoy ourselves." She took a bite, and he watched her face contort as she swallowed.

With a glance at the guards at the edge of the trees, Isaak discreetly tilted his plate and let the jellied lump slide onto the forest floor, nudging it beneath the table with his boot.

Ehri grinned and followed suit.

Together, they endured several courses and many jellies, celebrated the solid and highly recognizable venison steak, and agreed that whatever the gray stuff was, it was delicious.

"It's difficult, isn't it?" she asked at last. "To sit here and pretend our countries are not enemies."

"Do they have to be?" said Isaak. The words sounded clumsy and unsophisticated. Or dangerously like a proposal.

"It isn't up to me," she said. "I am not a queen. I am not anyone."

"You're a princess!" Isaak exclaimed.

Ehri touched her fingertips to her headdress. "But do you ever feel like . . . well, like a fraud?"

Every day. But what would Nikolai say? Isaak suddenly didn't care.

"Yes, I do. All the time."

Ehri leaned forward. "If people didn't bow to me, if they didn't dress me in silks and kiss my hem, would I still be a princess? Or would I just be a girl with a fancy colander on her head?"

Isaak laughed. "It's a good question. All I know is, I don't feel like a king."

"What *do* you feel?"

"Tired," he said honestly. "Ready for a cabbage roll."

"We've just eaten seven courses."

"Are you full?"

"Not remotely. Perhaps dessert is another steak?"

Isaak laughed again. He took a sip of the iced wine that had been served with the last course and asked Ehri the same question he'd been putting to himself. "If you were destined to be queen and not your sister . . ." Ehri's brows rose, and Isaak knew he was in tricky territory. Monarchs did not speculate idly. "How would you rule the Shu?"

Ehri toyed with the stem of her glass. Isaak had the urge to take her hand, but he knew that wasn't permitted. Strange that a king could command an army but he couldn't hold the hand of a girl he liked. And he did like Ehri. He'd been smitten with Genya, overwhelmed by her status and the idea that such a woman might take notice of him. Ehri was different. It was true that he barely knew her. She was a princess born of ancient royal blood. She sat before him wearing enough emeralds to buy and sell the entirety of Isaak's hometown. But she surprised him at every turn. She was warm and thoughtful and seemed to care as little for pretense as he did. If they'd been two ordinary people, if they'd met at a village dance instead of in a room surrounded by courtiers . . . Isaak had to wonder at himself. *As if you'd ever have had the nerve to talk to a girl like this.* But maybe Ehri—kind and funny Ehri—would have taken pity and granted him a dance.

"How would I rule?" Ehri mused, lifting the glass to her lips.

"You must have considered it?"

"Those are dangerous thoughts for one such as me." Ehri shook her head slowly, the emeralds glinting in her hair. "The things I imagine, the things I would hope for are not the musings of a queen."

"A princess, then."

Ehri smiled. "More like an artless girl. An end to war. A chance for the common people to choose their own futures. A world in which families aren't torn apart by hardship . . . or duty. I must sound very foolish to you."

"Not at all," said Isaak. "If we don't dream, who will?"

Ehri nodded, but her smile was tinged with sadness. "If we don't dream, who will?"

The last course had been served. Soon guards would come to fetch them away. As anxious as Isaak had been, he found he was sorry the evening was over.

"Will you return home immediately after the ball at the end of the week?" he asked.

"Yes." He didn't think he imagined the regret in her eyes.

"Meet me in the conservatory during the ball," he said before he could stop himself. "Otherwise we'll never have a real moment alone." He was shocked to hear the words leave his mouth.

He was even more shocked when she said yes.

30

NIKOLAI

THEY WAITED BENEATH A FLAT gray sky. It might have been dawn. It might have been dusk. Magical things happened at the in-between times. Morozova's sacred amplifiers had appeared at twilight. The stag. The sea whip. The firebird. Perhaps the Saints were the same.

Nikolai stood on the sands flanked by Zoya and Yuri above the spot where warrior priests had once come to be transformed, where the Darkling had torn the world open and created the Fold, and where, years later, he had finally been defeated. If there was power in this place, Nikolai could only hope that it was friendly and that it would help to destroy the remnants of the curse the Darkling had left behind.

Elizaveta's gown of roses bloomed dark red around her, a high collar of blossoms and buds framing her face as her bees hummed in her hair. Grigori's massive body folded and unfolded in a shifting mass of limbs. Nikolai wondered what form he would choose for his brief mortal life.

Juris was nowhere to be seen.

"The dragon couldn't be bothered to attend?" he whispered to Zoya.

"He wants this more than anyone," she said, and glanced up at the black stone of his spire in the distance. "I have no doubt he's watching."

Elizaveta nodded at both of them as her insects buzzed and clicked. "Are you ready, my king?" she asked Nikolai. "We cannot entertain the possibility of failure."

"A shame," Nikolai murmured. "My failures are so entertaining." He raised his voice and said, "I'm ready."

Yuri stood beside Zoya, his whole body vibrating with tension or fervor. In his shaking hands he held the pages of text he had continued to translate without Tolya's help. Elizaveta had insisted he remain with Nikolai and recite the ceremony.

"Is that entirely necessary?" Zoya had demanded.

"The words are sacred," Elizaveta had said. "They should be spoken as they once were. Yuri has his role to play in this too."

The monk pressed the pages to his chest now. His eyes looked wide and startled behind the lenses of his spectacles. "I find . . . I find I do not know what to pray for."

Nikolai gave his shoulder an encouraging squeeze. "Then pray for Ravka."

The monk nodded. "You are a good man. I can have faith in the Starless One and have faith in that too."

"Thank you," said Nikolai. He wasn't going to enjoy disappointing Yuri. But whether Nikolai lived or died this day, there would be no Sainthood for the Darkling. He would have to find some other way to appease the monk. Yuri was a boy in search of a cause, and that at least was something Nikolai could understand. He turned to Zoya. "You have the order? If the monster takes me——"

"I know what to do."

"You needn't sound quite so eager."

To his surprise, Zoya seized his hand. "Come back," she said. "Promise you'll come back to us."

Because he was most likely about to die, he let himself cup his hand briefly to her extraordinary face. Her skin felt cool against his fingers.

"Of course I'll come back," he said. "I don't trust anyone else to deliver my eulogy."

A smile curled her lips. "You've written it already?"

"It's very good. You'd be surprised how many synonyms there are for *handsome*."

Zoya closed her eyes. She turned her face, letting her cheek rest against his palm. "Nikolai——"

The hum of Elizaveta's insects rose. "It's time," she said, and lifted her hands. "Nikolai Lantsov, prepare yourself."

Zoya released his hand and stepped away. He desperately wanted to pull her back into his arms and ask her what she'd intended to say.

This is not a goodbye, he told himself. But it certainly felt like one.

Thunder rumbled over the gray sky. A moment later, Nikolai realized it wasn't coming from above but from below. The ground began to tremble, and a sound like distant hoofbeats rose from somewhere deep within the earth. It grew, an oncoming stampede that shook the sands. Elizaveta grimaced, perspiration gleaming on her brow.

She loosed a shout and the thorn wood burst from the sand. The stalks surrounded Nikolai and Zoya, twining and twisting, the thicket growing up around them as if woven on an invisible loom. Yuri began to chant.

"Have you never wondered at the power of the woods?" asked Elizaveta, her face glowing as she drove the brambles higher. "The magic at the heart of so many stories. The prick of a thorn? The magic a single rose can carry? These trees are older than anything else in the world, sprung from the first making, before man and animal and anything else. They are old as the stars, and they belong to me."

Gold seemed to drip from the thorn wood stalks, pooling at the bases of their trunks, then flowing in sinuous rivers toward Zoya. The sap formed a sphere around her, hardening into amber. Nikolai saw her press her hands to the sphere's sides as liquid began to rise over her ankles. The stalks around them creaked, twining against each other, the sound merging with the jagged syllables of ancient Ravkan.

Save her. The impulse was always the same, one that somehow both he and the dark thing within him could agree upon. Maybe because the Darkling had once valued Zoya and fostered her power. But Nikolai had known it would not be difficult to call the beast this time. It had been waiting, barely leashed, gnashing its teeth.

"Draw your sword, my king!" cried Elizaveta.

Nikolai drew the saber at his side and felt the monster rise. *Remember who you are.* Claws shot from his hands and he roared as his wings burst from his back.

The demon's hunger filled him, the desire to rend flesh, to feed, stronger than it had ever been. Before Nikolai could succumb and lose all sense, he slashed his sword through the nearest branch, slicing a thorn free of its stalk. It was nearly as long as his saber. He sheathed his blade and took the thorn in his taloned hands. Could he really do this? Could he really drive it into his own heart?

Both of their hearts. Slay the monster. Free himself.

He heard the creature scream as if understanding his intent. *Only one of us will survive this*, Nikolai vowed. *It is time you met the will of a king.*

What king? said a dark voice within him. *It is a bastard I have come to kill.*

Was it his hand that held the thorn blade? Or was it the monster that kept the point poised above his heart?

Nikolai Nothing, said the voice. *Liar. Fraud. Heir to no one. Pretender to the throne. I see who you are.*

But Nikolai knew those cruelties. He'd borne them his whole life. *It takes more than blood to make a king.*

Tell me what it takes to rule, the thing said in that taunting voice. *Courage? Valor? Love for the people?*

All of that. Nikolai strengthened his grip. He could feel the weight of the thorn in his palm. *And a solid sense of style.*

But the people don't love you, bastard. Despite your constant striving. The voice sounded different now. Cool, familiar, smooth as glass. *How long have you been begging for their love? Little Nikolai Lantsov playing the clown for his mother, the sycophant for his father, the handsome courtier for Alina? She was an orphan, a* peasant, *and even she didn't want you. And yet you continue, pleading for scraps like the commoner you are.*

Nikolai managed a laugh, but it did not come easy. *I've met enough commoners and enough kings to not take that as an insult.*

What do you think they saw in you to make you so unworthy? All of those medals earned, your fleet of ships, your heroic deeds, your earnest reforms. You know it will never be enough. Some children are born unlovable. Their mothers will not suckle them. They are left to die in the forest. And here you are, come to weep your last, alone in the thorn wood.

I'm not alone. He had Zoya, even Yuri for that matter, and Grigori and Elizaveta watching over them. *I have your delightful company.*

Now the dark voice laughed, low and long, mirth overflowing in a black tide. *Go ahead and do it, then. Drive the thorn into your chest. Do you really think it will matter? Do you really think anything can make you the man you were before?*

Before the war. Before the Darkling had set this curse upon him. Before Vasily's murder, the revelation of his father's crimes, the ambush at the Spinning Wheel, the countless battles that had cost so many lives.

How do you think I was able to take hold of your heart and burrow so deeply? You gave me fertile soil and so I took root. You will never be what you were. The rot has spread too far.

That's a lie. Elizaveta had warned Nikolai that the demon would try to trick him. So why did the words ring true?

Oh, you make a good show of it. Compromise, patience, an endless performance of good works to prove you are still the confident prince, the brazen privateer, whole and happy and unafraid. All that work to hide the demon. Why?

The people . . . The people clung to superstition. They feared the strange. Ravka could not afford another disruption, another weak king.

Another weak king. The voice was knowing, almost pitying. *You said it yourself.*

I am not my father.

Of course not. You have no father. I'll tell you why you hide the demon, why you cloak yourself in compromise and diplomacy and dribbling, desperate charm. It is because you know that if they saw you truly, they would turn away. They would see the nightmares that wake you, the doubts that plague you. They would know how very weak you are and they would turn their backs. Use the thorn, drive me out. You will still be a broken man—demon or not.

Was this the real fear that had chased him all these long months? That he would find no cure because the disease was not the demon? That the darkness inside him did not belong to something else but to him alone? He had been a fool. What he'd endured in the war, the choices he'd made, the lives he had ended with bullets and blades and bombs—there was no magic that could burn that away. He'd been human then. He had no demon to blame. He might purge the monster from his body, but the mess of shame and regret would remain. And what would happen when the fighting started up again? The thought made him impossibly weary.

The war was supposed to be over.

The demon's laughter rolled over him. *Not for you*, said the voice. *Not for Ravka. Not ever.*

Nikolai knew he had come here with a purpose. Drive the monster out. Save his country. Save himself. But those were not necessarily the same thing. He could not go back. He could not heal himself. He could not take back the part of him that had been lost. So how was he to lead?

Lay down the thorn.

The thorn? Nikolai could no longer feel it in his hand.

Lay down the thorn. Not every day can end in victory. Not every soldier can be saved. This country won't survive a broken king.

Nikolai had always understood that he and Ravka were the same. He just hadn't understood how: He was not the crying child or even the drowning man. He was the forever soldier, eternally at war, unable to ever lay down his arms and heal.

Lay down the thorn, boy king. Haven't you earned a bit of rest? Aren't you tired?

He was. Saints, he was. He thought he had grown used to his scars, but he had never grasped how much of his will it would take to hide them. He had fought and sacrificed and bled. He had gone long days without rest and long nights without comfort. All for Ravka, all for an ideal he would never attain and a country that would never care.

A bit of peace, whispered the demon. *You have the right.*

The right to wash his hands of this endless struggle and stop pretending he was somehow better than his father, more worthy than his brother. He was owed that much, wasn't he?

Yes, crooned the demon. *I will see Ravka safe to shore.*

Zoya would never forgive him, but Zoya would keep marching on. With losses and wounds of her own. Zoya would not rest.

Steel is earned, Your Highness, she had said, his ruthless general.

What had he earned? What was he owed? What was his *by right*?

He knew what Zoya would say: *You are owed nothing.*

Steel is earned. Remember who you are.

Bastard, hissed the demon.

I am Nikolai Lantsov. I have no right to my name.

Pretender, howled the dark voice.

I am Nikolai Lantsov. I have no right to my crown.

But each day he might endeavor to earn it. If he dared continue on with this wound in his heart. If he dared to be the man he was instead of praying to return to the man he'd once been.

Maybe everything the monster said was true. All Nikolai had done or would do for his people might never be enough. A part of him might always remain beyond repair. He might never be a truly noble man or a truly worthy king. In the end, he might be nothing more than a good head of hair and a gift for delusion.

But he knew this much: He would not rest until his country could too.

And he would never, ever turn his back on a wounded man—even if that man was him.

Nikolai Nothing, snarled the demon. *Ravka will never be yours.*

Perhaps not. But if you loved a thing, the work was never done. *Remember who you are.*

Nikolai knew. He was a king who had only begun to make mistakes. He was a soldier for whom the war would never be over. He was a bastard left alone in the woods. And he was not afraid to die this day.

He seized the thorn and drove it into his heart.

The monster shrieked. But Nikolai felt no pain at all—just heat as if a blaze had ignited in his chest. For a second he thought he might be dead, but when he opened his eyes, the world remained—the thorn wood, the twilight sky, the golden sphere. He had a brief moment to wonder why Elizaveta hadn't freed Zoya yet. And then he saw the monster.

It was a shape of pure shadow that hovered in front of him as if suspended in a mirror. Its wings beat gently at the air. In the place where the creature's heart would be, a slender shard of light glowed. The thorn. So this was the demon. The dark thing that had driven him, played with him, stolen his will. *I am the monster and the monster is me.* They were not as separate as he would have liked to pretend, but he remembered Elizaveta's words: *Only one of you will survive.*

It was time to slay the demon and put an end to this. He reached for his sword.

But he could not move his arms, could not move his legs. The thorn wood had grabbed hold of him, its stalks clinging tightly to his limbs, its spikes digging into his flesh.

Sap was still filling the golden sphere around Zoya despite the fact that he'd already called the monster. She was shouting and pounding her fists against its sides.

Something was very wrong.

He screamed as a sudden, searing bolt of pain shot through his hand. He looked to his left and saw a thorn impaling him through the palm. Another followed through his right hand and then each of his legs.

"I know the pain is bad," said Elizaveta as she drifted through the thicket. "But the thorns will keep you from forcing the darkness to recede."

"What is this?" Nikolai panted. Pain speared through him as he tried to break free.

"I had hoped you might simply let the monster overtake you. That your demon would win. It would have made all of this easier."

Nikolai's mind struggled to make sense of what Elizaveta was saying. "You're a prisoner here," Nikolai said. "After all this, you cannot mean to stay!"

"Certainly not. The boundaries of the Fold will remain intact, and here my brethren will be held captive still. But I will be free because I will be bound to him."

Nikolai did not need to ask who she meant. "The Darkling."

She nodded once. "The true king of Ravka. His spirit lived on with his power. It is only in need of a vessel."

The thicket parted and Nikolai saw a pale body borne atop a bier of branches.

It cannot be. He had stood on the shores of the Fold and watched the Darkling burn—and yet here his body was, whole and uncorrupted. It had to be some kind of illusion, or a brilliant facsimile.

Yuri stood beside the bier, the pages of liturgical Ravkan discarded. He wore a robe of black roses emblazoned with the sun in eclipse. "Forgive me," he said, his face contrite. "I wish it did not have to be so. I wish you could both survive this day. But the Starless One is Ravka's greatest hope. He must return." *I find I do not know what to pray for.*

"Go on, Yuri," Elizaveta said. "This honor is yours."

Nikolai remembered Yuri babbling when they had first come to the Saints' Fold. *All is as was promised.* He thought of the curling vine Elizaveta had so soothingly laid across Yuri's shoulders. She hadn't been trying to comfort him. She'd been afraid of what else he might say. *Yuri has his role to play in this too.* He'd said the Darkling had come to him in a vision.

Yuri approached the shadow beast and reached for the glowing shard wedged within its heart. Nikolai knew with sudden surety that if he pulled the thorn from the monster's chest first, it would be an end to everything.

"Don't, Yuri." He did not like the pleading in his voice. It did not become a king. "Don't do this."

"You are a good man," said Yuri. "But Ravka needs more than a man." He reached up and grabbed the thorn.

No. Nikolai would not allow it. He had opened the door. It was time to walk through. The monster was not the Darkling, not yet; it was something else still, something that longed for its own life, that had its own appetites, that he had lived with for three years.

Why do you hide the demon? Because it was angry, hungry, full of broken animal longing. And though Nikolai might not like it, those things were all a part of him still. *Like calls to like.* He had fought the demon. Now he would feed it.

Nikolai shut his eyes and did what that dark voice had told him to do. He let go of the perfect prince, the good king. He reached for all the wounded, shameful things he'd been so sure he had to hide. In this moment, he was not kind or merciful or just. He was a monster.

He left his mortal body behind.

When Nikolai opened his eyes, he was looking at Yuri from a different angle—close enough to see the smudge on his glasses, the wiry hairs of his scrabbly beard. Nikolai felt his wings beat the air, felt his demon heart race. He released a snarl and launched himself at the monk.

31
NINA

THEIR TIMING HAD TO BE PRECISE. The Wellmother and her Springmaidens would see to their charges on the factory ward and return sometime in the hours after midnight. Nina did not want to risk crossing paths with them, but she also needed to make sure they would have time to retrieve the girls, set the explosives, and get through the checkpoint on the road leading into town. If the guards at the checkpoint got a sign that something was wrong at the factory, they might well decide to investigate the vehicles passing through. And if that happened, there would be nowhere to hide.

Two hours before dawn, Hanne bound her breasts and pulled a pinafore over one of her stolen military uniforms. She kept a shawl wrapped around her head.

She and Nina slipped out through the kitchens and went to meet

Leoni and Adrik at the abandoned tanning shed where they were waiting with the enclosed wagon they'd secured. They helped Adrik into his uniform and stuffed his loose sleeve with cotton batting, pinning the end into his pocket to disguise his missing hand. Hanne tucked her pinafore away and took the driver's seat with Adrik beside her, while Nina and Leoni, both attired as Springmaidens, climbed into the back.

They were silent as they rode through the dark. Nina had laced her sleeves with bone shards, and she reached out to them now with her power, craving the peace they provided. She understood the risks she had asked the people around her to take, the danger she was putting them all in.

When they rolled to a stop, Nina knew they'd reached the checkpoint at the base of the hill. She peered through the slats and saw Hanne flash the order they'd forged to the men at the guardhouse—it bore Brum's stolen seal. Nina held her breath, waiting. A moment later, she heard a snap of the reins and they were moving once more.

The road leading to the eastern entrance was straight but rocky, and Nina felt her heart pounding with the hoofbeats of their horses as they made slow progress up the hill. There was no turning back now. She had lied not only to Hanne but to Adrik and Leoni as well about what she intended to accomplish today. The idea had come to her during her long dinner with Jarl Brum. It might be madness. It might fail spectacularly, but Nina had started to wonder if they'd been trying to fix Fjerda with the wrong tool.

Finally the horses slowed and Nina heard the voices of the guards. The wagon halted again. They had arrived at the eastern entrance to the fort. The whispers in her mind rose, guiding her on. *Nina*, they chorused. She shivered. The dead knew her name.

Justice, they demanded. She thought of the graves that surrounded this place, all the women and girls and children who had been lost here.

You will be the last, she promised.

Matthias had once begged her to save some mercy for his country, and she had vowed she would. But the girls in that ward were Fjerdans. Their children were Fjerdans. They were citizens of Gäfvalle and Gjela and Kejerut. The people of this country needed to be reminded of that.

The guards were looking over the order, taking their time. "Tell them to get moving," whispered Adrik.

"*Sedjet!*" Hanne barked. *Hurry up.* She'd lowered the timbre of her voice and for a moment she sounded chillingly like her father.

"What's the rush?" asked one of the guards. "Why do you need to move the prisoners now?"

"Not everyone knows about the work Commander Brum has authorized here," said Hanne, following the script Nina had laid out for her. "We got word the local governors are coming to the factory to investigate complaints about poisons in the river. We don't need more trouble."

"Bureaucrats," grumbled the guard. "Probably just looking for another bribe."

Another bribe? Did that mean local officials had been paid to look the other way about the fouling of the river—or about the girls in the abandoned wing?

A moment later the gate creaked open.

"Leave it that way," said Hanne. "Time is short."

"Wait a minute," said the guard. He threw open the back doors of the wagon and peered at Leoni and Nina in their pinafores. "What are these two doing here?"

"For Djel's sake, do you think I'm going to take care of a bunch of crying women and shitting infants?" said Hanne. "Maybe you'd like to come along and wipe their asses?"

Saints, she really was a natural.

The guard looked utterly horrified. "No thank you."

He slammed the doors shut, and in the next second, they were rolling through the gate into what had once been the eastern loading dock for the factory.

"Let's go," Adrik said, herding them to the big double doors. "That all took longer than it was supposed to."

Leoni dripped acid onto the locks to the ward and they fell with a hiss and a clang.

Gently, Nina pushed the doors open. They moved into the darkness, down the hall, toward the dim glow of a lantern. She could smell bodies, the tang of sour milk, soiled diapers, the old industrial smells of grease and coal.

The ward was full of the muzzy sounds of sleep, soft snores, the moan of a woman turning in her bed. A girl in a thin shift lay awake near the lantern, eyes hollow, skinny arms cradling her belly like a giant pearl.

When she saw Nina and Leoni her face broke into a happy, hopeful smile. "You're here early!" she cried. "Do you have my dose?"

"Where's my dose?" said another, rising from her blankets.

"Saints," muttered Adrik as lanterns were lit along the row of beds and the horror of the ward came into view.

Adrik looked sick. Leoni's eyes were full of tears.

Hanne had clapped a hand over her mouth. She was shaking her head.

"Hanne?" Nina murmured.

"No." She shook her head harder. "No. He didn't do this. He couldn't have. He must not have known."

A baby began to cry. The reality of the girls' need, of their clumsy

452

bodies, their hopeful expressions felt overwhelming. Why had Nina believed they could get away with any of this? But she had chosen this course—for all of them.

"Sylvi," Hanne said on a sob.

Sylvi Winther, Nina remembered, one of the people Hanne had nursed in secret.

The hollow-eyed girl looked up, but there was no recognition in her eyes. Hanne went to her side, but the girl shrank back, confused.

"It's me," said Hanne. "I . . ." And then she remembered her uniform, her altered face. "I . . . I'm sorry."

"Come on," Nina said. "We need to move." From her pocket, she drew the sedative Leoni had mixed. It was milky white, boiled from the stalks of *jurda* plants instead of the leaves.

"That doesn't look like my dose," said the girl by the lantern, frowning.

"It's something new," said Nina soothingly. "We're taking all of you to a new base."

"All of us?" one of the girls asked. "The babies too?"

"Yes."

"Does the new base have windows?" asked Sylvi.

"Yes," said Hanne, her voice raw. "And fresh food and sea breezes. It will be a hard journey, but we'll make it as comfortable as possible." At least that much was true.

One by one they offered the girls their doses and began to lead them to the cart.

Adrik consulted his watch. "Get going."

He raised his arm, and Nina's ears popped as he dropped the pressure in the factory to create an acoustic blanket and mask their movements.

Nina knew the layout of the factory floor best, so she would take

Leoni to set the explosives while Adrik and Hanne finished loading the prisoners and their infants. She helped Leoni stack the makeshift bombs in a basket beneath a pile of soiled linen and they crept deeper into the heart of the fort. It was blessedly silent, the day not yet beginning, and thanks to Adrik, their footsteps made no sound to break the quiet.

Nina dashed ahead to the main body of the factory and into the western wing, as close as she dared to the barracks and the kitchens. She didn't want to risk running into any patrols. She set the small explosives along the wall as she headed back, all of them connected by a long fuse.

Nina had just planted the last of her bombs when she heard a cry. *Leoni.* She raced back to the main hall on silent feet. As she entered, she heard voices and shrank up against a dusty vat, peering around it.

Leoni stood with her back to Nina, arms raised. Jarl Brum had a pistol trained on her. Nina clung to the vat, staying as still as possible.

"Who sent you?" he demanded. "You will give me answers or I will bleed them out of you."

"You disgust me," Leoni said in Zemeni.

Their voices had a strange, muffled quality. Did Brum hear it? Did he know Grisha power was at work? Slowly, Nina crept down the row of machinery. If she could get behind Brum, she could disarm him.

"I don't speak your ugly tongue," he said. "And I know you understand more than you pretend to."

Leoni smiled, the expression startling in its beauty. "And you understand less than you will ever know."

"I knew you weren't just traders. Where is your compatriot? And what about the guide, Mila Jandersdat? Does she know you're spies?"

"You're so very bald," Leoni said, still in Zemeni. "That won't be the worst thing Mila Jandersdat does to you."

"Was she a part of this?" Brum growled in frustration.

"How many girls?" Leoni said, switching to clumsy Fjerdan. "How many did you hurt?"

"Those aren't women," Brum sneered. "They're Grisha, and I'll be happy to give you your first dose myself. The might of Fjerda is about to descend on you."

He reached for a lever in the wall, and Nina knew an alarm was going to sound.

"Wait!" she shouted, unsure of what she intended—and at that moment Jarl Brum crumpled to the ground.

Hanne stood behind him holding a wrench and breathing heavily. "He knew," she said brokenly. "He knew." Then she fell to her knees beside him and cradled his bleeding head. "Papa," she said, tears sliding down her cheeks. "How could you?"

"Come on," said Nina. "We have to get the girls and get out of here."

Hanne ran a sleeve over her eyes. "We can't leave him to die."

"You saw what he's responsible for."

"What the *government* is responsible for," said Hanne. "My father is a soldier. You said it yourself, this country made him this way."

Nina didn't know if she wanted to laugh or scream. Jarl Brum was the commander of the *drüskelle*, the mind behind the torture of countless Grisha. He was not just a soldier. *Save some mercy for my people.*

"We need to go," said Leoni. "If we don't light the first fuse soon, the bombs won't go off in time. Assuming they go off at all."

"He's my father," said Hanne, her eyes full of that fierce determination Nina loved so much. "I won't leave him."

Nina threw up her hands in exasperation. "Fine, help me lift him."

They hauled Brum's body down the hall and through the ward. The man was enormous and Nina was tempted to drop him just for the satisfaction of it.

"So Commander Brum did *not* leave town?" asked Adrik, letting his arm fall to his side. Nina's ears crackled and sound bled back into the ward.

"I guess he wanted to say goodbye," she muttered as they dragged him into the back of the wagon. The girls looked at him with vague interest. The sedative had definitely set in.

"What about your sister?" said Hanne.

"She's not here," Nina said. "She must have been moved."

"How can you be sure?"

"We need to go," insisted Nina. She hopped down and ran back to the ward to set the fuses.

She lit the last of them and was about to join the others at the loading dock when a voice shouted, "Stop!"

Nina turned. The Wellmother was racing down the ward, flanked by soldiers armed with rifles. Of course Brum hadn't been alone.

"You!" said the Wellmother, her face red with rage. "How dare you wear the attire of a Springmaiden? Where are the prisoners? Where is Commander Brum?"

"Gone," Nina lied. "Beyond your reach."

"Seize her!" said the Wellmother, but Nina was already raising her hands.

"I wouldn't," Nina said, and the soldiers hesitated, confused.

Around her, she felt the cold tide of the river, eddying in deep pools—the graves of the unnamed and abandoned, buried without ceremony, women and girls brought here in secret, who had suffered and died and been left to the dark with no one to mourn them.

Come to me, Nina commanded.

"She's just one girl," snapped the Wellmother. "What kind of cowards are you?"

"Not just one girl," said Nina. The whispering rose in her. Fjerdan women. Fjerdan girls, crying for justice, screaming in the silence of the earth. She opened her mouth and let them speak.

"*I am Petra Toft.*" The words came from Nina's lips, but she did not recognize her own voice. "*You cut me open and took the child from my womb. You let me bleed to death as I pleaded for help.*"

"*I am Siv Engman. I told you I had miscarried, that I could not carry a child to term, but you made me conceive again and again. I held each stillborn in my arms. I gave each one of them a name.*"

"*I am Ellinor Berglund. I was your student, placed in your care. I trusted you. I called you Wellmother. I begged for your mercy when you discovered my powers. I died begging for another dose.*"

"What is this?" said the Wellmother, her hands clasped against her heart. She was shaking, her eyes wide as moons.

Woman after woman, girl after girl, they spoke their names, and Nina called them on. *Come to me.* Up through the earth, clawing through the soil, they came, a mass of rotting limbs and broken bones. And some of them crawled.

The doors to the ward slammed open, and the dead poured through. They moved with impossible speed, silent horrors, snatching the rifles from the Fjerdan soldiers even as they tried to open fire. Some were nearly whole. Others were nothing but bones and rags.

The Wellmother backed away, her face a mask of terror. She stumbled on her pinafore and fell to the stone floor. An infant pulled itself toward her on all fours. Its chubby limbs were still intact despite its blue lips and vacant eyes.

The dead had made quick work of the guards, who lay bleeding in silent heaps. Now they advanced on the Wellmother. Nina turned to go.

"Don't leave me," the Wellmother begged as the baby seized hold of her skirts.

"I told you I would pray for you," said Nina as she closed the door and issued her final command to her soldiers: *Give her the mercy she deserves.*

Nina turned her back on the Wellmother's screams.

"Go!" commanded Nina as she clambered into the back of the wagon. The time for subtlety had passed. They burst through the eastern entrance and onto the road. When Nina turned to look, she expected to see the guards raising their rifles to fire at them. Instead, she saw two bloodied bodies in the snow and a trail of pawprints leading into the trees.

Trassel. Her mind said she was a fool to think so, but her heart knew better. Now she understood why he'd never taken the food she'd left out. Matthias' wolf liked to hunt his prey. From somewhere up the mountain, she heard a long, mournful howl, and then a chorus of replies echoing over the valley. The gray wolves he had saved? Maybe Trassel would have to stay alone no longer. Maybe he'd finally said his goodbyes too.

Leoni was staring at Nina as they sped away from the factory. She had a baby clutched in her arms.

"Remind me to never make you mad, Zenik," she said over the rattling of the cart wheels.

Nina shrugged. "Just don't do it by a graveyard."

"What's happening?" asked one of the girls drowsily.

"Nothing," said Nina. "Close your eyes. Rest. You'll get another dose soon."

A moment later, the air filled with the clamor of bells. Someone at the factory had sounded the alarm. There was no way they were going to make it through the checkpoint, but they couldn't stop now.

They careened down the hill. Brum lay beneath a blanket, his body rolling this way and that as the cart jounced over a ditch.

Nina leaned forward and pulled on Hanne's jacket to get her attention.

"Slow down!" she shouted. "We can't look like we're running."

Hanne pulled back on the reins and glanced over her shoulder at Nina. "What *are* you?" She didn't sound scared, just angry.

"Nothing good," said Nina, and sank back to her seat in the wagon. Explanations and apologies would have to wait.

The wagon slowed and she peered through the slats. They were coming up on the checkpoint. She had known the timing had to be right, and now—

"Halt!"

The wagon rolled to a stop. Through the slats, Nina saw a group of Fjerdan soldiers, rifles at the ready. Behind them, a little farther down the hill, a long line of men and boys were headed to the fishery to work. They carried their lunch pails and chatted in easy conversation, barely sparing a glance for the guards or the wagon.

"We are operating under orders from Commander Brum," said Hanne gruffly. "Let us through!"

"You will stand down or you will be shot."

"We're transporting—"

"Commander Brum came through here nearly an hour ago. He said no one was to pass without his direct say-so." He turned to another guard and said, "Send someone up to the factory to find out what's going on."

Then he disappeared from view. A moment later, the doors to the cart swung open.

"Djel in all his glory," the soldier said as the early-morning light fell on the women packed into the wagon. "Seize the drivers! And get these prisoners back up the mountain."

The baby in Leoni's arms began to wail.

32

ZOYA

ZOYA DID NOT SCREAM. She stifled her panic as the sap rose over her rib cage and ceased her pounding on the golden sphere. She could not comprehend what she was seeing. Three years ago, she had watched the Darkling's body burn to ash. She had whispered her aunt's name as he had vanished in the heat of Inferni flames beside the body of Sankta Alina.

But it had not been Alina Starkov who lay on that pyre, only a girl tailored to look like her. Had the Darkling's supporters used the same trick?

She did not understand the extent of what Elizaveta intended, only that Nikolai would not live through it. And that Yuri had betrayed them, the pious little wart. *You always knew what he was*, she scolded herself. *You knew at which altar he chose to worship.* But she had ignored him, dismissed him, because she had never truly seen him as a threat. And maybe because she hadn't wanted to see her own foolish idealism reflected in his fervent eyes.

She watched Yuri approach the shadow creature that hovered like a strange ghost in front of Nikolai. She had sensed the Darkling's presence that night in the bell tower, but she hadn't wanted to believe he could return.

Blind. Naive. Selfish. Zoya held her breath as Yuri reached for the glowing thorn—but suddenly the monster was attacking the monk. She looked at Nikolai's body splayed against the thorn wood like an insect pinned to a page. His eyes were closed. Could he be controlling the creature?

There was no time to think on it. Zoya had tried to batter the sphere with the power of the storm to no avail. Now she focused on the sap that made up its walls, sensing the small parts that comprised it, the way its matter was formed. She was no Tidemaker. Before Juris this would have been beyond her. But now . . . *Are we not all things?* She concentrated on forcing those tiny particles to vibrate faster, raising the temperature of the sap, disrupting the structure of the sphere. Sweat poured from her brow as the heat rose and she feared she'd cook in her own skin.

In a single moment, the sphere's structure gave way. Zoya cast the scalding liquid away on a gust of air before it could burn her skin, and then she was running, letting the wind carry her over the sands to the palace.

What are you running to, little witch? To Juris. To help. But what if the dragon already knew what Elizaveta intended? What if he was watching her from his black spire even now and laughing at her naiveté?

The wind faltered. Zoya's steps slowed. She gazed up at the black rock. How long could Nikolai use the monster's form to keep Yuri and the Saint at bay? Was Zoya racing toward an ally or walking into a trap, squandering valuable time? Another betrayal. She wasn't sure she could bear it. But she would have to. She wasn't powerful enough to face Elizaveta on her own. She needed the dragon's wrath.

There was no time to trouble with the palace's winding passages, and she doubted she could find her way. Instead she let the storm lob her up, high into the sky and the mouth of Juris' cavern.

The room was empty. The fire in the grate had gone out.

That was when she saw the body. Juris lay on the floor in his human form, his broadsword discarded next to him. The gleam of his black scale armor seemed dull in the flat twilight.

"Juris!" she cried. She slid to her knees beside him.

He opened his eyes. They flickered silver, the pupils slitting.

"That Elizaveta," he said on a wheezing gasp. "Such an actress."

"What happened? What did she do to you?"

He released a sound that might have been a laugh or a moan. "She offered me wine. After hundreds of years. Honey mead made from fruit born of her vines. She said she had been saving it. It was sweet, but it was not wine."

She looked at his charred lips, his blackened tongue, and understood. "It was fuel."

"Only our own power can destroy us. My flames burned me from the inside."

"No," Zoya said. "*No*." Her heart was too full of loss. "I'll get Grigori. He can heal you."

"It's too late." Juris seized her wrist with surprising force. "Listen to me. We thought we had convinced Elizaveta to give up her power, but that was never her intent. If she breaks free of the bounds of the Fold, nothing will be able to control her. You must stop her."

"How?" Zoya pleaded.

"You know what you must do, Zoya. Wear my bones." She recoiled, but he did not release his grip. "Kill me. Take my scales."

Zoya shook her head. All she could think of was her aunt's resolute face. Zoya had been responsible for her death. She could have stopped the Darkling, if she'd looked closer, if she'd understood, if she hadn't been consumed by her own ambition. "He doesn't get to take you from me too."

"I am not your aunt," Juris growled. "I am your teacher. You were an able student. Prove to me that you are a great one."

She could not do it. "You said it was a corruption."

"Only if you give nothing of yourself in return."

The truth of that hit her, and Zoya knew she was afraid.

"A little faith, Zoya. That is all this requires."

A bitter laugh escaped her. "I don't have it."

"There is no end to the power you may obtain. The making at the heart of the world has no limit. It does not weaken. It does not tire. But you must go to meet it."

"What if I get it wrong all over again?" What if she failed Juris as she had failed the others? Her life was crowded with too many ghosts.

"Stop punishing yourself for being someone with a heart. You cannot protect yourself from suffering. To live is to grieve. You are not protecting yourself by shutting yourself off from the world. You are limiting yourself, just as you did with your training."

"Please," Zoya said. She was the thing she'd always feared becoming: a lost girl, helpless, being led up the aisle of the chapel in Pachina. "Don't leave me. Not you too."

He nudged his broadsword with one hand. "Zoya of the lost city. Zoya of the garden. Zoya bleeding in the snow. You are strong enough to survive the fall."

Juris released a cry that began as a scream and became a roar as his body shifted from man to dragon, bones cracking, scales widening, until each was nearly the size of her palm.

He enfolded her in his wings, so gently. "Now, Zoya. I can hold on no longer."

Zoya released a sob. *To live is to grieve.* She was a lost girl—and a general too. She hefted the broadsword in her hands and, with the power of the storm in her palms, drove the blade into his heart.

At the same instant, Zoya felt the dragon's claws pierce her chest. She cried out, the pain like the fork of a lightning bolt, splitting her open. She felt her blood soaking the silk against her body, a sacrifice. Juris released a heavy sigh and shut his glowing eyes. Zoya pressed her face to his scales, listening to the heavy thud of his heart, of her own. Was this death, then? She wept for them both as the rhythm began to slow.

A moment passed. An age. Juris' claws retracted. She could hear only one heartbeat now, and it was her own.

Zoya felt no pain. When she looked down, she saw her *kefta* was torn, but the blood flowed no longer. She touched her fingers to her skin. The wounds Juris had made had already healed.

There was no time for mourning, not if Juris' sacrifice was to mean something, not if she had any hope of saving Nikolai and stopping Elizaveta. Zoya would have her revenge. She would save her king.

She grabbed a dagger from the wall. Before her tears could begin anew, she scraped the scales from the ridge that ran over Juris' back.

But what was she to do now? She wasn't a Fabrikator. That was Elizaveta's gift.

Are we not all things?

Zoya had broken the boundaries within her order, but did she dare challenge the limits of the orders themselves?

Anything worth doing always starts as a bad idea. Nikolai's words. Terrible advice. But perhaps it was time to heed it. She focused on the scales in her hand, sensed their edges, the particles that comprised them. It felt alien and wrong, and she knew instantly that this work would never be natural to her, but in this moment her meager skill would have to be enough. Zoya let the scales guide her. She could feel the shape they wanted to take, could see it burning clearly in her mind like a black wheel—no, a crown. *Juris*. Pushy to the last. She shoved the image aside and forced the scales to form two cuffs around her wrists instead.

As soon as the scales touched, sealing the bond, she felt Juris' strength flow through her. But this was different than it had been with the tiger. *Open the door.* She could feel his past, the eons both he and the dragon had lived flooding through her, threatening to overwhelm the short speck of her life.

Take it, then, she told him. *I am strong enough to survive the fall.*

She felt Juris' restraint, felt him draw back, protecting her and guiding her as he had done over the past weeks. As he always would.

The dragon was with her. And they would fight.

33

NINA

OVER THE GUARD'S SHOULDER, Nina saw the fishermen turn their heads toward the sound of a crying baby.

Hurriedly, the guard tried to slam shut the doors.

"Help!" cried Nina. "Help us!"

"What's going on over there?" said one of the men.

Bless Fjerda and its belief in helpless girls. They were taught from
a young age to protect the weak, particularly women. That kindness
didn't usually extend to Grisha, but the dead had spoken, and Nina
intended to let them keep speaking.

Another baby began to cry. "That's it, kid," Nina whispered. "Do
your thing."

Now the fishermen were moving up the side of the hill toward
the checkpoint.

"This is none of your concern," said the guard, finally succeeding in closing the wagon doors.

"What do you have in there?" a voice asked.

Nina peered through the slats. Hanne and Adrik had been yanked from the wagon and were flanked by armed men. The crowd of locals around the cart was growing.

"Just a shipment for the factory," said the guard.

"So why is the wagon headed down the mountain?"

"Get this wagon turned around and get going," the guard growled to the soldiers now perched in the driver's seat. The reins snapped and the horses took a few tentative steps forward, but the fishermen had moved into the road, blocking the wagon's path.

"Show us what's in the wagon," said a large man in a red cap.

Another stepped forward, hands spread in an open, reasonable gesture. "We can hear babies crying. Why are you trying to take them to a munitions factory?"

"I made it clear that it's none of your concern. We do not answer to you, and if you insist on interfering with the business of the Fjerdan military, we are authorized to use force."

A new voice spoke from somewhere Nina couldn't see. "Are you really going to open fire on these men?"

Nina moved to the other side of the wagon and saw more of the townspeople had gathered, drawn by the commotion at the checkpoint.

"Why wouldn't they?" said a woman. "They already poisoned our river."

"Be silent," hissed a soldier.

"She's right," said the tavern owner Nina recognized from their first day in town. "Killed that girl up at the convent. Killed Gerit's cattle."

"You want to shoot us, go ahead," said someone. "I don't think you have enough bullets for us all."

"Stay back!" cried the guard, but Nina heard no gunfire.

A moment later, the wagon doors were pried open once again.

"What is this?" said the man in the red cap. "Who are these women? What's wrong with them?"

"They're . . . they're sick," said the guard. "They've been quarantined for their own good."

"There's no disease," said Nina from the shadows of the cart. "The soldiers have been experimenting on these girls."

"But they're all . . . Are they all pregnant?"

Nina let the silence hang, felt the mood of the crowd shift from suspicion to outright anger.

"You're from the convent?" the man asked, and Nina nodded. Let this miserable pinafore and these awful blond braids lend her a bit of credibility.

"These prisoners are not women," sputtered the guard. "They're Grisha. They are potential threats to Fjerda, and you have no right to interfere."

"Prisoners?" the man in the red cap repeated, his face troubled. "Grisha?"

The crowd moved forward to stare at the women and girls. Nina knew the power of the prejudice they carried with them. She'd seen it in Matthias, felt the weight of it. But she'd also seen that burden shift, that seemingly immovable rock eroded by understanding. If that could happen for a *drüskelle* soldier who had been raised to hate her kind, she had to believe it could happen for these people too. The girls in this wagon were not powerful witches raining down destruction. These were not faceless enemy soldiers. They were Fjerdan girls plucked from their lives and tortured. If ordinary people could not see the difference, there was no hope for anyone.

"Cille?" said a young fisherman pushing forward through the crowd. "Cille, is that you?"

A frail, sallow-skinned girl opened her eyes. "Liv?" she said weakly.

"Cille," he said, tears filling his eyes as he climbed up into the wagon, his head banging the ceiling. "Cille, I thought you were dead." He knelt, gathering her up in his arms.

"Get down from there immediately," commanded the guard.

"What did you do to her?" the young fisherman cried, his cheeks wet, his face nearly purple with rage.

"She is Grisha and a prisoner of the—"

"She's my *sister*," he roared.

"Is that Idony Ahlgren?" the man in the red cap asked, craning his neck.

"I thought she went to Djerholm to serve as a governess," said a woman.

Nina glanced up at the factory. How much time had elapsed? "Ellinor Berglund," she said. "Petra Toft. Siv Engman. Jannike Fisker. Sylvi Winther. Lena Askel."

"They took Cille!" cried the young fisherman. "They took all of them!"

A shot rang out. The checkpoint guard stood holding his rifle in the air.

"That is enough! You will clear the road or we will—"

Boom. The first explosion rocked the mountain.

All eyes turned to the factory.

"That sounded a lot bigger than it was supposed to," said Leoni.

Boom. Another blast, then another. *Right on time.*

"Sweet Djel," the red-capped man said, pointing up toward the old fort. "The dam."

"Oh Saints," said Leoni. "Something's wrong. My proportions must have been off, I——"

Another *boom* sounded, followed by a terrifying roar. All of a sudden people were screaming and running down the hill. The young fisherman took his sister in his arms and leapt from the back of the wagon.

"We have to get out of here!" he yelled.

"There's no time," said the man with the red cap.

Nina and Leoni clambered out of the back of the wagon. High above, dark columns of smoke rose from the flames at the factory. But far more frightening was the wall of water rushing toward them. The dam had shattered, and a snarling wave frothed and foamed down the mountain, uprooting trees and crushing everything in its path.

"Maybe it will lose momentum," said the fisherman, hugging his sister close.

"Move!" shouted Leoni. "That water is loaded with poison! Anyone it touches is done for." The guilt and fear on her face hurt Nina's heart, but this was the way it had to be. Fjerda didn't need mercy. It needed miracles.

"We did this," said Hanne. "We have to stop it."

Some of the townspeople were scrambling up the hillsides, but the wave was coming too fast.

"Get behind me!" Adrik yelled at the crowd.

"Now!" Nina commanded in Fjerdan when the people hesitated.

"Leoni," Adrik said as the people crowded in, forming a wedge behind him. "Can you do it?"

She nodded, determined, touched her fingers to the jewels in her hair, lips moving in a whispered prayer. Nina could hear Leoni's warning in her head: *Poisons are tricky work.*

The wave thundered toward them, churning with foam and bits of debris, so tall and wide it seemed to block out the sun.

"Get ready!" Adrik cried.

Leoni spread her arms.

Adrik thrust his hand forward, and the wave split, cleaved by the force of the gust he summoned, passing around the townspeople in an angry flood.

As the water passed, Leoni raised her hands and Nina saw a yellowy cloud appear in the air around her. She was drawing the poison from the water.

Grisha. Nina heard the word rise from the crowd. *Drüsjen.* Witches.

The cloud of poison grew above them as the water tumbled on and on. At last the tide had exhausted itself, but Leoni continued to draw the poison out until the flood had slowed to a trickle.

She stood with arms raised in the sudden silence as the crowd stared upward at the lethal mass of muddy yellow powder hovering over their heads.

"*Pestijla!*" they cried out. "*Morden!*" Poison. Death.

"No," Nina murmured to herself. "Opportunity." She reached into the waters of the flood, seeking the materials she needed, her power touching on the bones of girls lost in the dark. She grabbed hold.

Leoni's arms were shaking, her lips pulled back in a grimace. Adrik whirled, focusing the wind, forming it into a tiny cyclone, gathering the poison and driving it into the empty guardhouse. With a twist of his wrist, the door slammed shut. He grabbed Leoni up against him before she could collapse.

In the new quiet, Nina could hear the babies wailing, people crying. She didn't know how much damage the water might have done to the buildings below.

The crowd was staring at Adrik and Leoni. The soldiers raised their rifles. Nina prepared to call the corpses from the factory to protect them. But she hoped, she hoped . . .

"Look!" cried the man in the red cap.

In the wake of the water, a great ash tree stood in the center of the road, its white branches stretching to the sky, its thick roots sprawling in the mud.

"Djel and all his waters," said the man from the tavern, beginning to weep. "It's made of bone."

The bones of the girls lost to the mountain, forged by Nina's power into something new.

"Praise Djel," said the young fisherman, and fell to his knees.

Nina was glad now that she could not hear Matthias' voice, that he could not witness the way she had used his god. The trick she'd pulled wasn't the act of a soldier with honor. It was a bit of theater, the low illusion of con men and thieves.

But she was not sorry. The work she and Adrik and Leoni had been doing, the work of the Hringsa, was not enough. No matter how many Grisha they saved, there would always be more they could not. There would always be Fjerda with its tanks and its pyres and men like Jarl Brum to light the match. Unless Nina found a way to change it all.

"Lay down your arms," said the man in the red cap as the village of Gäfvalle went to its knees. "We have seen miracles today."

"Praise Djel!" shouted Nina. She knelt before Adrik and Leoni in her Springmaiden pinafore. "And praise the new Saints."

34

ZOYA

ZOYA SPED ACROSS THE SANDS, praying she was not too late. She had once thought only a Grisha in the grip of *parem* could fly. Now she arrived on the storm, borne aloft by thunderheads. It was almost as if she could feel Juris beneath her.

The sight that greeted her was horrifying.

Grigori had spread himself over the thorn wood in a great dome, built and rebuilt of sinew, trying to keep Elizaveta and Yuri away from Nikolai and his shadow self. Zoya saw Elizaveta's thorns stabbing through Grigori's flesh, her stalks writhing like serpents, lashing out to puncture him again and again.

But when the Bodymaker began to scream, Zoya realized it was not the thorns that had undone him, but the insects Elizaveta had set upon his body. Tiny holes and furrows began to appear on his flesh as burrowing insects consumed him. His body broke apart, trying to escape itself. He shook and trembled and then opened a thousand mouths to cry out as he was devoured.

Yuri stood behind Elizaveta, like a child hiding behind his mother's skirts, his hands pressed to his lips as if to stifle his own terror. Stupid boy. Had he known what Elizaveta intended to unleash? Had his Starless Saint promised him less bloodshed, or did a fanatic not care?

The Bodymaker shuddered and collapsed. Elizaveta gave a shout of triumph and descended upon the pinned bodies of Nikolai and the shadow creature, both of them now held in place by the vines of the thorn wood.

Zoya took two broken pieces of obsidian from her sleeve and cracked them together. The spark was all she needed. A gout of flame roared toward Elizaveta, who reared back in surprise.

Then the Saint's lips quirked in amusement. "I thought you were wise enough to run, Zoya. You're too late. The Darkling's spirit will soon reenter his body. There's no reason for you to be a casualty of this battle."

"My king lies bleeding. I am his subject and his soldier, and I come to fight for him."

"You are Grisha, Zoya Nazyalensky. You need be subject to no one and nothing."

Zoya could feel the pull of power even now. It would always be with her, this hunger for more. But she had made the acquaintance of tyrants before. "Subject to no one but you? The Darkling?"

Elizaveta laughed. "We will not be rulers. We will be gods. If it's a crown you want, take it. Sit the Ravkan throne. We will hold dominion over the world."

"I saw his body on the pyre. I watched him burn."

"I stole him from the sands of the Fold and left a facsimile in his place. It was well within my power." Just as Zoya had suspected. And she didn't care about the particulars. But she wanted to keep Elizaveta talking.

"You preserved his body?"

"In the hopes that he might be resurrected. I stored him in my hives. Yes, I know you were ready to believe my little story about my wound, my weariness. But you didn't dare walk down that dark corridor, did you? No one wants to look too closely at another person's pain. Did you really believe I would sacrifice an age of knowledge and power to become a mortal? Would *you*, Zoya?"

No. Never. But the power she was tied to now did not need to be seized or stolen. "And what will you do with the world once you possess it?"

"Is this where I present my grand vision for peace? For a unified empire without border or flag?" Elizaveta shrugged. "I could make that speech. Perhaps the Starless One will make that our endeavor. I know only that I want to be free and that I want to feel my power once more."

It was a need Zoya understood, and she knew the questions to ask, the same questions she had posed to herself when the dark crept in.

"You don't have enough of it?" Zoya asked, moving slowly around the circle of the wood. The shadow creature's chest no longer glowed—so someone had managed to remove the thorn. Its shape was leeching slowly into the Darkling's supine body. Nikolai lay dying, impaled on the thicket as his blood drained into the soil.

"What is power without someone to wield it over? I have lived in isolated splendor for too many lifetimes. What is it to be a god without worship? A queen without subjects? I was the witch in the wood, the queen on her throne, the goddess in her temple. I will be once more. I will savor fear and desire and awe again."

"You'll get none from me," said Zoya. She raised her hands and her sleeves fell back. Black scales glittered in the twilight.

Elizaveta gave a beleaguered sigh. "I should have known Juris would hold on long enough to do something noble and misguided. Well, old friend," she said, "it will not matter." With a sweep of her arm, two iron-colored stalks shot toward Zoya, their thorns gleaming like the barbed tail of a sea creature.

Zoya drove her hands upward, and a ferocious whirlwind caught the stalks, twisting them around each other and yanking them from the thorn wood by the root. Zoya flung them back at Elizaveta.

"How fierce you are," said the Saint. "Juris was right to make you his student. I'm sorry his knowledge will die with you."

This time half the wood seemed to rise up, a snarling mass of fat, thorny stalks. Zoya pulled moisture from the air in a cold wave, coating the stalks in frost, freezing their sap from the inside out. With a rumbling gust of air, she shattered them on the wind.

"Such power. But you cannot defeat me, Zoya. I have the advantage of eternity."

"I'll settle for the advantage of surprise."

Zoya raised the sands for cover and let herself plummet in a flash to the thorn wood. As Elizaveta had talked, Zoya had drifted to the far side of the circle, to the bier on which the Darkling's perfectly preserved body rested. She had the briefest moment to take in the beautiful face, those elegant hands. Zoya had loved him with all the greedy, worshipful need in her girlish heart. She had believed he prized her, that he cared for her. She would have done anything for him, fought and died for him. And he had known that. He had cultivated it as he had cultivated his own mystery, as he had nurtured Alina Starkov's loneliness and Genya's desire to belong. *He used us all, just as he is using Elizaveta now. And I let it happen.*

She would not let it happen again. She lifted her arms.

"No!" cried Elizaveta.

"Burn as you were meant to," Zoya whispered. She thrust her arm down, and, as easily as if she were summoning a soft breeze, lightning flowed in a precise, earsplitting crack. It struck the bier in a blaze of sparks and blooming flame. Zoya saw a shadow emerge from the fire, as if trying to flee the heat.

"What have you done?" Elizaveta screamed. She hurtled at the Darkling as the thorn wood tried to lift him to safety, away from the blaze.

But Zoya focused the heat of her flames until they burned blue as Juris' dragon fire. The thorn wood began to collapse in on itself.

Stalks twisted around Zoya's ankles, but she gathered her sparks and burned them away, singeing herself in the process. Fire was going to take some practice.

Elizaveta had thrown herself on the pyre to try to retrieve what was left of the Darkling's body. Zoya knew that though the flames might cause Elizaveta pain, they would not stop her. Only Elizaveta's own power turned against her would be enough to end a Grisha that ancient. Zoya had just a few minutes to act.

She found Yuri running from the flames and snatched the glowing thorn from his hand. "I'll deal with you later," she snarled, swiping two dunes to surround him in a strong gust. They buried him to the neck.

The remnants of the shadow creature hovered between Nikolai and the blaze of the Darkling's bier as if unsure. It was barely visible now, its wings shredded, its clawed hands hanging limply by its sides. She drove the glowing thorn back into the place where its heart should be.

Nikolai came to consciousness with a gasp. "Take it out of me," he rasped, ducking his head toward his chest where the real thorn was lodged. "End him."

And what if I end you too? There was no time to hesitate. Zoya yanked free the thorn. Nikolai howled as black blood poured from his chest. Zoya was slammed backward by the lashing trunk of a tree.

All around her, the thorn wood burst into bloom as Elizaveta rose shrieking from the Darkling's final funeral pyre. She was a swarm of bees. She was a meadow in blossom. She was a woman mad with grief. The thorn wood twisted around Zoya's wrists, binding her tight as Elizaveta hurtled toward her, locusts streaming from her mouth, her hands extended, reaching for Zoya's throat.

It's all right, Zoya thought. *I saved Nikolai. I kept Elizaveta confined to the Fold.* She had stopped the Darkling at last. Let Elizaveta take her heart. But Juris' voice roared within her, and she could almost see his sneer: *I gave up my scales for this? We are the dragon. We do not lie down to die.*

Zoya felt the branches squeeze tighter. The thorn wood was Elizaveta's creation. But the sap within it flowed like blood, like a river moved by tides.

Elizaveta screamed her rage, and the buzz of insects filled Zoya's ears.

Zoya focused on the sap running through the branches of the thorn wood, the sap that had drowned her again and again, and she pulled.

The stalks turned, the vicious spikes of their thorns jutting toward Elizaveta too quickly for her to change course or shift form. Her body struck the lances of the thorns with a dull, wet thud. She hung, bare inches from Zoya, impaled on the claws of her own creation.

Zoya twisted the thorns and watched the light vanish from Elizaveta's eyes. She could have sworn she heard the dragon snarl his approval.

Ravka might fall. The Grisha and the Second Army might scatter. But the world would be safe from Elizaveta and the Starless One.

She thought of the cubs in the snow, of Liliyana shelling hazelnuts by the fire, of the Hall of the Golden Dome back at the Little Palace, crowded with Grisha, laughter echoing off its walls before the Darkling attacked. She thought of Nikolai facing the demon, the thorn like a dagger in his hands.

This time I saved you, she thought as she collapsed. *This time, I got it right.*

35
NINA

IT WOULDN'T BE SAFE FOR THE GRISHA
women and their children, or for Adrik and Leoni, to remain in
Gäfvalle, no matter how the townspeople felt. The surviving soldiers
at the factory would rally. Troops would be sent to impose order in
the aftermath of the disaster. They all had to be gone before then.

In the chaos, Hanne returned to the convent to restore her features and change back into her pinafore, pretending to be just as startled as the others at the terrors visited upon the town. No one could
find the Wellmother, so it was easy for Hanne to slip away once more
and return to the crossroads, where she found Nina instructing a
young fisherman who had agreed to drive the wagon to port.

Nina had known this reckoning was coming, and as soon as the
fisherman had gone to see his sister resettled in the wagon, she turned
to face Hanne's anger.

But Hanne was calm. Her voice was steady. "I haven't been asking the right questions, have I? I asked what you were, not who."

Nina had changed back into one of Mila's dresses. She smoothed her hands over the heavy skirts. "I think you know."

"Nina Zenik." Hanne's copper eyes were hard. "The girl who maimed my father. The Corpsewitch."

"Is that what the Fjerdans are calling me now?"

"Among other things."

"I'm an agent working for the Ravkan government. I came to this country to free people like you, people with Grisha power living in fear."

"Why didn't my father recognize you?" Hanne asked.

"I was tailored before I came here. This," Nina said, gesturing to herself, "isn't me."

"Is *anything* about you real?"

"The skills I taught you. Everything I told you about the way this country works, about the corruption at its core." Nina took a breath and tapped her hand to her heart. "This is real, Hanne."

Hanne looked away. "You used me."

"I did," said Nina. "I won't deny it."

Hanne's gaze swung back to Nina. She folded her arms. "You're not sorry, are you?"

"I'm sorry for the hurt I caused. I'm sorry to have lost your trust. But we are soldiers, Hanne, warriors born. And we do what has to be done. There were lives at stake. There still are. I don't believe this is the only place where your father's men are experimenting on Grisha."

Hanne swallowed, and Nina knew she was remembering the girls in their beds on the ward, the babies in the cribs, their suffering. "There are more?"

"More bases. More factories. More laboratories. I won't pretend that all Grisha are good. Or all Ravkans. They aren't. Maybe I'm not. All I know is that what your father and his men are doing is wrong. They have to be stopped." She laid her hand on Hanne's shoulder, afraid she might pull away. "We could stop them."

Hanne looked up at the factory, at the wagon full of prisoners, at the great ash towering over the road with its finger-bone branches. She ran a hand over her shorn scalp, the stubborn lines of her face more pronounced without the thick cloud of her hair to soften them. When her gaze returned to Nina, there was new fire in her eyes. "Save them all," she said.

Despite the sorrows and dangers of the day, despite the challenges that lay ahead, Nina felt a new lightness overtake her. "Save them all."

"But Nina," Hanne said. "No more lies."

"No more lies," she agreed, and Nina wished, with all her heart, that could be true.

"What do we do first?" asked Hanne.

"We see to your father."

"I won't kill him."

Nina felt a smile curling her lips. "That is the very last thing I'd have you do."

When Hanne had gone to drag the still-unconscious Brum up the hill into the woods, Adrik turned to Nina.

"No more lies?" he said.

"Eavesdropping, Adrik?" She looked over his shoulder. "Is Leoni in the wagon? Is she all right?"

"She is. No thanks to you. Leoni didn't make a mistake with the fuses. You caused that accident," he said. "You rigged those explosions to blow the dam. You put me and Leoni and countless innocent civilians at risk."

It was true. She'd done a contemptible thing. So where was her regret?

"Do you know what I learned in Ketterdam?" Nina asked, gazing at the tree of bones she had built. "No one is innocent. You turned the tide today, Adrik. You didn't just hold back the waters—you changed the way these people see Grisha. You performed a miracle."

"It wasn't a miracle. It was skill and luck and a fancy prop you built out of body parts."

Nina shrugged. "The Fjerdans won't accept us as people, so maybe it's time they saw us as Saints. And this is how we'll do it, town by town, miracle by miracle. They're already whispering your name here, just as they whisper Sankta Alina's name. I guarantee tomorrow there will be shrines dedicated to you all along this road." She raised a brow. "You might not like what they're calling you, though."

"I don't like any of this," he said, but then his curiosity got the better of him. "Tell me."

"Sankta Leoni of the Waters." She paused. "And Sankt Adrik the Uneven."

Adrik rolled his eyes. "We need to go, Nina. Time is short."

"There's something else," said Nina, though she knew Adrik would never forgive what she told him next. "I didn't share all of the information in Brum's letter."

Adrik went very still. "What have you done, Nina?"

"There was talk of an assassination plan against the king."

"By the Fjerdans?"

"It wasn't clear. It only said that Lantsov wouldn't be a problem for someone named Demidov. That their spies believed the situation would resolve itself without interference soon."

Adrik cursed. "We have to get to Hjar as soon as possible. How could you keep a threat to the king's life to yourself?"

What difference could it make? There were always threats to the king's life. Nikolai had Tolya and Tamar to watch over him, and Adrik would have insisted on calling off the plan so they could travel to Hjar and locate a member of the network with access to a flyer who could get word to the capital. The king of Ravka had plenty of people to protect him. The girls on the mountaintop had only Nina.

"It was one day lost," she said. "There's time to get word to the king."

"That was not your call to make. But I won't debate it with you now. You can answer for what you've done back in Ravka."

"I'm not going with you."

"Nina—"

"I know what I need to do, Adrik, and I won't get a chance like this again. Ravka made me a soldier. Ketterdam made me a spy. Hanne can help me become something else entirely."

"Nina, you can't mean to—"

"I do."

"We'll have no way to reach you there. You'll be without allies, without resources. If things go wrong, you won't have any way out."

Nina glanced up at the smoldering wreckage of the factory. "Then I'll just have to blow a hole in the wall."

36

NIKOLAI

THE THORN WOOD WAS BLEEDING. The sap that flowed from its trunks was no longer gold but red, as if with Elizaveta's death it had died too. Its stalks began to shrivel, its thorns wilting. Nikolai pulled himself free, and the blood from his hands and legs dripped onto the sand. His chest throbbed, and yet the only sign that he'd driven a spike through it was a star-shaped scar. One more to add to his collection.

In the distance, he could see the great palace crumbling, its spires collapsing. *What will be left?* he wondered And how were he and Zoya going to get free of this place?

He stumbled over to her. She lay on a wilted bed of thorn trees and red quince blossoms, her hair splayed around her face. Before her, a dark pile of dead bees was heaped amid the branches. *Sankta Elizaveta.* Only a few feet away, he saw a mound of bones, both bear and human, blowing away to ash. Would this whole world crumble to dust?

He knelt beside Zoya and checked her pulse. It was steady. He was surprised to see two fetters of black scales at her wrists.

"Zoya," he said, shaking her gently. "Commander Nazyalensky."

Her lashes fluttered and she looked up at him. Nikolai reared back. For a moment, he thought he'd seen . . . No, that was impossible. Zoya gazed at him with vibrant blue eyes.

"Are you all right?" he asked.

"Fine," she replied.

"You're sure?"

"Which one of us gets to kill the monk?"

"You're fine."

He helped her to her feet and they made their way to where Yuri lay buried up to his neck in sand. At some point the rat had fainted. Blood trickled from his nose.

Nikolai sighed. "I hate to say it, but we're going to have to let him live. I need all the information we can garner on the Cult of the Starless and how the Saints brought us here. I think it may have been Elizaveta who unlocked my chains the night I got free from the palace."

"How?"

"She said their power could extend beyond the Fold, but only where the people's faith was strongest. Yuri was at the palace that night. Maybe Elizaveta used him to send her vines or her insects past my guards."

Zoya snorted. *"You're* the one who invited him in."

"You can choose our next dinner guest. I want answers, so the monk lives. For now."

"Perhaps some light torture, then? Or you could just let me kick him in the head for the next hour."

"I'd like nothing better, but I'm not feeling my best, and I'd prefer not to die in these clothes. We need to see if we can find our way out of here."

Zoya pulled the dunes away from Yuri, and they dragged him onto his back. They bound his hands with strips of fabric from Zoya's *kefta* and gagged him for good measure.

"Nikolai," Zoya said, laying a hand on his arm as she summoned a pallet of air on which to carry the monk. "Did it work at least? Are you free?"

Nikolai winked at her. "As free as I'll ever be."

He didn't have the heart to tell her he could still feel the monster somewhere inside him—weakened, licking its wounds, but waiting for the opportunity to rise again.

Whatever power had bound them in permanent twilight had died with the Saints. Nikolai and Zoya had been walking less than an hour when they saw the first twinkle of stars.

They continued on, despite their wounds and their fatigue, until at last they saw lights in the distance, and eventually the dead gray sands of the Fold gave way to soft meadow. Though Nikolai would have liked nothing better than to foist himself on the hospitality of a farmer, they couldn't risk discovery. They took shelter in an old equipment shed. It was damp and uncomfortable, but it was either that or rest beneath the branches of a plum orchard, and Nikolai had no desire to be anywhere near a tree.

It was a pleasure to close his eyes and feel sleep fall over him. He would never take it for granted again.

Zoya set out before dawn for Kribirsk and returned more quickly than expected with horses, a pack full of traveling clothes, and a young Grisha Healer to see to Nikolai's wounds.

"I'm sorry, Your Highness," the boy apologized as he sealed the punctures in Nikolai's hands. "This will most likely leave a scar. I'm still training."

"A roguish scar?" asked Nikolai.

"Well . . . a deep one?"

"Just as good."

When he was done, Zoya sent him on his way. "Speak of this to anyone and I will consider it treason." She trained her hard gaze on the boy and said, "That is a hanging offense."

He stumbled backward through the doorway. "Yes, Commander. Of course, Commander."

Zoya frowned and shook her head. "I swear they come through training softer and softer. One little glare and he was about to call for smelling salts."

Nikolai said nothing. This time there'd been no mistaking it. When Zoya had glared at the boy, her eyes had flashed silver, and her pupils had turned to slits. For a moment, he had been looking into the eyes of the dragon. Just what had Zoya done to get them free? That question would have to wait until they were safely back at the palace.

They pushed through their exhaustion and rode hard the rest of the day. Occasionally, Nikolai felt a jab in his chest, as if the thorn were still lodged there. Yuri sat silent and shivering in his bindings, his hood pulled low over his face.

They soon learned that whatever had happened on the Unsea had been felt throughout Ravka, maybe beyond. Earthquakes had been reported as far north as Ulensk and as far south as Dva Stolba. Nikolai knew there would be other consequences. Three of the world's most powerful Grisha had died, and the ritual had definitely not gone as planned.

Before they entered Os Alta, Zoya bound Nikolai's hands and

attached ropes to the bridles of his and Yuri's horses so they would both look like prisoners as she led them through the lower town, across the great canal, and onto the broad boulevards that would take them up the gentle slope and through the golden gates to the palace. They saw no mourning banners, no flags flown at half-mast. No one was rioting in the streets. Either Nikolai was decidedly less popular than he'd hoped, or somehow Genya and David had managed to keep his disappearance a secret.

Nikolai felt torn between anticipation and dread. When Zoya had gone to Kribirsk, he'd ungagged the monk and had quickly understood that, as bad as things were, they were going to get much worse. *Open the door.* He'd done it, and something terrible had stepped through.

And yet, at his first glimpse of the crowned double eagle perched atop the gates and the gilded rooftop of the Grand Palace in the distance, his heart lifted. He was home. He had survived, and even if he wasn't cured, somehow he and Zoya and the others would find a way to move forward. The demon inside knew him well, but now Nikolai knew the demon too.

Zoya rode up to the guards on duty, tossed back her hood, and said, "Open for your commander."

The guards instantly came to attention. "*Moi soverenyi.*"

"I am weary and I have prisoners to present to the other members of the Triumvirate."

"Do they have papers?"

"I will take responsibility for them. But if you make me wait any longer for a hot bath, I will also take responsibility for your slow death."

The guard cleared his throat and bowed. "Welcome home, Commander."

The gates swung open.

It was clear some kind of big party was in progress. The walkways were lit with lanterns and music floated down from the sparkling windows of the Grand Palace.

"Is it possible they actually went through with it all?" Zoya said in disbelief.

"How can you throw a ball for a king who isn't here?" Nikolai asked. They couldn't possibly have attempted to tailor someone to take his place, could they? There wouldn't have been time to train him, especially for an event with so much riding on it.

"Maybe they dressed up a scarecrow and put your crown on its head," said Zoya.

"I should adopt that strategy at council meetings."

They weren't sure what might be waiting for them inside, so they checked the monk's bindings and gave him a drop of Genya's sleep concoction for good measure. They stashed him behind a hedge and agreed to split up until they found a member of the Triumvirate or someone they could speak to without causing an uproar.

Nikolai made his way along the southern flank of the palace, keeping to the shadows as music drifted back to him from the party inside. He glimpsed movement in the conservatory. A couple meeting for an assignation? He'd leave them to it. He hastened along the glass wall dotted with miniature orange trees and was about to turn the corner when he saw . . . himself.

A bolt of panic shook him, his mind racing with confused thoughts. What if he wasn't Nikolai anymore? What if he was just the monster? What if he was still caught in the twilight Fold and this was all a dream? He looked down at his hands—scarred but human, without claws. *I am Nikolai Lantsov. I am here. I am home.*

He looked back through the glass. The other him was standing amid the fruit trees and fountains of the conservatory, medals glinting from the pale blue sash across his chest. So this was why there was no panic in the countryside or cities, no flags of mourning raised. They'd used his plan. Genya had tailored some poor sap to play the role of the king.

Nikolai was at once thrilled and insulted. To think that someone could take his place so easily, well—a lesser man might have found it humbling. And yet his mind couldn't help but spool out the possibilities. He could have this actor sit through state dinners and the openings of orphanages and concert halls. Nikolai could be in two places at once. But what was his new twin doing away from the other guests?

The answer presented itself in an elaborate green gown and emeralds—a girl. A very pretty girl in what appeared to be very expensive jewels. Was this the princess Ehri Kir-Taban? There were no chaperones in sight.

His stand-in was pacing, talking rapidly. Nikolai couldn't hear what he was saying, but to his great horror, it looked very much like a declaration of love. What was this pretender getting them into? And had Genya and David sanctioned such a thing? This was the moment for a well-timed interruption, but exactly how was Nikolai supposed to accomplish that without upending the whole charade?

Maybe I'm wrong and they're discussing matters of state, Nikolai thought hopefully.

At that moment, the couple strode toward each other. The false king of Ravka took the princess in his arms. She tilted her face up to his, her eyes sliding closed, her lips parted. That was when Nikolai saw the knife in her hands.

37

ISAAK

ISAAK'S PALMS WERE DAMP. It had not been easy to evade Tolya and Tamar. The twins were seasoned mercenaries with a gift for appearing when they were least wanted.

But at his first glimpse of Ehri in the conservatory, he knew he would have gladly dodged a thousand trained soldiers to be here right now. He had no idea how she had lost her guards or how much time he would have with her before they were discovered. He only knew he wanted to look at her forever. Her gown was the color of green pears, its elaborate folds embroidered with falcons. Emerald combs glittered in the dark fall of her hair.

"Nikolai?" she asked, peering into the dimly lit conservatory.

Isaak, he wanted to beg her to say. What would it be like to hear her call him by his real name?

"I'm here," he whispered. She turned and smiled, and it was like a fist to his chest. "I wasn't sure you'd come."

"I wasn't sure I'd be able to. My ladies have been fussing over me since sunrise. I didn't think I'd find a second alone to escape them."

"I'm glad you did." That was an absurd understatement, but he couldn't think of anything else to say.

She took a step toward him, and without thinking, he took a step back, maintaining the distance between them. He saw the hurt on her face and felt like the worst kind of dolt.

"I'm sorry," he said quickly, though he knew apologies did not come easily to kings.

She clasped her hands in front of her. "Did I . . . did I misunderstand?"

"No," he said. "*No.* But there's something I need to tell you." Isaak turned on his heel, pacing in front of the orange trees, their sweet-smelling blossoms clouding the air. He had planned countless things to say, but none of them seemed right in this moment. He was a poor boy from a small town. He was a palace guard. He'd thought he was happy. He *had* been happy until all this began. But now?

Isaak wished he could take her in his arms and kiss her, but he couldn't do that when every word he'd spoken to her was a lie. And yet he couldn't tell her the truth—not when he might put an entire nation at risk.

"Ehri . . ." he began. "If I were not a king . . ." he faltered. What was he trying to ask her exactly? He tried again. "What is it you like about me?"

She laughed, and his breath left his chest in a grateful rush at the sound. "Is this a test? Or does your pride just need stroking?"

"My pride is always in need of tender attention," he said, then cursed beneath his breath. That was Nikolai talking, and he did not want to be Nikolai tonight. "Wait. I'll tell you what I like about you. Your nerve. Your way with a practice sword. That you always say what you mean. The way you look when you tell stories of your house by the lake."

She tilted her head, and for a moment an expression of such sadness flashed across her face.

"What is it?" he said, wanting only to wipe whatever had caused her pain from her mind.

"Nothing," she said. "Only that I wish this moment could last."

He wanted to tell her it could, but he didn't know if that was true. He could offer her nothing. And here was the sticky reality: He had no idea what the Triumvirate truly wanted from him. Would they ask Isaak to play this role forever as they ran Ravka? He'd thought there was no way he could be the king they needed, but when he'd dined with Ehri, he'd started to wonder if maybe, with her by his side, he *could*. Would Genya and the others ever permit such a courtship? If they refused, would he have the courage to stand against them? And even worse, the thought that had kept him awake since that happy night on the island: What if the real king returned and chose Ehri as his bride? Would Isaak have to watch him court and marry her? Would he stand at attention in the chapel at the royal wedding? Would Ehri ever realize that the man she wed was not the man who had stood here in this conservatory, on this night, with his heart full of longing?

"I wish it could last too," he said. "I wish there was no one in the world but you and me, that there were no countries, no kings and queens."

He took a step closer, and then she was gliding into the circle of his arms. She was lithe, almost wiry. She was perfect.

"Ehri," he said as he drew her to him, as she tilted her beautiful face to his in invitation. "Could you love me if I was not a king?"

495

"I could," she said, and he didn't understand why her eyes were suddenly full of tears. "I know I could."

"What's wrong?" He cupped her cheek, brushing away the tears with his thumb.

"Nothing at all," she whispered.

He felt a jolt, as if she'd shoved him, and looked down. Something was sticking out of his chest. His mind made sense of the shape as the pain hit. A dagger. The white handle was carved with a wolf. He heard a furious rapping against the glass, as if a bird were trying to get into the conservatory.

"Why?" he asked as he slid to the ground.

She fell with him, going to her knees, her tears flowing freely now. "For my country," she said as she wept. "For my brother. For my queen."

"You don't understand," he tried to say. A laugh emerged from his lips, but it sounded wrong, like a bubble popping.

"Forgive me," she said, and yanked the dagger from his body.

Pain flooded through him as he felt the warm gush of blood from his wound.

She pressed a soft kiss to his lips. "My only comfort is that you never could have been mine. But know that I would have gladly been yours."

"Ehri," he moaned as the world began to go dark.

"Not Ehri."

From somewhere he could hear shouting, the sound of hurried footfalls running toward them.

"Everyone mourns the first blossom," she recited softly.

Who will weep for the rest that fall?

Isaak watched, helpless, as she grasped the dagger and drove the blade into her own heart.

38

NINA

NINA DRESSED WITH CARE. Her gown was palest lavender, modestly cut, perfectly suited to Mila Jandersdat's coloring and generous figure. She wore no jewelry. What baubles could a poor widow afford? But a Fjerdan woman's greatest adornment was her virtue. Nina smiled at the girl in the mirror, the expression sweet and guileless.

She smoothed her flaxen hair into a tidy braided crown that would have made the Wellmother proud and found her way to the solarium. The great glass windows were ringed with frost, and through them she could see the ice moat and beyond it, the glittering spires of the White Island. The Ice Court was as dazzling as she remembered.

She heard footsteps behind her and turned to see Jarl Brum approaching, his wife on his arm. They were a remarkably handsome couple, tall and fine-boned.

"Enke Jandersdat," he said warmly. "My savior. Please allow me to introduce you to my wife, Ylva."

Nina curtsied. "It is my greatest honor."

Brum's wife took Nina's hand. Her thick chestnut hair fell nearly to her waist, and she wore a gown of gold silk that made her brown skin glow like autumn. Nina could see where Hanne had come by her beauty.

"The honor is mine," said Ylva. "I understand my husband owes his life to you."

Once the wagon was long gone, Nina and Hanne had awakened Brum. They'd told him that they'd come running after the explosion and found his body by the side of the road. He was lucky to have escaped the waters and the disaster at the factory with little more than a bad bump to the head. Whatever suspicions Brum had held regarding Mila Jandersdat, they'd been cured by the fact that she had remained in Gäfvalle when the Zemeni couple and the Grisha prisoners had fled.

Nina and Hanne had waited patiently at the convent while Brum had returned to the factory to see who had survived and put everything he could to rights—and, Nina suspected, to make sure there was no evidence of his failures. An industrial accident that had resulted in the deaths of valued captives was one thing, but a successful Grisha escape attempt after his humiliation at the Ice Court the previous year would have spelled disaster for his career. And it was very important to Nina that Jarl Brum did not lose his favored position in the Fjerdan hierarchy. For the plan she had in mind, she would need every one of his connections and every bit of his access to highly placed bureaucrats, military commanders, and noblemen.

"I did nothing," Nina said to Ylva. "It was Hanne who showed true courage."

"And that is another debt we owe you," Ylva said. "Jarl tells me you are responsible for the remarkable change in our daughter."

"I cannot take praise for that! I credit your own influence and the steady tutelage of the Wellmother, may Djel watch over her."

The Brums nodded solemnly, then Ylva's face broke into a wide smile.

"Hanne!" she exclaimed as her daughter entered the room.

The truth was that Nina deserved plenty of credit for Hanne's transformation. She'd taught her to dress to suit her long, lean figure; taught her to stand with her shoulders back and walk with a lady's grace; and of course, Nina had taught her to act. As for Hanne's trust, she would find a way to earn it and maybe even be worthy of it. Somehow.

Ylva embraced her daughter as Brum said to Nina, "Hanne tells me she is at last prepared to put aside her foolish ways and find a husband. I do not know what magic you worked on her, but I am grateful. She is so much changed."

She was perfect before, thought Nina. *Or would have been if you hadn't pruned and plucked at her like an overeager gardener trying to mold an unruly shrub.*

Nina smiled. "I think it was only a matter of time before Hanne discovered who she was truly meant to be."

"You must learn to take a compliment, Mila." He pressed a kiss to her knuckles. "I hope you will in time." He clapped his hands together. "Shall we dine?"

Hanne turned to her father, her face happy and serene. She wore deepest russet, and her freckles looked like pollen on her cheeks. Her hair was still closely shorn.

"I'm afraid a number of generals have come to discuss boring matters of war. Vadik Demidov himself will be arriving in the capital soon," said Brum. Nina hoped so. She intended to learn all she could about the Lantsov pretender and Fjerda's plans for battle. "We will try not to put you ladies to sleep."

"We will be happy to talk amongst ourselves, Papa," said Hanne. "There are new dress designs from Gedringe to discuss."

He smiled indulgently at her and took his wife's arm.

As soon as his back was turned, Hanne winked at Nina, her gaze snapping fire.

"Shall we?" she said.

Nina slid her hand into Hanne's as they followed Ylva and Jarl Brum into dinner.

They would build a new world together.

But first they had to burn the old one down.

39

ZOYA

ZOYA HEARD THE UPROAR and ran toward it. She'd sensed the wrongness of the night even before she heard Tolya's shout. She felt it on the air, as if the crackle of lightning she controlled so easily now was everywhere, in everything. It had been that way since she'd claimed Juris' scales. He was with her, all of his lives, all he had learned, the crimes he'd committed, the miracles he'd performed. His heart beat with her—the dragon's heart—and she could feel that rhythm linking her to everything. *The making at the heart of the world.* Had she really believed in it before? Maybe. But it hadn't mattered to her. Power had been protection, the getting of it, the honing of it, the only defense she could grasp against all the pain she had known. Now it was something more.

Everything was different now. Her vision seemed sharper, as if light limned each object. She could smell the green grass outside,

501

woodsmoke on the air, even the marble—she'd never realized marble had a scent. In this moment, running down these familiar halls toward the clamor in the conservatory, she didn't feel fear, only a sense of urgency to make some kind of order out of the trouble she knew she'd find.

But she couldn't have anticipated the mess awaiting her. She closed the doors to the conservatory behind her and clouded the glass with mist in case of passersby. Security had fallen to pieces without her here. No surprise.

Tamar knelt beside a Shu girl with a dagger in her chest. Genya was crying. Tolya, David, and Nikolai, still dressed in his prisoner's shroud, stood around another body—a corpse that looked very much like the king. Everyone was shouting at once.

Zoya silenced them with a thunderclap.

As one the group turned to her, and instantly they had their hands up, ready to fight.

"How do we know it's really you?" said Genya.

"It's really her," said Nikolai.

"How do we *know* it's really *you*?" Tamar growled, not interrupting her work on the Shu girl. It seemed a hopeless cause. The girl still had color in her cheeks, but the dagger looked as if it had pierced her heart. Zoya refused to look more closely at the other body. It was too hard not to think of Nikolai pinned to the thorn wood, his blood watering the sands of the Fold.

"Genya," said Zoya calmly. "I once got drunk and insisted you make me blond."

"Intriguing!" said Nikolai. "What were the results?"

"She looked glorious," said Genya.

Zoya plucked a bit of dust from her sleeve. "I looked cheap."

Genya dropped her hands. "Stand down. It's her." Then she was hugging Zoya fiercely as Tolya clasped Nikolai in his massive arms and lifted him off his feet. "Where the hell have you been?"

"It's a long story," said Nikolai, and demanded Tolya set him down.

Zoya wanted to hold tight to Genya, take in the flowery scent of her hair, ask her a thousand questions. Instead, she stepped back and said, "What happened here?"

"The dagger is Fjerdan," said Tolya.

"Maybe so," said Nikolai. "But it was wielded by a Shu girl."

"What do you mean?" said Tamar as she worked frantically to restore the girl's pulse. "She was attacked too."

"Is it her heart?" Zoya asked.

"No," said Tamar. "That would be beyond my skill. The dagger struck a little too far to the right."

"Can you save her?" asked Genya.

"I don't know. I'm just trying to stabilize her. It will be up to our Healers to do the rest."

"I saw it all happen," said Nikolai. "She attacked him—me? Him. Then turned the blade on herself."

"So the Shu are trying to frame Fjerda?" said Tolya.

Genya's tears began anew. She knelt and put her hand to the impostor's cheek. "Isaak," she murmured.

"Who?" said Zoya.

"Isaak Andreyev," Nikolai said quietly, kneeling by the body. "Private first class. Son of a schoolteacher and a seamstress."

Tolya brushed his hand over his eyes. "He didn't want any of this."

"Can you restore his features?" asked Nikolai.

"It's harder without blood flow," said Genya. "But I can try."

"We owe that at least to his mother." Nikolai shook his head. "He survived the front. He was meant to be past harm."

Genya bit back a sob. "We . . . we knew we were putting him in danger's way. We thought we were doing what was right."

"The princess is breathing," Tamar said. "I need to get her to the Corporalki in the Little Palace."

"This makes no sense," said Genya. "Why not just murder the king—or the man she believed was king? Why try to kill herself too? And why would a princess sacrifice herself to do the job?"

"She didn't," said Nikolai. "Get me fresh clothes. I'll return to the party to close out the festivities. I want to have a word with Hiram Schenck. He's the highest-ranking member of the Kerch Merchant Council here, yes?"

"Yes," said Genya. "But he isn't happy with you."

"He's about to be. For a time. Keep the doors to the conservatory locked, and leave Isaak's body here."

"We shouldn't—" Tolya began, but Nikolai held up a hand.

"Just for now. I swear he will have the burial he deserves. Bring the Shu delegation to me in my father's rooms in one hour's time."

"What if Princess Ehri's guards raise the alarm?" asked Genya.

"They won't," said Zoya. "Not until they know their plan has succeeded and the king is dead."

Nikolai rose, as if his wounds no longer pained him, as if the horrors of the last few days had never been, as if the demon inside him had been conquered after all. "Then long live the king."

Two hours later, the festivities had dwindled to a few happy drunks singing songs in the double-eagle fountain. Most of the guests had gone to their beds to sleep off their indulgences or had snuck off to some quiet corner of the gardens to indulge in more.

Zoya and the others had returned to the conservatory, and when

Nikolai entered he was dragging along a terrified-looking Shu guard. She had a pinched, homely face and wore the uniform of the Tavgharad, her long black hair tied in a topknot.

"Mayu Kir-Kaat," said Tamar. "What is she doing here?"

At the sight of the body on the floor beside the lemon trees, the guard began to shake. "But he . . ." she said, staring at the dead king and then back at Nikolai. "But you—where is the princess?"

"What a fascinating question," said Nikolai. "I assume you're referring to the girl we found with a dagger in her chest just half an inch shy of her aorta—due to luck or a lack of follow-through, you be the judge. She is currently recovering with our Healers."

"You must return the royal princess to our care," sputtered the guard.

"She is no such thing," said Nikolai sharply. "And the time has come and gone for such deceptions. An innocent man died tonight, all so you could start a war."

"Is he going to explain any of this?" whispered Genya. Zoya was wondering the same thing.

"Gladly," said Nikolai. He gestured toward the guard. "I'd like all of you to meet the real Princess Ehri Kir-Taban, favored daughter of the Shu, second in line to their throne."

"Lies," hissed the guard.

Nikolai seized her hand. "First of all, no member of the Tavgharad would allow a man to snatch her wrist like the last sugared plum." The guard gave a belated tug to try to get her hand free. "Second, where are her calluses? A soldier should have them on the pads of her palms, like Isaak. Instead, they're on the tips of her fingers. These are the calluses you would get from playing—"

"The *khatuur*," said Zoya. "Eighteen strings. Princess Ehri is a master."

"So they planted an assassin in place of the princess in order to get close to the king," said Tamar. "But why would she try to kill herself off too?"

"To cast more suspicion on the Fjerdans?" asked Genya.

"Yes," said Nikolai, "and to give the Shu a reason to go to war. Ravka's monarch dead, a member of the Shu royal family slain. The Shu would have every excuse they needed to march their armies into our leaderless country and use it as a base to launch an attack on Fjerda's southern border. They would arrive in force with no intention of ever leaving."

Now the guard—or rather the princess—closed her eyes as if in defeat. But she did not weep and she did not tremble.

"What was to become of you, Princess?" Nikolai asked, releasing her hand.

"I was to have a new name, a quiet life in the countryside," she said softly. "I have never cared for politics or life at court. I would be free to pursue my music, fall in love where I wished."

"What a lovely picture you paint," said Nikolai. "Were it not a danger to my country's future, your lack of guile would be charming. Did you really believe your sister was going to leave you to rusticate in some mountain village? Did you actually think you would survive this plot?"

"I have never wanted the crown! I am no threat to my sister."

"Think," Zoya snapped, losing patience. "You are popular, adored, the daughter everyone wants on the throne. Your death is the thing meant to rally an entire nation to war. How could your sister let you live and risk discovery? You would be nothing but a liability."

The princess lifted her pointed chin. "I do not believe it."

"Your guards have been secured," Zoya said. "I suspect one of them had orders to make you disappear before you ever made it to your pastoral retreat. You can question them yourself."

Ehri somehow lifted her chin higher. "Will I face trial or simply be executed?"

"You should be so lucky," said Nikolai. "No, I have a far worse fate for you in mind."

"Am I to be your hostage?"

"I'm not much for pet names, but as you like."

"You truly mean to keep me here?"

"Oh, indeed. Not as my prisoner but as my queen."

Zoya was surprised at the way those words pricked at—what? Her heart? Her pride? She had known this end was inevitable. It was the course she had fought and harangued for. So why did she feel like she'd left her flank open yet again?

"Our engagement will earn me a glorious dowry," said Nikolai, "and your popularity among your people will keep your sister from harassing our borders."

"I will not do it," said Ehri, her face ferocious—the countenance of a queen.

"It's that or execution, my dove. Think of it this way: You won't be hanged, but the price is a life of luxury and my sparkling company."

"You might consider the gallows," said Zoya. "Quicker and less painful." It felt good to say the words, to tease him while she still could.

Nikolai nodded to Tolya and Tamar. "Get her back to her chambers and keep a close eye on her. Until we announce the royal engagement, there's a good chance she'll try to bolt or kill herself."

"What do we do with the injured girl?" said Genya once the princess had been escorted out of the conservatory and the twins had returned.

"Keep her under *heavy* guard at the Little Palace. Even wounded, she's a member of the Tavgharad. Let's not forget that."

"Did the real Mayu ever really mean to defect?"

"I think so," said Tamar. "She has a brother, a twin. I think he was taken to be trained for the *khergud*. She may have hoped to get both of them out of Shu Han."

"*Kebben*," said Tolya, resting a hand on his sister's shoulder. It was a word Zoya didn't know. "If she was found out, maybe she used her own life to barter for her brother's freedom."

"Should make for an interesting chat once she's conscious," said Nikolai. He knelt once again by Isaak. "I'll write a letter to his mother tomorrow. We can at least give him a hero's pension and make sure his family wants for nothing."

"And the body?" asked Tolya quietly.

"Take him out through the tunnels to Lazlayon."

Genya brushed her fingers over Isaak's lapel. "I'll begin work on him right away. He . . . he didn't hesitate. When we told him what was at stake he . . ."

Tolya lifted Isaak's body carefully in his huge arms. "He had the heart of a king."

"What did you tell Hiram Schenck?" asked Genya, wiping fresh tears from her scarred cheek. "His grin was as big as a melon rind."

"I gave him the plans for our submersibles."

"The *izmars'ya*?" said Tamar.

"Armed?" asked Tolya, his face distressed.

"Afraid so. As I understand it," said Nikolai, "the Apparat has gone missing and Fjerda is marching in support of a Lantsov pretender. Is he good looking?"

Tamar frowned. "The Apparat?"

"The Lantsov pretender. I suppose it's of no matter. But yes, I gave Schenck the real plans. We're going to war. We'll be in sore need of Kerch funds as well as our new Shu friends."

"The Zemeni—" protested Tolya.

"Don't worry," said Nikolai. "I gave Schenck what he wanted, but he's going to discover it's not what he needs. Sometimes you have to feed the demon."

"What does that mean?" asked Genya. "And are you going to tell us where you went?"

"Or if you found a cure?" said Tamar.

"We did," said Nikolai. "But it didn't quite take."

"So the monk was no help at all?" asked Tolya.

Nikolai's gaze met Zoya's. She drew in a long breath, then nodded. It was time the others knew. "We have some bad news."

"There's more?" asked Genya.

"It's Ravka," Nikolai and Zoya said together.

"There's always more," she heard him finish as she vanished into the antechamber to retrieve their prisoner, hands tightly bound. She'd woken him with Genya's red bottle, enjoying the way he startled, the brief confusion in his eyes.

"Yuri?" said Genya. "What did he do? Bore someone to death?"

Zoya tugged at the rope, and the monk stepped fully into the light. His hood fell back.

Genya gasped, edging away, her hand flying to the patch that covered her lost eye. "No. It can't be. *No.*" Nikolai placed a steadying hand on her shoulder.

The monk was still too tall and too lean, but he moved with a new grace. His face was clean-shaven and his glasses were gone. His hair looked darker, smoothed back from his brow, and the very shape of his features seemed to have altered, the bones winnowing to sharper, more elegant lines. His eyes flashed gray, the color of quartz.

Tamar stepped in front of Genya as if to shield her. "Impossible."

"Improbable," said Nikolai gently.

When Zoya had destroyed the vessel that Elizaveta had so lovingly preserved, she had seen a shadow leave the fire, but she hadn't understood what it meant at the time. The Darkling's power had fractured—part of it had remained in the wounded shadow soldier that the ritual had almost destroyed and that still lived on in Nikolai. But the rest, the spirit that had begun to bleed from that soldier into the body Elizaveta had prepared . . . Zoya should have known the Darkling would not miss his chance at freedom.

Yuri had gotten his wish. He'd helped his Saint return. Had the young monk given himself up willingly? Joyously? Or in those final moments of fire and terror, had he begged to keep his life? Zoya knew there would be no mercy from the Starless Saint. The Darkling was not in the business of answering prayers.

Nikolai had made the discovery in the shed where they'd taken shelter, in the hours when Zoya had been trekking to Kribirsk.

"Let me kill him," she'd told Nikolai when he'd shown her. "We can bury his body here. No one ever has to know he . . ." She had stumbled over the words. *He has returned.* She could not say it. She refused to.

"If we kill him, I may never be free of the demon inside me," Nikolai had said. "And we are about to be at war. I intend to use every resource we have."

They'd kept him gagged throughout their journey back to Os Alta, but just the amusement in those familiar gray eyes had made her want to snap his neck.

Nikolai insisted there was a way to use his power. Zoya wanted to watch him burn all over again.

So she would wait. She could be patient. The beast inside her knew eternity.

Now Zoya looked at Genya with her scarred hands pressed to her mouth, at Tolya's fury, at Tamar with her axes drawn. She looked at her king and the woman who would soon be his wife.

We are the dragon and we will bide our time.

"So many of my old friends, gathered in one place," said the Darkling from the mouth of a loyal, gullible boy, another fool who had loved him. "It's good to be home."

© Taili Song Roth

LEIGH BARDUGO

is a No.1 *New York Times*-bestselling author of fantasy novels and the creator of the Grishaverse. With over two million copies sold, her Grishaverse spans the Shadow and Bone Trilogy, the Six of Crows Duology, *The Language of Thorns*, and *King of Scars* — with more to come. Her short stories can be found in multiple anthologies, including *Some of the Best from Tor.com* and *The Best American Science Fiction and Fantasy 2017*. Her other works include *Wonder Woman: Warbringer* and *Ninth House*. Leigh was born in Jerusalem, grew up in Los Angeles, graduated from Yale University, and has worked in advertising, journalism, and even makeup and special effects. These days, she lives and writes in Hollywood, where she can occasionally be heard singing with her band.

The second book in the King of Scars Duology will be coming soon.

leighbardugo.com

ACKNOWLEDGMENTS

First, to my readers, new and old, who have made it possible for me to continue this journey through the Grishaverse, thank you. I could not ask for better travel companions.

Many thanks to the magnificent crew at Imprint: my ingenious editor Erin Stein, who let me pitch her this book over lunch at San Diego Comic Con; design warlords Natalie C. Sousa and Ellen Duda; John Morgan; Nicole Otto; Raymond Ernesto Colón; Melinda Ackell; Dawn Ryan; Weslie Turner; and Jessica Chung. I would be lost without the MCPG genius strike force: Mariel Dawson, Morgan Dubin, Molly Ellis, Teresa Ferraiolo, Julia Gardiner, Kathryn Little, Katie Halata, Lucy Del Priore, Allison Verost, Melissa Zar, the Fierce Reads team, Jennifer Gonzalez and the sales team, Kristin Dulaney, and the ever intrepid Jon Yaged.

All the love and gratitude to my New Leaf Literary family: Pouya Shahbazian, Hilary Pecheone, Devin Ross, Joe Volpe, Kathleen

Ortiz, Mia Roman, Veronica Grijalva, Abigail Donoghue, Kelsey Lewis, Cassandra Baim, and, of course, Joanna Volpe, who has held my hand and had my six at every turn. And a special thank-you to Melissa Rogal, slayer of giants.

I want to thank Holly Black and Sarah Rees Brennan, who provided invaluable feedback on the early drafts of this manuscript; Morgan Fahey, who helped me sort my saints and name my kings; Rachael Martin, who offered guidance and encouragement on the final draft; Robyn Bacon, who makes a killer potpie and a glorious Baked Alaska; Ziggy the Human Cannonball, who makes me laugh and laugh; and Erin Daffern, who keeps me moving even when I really, really want to stay still. Thanks also to Marie Lu, Rainbow Rowell, Robin Wasserman, Cassandra Clare, Sabaa Tahir, Robin LaFevers, Daniel José Older, Carrie Ryan, Christine Patrick, Gretchen McNeil, Julia Collard, Nadine Semerau, the Petty Patties (long may they reign), and to Eric for every aloha.

Thank you to Emily, Ryan, Christine, and Sam for all of the love and patience, and to my weird and wonderful mama, who weathers my storms.